To Bill

Great Working w...

Find your truth.

D1552508

# San Lorenzo's Truth

## Marc B. Massoglia

**Chestertowne Press**

# Dedication

This book is dedicated to my wife, Kathy.

# San Lorenzo's Truth

# Prologue

**Rome**

**August 10, 258 A.D.**

"This is a good day for an execution," the Prefect said to the two guards standing closest to him atop the Temple of Antoninus and Faustina. He surveyed the crowd assembling below in the Forum and with a nod of his head, the men scuttled off.

In short order, the two Prefect guards returned to the foot of the temple producing a metal lattice used for grilling large racks of meat. As sweat poured from their faces and limbs in the fetid air, they made quick work lashing the stripped and beaten man to the gridiron. Three more guards joined the effort and the five lifted the contraption, side-stepping, their muscles bulging and veins popping, toward the burning coals. There, a sixth guard had heaped red hot coals from a local kitchen onto the makeshift pit. A stream of blood flowed from the doomed man's nose and the gash above his eye. Purple and blue bruises rose on his skin above his ribs and when he coughed, he spat blood.

For over an hour, Lorenzo, a deacon of the Christian church, remained lashed to the metal structure, his back hovering above the intense heat. While his skin bubbled and charred, he swallowed his pain and gave strength to his followers. Lorenzo did not scream, but when the agony was too great, he released small moans. The odor from Lorenzo's burning hair and smoldering skin filled the Forum and caused many observers to back off to avoid the nauseating smell.

Every time the guards fed the fire, Lorenzo writhed in new pain.

Eventually, the Prefect, dressed in his white tunic and ornate metal breastplate with a red sash which clung to him in the humidity of the mid-morning sun, waded through the vile stench of singed human flesh and approached the damned. The Prefect resisted the urge to wipe the sweat from his face in front of the gathered crowd, lest he show weakness.

Splayed on the gridiron, slowly roasting, the doomed man took shallow breaths. Sweat leaked from every pore in his body's vain attempt to quench the searing heat.

When Lorenzo noticed his presence, the Prefect smiled with satisfaction. He called so all could hear. The bar of cruelty for Christian leaders had been raised and he wanted potential replacements to heed the warning. "Lorenzo, Deacon of the Roman Christian Church, what do you have to say for yourself?"

Lorenzo took three rapid breaths to gather his remaining strength. With all the force that remained in his weakened body, he declared "Turn me over..."

"What?" asked the Prefect, who snickered and turned toward the remaining crowd to make certain they recognized his dominance. "Turn you over to whom? There is no one in the Roman Empire, except the Emperor, of greater authority. To whom shall I turn you over?"

Lorenzo pushed out the words with the very last energy that remained, "Turn me over...I'm done on this side."

The Prefect's faced tightened and body went rigid with fury but it was too late for reprisals. With that comment, Lorenzo smiled, dropped his head to one side, and breathed his last.

One of the Christian leaders, observing from a distance and trying not to be noticed, grabbed a writing implement and scribbled two words on papyrus. Handing it to a young man traveling with him he said, "Bring this to Dionysius. He will know what to do."

"Yes, sir," said the young man but not before reading the note which said, "*assus est*", he is roasted."

# Chapter 1

The plan was to close the deal, take the money, and return home a hero. At least that *was* the plan. Max's dream opportunity, his daughter's best hope, had turned into a nightmare.

Max closed the heavy apartment door and heard the lonely echo rumble down the stairwell. He took the staircase which wound around the elevator shaft; one of those exposed old fashioned types that he had only seen in the movies. Last night, he and his aunt rode it to her fifth-floor apartment. This morning, Max chose the stairs, unwilling to chance getting trapped in that ancient metal box and miss his meeting.

The highly polished marble steps looked slippery and he stepped cautiously at first before increasing his pace, going faster and faster, descending around the exposed steelwork – spinning at the limit of control. The rapid rush down five flights released some of his nervous energy and dizziness overcame him by the time he hit the lobby.

A cardboard mailing tube, too long to fit completely inside, protruded from Max's messenger bag. Three times during the descent and again before stepping out onto the street, he took advantage of the easy access to touch it and ensure its safety. Its contents had caused him a lot of trouble so far. He expected that today, it would very likely cause him much more... especially if he considered losing his job, his family and his freedom a lot more trouble.

After three days of scrambling, he'd just about run out of options. Max rubbed his head –a useless attempt to relieve the stress. His brain hurt from thinking and he didn't know how much longer he could operate. Quitting would be so easy. Maybe he should just resign himself to his fate.

No. If he did, his innocent family would suffer the most from his choices. As Max crossed the street, he committed, for the sake of his wife and three kids, to try to resolve the mess he created. Guilt and self-preservation propelled Max to make one more play before the authorities, or some other force put an end to his run.

Max had memorized the city map in order to not appear like a tourist while out – not that there are many tourists in Torino in November or any time for that matter. His route would take him near St. John the Baptist Cathedral, home to the city's most famous relic, the Shroud of Turin. The faithful believed that a miracle imprinted the image of Jesus on the burial cloths.

A miracle, divine intervention, Max thought, is what I need. That, and faith.

Among the baroque and art nouveau architecture of the city, Max blended in with the shoppers who hurried along the arcaded walkways patronizing the city's famous art-deco cafés and luxury boutiques. He didn't have the time, the money or the language skills to shop there but he did slow down to admire the pastries in one window. The smell of burnt sugar and orange zest flowed out of the door. He thought back to home and how much his wife, Laura, would love this place.

The hairs on the back of his neck raised and his ears itched.

Something had caught his attention and he twisted his head scanning the crowd to see what it was. He recoiled a few steps placing his back to the store window.

Max saw nothing – he sensed it.

He touched the mailing tube and looked around, visually retracing his route and peering forward to the sidewalk ahead. Nothing seemed out of the ordinary but the feeling of uneasiness remained.

Could the homicide detectives have followed him here? Unlikely, but not impossible.

Max froze from indecision.

His chest tightened.

His breath shallowed.

The covered sidewalk ran on for several more blocks. He could continue in that direction or veer off down a narrow road toward the Cathedral. If he was being followed, the latter would be better for exposing the tail.

I'm being ridiculous.

It was too early for panic...but not too early for concern.

Unconsciously, his next steps were brisker and his long legs carried him the distance of several storefronts in only a few strides.

That's when he noticed it – out of his peripheral vision, across the street – a man wearing – what? – a yellow Members Only jacket? It struck Max as odd because the color was so bright and that a zip-up nylon jacket with narrow epaulets and collar strap was fallen fashion. Once so incredibly popular and a staple of the hip, it had been out of style, at least in the States, for at least fifteen years and now marked the wearer as hopelessly uncool. But he had seen the man before...or at least the jacket. He couldn't remember when. It could have been in Basel or Zurich or Milan, any of the places he'd been in the past 48 hours. But now he saw it again in Torino, Italy.

His heart raced as if he had just completed a 5K run instead of only taking a few steps. Max's ribs hurt as he gasped for air. He forced himself to stop, gather himself and look at the window display. At six-three, he couldn't hide very easily. His actions needed to be his camouflage.

The store's lighting, designed to highlight the rich leather handbags, allowed for an excellent mirror effect. Max peered into the window and could make out the reflection of the yellow jacket on the other side of the street, under the portico. The man's face was obscured but it appeared that he, too, had stopped and was looking at him.

Max swallowed his fear. The concern ripened to panic as the evidence mounted.

The crowded shopping arcade would probably discourage a direct confrontation but the crowds could also act as a good screen and distraction for a more surreptitious theft of the mailing tube from his bag. The second outcome, Max knew, was far worse than any physical violence.

After only a brief hesitation, Max left the covered portico. Better to be out in the open to ward off an attack. He walked down the smaller street with narrow sidewalks on both sides and a tram track running down the center. Up ahead, an old man in a plaid cap and overcoat smoked a small Italian cheroot cigar in the doorway of a café. The smell of warm anisette-flavored tobacco and espresso heightened Max's senses.

Without looking behind him, he sensed the yellow jacket had followed his change in direction and kept pace. An escape into a café? No. There were no odds in escaping by way of a place with only one way in and one way out.

He kept walking toward the Cathedral, keeping his pace brisk, yet unhurried.

The feeling of pursuit only got stronger. A recent rain had freshened the streets and the sun bounced off the cobblestones. Max knew that the yellow jacket was behind him somewhere.

Sprint away? But where was safety? And could he even outrun his pursuer?

His antennae up and alert and pulse quickening, the other part of Max's psyche argued that he was being foolish and imagining threats that didn't exist. A yellow jacket is not unique; plenty of people wear them. No rational person believes that seeing one equals a threat. Perhaps, he was just being paranoid.

The narrow street opened up to the piazza. The sun shined brighter here as the reflection from the wet pavement gathered with the light from above to blind Max. He squinted to make out the nearest escapes; one behind him and the other at the steps of the Cathedral entrance about eighty meters in front of him. He walked toward the Cathedral's main entrance. Going back on his vow, he now acted a tourist, covering his eyes like a sailor trying to make out land and swiveling his head from side to side to get a better view of his surroundings.

He touched the mailing tube again – still there.

Max meandered toward the south side of the Cathedral, where, in the great expanse of the piazza, he remained visible from all sides. His palms sweat as he pushed himself to keep moving. In this direction, he'd have the choice to either enter the Cathedral through a side entrance or leave the piazza entirely through a brick archway that led to another, larger square.

Max stopped about equidistant between the two options and pretended to look around as a tourist would. His actions finally gave him a good opportunity to check the theoretical pursuer and assess his intentions. Peering through the glare, he saw it. Looking directly at the man in the yellow jacket, Max finally saw that the man occupying it was closing the gap with intent to do harm.

Fear clenched his heart and the blood drained from his face. Max's hand tremored in a slight, yet uncontrollable, shiver. A million thoughts populated his mind as he prepared to be attacked by the man in the yellow jacket.

The plan *was* to close the deal, take the money that would save his daughter, and return home a hero. Now, the plan was survival.

That's when a stab of lightning pain shot across his head.

That's when the cobblestone got closer and closer – the specks of granite glinting in the sun seemed like stars.

That's when Max's world went blank.

# Chapter 2

**Torino, Italy**

**Seven Years earlier - Winter 1990**

Either the alpine wind sweeping down into the Piedmontese valley or his nervousness caused Pier Luigi to shiver. This morning, he and his wife, Franca, walked the several blocks from their rented apartment to the Capitular Archives and crossed the piazza whose damp paver stones twinkled like sunbursts damp from the tentative morning sun. By the time they entered the side door into the vestibule and presented themselves at the guard's desk, Pier Luigi's chills had turned to profuse sweating.

The scrawny, unshaven guard looked up from his daily inspection of the newspaper and a story of the super-rich, Fiat-financed team's star striker's battle with cocaine addiction. Pier Luigi saw the look on the man's face and could sense what he must have thought of the couple – Beauty and the Beast. The mismatched pair presented their identification for inspection as the guard pulled his attention away from the paper and regarded the visitor's proffered identification with practiced ambivalence. The guard had been told to expect the married couple, professors of antiquities, but had probably not expected their appearance to be so...different.

The husband, Pier Luigi Scarsi, presented his papers for inspection first. The guard observed the short, doughy professor. The professor had a large nose and bigger ears and tried to hide his lack of a chin with a large, gray-flecked beard which made him look gnomish rather than distinguished. While the wife fumbled through her purse retrieving her documents, the guard pointed to an open log book for Pier Luigi to sign.

"Do you need to look at my bag?" Pier Luigi asked.

"Not when you enter. But when you leave, I will inspect every bag," said the guard.

The guard reviewed the woman's identification more carefully. Pier Luigi knew most people never guessed that she was as old as forty-one. Franca Làconi's dark haired and statuesque beauty immediately brought to mind the Italian sex goddess of the sixties, Sophia Loren. Pride and embarrassment bled together as the guard looked back at him…the gnome.

After copying the pertinent information from the professor's identification into an oversized ledger, the guard stamped the date and handed the visitors laminated badges. The University of Padua professors of Antiquities had been invited to inventory a small section of the manuscripts, books, and documents held at the Capitular Archives of the Archdiocese of Torino. The guard mumbled for them to wait in the vestibule where the couple could wait for their new employer to arrive.

Pier Luigi leaned on one foot then the next as he watched the scruffy guard eye his wife and then look back at him. It happened all the time. Pier Luigi saw the snigger, the twitch of a smile, the snort, or what poker players called a 'tell'. He saw it every time they were together – even when it never happened. Pier Luigi knew he was nobody's idea of handsome. Yet, despite the obvious mismatch in physical stature, or perhaps because of it, Franca gravitated to him. Perhaps because of his strange looks, his clever wit, intellect and rakish charm had won her over. Perhaps not.

Maybe one day, he thought, she'd wake up and see she'd made a mistake.

However now, after years of courtship and many years of marriage, the professors were respected antiquarians whose various published academic discourses had received praise from their peers and had led them to this job. Neither of them was nervous about the work. At least, not about the official work for which they were being paid.

The building they entered housed the archives and joined, through a labyrinth of hallways and connecting rooms, the Cathedral of St. John the Baptist. Originally the site of an ancient Roman Theatre and the site of Catholic churches going back to the year 591, the archives contained an expansive and rich trove of important historical documents and artifacts.

A phone rang. The guard looked up at the couple. The ringing was coming from one of them and the sound echoed off the walls creating a cacophony that surely half the world could hear. Franca checked her purse and shot her husband a look when she realized it wasn't hers.

Pier Luigi fumbled, put down his bag and finally dug out his mobile phone, answering it on the sixth ring. "*Pronto, chi parla?*" he answered. He looked up at Franca and the guard and then looked down the hallway before drifting away from the guard's desk.

"Yes, Yes, I know. No, No this is not a good time to speak," he said in English as both the guard and his wife looked on.

"Yes. Of course. I will call you." A muted and indistinguishable voice could be heard on the other end. Pier Luigi's head nodded like a bobble head doll as he strained to end the conversation.

"I have nothing now. As I told you..." More waiting. Pier Luigi's pushed his head down but his eyes stayed on the guard who in return squinted while observing the English-speaking Italian professor. "Yes, I will call. Ciao, Ciao."

Franca looked at Pier Luigi and raised her eyebrows while tilting her head.

Yes. Pier Luigi gave the slightest nod.

Franca turned to the guard and offered a movie star smile, good enough for the red carpet.

Her husband returned his phone to the bag after powering it off and pulled out a handkerchief to wipe his brow. Before his anxiety became debilitating, footsteps from down the long corridor echoed off the tile floor and high barrel ceilings. Monsignor Pregliasco approached them with a smile; a warm two-handed handshake for Pier Luigi and the customary kiss on both cheeks for Franca. His hair was thin and combed straight back. His barrel chest and hearty grip conveyed a powerful physical presence balanced by his heavy jowls and lively eyes which exuded a quality of frankness and fairness of a man on a mission. He motioned for them to follow.

"Thank you for coming today. I'm so pleased that you agreed." He spoke in clipped sentences. He placed his hands together in a gesture of prayer and thanks. "We have a lot of important work to do. I can't wait for you to get started. The collection is vast. It's overwhelming my ability to inventory it. Hundreds of years of wars, fires, thefts and political power grabs have both added to and reduced the collection. Your expertise will be especially helpful."

"We are pleased to be here. Thank you," answered Pier Luigi.

"We have Cardinal Burtone to thank. He is the one promoting the idea of digitizing the Church's collection. He requested that the work should begin with the Capitular Archives of the Archdiocese."

Pier Luigi nodded.

"To tell you the truth, I had an in," the Monsignor continued while sharing a conspiratorial smile. "Cardinal Burtone grew up nearby and I'm from Ivrea; so we are neighbors. He asked me to oversee this effort."

"I, myself, grew up only a few kilometers from there, in Strambino,"

Pier Luigi said.

"I know. Why do you think you were chosen?" He let out a belly laugh and pushed out his elbow to tap the professor. "No. Seriously, being Piedmontese didn't hurt, but you two came highly recommended."

"Thank you," responded Franca. Her eyebrows furled and she took an unconscious step backward. Pier Luigi blanched. He knew she had fought for education and respect all her life but the nagging self-consciousness of her upbringing on a backwater island in an overlooked province still made her feel left out. He reached a hand out to her which she ignored.

"Now, the first step in this process is to find out, once and for all, what these archives actually possess. Over the centuries, numerous inventories had been conducted but a full- fledged, comprehensive inventory has never been completed. I hope that you will be able to complete the task of inventorying the tens of thousands of individual items soon so that we can begin the digitization process in summer. My goal is to finish the task before I retire...or die." He finished with another hearty chuckle. "Come. Let me show you where you will be working."

They set off down the wide, dimly lit corridor whose only source of light came from the high window transoms that ran atop the solid wall to the left. The three passed several unoccupied rooms as the Monsignor spoke to the professors about the importance of their task.

Before reaching their destination Franca asked, "Cardinal Burtone is in Rome at the Congregation for the Doctrine of the Faith, is he not?"

Monsignor Pregliasco stood back in surprise. "Yes, he is."

"What does your inventory of antique breviaries, missals, bible and such have to do with that defending the Church against heresy?"

Monsignor Pregliasco's head wobbled in shock by the professor's abrupt question and even more so by her knowledge of the Roman Curia, but answered, "You know Church organization very well Profesoressa Làconi." The Monsignor, unaccustomed to being questioned by lay people, bristled at explaining himself. Deciding that the truth may help stress the importance of the job, he offered, "This project is more personally motivated by the Cardinal's love of books and antiquities than his official duties."

The three continued to make their way down the hall. It really didn't matter for their purposes who had hired them to complete the task but they listened just the same. "I know that when he was a small child, the future Cardinal was very sick. His life was saved by a local doctor. That doctor's daughter and the Cardinal were good friends. They grew up in a small town called Romano Canavese; very close to where you are from, Professor Scarsi."

Pier Luigi smiled. "It is really just a village. But yes....it is just next door to Strambino."

Pregliasco continued, "Because it was her father who saved his life, the bond of friendship grew stronger. They remain friends even today." The Monsignor stopped at the last door on the right which stood a few meters away from a large atrium and turned to his guests to finish the story and make the point of connection. "Would you believe that his childhood friend, the daughter of the doctor who saved his life, married a famous and influential rare and antique bookseller here in Torino?"

"What a coincidence," Pier Luigi said and rolled his eyes at Franca when the Monsignor wasn't looking. He didn't understand the point of the story.

The Monsignor smiled and continued, "Not a coincidence, the childhood friend's husband, Arturo Principe, owns one of the most world-renowned and respected rare and antique bookshops. He has been very influential with the Cardinal in encouraging the Church to do more to protect the antique books and to become better stewards of the histori-cal items that they had been given."

"So, the Cardinal is using his influence to preserve antique books?" Franca asked.

"*Exacto*," The Monsignor replied as he opened the door and invited the professors to enter.

Pier Luigi had no interest in the workings of the Roman Curia and instead marveled at the towering heights of the ceilings. The entire building seemed to be designed for giants; the door being able to accommodate two of his height's walking upright.

Franca, on the other hand, furled her brow in concern. She leaned over to her husband and whispered, "Why would someone as influential as Cardinal Burtone be involved in the oversight of the project?"

Pier Luigi shrugged, unsure of how much to worry out this new information.

The couple stepped into the small room's only entrance. The sparsely furnished room contained only a large table in the center, a side table on which a computer sat, and two solidly built but well-worn chairs. On the opposite side, two tall, narrow windows opened to the courtyard below. A severe looking middle-aged man in clerical garb with a full head of gray hair and large caterpillar-sized black eyebrows looked up from his work as they entered.

"This is Fr. Paolo Giorgi," said the Monsignor indicating the man dressed in a cassock. The man went back to aligning papers and logbooks on the table. "He will be assisting you in this task." The professors smiled and the cleric nodded with his eyes. No pleasantries were exchanged. "The log books here," indicating the large format, handwritten books that Fr. Giorgi was adjusting, "are for you to cross-reference the items. All information should be recorded into the computer for a final and complete inventory of the archive's possessions."

"I understood that we would be working in the archives themselves," Pier Luigi said.

"I'm afraid we cannot allow that," the Monsignor replied. "No one may enter the archives from outside our Order. I'm sure you understand." Pier Luigi did – he also understood that this new security measure would make their task much more difficult. "The items we have in our trust and care have incredible historical and spiritual importance and we cannot risk any…" The Monsignor struggled with the next phrase trying not to offend his guests whose help he had enlisted, "misplacement of the items."

A nervous moment passed.

The Monsignor put on a big smile and continued. "We've tried to make you comfortable here and there are facilities," indicating the bathroom. "You should have everything you need to make yourselves comfortable while you complete your work."

Pier Luigi looked around noticing the plastered walls, graying with age and adorned with nothing but a crucifix above the door to the washroom. He wondered if he would consider this plain room a luxury should his plan fail.

Monsignor Pregliasco noticed the professors' strained expression and quickly added, "Fr. Giorgi will be able to retrieve the items from the stacks. He has spent years here in the archives and will be most helpful in the process. I'm sure that this arrangement will be the most efficient and quick."

Pier Luigi gave his wife a brief glance which indicated his distress at the new arrangements and turned back to say, "Yes, this will work fine, thank you."

"Very well, I will leave you to do your work." As the Monsignor was leaving he pressed the professors to commit, "Do you agree that we may be able to start the digitizing process by summer?"

"We have leave from the university for this semester and have leased the apartment for three months. We do not expect it to take longer," Pier

Luigi answered.

"Very well, thank you," the Monsignor said as he was leaving the room. "If you need anything please let Fr. Giorgi know and I will see what I can do."

After the Monsignor had left, Fr. Giorgi spoke his first words, "I expect that you will start by transcribing the log books into the computer format." Pier Luigi and Franca nodded. "The archives are classified already but I will continue to prepare them for your inspection. When we are ready to begin the physical inspection, I can bring the items you request down on a cart and then return them when completed," said Fr. Giorgi.

When Fr. Giorgi first learned of the plans to bring the couple in, he had complained bitterly about inviting outsiders to do the task of the Order. He had only relented when he was told that the Cardinal himself insisted on getting expert outside opinions for the inventory.

Fr. Giorgi continued with his instructions. "Unfortunately, I cannot allow you to go beyond this room into the rest of the library. These are our protocols. Lastly, while the books are here in this room, neither of you are to leave the room without my permission..."

He had cut himself off and decided to restate. "Please don't leave without discussing with me first...for security's sake. I'm sure you understand." The cleric took his leave.

"What a *stronzo* that guy is!" Franca said after the cleric had left. "What does he think? That we are amateurs! We are recognized and accomplished experts in this field and he treats us like school children. Does he not know our credentials?"

"Relax. He's just not happy that outsiders have come to do his work," Pier Luigi walked over to touch Franca's arm. "He's not attacking our self-worth. He just sees us as a threat to his status in the library," Pier Luigi said, making sure to indicate that he too recognized the perceived slight. He knew that the cleric's cold reception combined with the Monsignor's familiar attitude with a fellow Piedmontese tapped into Franca's insecurity about her upbringing. For all her credentials and professional success, Pier Luigi knew she needed reassurance. His touch became a hug. "Don't get so upset."

It wasn't the first time that class distinction of their families had caused problems. Pier Luigi tried to empathize. But he couldn't. After all, what Franca thought of the dusty ferry town where she grew up, was paradise to Pier Luigi. To Franca, the cluster of rocks off of the southwest corner of Sardinia was a symbol of inequality. To her, the island represented a prison of ignorance where the children of brutish chambermaids and fishermen tortured her existence and made fun of her intellect. To Pier Luigi, the arid landscape crisscrossed by stone fences surrounded by crystal clear turquoise seas was a magical place where he could take pleasure in relief from scholastic pressure and enjoy the rare love and warmth of his usually emotionally cold parents.

The island transformed every year in August with the arrival of hordes of wealthy northern tourists. During the middle of the dry season; when brown permeated the landscape and fine dust accumulated the green leaves of the trees, Pier Luigi's family descended, not for verdant land but, to enjoy the sun, the brilliantly hued water, and the cliffs which rose dramatically from the sea. The visitors used their boats, not to earn a living fishing but to enjoy the numerous grottos, underwater caves and to explore hidden beaches.

Back home in a town at the foot of the Alps, Pier Luigi's parents pushed him to pursue math and the sciences. They wouldn't listen to his pleas to study his passion, literature. Instead, they regimented his daily activities and pressed him to achieve the lofty academic goals they had set for him. On the few occasions he was allowed free time, he played soccer with his friends. Not that he was athletic. On the contrary, the chubby boy was physically weak and uncoordinated. But his quick wit, kind manner and ability to make others laugh gained him a margin of acceptance by the other boys.

But on the island, everything was different – his business-obsessed father did not hound him about schoolwork and his socialite mother seemed pleasant and attentive to his needs. While Franca holed up in a pew, the Scarsi family boated, finding anchorage off the small inlets which dotted the island. Pier Luigi looked up in awe and dreamed as the massive cliffs presented a grand canvas of rocky outcropping whose colors and shadows changed based on the sun's location. In the gentle breezes, Pier Luigi smelled freedom from the regiment of scholastic demands. In the dusty rocks, Pier Luigi saw heaven.

But the lives of the locals and tourists remained as separate as fingers on different hands; only coming together for work. To Pier Luigi, the times on that island represented the happiest of his life, to Franca the most miserable. Where he saw a quaint town and summer resort, she saw a circle of poverty and dead-end jobs. The differences in their upbringing only pronounced Franca's insecurity and fed the seeds of envy. Their very differing views were a fissure in their relationship which, like tectonic plates, could exist without harm for some time before an earthquake eventually happened.

"Come on and cheer up. We're the Antiquities Power Couple," he said – an inside joke.

"Like such a thing exists," she said. "Half of the students are studying to become professors, so the university doesn't need to pay us much. We can always be replaced."

"You sound like an economics professor now," he said. He became serious and looked into her eyes, "That's why we need to do what we planned. Besides, we somehow need to pay for our apartment and the beach house. You know, keeping up with all your wealthy society 'friends' costs more money than we make."

"Who is being the economist now?" She broke away from his embrace and busied herself with her purse. "They're your friends, too." Her frown worked overtime. "It's just not fair."

Pier Luigi knew that spending at the rate of their clients and peers had left them with significant debt. The pay from this project to inventory the Archdiocese's archives would help. But barring a newfound resolve to practice financial self-discipline and a moderate lifestyle, nothing would solve their financial woes except for what they had in mind.

Franca balked when he first presented the idea, Pier Luigi remembered. He tried to explain the financial situation, that lifestyle choices, like the vacation house in Cote d'Azur, caused this problem. Franca spat back that Pier Luigi, too, spent much of the money and enjoyed the very same lifestyle that he was now condemning. Pier Luigi insisted that he would have been just as happy vacationing with his family. Franca retaliated with scorn, seeing every attempt to cut back spending as a personal affront and proof that he no longer loved her.

The opportunity to inventory the antiquities collection helped. It certainly paid better than the university. But when the couple celebrated their financial windfall with lavish spending, they began the project in even greater debt than before they accepted the position.

"I don't feel good about this....this Father Giorgi. He will make our task more difficult to accomplish," Franca said.

"Cheer up. Once Giorgi gets accustomed to us, we'll find the security gaps and then we can do as we planned." He hesitated and then a little more tenderly said, "Besides, who could resist a beautiful woman like you?"

"He's not interested in me." She said and cast her face down in a frown. "Did you see the way he totally ignored me?"

"You are irresistible to all men, even men of God," he added without irony. "Come on...don't be silly," he continued to smooth his hand over her back. "Once Giorgi believes that we are only here to serve his interests, he will become more open. You will see. I can be very persuasive. Remember, I persuaded you." He laughed.

"*Va bene*," she said wrapping her arms around him and nestled her head in his shoulder.

The two began their work.

# Chapter 3

**St. Augustine, FL**
**September 1997**

"I'm afraid, Max, that some people are going to lose their jobs," the big man said from across the massive desk.

While waiting in the big boss's office, Max had been day dreaming about redecorating it when he took over. Now, he hoped he was still dreaming. A cold wave of dread washed over him. Beads of sweat sprung from his pores and he could feel the chill from the over eager air-conditioning vent above him. Maybe the blasting arctic air will keep him from losing consciousness.

Only moments ago Max was bouncing his feet on the deep pile carpet of the executive floor– so different than the flat industrial crap they had down on his floor. Wasn't it bad enough that when Max's elevator arrived on the executive floor that little shit, Vince – assistant to the vice president – Lolli, called out in mock alarm, "Minion Alert! Minion Alert?" He heard his big boss say one time at a cocktail party that if you couldn't see the corner office from yours by the time you were forty, you'd never get there. Well, Max was closing in on that age and nowhere near the destination. Worse, he was being accosted as an interloper for just appearing on the executive floor.

"One of the most poorly kept secrets is that we're headed for a re-org," the big man continued while leaning back on his leather throne. "All the directors have been asked to submit one primary and one alternate name for headcount reduction." Max's normally open, big-toothed smile, closed and his pulse rose quickly. He felt his face flush red and he shifted his gangly body in his chair.

"Your name is on the list," the big man finally said.

Max's chest constricted and felt all the color leave his face "Wha... What? I can't lose my job." Max stammered as he jumped forward. The big man put his hand up to hold off comments. Theodore Armistead Buford was an imposing man who carried himself in such a way that no one ever tried to call 'Ted' or 'Teddy'. Just shy of fifty years old, his blond hair was tightly cropped and thinning a bit on top. He had broad shoulders and walked with a slight limp that, rather than detract from his vigor, actually projected a greater sense of power.

"Now, there's been some pushback from me and a few others about the list. But ultimately, Wilson is your director and gets to pick his team. His recommendation to let you go will hold a lot of sway.

That rat bastard weasel, Max thought. A flush of heat resumed to his face with the rising anger. "But that can't be! I'm the top performer in the group. Wilson and I were up for the same position only a few months ago before he got it."

"Now being on the list doesn't mean you'll be fired. But it's third and long." The big man grabbed an autographed football from one of the several lined up on the credenza behind him. He spun it and tossed it to himself. The entire corner office contained memorabilia from the man's Alma Mater. Even a piece of artificial turf from the stadium adorned the walls. There was no way of telling by the décor that Theodore Armistead Buford wasn't the university's athletic director instead of being the area vice president, or AVP, of RK Trucking.

Earlier today, when the big boss had called him into the gigantic corner office, Max thought it was a good sign. Now, it clearly was not.

"Let me ask you a question," the big man said. To Max, this was not fact finding query –it was an accusation. People didn't ask Max questions because they were curious; they asked him questions to find the guilty party.

Theodore almost reclined in the chair as he palmed the ball in his left hand. The transformation was on. Just a good ole Palatka boy, talkin' man to man, honest, just askin' to learn. No need to worry. Max knew better – when the big boss talked country, it was time to worry. Theodore tilted his head to the side and asked, "D'you think I don't know what's goin' on?"

"I'm not sure what you mean, sir." Max had difficulty keeping his voice level. He straightened in his seat.

Theodore continued to stare as a cat might at a cornered mouse.

Max's eyes darted around the room to avoid the man's gaze. Lose his job? Max took shallow breaths to tamp down a wave of nausea. His teeth started to itch.

Theodore leaned way back in his seat and reached behind him to put the ball back on the credenza. He turned faced Max and leaned forward placing his elbow on the arm of his chair. He kept his wrist loose as if any moment he could flick it and dismiss Max as a Roman Emperor would send Christians to the lions. He made sure that he had his subordinate's full and undivided attention.

Max's condition changed from squirming to panic.

"You know exactly what I'm talkin' about," Theodore said. "You don't think I see?"

Max's face turned hot and his heart raced.

"You gettin' in a little later, leavin' a little earlier, takin' a little longer lunch. Makin' snide remarks during the weekly meetin's." The letter 'G' didn't exist on Theodore's roll. "You tryin' to stick it to Wilson. Aren't you?"

"Well I, I ..." Max stammered. Of course, Max had done what Theodore accused...he just didn't think it was that obvious. He didn't think that the weasel would have complained about him – but then, he was a weasel. If Theodore had recognized the behavior, Max was being too obvious.

"Look, I know you're upset that you didn't get the director's spot. It was a hard decision but, at the end of the day, Wilson got the startin' job. He's worked here longer, been in different departments, and spent his time on the practice squad. Frankly, he's more mature." Max blanched at the shot to his maturity. "Don't think of it as being on the bench. I still need you workin' the special teams and handlin' the clipboard."

"But I'm creative..."

"Yes, you are. I appreciate that. You got a gun on you, son and you can throw the ball down the field, for sure. But you gotta be able to deliver it in the seams to be a starter."

"But I'm a better sales person and…"

"There you go. Talkin' when you should be listenin'. That's a sign that you're not mature enough to lead the team."

"But I…"

"There is no 'I' in 'TEAM'!" Buford bellowed.

"But there is one in 'WIN'," Max blurted out before he could think better of it.

Theodore flushed and yelled, "You wanna to go out on your own?" He waited as he watched Max squirm. "I'm sure you'll be successful. Lots of entrepreneurs are. Make this whole downsizin' thing a whole lot easier!"

Max leaned forward in supplication, "No, no, no. That's not what

I meant. I'm sorry I was only trying to be funny. I need this job and the insurance. I've got three kids and a wife to support at home."

"You want to be a show-boater?" Theodore continued, avoiding Max's home responsibilities. "I'll have you return punts. But it takes more than that to lead the team. You can't throw the ball, catch the ball and block at the same time. You need to work together. You want the starting job as QB? You gotta show maturity and better judgment."

Max flinched at the accusation of immaturity. It was his Achilles Heel and the dressing down stunned him.

"And I can tell you that pissin' off Wilson won't make you a more attractive candidate for the next promotion." Boy, did he sound like Laura, Max thought.

"I understand. I'm sorry."

"Well, all right. But it's your demeanor and perception that you need to improve. You got a long career ahead of you. This is a minor setback, a five-yard false start penalty in the first quarter. It can be overcome if you don't compound the mistakes. First rule when you're in a hole is to stop diggin'! And let me tell you, young man," Theodore continued. "You got way more advantages than I did at your age. Daddy was a potato farmer in Palatka. I'm the youngest of twelve and the first to go to college. Shoot, the first time I left the state was when they invited me to play ball in Knoxville. The only thing I learned in college was how to tackle… and not even that well. Had to start here at RK as an assistant dispatcher working the night shift."

Max knew the story. He also knew that Theodore had no enemies in the company – he had disposed of them during his climb up the ladder. Theodore may have escaped a life of a North Florida potato farmer but never abandoned his twang which he used to disarm opponents. "You gotta good education, you're young, hungry, know the business, and you got a sharp mind. Heck, you even look the part," he chuckled, "good lookin' guy, tall and lean with a good head of hair."

Theodore dropped the heavily affected accent and got more serious; the g's returned. "Now your timing for this little temper tantrum couldn't be worse. Corporate is asking for headcount reduction and we will be losing good people. It's up to you to make sure you aren't one of them."

Max looked around the room failing to focus on any particular item, his head spinning from the discussion. A few weeks ago, he was one of the leading candidates for promotion and now he was on the chopping block with the victor swinging the ax. "I understand and will straighten up. I won't let you down," Max said.

Relieved yet not totally convinced, Theodore said, "That's what I want to hear. I can only do so much. You got to take it one game at a time and leave it all out on the field…is all I can ask. And to that…you can start by proving your maturity and value at the Refrigerated and Frozen Food Conference."

Max had almost forgotten. Months ago, he had contacted the conference organizers and offered his services as a speaker. When they accepted, Max cajoled his former boss for approval to attend. He passed the buck to Buford.

"Your trip to Zurich, Switzerland has been approved." Even on the edge of being fired, the prospect of an international business trip buoyed Max's spirits.

"Thank you. It's a good opportunity to get our company's name out there," Max responded with a toothy smile.

"Yeah, well it's also the week before a final decision will be made on the job cuts. So this could be either a place for you to shine or a swan song. Now I'm calling an audible and putting you in. Give it a hundred and ten percent and don't let me regret sending you. Think of it as the NFL combine – your chance to show us what you can do."

"I won't let you down, Mr. Buford."

Theodore nodded and looked to his desk picking up a file. "We'll see soon enough."

# Chapter 4

Max clenched his eyes creating total darkness while his skin seared from the hot water pounding his back. A few moments of calm. Soon, the peace and quiet would end.

"Let me ask you a question," his wife, Laura, demanded as Max stepped out of the shower and stood towel-less on the fringed, pea green bath mat. "What did you do with the three thousand dollars?" His wife leaned cross-armed against the closed door. Back a few years, unclothed conversations in a steamy bathroom were naughty and stimulating. Now, they were confrontations Laura forced Max to have to get out of sight from their three children who were always underfoot in the two bedroom, 1930's built bungalow they occupied on Anastasia Island.

"Did you give the money to Kevin?" Laura said knowing Max's fascination with new business ventures. The current scheme involved the manufacturing of stackable, modular, vaccine storage trays with spring loaded dispensing rows that Max's old college roommate had assured were in great demand in hospitals and pediatrician offices. When Kevin proposed starting a business to supply the trays, Max jumped at the chance to double, triple, even quintuple his money without much consideration to the fact that he didn't know anything about the medical accessories market.

Max's heart rate kicked up as he stood exposed, both literally and figuratively. "It's not giving. It's investing."

"Do you have any idea, Max, how tight we are?"

"I know, I know. Why do you think I'm doing this? It's to make more money, to pay our bills, to have a better life…for all of us." Max knew this was not the time to mention Theodore's warning.

"You don't know! If you did, you'd know we don't have the money for your fantasy projects."

"Hey, that's not fair. We'll make enough profits from the trays to pay for all of our bills plus some," Max said. "Maybe we can even take a trip. You and me. You know? Like a honeymoon." The honeymoon that we never had, Max thought, because we got married senior year of college only months before the arrival of our daughter, settling for a February wedding in her mother's living room and a "reception" at the Golden Palace Chinese restaurant next to the TJ Maxx. The only consolation for Laura was that the college graduation gown hid her six-month form.

"You think I'm an idiot? We don't need a trip!" She said 'trip' with great affectation and air quotes. "We need to pay some of these damned bills and get crap around here fixed. And what about Sam's treatment?" Without waiting for an answer she sneered, furrowing her brow "Besides, what do you even know about vaccine storage?"

"The trays are really cool. There's nothing else like it on the market. I've got a line on some distributors that might be interested. Kevin has some guys, too. The margins are really good so we don't need to sell many to break even."

"Is this going to be like the diet mints? What a scam that was! Or the inflatable light that looks like a condom?" she asked staring him down. She could have mentioned the non-stick pans or the phone cards or many other business ideas but it was hard for her to keep track of all of them. "What about the glues and electrical products from South Africa that were supposed to sell?"

Her face reddened and eyes became swollen as she turned toward the steamy mirror and tossed a bath towel toward Max. "You know? I don't even care." Tears rolled down her face. "You do what you want! I'll just have to take care of the kids by myself."

"Look!" Max opened his mouth and forced a breath causing an audible whistle. Getting worked up never worked, but he did it anyway. "I could go through those business plans point by point and they were good ideas at the time. I'm not dumb. I know business."

Laura pursed her lips and shook her head.

"You're right," he continued. "Some of those were not the greatest ideas."

Same conversation, different day, with minor changes in the details. Same result – frustration all around. Max strained to keep his voice down, "I'm busting my butt to try to provide the best income I can for us. I've got to take chances to make money…so I don't have to work in cubicle city all day. I should be going to the meetings in New York. I should be running that place! If they're not going to recognize it, I'll have to do my own thing. I can do more – for me, for us."

Laura opened the door and stepped out of the bathroom, flicking her hand dismissively over her shoulder, "Well, you should concentrate on the job you have instead of spending your efforts elsewhere and maybe they will!"

"Laura, wait," Max implored, following behind her in his towel stepping past the laundry basket and the pile of library books neatly stacked against the wall.

Laura spun and glared at Max speaking in a low rumble, "You don't think your bosses see that you're distracted?"

"Don't give me that," Max said. "I'm the best salesperson in that office. My numbers are the best. They're lucky to have me!"

Laura proceeded to the kitchen and threw the bread soaking in the egg mixture onto the pan. "Then why did they promote Wilson and not you?" she said, working the pan while insisting on an answer. "Huh?"

"Wilson's exactly the kind of weasel they promote into those positions. He stands there tapping his watch if I'm only a minute late back from lunch." Laura rolled her eyes believing neither the description of Wilson's actions nor Max's concession of being only a minute late. "I didn't want that job anyway. It's all reports and crap like that."

"You're impossible," she said turning to the stove. "Shit! It's burnt." She flipped the burnt ones onto a plate and dropped them in front of Max. After putting new bread, freshly dripping with egg, onto the pan, she said, "Just tell me that this is the last of the investment in those trays. I don't want any more of our money going to Kevin's plans. Matter of fact, no more crazy schemes of any kind! And concentrate on work…you know? The one that pays you."

"Okay. I won't. I will, I promise," Max stammered. The calm had returned. "When we get this batch sold, we'll make three thousand dollars plus our initial money back."

"We could use it. I received a package from CHOP yesterday. They're willing to take Sam. The timing is right for the greatest chance of success."

"Great, let's sign her up for it."

"Dammit, Max! We already went over this. Your insurance doesn't cover the surgery and it's the only known way to totally cure her. The medication only treats her flare-ups. It's not a cure. And we have enough trouble just paying those deductibles."

"Let's get the paperwork going and we'll figure it out."

Laura tilted her head looking at Max as if observing colossal stupidity for the first time. "It's ten grand for the surgery and that doesn't even include travel, hotels, meals, daycare for the boys…it's really expensive and your crap insurance doesn't cover it. We can't just 'sign her up for it'." The anger and disdain returned in spades.

"We're not that bad off. I have my bonus coming in a few months."

"You have no idea what I go through, Max, because you never see a bill."

Thinking about bills, Max looked over at the corner where twin boys played quietly, speaking a language which only they could understand. He scooped them up in each arm and brought them together, snuggling his head in between them. They fussed slightly as he breathed in their fresh morning smell and smiled. After a moment, he bent down to place them back in their pen; his smiled tempered remembering his Uncle Jimmy's saying, 'when they're little, they're little expenses. When they're big, they're big expenses'.

Laura continued, "Yesterday, I got a call from a collector about the emergency room visit we made with Sam last month."

"Just ignore them," Max said. And then looked at his wife's crushed face and slumped shoulders. He stepped toward her and held her, "At least Sam is okay now – and things will turn around. All I need is for one of these deals to hit and we'll be able to pay for the surgery; no problem."

Samantha arrived prematurely, surprising the newlyweds, their families, and the doctors. Ten years old now, she still suffered health issues from the Congenital Cystic Adenomatoid Malformation (CCAM) diagnosed before birth. Their oldest child's chest contained benign lung lesions which appeared as cysts or lumps in the chest and caused intermittent breathing issues. While the condition can be treated with medication, the only curative solution was surgery at the Children's Hospital of Pennsylvania (CHOP). Samantha seemed constantly behind the eight ball; struggling to breath with poorly developed lungs due, perhaps, to insufficient time in the womb. Laura blamed herself for the premature delivery believing that planning a wedding, studying for finals and dealing with a disappointed family may have caused Samantha to be born with the chronic disease.

Sometimes, Max thought, the same could be said of his marriage to Laura. They loved each other but perhaps their relationship never had enough time to develop and mature. When Laura became pregnant, they were thrust into the responsibilities of parenthood before the obligations and self-sacrifice of marriage could be mastered. Maybe that was why now, as the pressure to provide for his family mounted, he felt most alone.

"Yeah, but what if she has another episode?"

"The hospital has got to take her in. They're not going to refuse a sick kid at the emergency room door."

"Great," Laura said sarcastically as she pushed away from Max and walked back toward the stove. "Now, we're a welfare case," she grumbled into the frying pan. She banged around setting the pans in proper order and getting the stove temperature right and then turned around to Max.

She stared at him with her beautiful green eyes, the beacons of attraction that first engrossed Max years ago. Usually flashing with life and joy, they now revealed pain and disappointment. He wanted to look away but couldn't.

Overwhelmed by the sense of futility, Laura broke down and started to cry, "I don't want to live like this!"

Max stepped toward her and held her tight. "I'm doing my best. Things will be all right. I'll get the money back from this investment… with profit. And things are really looking up at work. Bonus is right around the corner."

"Are you okay, Mommy?" Samantha had just walked into the room.

"I'm fine, honey," Laura said, trying to pull herself together. "Your breakfast is on the table. Go and eat and make sure you drink all of your orange juice. Did you put your homework in the red folder?"

"Yes," Samantha said as she walked to the table, making sure to put her American Girl doll on the seat next to her first.

"I've got to get to work." Max disengaged himself from Laura.

"Okay, don't be late," she said wiping a tear from her eye and trying to regain her commanding tone. "Wilson won't be happy."

"That guy is such a weasel," Max replied deciding not to mention the headcount list Wilson was making.

As he grabbed his coat and walked toward Samantha to kiss her good-bye, Laura said, "Well, he is your boss so you can't piss him off."

"Ha-ha. Weasel," Samantha laughed. "You're funny, Daddy."

"Well, I'd like to have that weasel's bonus," Laura said.

He walked over to where the boys were playing and picked each up and gave them a hug and kiss.

"Weasel, weasel, weasel," Samantha sang until interrupted with a coughing fit.

# Chapter 5

"Let me ask you a question," Edgar leaned forward and stared directly into Max's eyes as he spoke. Max recoiled at the phrase. Edgar was just a friend – an acquaintance really – guy who owned a used book shop in the historic section of town. They'd struck up a conversation a few weeks ago and followed up with this lunch. The question shouldn't make him nervous. Except it did.

Max had a little extra time as Wilson and his AVP were both out today, but he still looked at his watch, conscious of the time. The two men sat at a sidewalk café having lunch on Avilla Street in St. Augustine. The narrow street, designed for the horse and buggy days, limited the automobile traffic and became a tourist attraction where several restaurants offered sidewalk table service. Flowering plants hung on the second-floor balconies and red, yellow, and green table umbrellas framed the cobblestone street to give it an old world feel on this unnaturally cool September day.

The two men's business attire confirmed that they were not tourists. Bald on top with the few remaining hairs combed straight back, Edgar's dark skin and almond shaped eyes announced his Mediterranean ancestry. Almost a head shorter than Max, his slight frame, paunch and sloping shoulders made him appear older than thirty-eight. His soft body, bald head, and round, open face made him look a bit like Charlie Brown – if Charlie were middle aged and more brown. But Edgar's quick smile and demonstrative facial expressions belied his intensity, cunning, and cut-throat nature.

Even though Max only knew Edgar a short time and didn't have a history to have done anything wrong, the question made Max anxious. The phrase, 'let me ask you a question' always gave Max a queasy feeling and put him on the defensive. When he was a kid, it as an opener adults used before launching into an object lesson followed by punishment. Max reviewed the files in his mind to ascertain what he might have done wrong.

"Let me ask you a question," Edgar repeated again. After looking up and down the block, Edgar leaned in closer under the sidewalk café umbrella and said, "Would you be willing to help me with something?"

Max let out a deep breath of relief. Help. Yes, that is something I can do.

Max nodded approval and blasted his perfect smile.

Edgar continued, "You are going to Switzerland and...I can't get away," he said indicating his shop across the street. "I'm tied up here and if you could go...as my representative...or partner," he said with an ingratiating smile, "it would be most helpful."

Max leaned forward and raised his eyebrows but his pulse skipped a beat and quickened when Edgar said, "Of course, I would pay you."

Max's mind was made up even before Edgar added, "It could be worth a lot of money."

Max tried to remain cool and impassive. His heart raced and he failed to suppress the smile expanding across his face. Forgetting his promise to Laura, he said, "I'm interested. What do I need to do?"

"I have an antique manuscript and I need your help in transacting its sale. I can arrange the meeting but I need you to be there to close the deal."

Max knew nothing about antique manuscripts but blurted, "Sure. No problem." And then added, "So what is this thing and how'd you get it?"

"It's a manuscript, a hand-painted illustrated page of prayers for a particular saint's day. And don't worry about how I got it," Edgar said a tad too steely.

Max's head rocked back a bit but Edgar caught himself and let out a big laugh, a staccato Ah-Ah-Ah, like a penguin. "I'm kidding. All very legitimate. I purchased it from very reputable professors of antiquities. Only the highest quality and unassailable provenance."

Max leaned back and smiled. Edgar continued, "But in this business, you can never be too careful. Not everyone is so honest."

# Chapter 6

**Torino, Italy**
**Winter 1990**

Pier Luigi and Franca had both spent years studying, researching, and writing academic treatises exposing the secrets of ancient literature. Rare books were their shared passion. Now, they sat meters away from thousands of books that had not been read or even handled in hundreds of years. Cataloging them in this first ever, exhaustive inventory should have been stimulating and the pinnacle of their careers. However, the need to identify targets of theft occupied all of Pier Luigi's thoughts.

Pier Luigi could see that even Franca now began to feel the weight of deceit. Both knew that if…when…their plan succeeded, some of these works would never return to the library. Tension grew every time the priest brought down a cart of items.

The Archdiocese asked for this inventory because they didn't know what items they possessed. The professors agreed that if they only stole items that failed to appear on any of the previous handwritten inventories, the items wouldn't be missed. So long as they physically made it out of the archive building undetected, the items would never be identified as stolen and the professors would never be pursued as thieves.

Pier Luigi, however, grasped that once they set their plans in motion, the course of their lives would be changed; with either success or failure, he'd become a criminal. The realization expunged any potential joy or intellectual stimulation from the task.

***

About nine weeks into the professor's assignment, on a chilly Thursday at mid-morning, Fr. Giorgi delivered a full cart. He explained to Professor Scarsi, "These items on the top shelf are not on the list that you provided but they come from the same area of the library as the others. I think that they may belong to the section you are inventorying now. Some of the works are quite important."

Pier Luigi saw that the top shelf contained nearly fifty items and glanced quickly at Franca. The large number of items meant that one less item would probably not be missed by Fr. Giorgi when he returned the cart and replaced the books on the Library's stacks. Franca saw Pier Luigi's eyes shoot up and his head nod slightly.

It troubled Pier Luigi that Fr. Giorgi had not succumbed to Franca's or his charms and still regarded the professors in an aloof manner. The cleric continued to remain vigilant and formal even after these many weeks of working together, an attitude that made taking an item unnoticed, difficult.

However, the fifty items brought down on this cart were a lot for their attendant to remember. He could not be expected to recognize a missing item or two. Pier Luigi nodded to Fr. Giorgi and glanced again at Franca indicating that this may be the time to make their move.

Without looking up or pausing, the priest stacked the books and manuscripts on the large table where Pier Luigi sat ready to start the inspection.

Earlier, back in their apartment, Pier Luigi pressed Franca on a key point, "We need to also consider the physical size of the item. We will need to carry the item out, most likely under our clothes, to get it past the guard and out of the building. It can't be too big or heavy." Franca nodded at the challenge. "Whatever we decide to take, a book, manuscript, whatever...it needs to be small enough to smuggle and valuable to the...."

"The book dealer? The one you met in London?" Franca interjected. "The one who called you earlier?"

"Yes," Pier Luigi said. "The one who has been calling me." He paused and then added, "Let's make sure the item we take is valuable to him...no sense going through all of this to bring him something he won't pay for."

Back in the archive's room, after a cursory glance, Pier Luigi recognized a few items that would meet his criteria.

He nodded to Franca indicating that, yes, this was it.

His gaze first landed on a volume containing a design for a new cathedral of Turin made by an architect at the end of the 19th century which, while not very important, may be interesting to certain collectors and would not be missed. Next, he spied a bible with leather bound cover. He discreetly lifted the cover and noticed minor staining, light discoloration, and a few fox marks.

"Inscription in brown ink on the first page," he said as he described the bible of Antonio da Romagnano. He looked over at Franca and realized without speaking that she too had recognized the items and their value.

Not wanting to draw attention to the targeted items, Pier Luigi closed the cover of the bible and, with practiced indifference, dropped the book onto a random pile of books. The professors then worked to record the many other documents in a proficient manner.

The volume containing the cathedral's plans was rather large but fairly thin, about the size of a notebook, and could probably be placed in Pier Luigi's pants under his belt, resting on his back. With his suit jacket on, it would be difficult for the guard to notice the smuggled item as they left the building. But first, they needed to distract the priest's attention.

"Fr. Giorgi," Franca said. "Could you please have someone bring in some water? It is very dry in here."

The priest jerked his head upward as if being awoken from a minor daydream and looked up from his inspection of the books on the table. The request was not that unusual as the professors had been, for the past few weeks, practicing different techniques to get their attendant to leave the room in preparation for this day. After earlier requests for water, Fr. Giorgi had suggested bringing in another side table for coffee and water so that the professors could partake when necessary and without disturbing the priest's work. However, Pier Luigi had refused, stating that the extra furnishings would crowd the already cramped room.

"Yes, of course," Fr. Giorgi responded and started to move toward the door. "With gas or without?" he asked. "With, please." Franca smiled. Maybe he wasn't immune from Franca's charms, after all, thought Pier Luigi.

The professors knew from past experience that the priest would be gone for no more than three or four minutes. As soon as the door closed behind him, the professors stood up. Pier Luigi moved deftly around the table to the volume with the cathedral's plans. He turned and handed it to Franca as he unbuttoned his pants and unclasped his belt. With the now loosed pants opened, Franca stuck the architect's volume under his belt and then wedged the saint's bible between her husband's back and the volume. Pier Luigi reversed the process, tucked in his shirt and re-tightened his belt, now on the more extended belt loop. The architect's volume now formed an angled 'V' from his lower back extending to his mid-back wedging the bible snuggly up against him and only created a six-inch projection which would be covered by his suit jacket.

Pier Luigi walked gingerly to the coat rack in the corner and put on his suit jacket. The two professors returned to their seats. Moments later, and surely less than the three minutes they had been counting on, Fr. Giorgi returned with a bottle of San Pellegrino and a glass. That he neither asked after Pier Luigi's thirst nor brought a second glass told him that, yes, Fr. Giorgi was not immune from Franca's charms.

The priest looked at the scene in front of him and hesitated for the slightest of moments. If he suspected any change, he did not voice his suspicion. Could Fr. Giorgi possibly recognize that Pier Luigi, formerly in shirtsleeves, was now sitting in the exact same location in a suit jacket? The professors looked sideways at the priest to see.

"Professor?" the priest said to Pier Luigi. "Are you feeling well?" Pier Luigi remained seated, unblinking, staring at the opposite wall. "Professor?" the priest asked again, stepping closer.

"Yes! Fine." Shaken, Pier Luigi's head swiveled like a lizard upon hearing a loud noise. He directed his stare anywhere but at the priest. "No. I'm fine," Pier Luigi said as he settled his gaze and picked up a $16^{th}$ century book of illuminations. He lifted it slowly to eye level before coming to a complete stop. Mesmerized, he remained unmoving like a statue, painfully aware of the stolen books strapped to his back. He kept his back arched and immobile in order to minimize any possible protrusion from behind. For a while, he forgot to breathe. Sweat begin to bead on his forehead and his heart pounded so fast that he knew everyone could hear it. His erect posture physically drained him and he stared absently across the room in the direction of Fr. Giorgi, unable to continue his work.

The priest stared at him and then back to Franca.

Pier Luigi waited for the priest to make the connection. For a second, he thought of taking the volume and bible out of his pants and replacing them on the table. He could joke and laugh that he had played a funny trick. He didn't have the nerve for this type of deception and he wished with all his might that he be transported to anywhere in the world… except for here.

Franca poured the offered San Pellegrino into her glass and took a long drink, making sure to smile at Fr. Giorgi. The priest continued to look at Pier Luigi and, for a moment, it seemed that he would say something. Franca exclaimed, "Thank you so much. It is amazing how thirsty I get." Fr. Giorgi nodded. His bushy eyebrow shot up while still keeping his attention on Pier Luigi. Franca began to type loudly in an attempt to draw attention toward herself instead of at Pier Luigi who, at this point, looked as if he'd just swallowed rat poison.

Her husband finally awoke from his paralysis when Franca, speaking to no one in particular, launched into a small dissertation about the item Pier Luigi was holding, "Pier Luigi, it looks like you are holding an interesting miniature from the 15th century. You know," she said trying to get the attention of Fr. Giorgi, "that the word miniature in this sense does not refer to the size of the document but is derived from the Latin 'minium', where red lead pigment, has been 'miniated' or 'delineated' and used in the decoration of medieval illuminated manuscripts."

Fr. Giorgi's head nodded in appreciation.

"Of course," she continued, "the etymological confusion of the term 'miniature' with 'minuteness' is strengthened because many of these codices are generally small. It's something that the public and even students of mine have difficulty separating in their minds."

"Enlightening," Fr. Giorgi remarked. "I imagine that I never thought of that. But it makes sense."

Pier Luigi relaxed his breathing and drew confidence from Franca's coolness in the face of discovery and personal ruin. He used her strength to boost his poise and regain the belief that he could pull off the heist. The moment of immediate danger had passed and the two professors continued cataloging the items on the table for another hour. The beads or perspiration on Pier Luigi's forehead were now visible and he could feel the sweat soaking his back and the documents strapped there.

"Fr. Giorgi," Pier Luigi said, "Could you please open the window a bit. I feel that it is quite hot." The priest complied and walked to the window saying, "You should take off your jacket if you are hot." Fortunately for the couple, the priest was facing the windows fiddling with the latches and could not see Pier Luigi's horrified expression. "You know the cold wind can cause you to catch a cold."

Franca shot Pier Luigi a glance that warned him to remain calm. It produced the opposite effect and terrified him. But eventually, his fear of failure and Franca's reaction to being caught allowed him to calmly reply. "Thank you…but no. I need the jacket to keep my reading glasses." He forced a chuckle as he pulled the glasses out of his breast pocket to prove his point.

The priest took his lunch at noon every day. He made it known during the preceding several weeks that he expected the professors to do the same. Normally, the professors were so engrossed in their work that they did not heed the noon hour quitting time without some sort of delay. Today, with the ancient books sticking to Pier Luigi's back and the physical strain and emotional stress of the past few hours, the professors were more than happy to accommodate the priest's lunchtime routine.

"*Allora,*" Fr. Giorgi said. "We will be taking lunch now." It was a statement more than a question.

"Yes, that sounds good," responded Pier Luigi. Franca shut down the computer and rose; grabbing her purse and adjusting the contents within. In fact, their abrupt acquiescence to Fr. Giorgi's announcement of the time was almost too accommodating and may have raised suspicion.

Pier Luigi, recognizing the shift in the priest's continence, remained at his seat for a moment before gathering his briefcase and standing. The priest stood near the door and pulled out his keys to lock it behind him. Franca departed the room first as the priest held the door open for her.

Pier Luigi followed and walked uprightly as he approached the priest holding the door; he made a conscious effort to keep the documents stuffed in his pants from protruding out of his jacket. Pier Luigi brushed past the priest and stepped across to the far side of the hallway, as the priest fumbled with his keys. With three rapid steps, Pier Luigi turned to position himself with his back, and the stolen items, to the wall. The priest finished locking the door and turned to the professors, "*Va bene*, so we meet back here at 1:30?"

Pier Luigi was quick to reply, "We might be a little later. I want to take Franca for a nice lunch at a trattoria near our apartment, it is our anniversary."

"How nice." The priest smiled with real joy. "Whatever you wish. When you come back, I will have the next set of documents brought down for your inspection. Take your time and enjoy your celebration."

Fr. Giorgi responded without suspicion. In fact, it could be described as cordial or even friendly. The priest left toward the interior of the building leaving the professors alone in the corridor. Franca and Pier Luigi gave each other a look of relief and proceeded down the hall toward the exit and the final test.

The corridor looked longer than usual. With each step Pier Luigi took, he felt the book slip slightly down his back and into his pants. He adjusted his gait to minimize the disturbance but that only seemed to make the slippage worse.

The couple approached the exit and saw the guard, the same as the first day's arrival and every subsequent day, sitting at the desk. This time, instead of having his head buried in the sports page, he had been staring intently at the couple as they approached. Of all the days for the sports news to be slow, thought Franca.

As Pier Luigi approached the guard's desk, the architect's volume slipped down and lodged in the bottom of Pier Luigi's pants, below the cut of his jacket. The bible was stuck to his sweaty back and being held in position with only the slightest of force from the architect's volume. Anyone viewing him from behind would wonder why two sharp edges were protruding from the seat of the man's pants. Fortunately, aside from an infrequent visitor or other clerics, this entrance was rarely used.

Pier Luigi tried to relax but his attempts just made him more anxious. He dared not reach around and adjust the items but the bible was perilously close to teetering over and spilling out of its wedged position and out of his shirt and onto the floor.

In a flash, he had the strangest, most random remembrance of his youth. He was at his grandmother's apartment pretending to give a Mussolini-type speech while overlooking the piazza and 18th century church designed by Carlo Andrea Rana – 'the frog church' kids called it because of the architect's last name. After lunch, he lay on the small cot in the sewing room and rested. Maybe he thought of the strange memory because, to keep the book in place, he had to wobble like a frog or maybe because all he wanted to close his eyes and be in the comfort of his grandmother.

Whatever the reason, the flash memory distracted him for a moment before being revived by the guard's words calling, "Professor? Professor! ….What is that...behind you?"

# Chapter 7

**Basel, Switzerland**
**Wednesday, November 12, 1997**

The train emerged from the tunnel and picked up speed on the final leg of its journey to Basel. In the late autumn morning with overcast skies, Switzerland looked nothing like the postcards. Max had expected to see snow covered mountain tops, girls with pigtails in lederhosen, and yodelers. Instead, he saw the ass-end of towns and industrial parks along the tracks that ran westward from Zurich.

With nothing to look at during the hour and ten-minute ride from Zurich Hbf, Max flipped through the Basel tourist guide map and mentally prepared for the meeting with the manuscript buyer Edgar had set up. Positioned on the Rhine near both the German and French Borders, Basel had roots in the Roman Empire and traced its history even further back into the time of the Celts. Known as a major industrial hub acknowledged for its pharmaceutical and chemical companies, as Switzerland's third-largest city, it also enjoyed the secretive Swiss banking regulations.

For nearly all of his thirty plus years, Max had envisioned himself an international businessman instead of a low-level functionary in an unglamorous industry. While he would admit it to no one, least of all, his wife, Max set his sights on being a cross between James Bond and Donald Trump; suave and debonair, razor sharp business acuity, comfortable in any part of the world…and rich.

His fortunate meeting with Edgar Shadi could help him realize those dreams – or so he hoped. Opening a Swiss bank account was a hell of a start. He could even become an international broker of antiques. Why not? Calls had been made and a Swiss bank account set up to act as a conduit by which all the parties in Edgar's scheme could be paid. In planning, Edgar had insisted on complete discretion and that all of their communication be done in person and not by email. "In fact," Edgar had said, "nothing should even be written down."

"Why the secrecy?" Max had asked. "Are we doing anything illegal?"

"Of course not; selling the manuscript is completely legitimate," Edgar assured his newfound partner. "But the taxman may want a cut of the proceeds. I think it best that we keep it off the books and tax-free. That's the reason for the Swiss bank account."

"Makes sense. Besides, I'd rather not have my company knowing anything about my extracurricular activities."

It took a lot of groundwork to get free from the Zurich conference and to make the Basel meeting. If all went well, though, it could be the start to a new life; the one Max dreamed of. At the least, it would result in an immediate end to his current financial problems.

As he had promised Theodore, Max had stopped deliberately antag-onizing Wilson but he wasn't sure if the damage wasn't already done. Max rationalized that weak leaders don't like strong outspoken team members to make them look bad. Comforting thoughts aside, Max knew he was on the bubble and the slightest hint of doubt in his job dedication would put him irrevocably out the door.

Max planned to travel to Switzerland alone and for the most part, his tactics worked out. As expected, his recently promoted supervisor, Wilson the Weasel, decided not to come citing familial duties. Unexpectedly, the big boss, Theodore Armistead Buford, chose to come instead. Perhaps, the big boss wanted to check out for himself if the trip was a boondoggle. Fortunately, Max's scheduled itinerary with prospective clients and vendor meeting impressed the boss.

Unfortunately, the big boss's attendance meant that in order to make the meeting with the book dealer, Max now had to arrive a day early, buy a roundtrip ticket from Zurich to Basel (at his own expense) and return in enough time to meet Theodore for the conference's opening cocktail reception at six, followed by client dinner with an American food broker. Based on his AVP's arrival time, the big boss should currently be occupied…for now. But Max would be incommunicado for the next five or six hours and missing the cocktail party or dinner would create more problems than he cared to imagine.

The train slowed as it approached the outer stations. This express train wouldn't stop until it reached the Basel Bahnhof SSB, the central meeting point for both the Swiss rail lines and the French railroads. The meeting with the banker was supposed to be near the railway station so it should be convenient. That is, as long as they hadn't meant the Basel Badischer Bahnhof which was the station used as the terminus for the German railroad in Basel. Then he'd really be screwed. A wave a dread washed over him.

As the train pulled into the station, Max looked through the window at the large blue signed printed BASEL SSB to make sure he was in the right spot. He closed the Ian Fleming novel, <u>Casino Royal,</u> and placed it in his olive green canvas messenger bag. He grabbed his suit jacket off the hook next to him, stood, and put it on. He touched the mailing tube to make sure it was still secure in his messenger bag.

It was.

Standing in the railcar's passageway, he patted his hands over his pants pocket and suit jacket to check that he had his wallet, passport and return train tickets. His passport was in his front right pants pocket along with his ticket. Max's wallet should have been in his suit jacket or back pants pocket but he felt nothing. He checked again patting himself all over.

No luck.

Passengers departed as Max checked the seat around him. He took his jacket off and almost turned it inside out searching. His wallet wasn't there.

Unlike the terminus type stations where the train backed into stub tracks inside a gargantuan building and waited a substantial amount of time between arrival and departure, Basel was a 'through station'. The train would stop on an island platform for only a brief time to let passengers off and the new passengers on. Max had to get off the train before it left for the next stop, somewhere in France.

People scurried onto the train. He didn't know how much time remained but he figured that he had probably already used up two minutes of the six or seven minute pause.

Max walked toward the railcar's exit and absently pushed around the passengers joining the train in Basel. A tall man with a loosely knotted tie putting his case in the rack above the seat glared as Max brushed by.

Max's mind raced and his pulse pounded. A slight dizziness overcame him and once on the station platform, he searched his bag again. He pulled almost everything out in a vain attempt to conjure up the missing wallet. His breathing became shallow and his vision tunneled.

The wallet was not there.

He looked up the platform to find the conductor milling around. No way would he help, Max thought but by observing the conductor's actions, he could tell how much time he had before the train departed. Max guessed that he had a few more minutes.

He decided to check his seat again and bound for the train. He leaped onto the car and pushed his way around a woman with a rolling suitcase, stopped between cars deciding which way to go to. He headed up the aisle and stopped at his old seat. A passenger had already taken it and Max blurted, "I'm looking for my wallet. It must have fallen out around here."

The passenger seemed uninterested or uncomprehending as Max got on his knees to search under the seats. His heart raced, his ears turned hot, and he had trouble breathing. Thoughts of doom rushed in faster than he could dismiss them. Recognizing that too much time had elapsed, Max gave up the search and sprinted toward the exit.

The train had begun to move. The doors closed as Max pressed through and jumped to the platform. Out of breath and soaked with sweat despite the cool temperature, he stood and watched the train depart.

Max closed his eyes and willed himself to remain calm. Panic is the ravine below the mountain goat path, just a slip or wrong step away. Max clung with all his might to remain on the path of calm but he was slipping fast. His throat constricted and eyes welled up. He exhaled a few blasts before taking a deep breath and quickly took stock of his situation. He was stranded on the platform in Basel with no driver's license, no credit cards, no phone calling card, and no money. He had a meeting to attend with Swiss bankers and a hard return time with the big boss back in Zurich at the cocktail reception. Luckily, he still had his passport and the return train ticket. Most importantly, he had the reason for his meeting rolled up in the mailing tube.

Taking a few more deep breaths, Max made his way to the escalator that took him to a passageway under the tracks and toward the station. As he walked up the slopping tunnel into the station's interior, he should have been excited about finally living his dream. Instead, he thought about the additional challenges his missing wallet would present. At some point, he'd have to call his wife and have her cancel the credit cards; a conversation he was not looking forward to.

A clacking noise caught his attention and he looked up at the large flip-flap display that showed the station's train departure schedule. The Solari boards announced the updating schedules as each position flipped in undulating row-by-row waves, creating the distinctive noise of European train stations. Flashing up on the board were all the destinations for the next few hours displayed on a 24-hour clock. Max recognized many of the destinations he had dreamed of… Paris, Milan, and Berlin among them. He searched out the Zurich-bound trains and saw the 1624 train, the one for his return trip, scheduled for track 4a. Even if everything went on schedule, he'd be cutting it close for his appointed time with Theodore.

In any normal circumstance, Max's face would have lit up like a kid seeing the tree on Christmas morning. All those years playing with a train set and now he was living the real life thing. The lost wallet sobered him and rather than gawk, he followed his Nonna's advice and moved briskly from place to place with a sense of purpose. It was big city advice his Nonna had given him as a kid when she picked him up in mid-town Manhattan from the Port Authority bus terminal – never look lost in a strange place, there's no better way to announce oneself as a target for thieves than to wander around aimlessly looking for directions and re-reading signs. If you are going to be lost, at least don't look it.

Max walked directly to the information counter but, after seeing the long line, decided not to wait. He stepped out of the station, past the bus lines, and into the city. He took a moment to look around; Baroque buildings mixed with post-war utilitarian structures faced the station.

People moved in an unrushed but businesslike cadence among the restaurants, shops, and offices. Max couldn't imagine anything further from the beach town he lived in and he allowed himself a slight smile with the knowledge that he was living the adventure he'd always wanted. His pulse quickened with the thrill of anticipation of the thrills and challenges that lay ahead.

Across the street from the station, stood a large terminus of electrified street trams. Max thought about taking one of the trams to his appointment but paying for it, without his wallet, was too much to tackle. Besides, if he made a mistake, he could end up in one of Basel's suburbs which sprawled into France and Germany. A taxi wouldn't do either. Without cash, he would need to walk to his meetings.

Max looked at his watch and realized that he was over an hour early. Prior to losing his wallet, he considered that his early arrival would allow him to transact business quicker and return on the earlier 1524 train to Zurich and give him extra time to get ready before meeting his boss. Those plans evaporated.

Even at mid-day, the gray overcast sky gave no indication of the sun and therefore no sense of time. The rain had just stopped or was about to begin, or this is how Basel usually is —Max didn't know. Being accustomed to his native Florida where the sun always made a daily appearance, this weather, more than anything else, gave him a sense of otherworldliness. The sense of separation and the lack of his wallet, coupled with the gravity of the impending meeting, increased Max's sense of anxiety.

James Bond wouldn't feel this anxious. Max suppressed his apprehension and stepped away from the station and the waiting taxis. Suffering from sensory overload, he absently stepped off of the curb to cross the street. Out of the corner of his eye, he spotted several other pedestrians, Basel folk on about their business, waiting for the light to change. A small alarm went off in Max's head reminding him that the Swiss are particular about obeying the traffic laws, even pedestrians. This Germanic trait, especially so close to the border, was well ingrained in its citizens. Rather than buck the cultural norms that would identify him as a foreigner, Max stepped back on the curb and bit his lip as he waited for the light to change.

Then an idea struck him.

# Chapter 8

Max crossed the busy street and entered the first hotel he saw. He approached the front desk where two female clerks, dressed in identical uniforms, busied themselves with paperwork. Although one clerk was shorter and stockier than the other, they looked similar with shoulder length hair and severe bangs that framed their round faces. Neither looked up from their paper filing to meet Max's gaze.

"Excuse me," he said. "I was wondering if you could help me. I lost my wallet and don't have any credit cards or my phone calling card. Do you know if there is an American Express office nearby?"

Neither clerk broke from their task. After many moments of silence, the shorter clerk responded, "Did you lose it here in the lobby? I can call the hotel security officer. He may be able to assist you."

"I didn't lose it here. I lost it on the train."

The women hesitated, deciding what to do next.

"What hotel room are you in," the shorter said as she typed on the computer to look up Max's reservation.

"I'm not staying here."

The women jockeyed to decide which one of them would give the brush off. Before they could choose, Max said, "I just need help in finding an AMEX office so that they can replace my card. Do you know where one is?"

Neither clerk responded.

"Or do you have a phone book so that I can look it up?"

The taller clerk stepped up, "You can call the number on the back of the credit card. It should be toll-free."

Max let out a guttural sound before stopping himself. Speaking each word distinctly so as not to lose control said, "I don't have the card. It was in my wallet...which was lost or stolen."

The shorter woman nodded to her compatriot and retrieved a phonebook from the shelf behind her. The two women flipped through the pages as Max stood peering over the raised counter. Both women bent toward the fine print in the book and pointed at different lines. After conferring in German for a few seconds, the shorter clerk answered, "There is an office at 4906 Zurcherstrasse."

"Is that far?"

"No," the taller woman responded. "About three kilometers. You can take a taxi."

Max swallowed his frustration. He replied through gritted teeth in forceful restraint, "I don't have money for a taxi. It was in my wallet." After taking a breath, he asked evenly, "Can you write the address down for me, please?"

The shorter woman complied and passed him the handwritten note.

"Thank you. Do you have a map of the city that I can use?

"The back of our card has a small map that could help." She handed Max the hotel's card with an extremely high-level sketch of the city's plan.

"Thank you," Max said as he left.

Following the broad outline of the proffered map, Max crossed the street and proceeded to the right. He found PeterMerianstrasse and cut through the park where several men lay on benches. He had read that

Switzerland had very lax laws on heroin use and assumed that the park's occupants were waiting for their fix. Max avoided their stares and walked briskly onto Sevogelstrasse until it hit Zurcherstrasse.

Navigating a foreign city boosted Max's confidence…and that was something he would need today. If he remembered correctly, this route would take him near the bank on 24 Angensteinerstrasses, which would be about a half-mile up on the left. Actually, he thought to himself, it would be about a kilometer on the left. In order to act European, he should at least measure distance as they do. In that case, it was probably nine degrees Celsius. Either way, the chill dug into his sun-loving bones; now that he thought about it.

The numbers of the buildings indicated that he was headed in the right direction but that he had a long way to go. As he walked, microdroplets of rain began hitting his face. A light rain soon followed the misting which grew steadier. As the rain fell harder, Max audibly cursed himself for not carrying an umbrella.

But he put his head down and pressed on. After only a few minutes, his hair dripped with runoff and his jacket held a sheen of rain droplets. Three kilometers was much more than he imagined. The leather soles of his shoes were soaked and his socks became damper by the step. Time was ticking and Max's breath labored and legs grew heavy knowing that every block he walked toward the AMEX office was a block he'd have to walk back.

Hopefully, by then, the rain would stop. He began doubting the direction. He had walked too long. Believing that he had made a mistake, he pulled out the address again. He was close. He walked another few minutes before finding the match. He had arrived at the correct address but didn't see a sign indicating an American Express office. Max walked through the front door and crossed the marble lobby to the receptionist.

"Hello," Max said with as much cheer as he could muster.

The brunette receptionist looked up with kindly eyes and smiled. "May I help you?"

"Yes. I hope. I'm looking for the American Express office." The receptionist looked confused. "I was told that this address," he said handing the note the hotel clerk had written, "is an office for American Express."

"No. I'm sorry this is a phone company."

Max closed his eyes, looked up and then dropped his head in resignation.

Opening his eyes he said, "I lost my wallet...or it was stolen...on the train. I'm here on business and wanted to get a replacement card."

The woman let out a sympathetic sigh. "Let me look up the American Express phone number for you." She lifted a phone book, scanned it and started dialing. "Here," she said handing Max the phone. "It is ringing."

Max took the handset with gratitude and spoke to the AMEX operator on the line. "Hello. My name is Max Agresta and I am in Basel, Switzerland. I lost my wallet and would like to get a replacement card. Do you have an office nearby where I could do that?"

"The closest office is in Zurich on 12600 Bahnhofstrasse."

"There is nothing here in Basel?" Max inquiry came out as a plea.

"No. I'm sorry. There is no office in Basel. We can have the card mailed to you in Basel if you'd like," the operator said.

"No, I'll be back in Zurich this afternoon. Can you give me the address again?" Max wrote it down and repeated it. "Thank you. Oh," almost forgetting to ask, "what time does the Zurich office close?"

"Six o'clock," she said.

"Thank you," Max said and hung up the phone. "I have a favor to ask," he said to the receptionist. "May I use your phone to call my wife?"

She nodded. "You are calling the States?"

"Yes."

"No problem. Dial 001 and then your number."

Max dialed and the answering machine clicked on after four rings, "Hey Honey. I'm okay but I had a little problem. My wallet was stolen on the train. You'll need to contact the credit card companies to let them know. Sorry for the trouble. I'm heading into a meeting and will call you when I'm back at the hotel. Love you."

Max handed the phone back to the receptionist and thanked her profusely for her help. He left to make his way to his appointment without his replacement credit card, without his money, wet and pressed for time. The only bright spot? It had stopped raining.

The walk back to the bank on Angensteinerstrasses was much shorter than he had expected or maybe his mind so occupied that he didn't realize how the time had passed. Modern, multifamily houses with large windows to let in whatever dim sunlight there might be sat on the south side of the tree lined street. The other half built with older homes and businesses that reminded Max of brownstones in Manhattan.

The bankers were expecting him after lunch and, even with his fruitless detour, he arrived on time; perhaps a little early. Max walked past the address and became concerned. He couldn't believe that he had made a mistake – again. The building with the address that he had committed to memory looked nothing like a bank.

The address appeared distinct from all the others on the street. It was the only one without a street level entrance and sat back from the sidewalk making it difficult to peek in as he walked by. The large mansion with a flight of stairs leading up to a large glass-door entrance looked more like a residence than an office and certainly not a bank.

The day had thrown too many curveballs. He didn't know how long he could cling to the path before succumbing to the ravine of panic. The planning of the fund's transfer, the jet lag, and the adjusting of schedules to get to Basel had taken a physical, financial, and mental toll. Missing this appointment would be detrimental to the deal with Edgar and catastrophic to Max's dreams. He worried about justifying the cost of a roundtrip train ticket to Basel when he had trouble paying the mortgage every month.

Max stopped a half a block away and leaned against a building. Another trick he had learned from his Nonna – when traveling in a strange place, reduce your angles of exposure to ward off pickpockets and con men. The pick-pocket had already gotten me, he thought, mentally putting the incident on his growing list of bone headed moves.

He opened his bag to search for his notes. Despite Edgar's strict instructions for exclusively verbal communication, Max did have a few cryptic scribblings in his planner. Among them, he hoped to find the address of the meeting.

He flipped page after page trying to decipher his own writing. Partial messages, phone numbers, doodles and freight rates filled the pages.

How could he be at the wrong address? The rocks from the mountain path fell from under him, his footing was shaky as the ravine of panic called. And then…there it was, '24 Angensteinerstrassee'.

That was it.

He had a phone number attached to the address but no way would he call it. There were payphones back at the station but how do you make a long distance call from a foreign country to a foreign country. "Or would it be a local call?" he wondered aloud. Max didn't know. But without his wallet, the point was moot.

He did have a cell phone but hesitated using it. Before he left for this trip to Europe, his company had issued him the temporary use of a European formatted phone. The accounting department and Wilson warned him to be careful with the phone use and that both outbound and incoming calls were charged at extremely high rates. Wilson issued direct orders that the land line in conjunction with his AT&T calling card is used for all business calls and that only one call home per day was permitted. The cell phone could be used for emergencies or whenever Theodore needed it and every call, including the number and duration, would surely be scrutinized by Rhonda in accounting.

Better to brave up and walk with authority into the specified address. The optimist in Max thought that it could still be the correct location. If this was the wrong place, it was too late to reschedule. He couldn't call Edgar for additional instructions as it was not even seven in the morning back home. If this wasn't the right place, the meeting would need to be scrapped. Any diversion would make him miss his meeting and loosen his tenuous hold on his job.

Walking up the steps of the building, Max tried to put all these thoughts out of his head. He approached the front door and could see an office through the side window. Buoyed by the sight of a receptionist, Max noticed the brass plaque on the building. Instead of fancy font announcing the presence of the private bank where he would sell the manuscript and earn a big commission, the sign pronounced his arrival at the consulate of Bosnia-Herzegovina.

He was at the wrong place.

Max's heart dropped to his left foot.

# Chapter 9

**Jacksonville, Florida**
**Wednesday, November 12, 1997**

"Very good," Customs Service Special Agent Grace Hemmer said. She cradled the phone between her shoulder and left ear while she arranged some files on her desk.

"Okay...let me know after your meeting." She paused and waited for the response.

"Yes. Of course. I understand that you will need to check with your resources to confirm the identity but..." Grace nodded her head as she drew angular shapes on her notepad.

"Okay, then call me when you get back home. That will be fine..... Oh, wait," Grace said as she saw the sticky about her dentist's appointment.

"That will be late afternoon here. Sorry, I have an appointment. Tomorrow?" she appealed. Upon hearing the confirmed time for continuing the discussion tomorrow she said, "Yes, same time."

Grace listened on the phone to the distant voice. "It's six o'clock here."

More conversation.

"Yes, this is my work phone but it's no problem, I get here this early every day." Grace smiled and nodded even though the man on the other end could not see her.

"Thank you for contacting me and please let me know what you learn. Your information will be very helpful in making my case. *Merci,*" she said thanking the caller in his language. "Talk to you tomorrow."

Although her group supervisor, Tom Merriman, didn't appreciate the regularity at which she went over his head to Cecil Pond, the Resident Agent in Charge (RAC) for the Jacksonville office, he had to appreciate the results Grace generated. Both Pond and Merriman received accolades from Washington for Grace's work in a political corruption case where her tireless efforts dug up enough damning evidence to convict State Senator McClay on corruption charges. Her tenacity in bringing the case to trial also earned her the respect of U.S. Attorney for the Middle District of Florida, Don Weidenfeld, who was pleased with the positive press attention he received from the conviction of a high-profile suspect.

Grace's reputation grew even larger when, she recovered an artifact stolen years ago from Italy and found in nearby Ponte Vedra Beach several months ago. Mr. and Mrs. Latzko believed that they had bought the manuscript from a reputable dealer and had no idea of its nefarious origins. When confronted with the fact of its origins, the couple returned it without incident. The Italian authorities, pleased with the cooperation they received from the Customs Service, bestowed a special commendation for her efforts. The local and international notoriety also received serious attention in Washington. Spurred by her disappointment in not getting a conviction, she redoubled her efforts on a local illicit trafficking of cultural property case that could lead to a prosecution and result in augmenting her reputation.

No doubt, Grace wanted to be taken seriously and, sometimes after finishing a bottle of Cabernet by herself, she would admit, feared. Her competitive nature, boldness in tackling problems and commitment to long hours, earned her a reputation of someone not to be crossed yet someone to be counted on to deliver. In the ten years, she had worked in the Service, she had succeeded in creating the persona she sought.

She knew there was more. When uncorking the second bottle she'd admit that she was an attractive woman – at least that's what a few interested suitors had claimed. Looking in the bathroom mirror of her Riverside apartment, she saw the green eyes that her one-time boyfriend and backup professional quarterback called stunning. Yes, she had good skin, high cheekbones and maintained her tall, lean, swimmer's frame with daily workouts. But work came first. She insisted that she be judged on her merit alone. She joined the U.S. Customs Service after swimming as an undergraduate in a midsized Division II school and earning her law degree from the University of Florida. She worked hard to minimize the display of her physique and natural beauty. She dressed in conservative, borderline frumpy clothes, applied no makeup, and wore her dirty blond hair in a practical, un-stylish manner.

Lest anyone fail to take her seriously at work, she rarely even socialized with the other agents. At thirty-three, she had no interest in a serious relationship as it would only distract her from her career goals. Plus, the long hours made it difficult for her to meet men in the 'civilian world' and she would not date co-workers. Instead, she poured energies into her work, building cases and gaining convictions. That aloof behavior, along with the good press she always seemed to get, resulted in a gap in trust and camaraderie among her coworkers and caused her to feel like an outcast.

Special Agents work on Law Enforcement Availability Pay (LEAP) which meant that they must be available 25 percent more than their normal work hours. Even so, it was rare to see anyone in the office before eight o'clock unless they were on surveillance or shift work – except

Grace. She had been at the office since six this morning as usual and was anxious to see if her boss had arrived yet. She needed some quality face time with him before her other less aggressive peers came in at eight. As soon as she saw his office light come on from across the office, she made a beeline to his door.

"Today's the big meet!" she exclaimed. At times, it seemed that the big boss appreciated her efforts but at other times she felt that he barely tolerated her.

"What?" RAC Pond said. He turned on his computer and settled into his office. Grace's habit of barging in first thing in the morning had become so common that he went about his morning routine without paying much attention.

"The San Lorenzo. The memo I emailed you last week?" She waited for acknowledgment to flicker in Pond's eyes. "The San Lorenzo is page 212 from the Missal of Ludovico da Romagnano," Grace explained. Without waiting for a reply, she blurted, "Anyway, my informant is meeting with the seller today."

"Huh?" Pond said. He gave a genuinely confused look. "Oh, yeah. I remember seeing something but I'm still trying to dig through my emails. What did Merriman say?" Pond asked. The hint was none too subtle; work through the proper chain of command and deal with her boss instead of directly through him. The question had the added benefit of covering for the fact that he hadn't read Grace's numerous memos, studies, reports and resource requests. Pond knew that when it was important, she would be standing at his door, like she was now, to inform him in person.

"I sent the memo to both you and Merriman. It's okay. I'll re-send it. Remember the Italian 15th century manuscript that we found a few months ago at the home of that Ponte Vedra couple and returned to Italy? The manuscript I'm tracking down is the San Lorenzo which is from the same Missal – it's just a different page."

"You mean the one where the Carabinieri Art Squad had a tip that an Islamorada art dealer sold an unsuspecting Florida couple a rare and ancient manuscript and you retrieved it, received an award from the Italian Consulate in Miami, and made every newspaper and magazine in the state?" Pond asked. "No, I don't remember."

"Very funny – but yes, that one. We never found out who sold it to the couple. I've always suspected that the culprit was here in our AOR," Grace said using the acronym for "area of responsibility" and trying to sell the excitement for her case. "Several weeks ago a French book dealer, Frederic Paquet, called me and said that he had been contacted about possibly purchasing a manuscript which fit the description of the missing page, known as the San Lorenzo. Apparently, finding it's an extra big deal because the page is supposed to settle some controversy."

"And let me guess, he didn't call the Italian authorities. Instead, he saw your picture in the paper, thought you were cute and decided call you instead?"

"No! I mean yes. He did see my picture in the paper, but what really caused him to call me was that the seller who contacted him is from here... or at least our AOR ... St. Augustine."

Pond leaned forward. If the crime took place in his Area of Responsibility, a case could be made for their involvement. "So the document is here and was sold here?"

"No. Basel." After receiving a blank stare from her boss, she continued, "Switzerland."

"Then it's got nothing to do with us."

Grace stood without reacting to his dismissal.

Pond continued, "It is Italian property, right? Have we received a mutual legal assistance treaty request from the Italian government for assistance?"

Grace stared without responding. She'd let Pond exhaust his objections before making her case.

"No?" Pond answered his own question. "Then it's not our case to worry about." Turning to other matters, Pond waved his hands to signify the end of the discussion. Grace didn't move from her position at the office door and so he continued with additional instructions, "Call what's his name… from the Carabinieri Art Squad; the guy you worked with on the previous recovery; the guy with the renaissance architect's name…" He squinted his eyes and pressed his fingers against his head like he had a brain freeze. "Bramante… ah, ah, ah…Bramante Buratti; that's the guy. Call him and give him the tip," Pond said.

"Renaissance architect?" Grace said. She twisted her face in mild derision.

"Yes. Bramante was a famous architect of the Renaissance who laid out the initial designs for St Peter's Basilica in a centralized Greek cross plan. Although, he doesn't get much credit because much of that plan was altered when Michelangelo changed the western end and modified the dome toward its completion," Pond answered, puffing out his chest at having one-upped his subordinate.

"How do you know all of that?" Grace said, surprised that her boss knew this arcane bit of trivia.

"Benefits of a classical education." Pressing his advantage, he continued, "Anyway, call the Commander of the Art Squad. Good looking guy. Well-dressed, if I recall." He decided to increase Grace's discomfort by adding, "It'll give you a chance to rekindle the romance. I seem to remember that you had a crush on him."

"I did not!" She started to feel her ears getting hotter. "And I will not call him." She took a couple of breaths.

"This is my case," she continued. In a voice that brooked no opposition, "I developed the contact, I developed the lead, I think it's only right that I ..." She saw her boss's admonishing look and paused before re-stating her case, "...*We* should pursue this as far as we can."

"Tell me again what you say is stolen? An old manuscript?" Pond changed the approach. "I know it's probably important to someone but we're talking about one page from an old book – one piece of paper. It's not that big of a deal." Pond rubbed his temple with his fingers and thought. Grace knew that if he was going to throw his weight behind this investigation, he'd like to know what he was fighting for and the significance. So far, Grace had not made any case that this one particular piece of paper's importance.

"The Missal is a liturgical book that contains all the instructions and texts for celebrating Roman Catholic Mass throughout the year. Basically, it's an instruction manual for priests. And in medieval times, the Missal was one of the church's most important possessions. Remember, this was before the printing press so the script and illustrations were hand painted and beautifully decorated by monks toiling away in obscurity. Each page of the Missal is a work of art and can be extremely valuable to a collector."

Pond took on a fatherly tone in his attempt to get her on track. "Listen, Grace..."

Grace interrupted, "I have a theory about who in St. Augustine is illegally fencing these stolen ancient texts. Let me check my notes. Plus, the world of 15th century manuscript sellers is extremely small. I mean, they're not producing any more of them. Once a collector dies, his estate sells it to a dealer. A meeting of the most important dealers could probably fit into our conference room..."

"I like your enthusiasm," he said, cutting Grace off and allowing for no additional interruptions. "God knows, I could use eight more of you in this office. That reminds me, did Merriman talk to you about helping in the Salvatierra case? I think your time and energy would be better served working on that. If you really want to move up the ladder, helping him will be the best way. Not show-boating with these headline-grabbing cases."

Pond dispensed the advice, knowing that Grace wasn't going to listen. And on the other hand, her success in bringing in the headline-grabbing cases could also help his position with Washington. "Anyway, this Carabinieri Art Squad specializes in investigating the theft and illicit trade of art. These guys are the best. They're very dedicated and have all the resources for completing the forensic analysis and monitoring the activities of art and antique dealers and bookstores. We're not equipped or tasked with doing that."

He looked at Grace and could see he was getting nowhere. "Grace, we got lucky on that last one. But, it basically fell into our laps. We need to stick to what we're good at. Give Bramante a call, let him know about your tip and if you're lucky, he'll send you a nice bottle of wine or something when he recovers the piece."

"But the stolen manuscript was here…in our AOR, right down the road from us. If someone from Florida is trying to sell the San Lorenzo, I want to know who it is and what other stolen rare documents they have. We have the right…and the responsibility, to bring them to justice."

"Well," considering it for a moment, "that's a good point. If you can make a case that someone in our area committed a crime and we can get an indictment, it may be worth pursuing." The long shot intrigued Pond and got him thinking about how a conviction would help Don Weidenfeld's bid for the open Congressional seat next fall. To a large extent, the Customs agents' and U.S. District Attorney's fortunes were tied together. The positive press from an indictment could only help them both. "But again, it's not in our wheelhouse. Let me know what your informant says and then we'll decide."

"Just give me a day to make my case on why we should make this bust and how it links back to St. Augustine residents," Grace said.

Pond grunted and turned back to his computer.

Grace assured him, "Don't worry bossman, I'll get a couple of local white collar criminals locked up for you so that you'll make the <u>Florida Times Union</u> and the <u>St. Augustine Record</u>. And I don't mean the Metro section." she promised.

"We'll see," Pond said without turning back around. He could afford to be noncommittal but knew that once Grace set her sights on a target, they were as good as in the bag.

# Chapter 10

**Basel, Switzerland**
**Wednesday, November 12, 1997**

Max stood slack-jawed in front of the door, his head became lighter like a balloon losing its air. The Bosnian-Herzegovina consulate? Panic rose as his chest constricted, his face became ashen and his skin clammy. For the second time today, he was not at the right location. His eyes welled up like the time an eleven-year-old Max learned of the cancellation of a much-anticipated Disney vacation. The ravine of panic and despair called but Max hung on the path of calm a bit longer. He pulled himself together. He'd come this far – might as well walk into the office and see what his mistake had been. He decided against ringing the doorbell and walked into the lobby to greet the receptionist. She looked up from her paper sorting and gave Max a polite but not committal look.

"Hello," Max said. "I'm here to see Mueller Wilhelm."

Max could feel his faced redden as she responded, "Do you mean Wilhelm Mueller?" Max nodded, embarrassed that he mixed up the man's name but relieved that the receptionist recognized it and that he might actually be able to salvage this meeting. Learning that he was in the right place made up for the embarrassment of getting the name wrong.

"Do you have an appointment?" the receptionist asked.

Max beamed the affirmative.

"Please." She pointed to the chair behind him and said, "have a seat and I will call for him." The receptionist picked up the phone and spoke a few words in German. "He will be out to see you in a moment." Not in the harsh German accent that Max expected from having watched so many war movies but a definite "V" sound on the word 'will' as if the word was 'ville'.

Max busied himself fixing his tie and coat. The pants dug into his waist and Max remembered that the last time he had worn this suit was to a funeral about ten months, and obviously several pounds, ago. The unfamiliar feel of the worsted wool combined with the constriction and dampness added to Max's discomfort. The receptionist sitting across from him made no sound as she plowed through her paperwork leaving Max alone with his thoughts. After a few minutes, he heard approaching foot-steps from down the hall.

Two men approached and the older said, "Hello, Mr....?"

Max stood to greet the bankers and replied, "Agresta."

"Yes, I am Mr. Mueller. This is Mr. Strauss," pointing to the younger man behind him dressed in bold pinstripes and an aggressive red tie and light pink shirt.

"Please. Will you come with me?" said the banker.

Mueller's hand enveloped Max's in a handshake. Even though slightly bent with age, Mueller stood a bit taller than Max. One could tell he had been a very impressive figure as a young man. He wore his charcoal suit and blue silk tie with a natural confidence of one who con-ducted his business in quiet hushed tones. His large face made his large nose seem appropriate and his light gray hair flecked with dark brown, slightly disheveled and exactly the look of a private banker that Max had been expecting.

They walked down the hall in silence and entered a large room. The building, at one time, must have been a private mansion of a wealthy industrialist, now converted to commercial affairs. The Bosnian consulate must be one of the other tenants that shared office space in the large building.

The younger banker showed Max to a large high back chair as Mueller sat opposite him on the dark red leather sofa. Mueller placed a file on the coffee table and hunched over it as he sought the right documents.

"Do you take coffee?" said Strauss as Max sat.

"Yes, black, no sugar."

Strauss backed out of the room once Max placed his request.

Max swiveled his head around the room which must have been the grand parlor back in the day. A large fireplace stood at one end of the room, above it hung a tapestry depicting a medieval stag hunt. Antique prints of manor houses and fox hunts lined the black walnut paneled walls richly stained by the decades of the smoke from the fireplace and fine cigars. The Persian rug, worn but of obvious quality, covered the center of the room. The room smelled of money and privilege. Max could get accustomed to this lifestyle and a wave of satisfaction spread through his core. His plans were becoming reality.

Strauss returned and sat on the sofa.

"Your colleague informed me that we will be opening up an account for you," said Mueller leaving no doubt who was in charge.

Max nodded.

"We have received the wire transfer of ten thousand dollars and it will be deposited into your account once we have signed the paperwork." Edgar fronted the ten grand to open the account and Max's commission would come from the sale of the manuscript.

"Thank you," Max replied.

"Please," Mueller said as he handed him some paper. "I have highlighted the account number. This is very important as your name will not be on the account. This number is the only way to identify the owner," Mueller explained.

Strauss reentered the room with a woman carrying a coffee service. "Please," she said as she slightly bowed to present the tray. Max reached for the coffee saucer and plate but ignored the creamer and sugar.

"Thank you," Max said as the woman quietly turned and left. Neither Mueller nor Strauss took a coffee which signaled a short meeting stripped of extraneous pleasantries.

Max signed the paperwork where necessary and looked to the banker for the next step. Strauss, who didn't have the experience or couth of the older banker asked, "When will you be depositing additional funds? As you know, we are not a normal bank." Emphasis on 'normal'. He continued by saying, "We usually do not handle such small amounts."

Mueller shot his partner a look which warned him to be more guarded. Strauss's comments were obviously true, but Max even recognized they did not have to be spoken so plainly.

"I believe that today, we are expecting a Mr. Paquet to inspect the manuscript I brought. He will be transferring additional funds once we finalize those details," Max said. He could hear his own words come out in the stilted manner of these bankers, proud of his ability to blend it.

"Yes, Monsieur Paquet phoned earlier for directions and will be here momentarily. If you will excuse us." Mueller said. It was not a question. "Please make yourself comfortable. When your guest arrives, I will have him brought in." Before Max could put his coffee down and rise to shake hands, the two bankers stood up and left the room.

Max sat back in the chair and let the feeling wash over him. The stress of the travel challenges, setbacks, and the uncomfortable feeling of wet feet vanished. The account had been set up, Edgar's deposit had arrived and the meeting for the sale of the manuscript was on schedule.

Once the manuscript was sold, the purchase price would be deposited. Max would then draw his commission and hand the numbered account information to Edgar; who could withdraw it at his leisure.

Better than the results of walking out with the cash for his daughter's surgery was the thought that this was just the beginning. Edgar mentioned that he had many manuscripts in his possession and that this type of transaction could become a regular occurrence. At this commission structure, a few of these deals per year would double his salary. Laura would be happy that the bills could be paid and, hopefully, she would be proud of him for being so enterprising. Max could now be thought of an international art and antiquities dealer…in addition to selling truck freight on the side.

Max smiled as he inspected the printed train schedule he had picked up and saw that he might be able to take the early train back to Zurich after all and have time to call home before meeting his boss at the conference cocktail party.

# Chapter 11

**Torino, Italy**
**Winter 1990**

"Professor? Professor! ....What is that...behind you?" the guard called.

Pier Luigi's heart pound in his ears and he shuffled backward toward the wall. His throat constricted at the guard's question.

Since the beginning of their project, the professors had attempted to befriend, or at least become familiar, with the guard. It had not worked; his disposition was as cold as the first day. On most days, the guard sat with his head buried in the sports tabloid and only lifting his head to demand their visitor badges and to check their bags.

However, today, the guard sat at his desk with the paper neatly folded on the desk. He stared at the couple and demanded again, "What is that behind you?"

Pier Luigi's chest tightened and his bowels loosened. His eyes dilated making it hard for him to see but he could make out the guard jumping up from his seat and moving around the desk toward them. Pier Luigi would never have thought the man could be so animated. His back nearly up against the wall, Pier Luigi turned toward the oncoming guard in fight or flight mode, careful not to knock loose the book hanging on his back.

The guard glanced at Pier Luigi and squinted. He took a step past him toward Franca. The guard bent down in an almost supplicant manner like a bow before royalty. Franca reeled back, threw out her arms and looked down at the strange man.

"*Professora*. I believe you dropped this," he said and handed her a black leather glove.

Franca reacted with calm. "Thank you so much. You have such sharp eyes." She batted her eyes. "I would have frozen without it." The guard grinned. Pier Luigi started making his way to the door. Franca shook her head slightly and scrunched her eyes while mouthing '*fa calma*', the message to stay calm. She engaged the guard further, "You got up so fast. I was scared for a second."

"I'm very quick. Even at my age." His head nodded side to side like Barney in Mayberry. "I used to be a striker for my club team," he said. Franca could see him puff out his chest.

"I'm not surprised," she said.

"I like to keep an eye out. Keep my wits sharp. You know," he said as he straightened his shoulders, "this is an important job."

"Terribly. Thank you. We all must protect the culture," Franca said.

"Yes. I agree. Here, let me take your badges."

Franca maintained her position as Pier Luigi handed his badge and presented his satchel for inspection. Without being asked, he held it open widely for easy inspection. He smiled trying to appear happy and carefree. The guard leaned forward and peered into the case. There wasn't much to see and after the brief inspection, he grunted approval.

"I will sign you both out. Have a nice lunch." Pier Luigi breathed easy as it appeared that Franca's charms were beginning to work. He shuffled around his wife and through the door; not bothering to hold it open for his wife. If the guard noticed the abnormal breach in etiquette, he didn't see. Franca blocked the view of Pier Luigi and his bulging pants bottom containing the smuggled books.

Once clear of the building's exit and out of sight, Pier Luigi reached behind his back and pulled the bible and the architect's plans out of his pants and stuffed them into his leather satchel. He shot a look of nervous relief at Franca and beckoned her to follow.

They walked without aim for several blocks. Pier Luigi wanted to be as far away from the archives as possible. When his heart rate had dropped to a more normal rate, he continued to walk at a slower pace.

The professors stopped in front of a flower shop on a quiet street and looked at each other. They had just entered the world's second oldest profession of art theft. Pier Luigi wanted to express the seriousness of the situation and began to speak when Franca cut him off.

"Well, that was fun!" she said. Pier Luigi's eyes twitched uncontrollably and his face had no color. His wife actually thought that dishonoring the trust of his employer, stealing rare artifacts and almost having one's life ruined by an overly suspicious cleric, was fun.

"How terrible." Pier Luigi's shoulders slumped and sweat ran from his temples. "I'll never do that again!" He wiped his brow with a handkerchief and looked around for danger before settling on his wife.

"Come on, Pier Luigi. Don't be so miserable."

"You want me to be happy with what we did?" Pier Luigi said. The immediate risk of discovery had passed and he was only now beginning to feel normal.

"Listen, we decided to do it and we succeeded," she said. "Where is your sense of adventure? We're like Bonnie and Clyde. But without the guns." She laughed.

Pier Luigi knew that she had always liked to bend the rules. But now, apparently, she relished breaking them. He found himself strangely even more attracted to her. He thought back to the time when she convinced him, back when they were dating, to make love on the hood of her car in front of his parents' house. He re-entered the house to a family gathering, flushed in the face with clothes a little more rumpled, horrified and convinced that everyone knew that he had done more than just walked his date to her car.

He smiled at the memory which was disrupted by Franca saying, "Did you hear me? Let's make the call."

He had almost forgotten… "Yes, yes. Please. Not so loud. Let me get my mobile." He pulled out his phone and powered it on, pulled a slip of paper from his billfold and, after putting on his reading glasses, carefully dialed the number. He waited several rings and was about to press the 'end' button when the man on the other end picked up.

Bolstering himself and trying to sound confident, he said, "*Ciao*, it is Pier Luigi Scarsi." He spoke English to the man he had met in London at a rare book show several months ago.

"Yes, well, you said that I should call you if I had anything of interest." He looked up and smiled at Franca who was leaning in close trying to hear the other end of the conversation. The game was on.

"Well, I'd rather show you. But let me say that they are special items. I think that your clients would be pleased to have them in their collection." He listened as the man on the other end of the line spoke.

"You are here now? Well, yes – if possible," he said. "Yes. I know where that is." A pause. "In half an hour? Yes. We can meet you there." Franca looked at her husband. She raised her eyes in a question. She wanted to know the details but could only hear her husband's side of the conversation.

"Yes, I'll have them with me. *Ciao*." His hand shook and pecked blindly before finally pressing the 'END' button. He replaced his glasses in his breast pocket and put away the phone slowly, aware that, for a brief moment, he had control over Franca with the information.

"He'll meet us in half of an hour at a café on Via Po near Ponte Vittorio Emmanuele."

When leaving the archives, they had actually walked in the opposite direction of the suggested meeting place. Pier Luigi and Franca reversed course and walked in silence, each preparing in their own way for the meeting.

To some extent, meeting the buyer distressed him more than the theft. What if this was a set-up? What if this buyer was actually a Carabinieri Art Squad undercover agent or informant ready to catch us in the act of selling stolen properties? The *Comando Carabinieri per la Tutela del Patrimonio Culturale*, better known as the Art Squad, was established in 1969 to protect Italian Culture by combating art and antiquities crimes. They had a solid reputation for thoroughness, persistence, and cross-border cooperation that made international art crimes difficult to get away with. Instead of looking for art thieves, maybe they've decided to set the bait and let the thief come to them?

Pier Luigi looked at Franca and almost mentioned his concern. No, he thought to himself. She'll only berate me for weakness. We've come this far. It couldn't be a trap. If we backed out now, all this risk was for nothing. Pier Luigi walked on silently, convinced that desire dictates logic.

They arrived in twenty-five minutes and the couple hesitated before entering the café. Pier Luigi had only met the man one other time and he wasn't certain that he would recognize him. As they made their way past the crowd standing at the bar drinking coffee, he saw the round-faced balding, Mediterranean man sitting alone at the back corner table. The man stared right at the professors and made a small nod of his head to acknowledge their presence. Michael Corleone's meeting with Solazzo and Captain McClusky flashed across Pier Luigi's mind.

Pier Luigi thought, as he walked the few steps, that the man had been closer to the café than he let on. He had wanted to arrive first to await them.

The couple presented themselves at the table and the man stood partially and shook both Pier Luigi's and then Franca's hands. In this crowded café and wanting to avoid eavesdroppers, the men continued speaking English, "Please." He smiled and opened his hand to indicate the two empty chairs. The couple took their seats and looked for a waiter to bring them coffee. "May I see what you have?" the man asked.

"Oh, yes, they are right here." Pier Luigi realized that the man had come to conduct business as quickly as possible. This was not a time for a social call. The coffee could wait.

Pier Luigi placed the two rare items on the table and tried his best to shield them from the view of the patrons at the bar. It was no matter; the table was tucked in the back of a café busy with office workers grabbing a coffee and a quick bite to eat while they caught up on local gossip. Nobody paid any attention to the three people huddled over a corner table.

"The volume contains a design for a new cathedral of Torino and was made by an architect at the end of the 19th century. It is an interesting piece and may be appealing to your clients," Pier Luigi said.

"Now, this is a much more important item," indicating the second piece. "It is the bible belonging to St. Antonio of Romagnano." Entering into his professor mode he continued, "Notice the numerous woodcut headpieces and initials included in this edition are mostly formed by interlaced patterns? Antonio…"

"Yes, I see," the man cut him off. "I will give you two thousand dollars."

"Certainly this bible is worth more than two thousand dollars," Pier Luigi threw up his hands and shifted in his seat. His face screwed up as if he was chewing cranberries.

"Two thousand for the both of them," the man responded. "The church plans are not worth much at all."

Pier Luigi looked over at Franca. The paltry offer was offensive and hardly worth the risk. Two grand would do nothing to help their financial situation.

Pier Luigi turned back to the man and was about to let his anger fly when Franca spoke for the first time, "These are very rare items and they will present no risk to you. We are experts in the field and we assure you that you will find a good market for them. They are certainly worth more than two thousand dollars," she said in a calm yet pressing voice.

"Where did you get them? My clients may want to know," said the man.

The couple looked at each other and Pier Luigi responded, "I thought that we had an arrangement that no questions would be asked?"

"As you wish," the buyer responded. "I am just asking to satisfy my curiosity. But without a solid history or recorded provenance, the value of the item is decreased because I must seek out...alternative markets for sale."

"You will find that the provenance of these two items is clean. There are no records of them anywhere," Franca said.

The man smiled and sat back a bit appraising the couple, the nervous, impulsive, hot-headed husband and the direct, composed wife. "What do you mean that there are no records of these items?"

Franca looked back and forth between her husband and the suspicious buyer.

"Professor Scarsi and I," her voice authoritative and formal, neck elongated and holding her head in a regal position, "have been asked to combine the inventories using all the known ledgers, records, and documents in the possession of the library." She smiled and leaned forward subtly pushing her husband back. "There are no records of these items in the Libraries at the Capitular Archives, so there is no risk of them being identified as being from there. They never existed in the archives which means that there is no risk of them being considered stolen. Therefore, they should be worth more money," she finished, sitting back in her chair to await the buyer's response.

"Yes, but where do I tell my customer's that they came from?"

"That is your business." Franca jumped forward to respond. "Say that you found them in your grandmother's attic. I don't know. I don't care."

She hesitated and then continued, "What I do know...is that you will be able to sell these for many times the two thousand that you offer us."

"If you know that they are worth so much more, why not sell them yourself?"

She scoffed at the idea. "We are professors of antiquities, not merchants."

"Yet you are trying to sell to me now?" The man smiled as he exposed her hypocrisy.

Franca's face flushed a little but Pier Luigi smiled; she had made their point. They were not pushovers and they were offering a great opportunity to the buyer. But Pier Luigi knew that their options were limited. Now that they had identified themselves as thieves to a man they barely knew, they were at his mercy. They could only protect themselves by linking the buyer to their guilt. While he knew that they would eventually accept any offer from the buyer, he hoped that his wife's little display of bravado would at least increase that offer.

"Very well. You make a good point. And I want you to be happy and bring me new items," the man said. "I'll give you five thousand dollars cash – now – for the items." He looked up as the professors looked at each other and, without a word, agreed to the price.

The man pulled his hard topped briefcase onto the edge of the small table, unlatched the two clasps and flipped open the top. He spent a few seconds with the contents and handed over a stack of hundred dollar bills to Pier Luigi saying, "I think that I am being very generous. I want to continue working with you and my generosity is a sign of good will." Although the buyer negotiated with the woman, he consummated the deal by handing the money to the man.

Before Pier Luigi could absorb the fact that he had the money in his hands, the buyer picked up the items and placed them into his briefcase. He shut the top, locked the clasps and started to stand.

"It was a pleasure," he said. "Please let me know if you have anything else that I might be interested in. I will be in town only another two days. Let me know and we can make the same arrangements."

The professors stood and followed him out of the café, bewildered by the abruptness of the transition. As the man gave no indication that the conversation would continue, the professors turned to walk down the street in the opposite direction of the buyer.

Before they had taken more than a few steps, the man hailed them saying, "Oh. Have you by chance inventoried the Missal Ludovico da Romagnano yet?" He bridged the gap between them and was now standing very close.

"What?" Pier Luigi said. He could feel a croak in his voice.

Mistaking the question for ignorance, the man explained, "The Missal is a liturgical book which compiles all the instructions and texts necessary for celebrating Mass throughout the year. This manuscript is said to be particularly beautiful." Pier Luigi and Franca were speechless and stared in disbelief. The buyer finished, "I would be very interested in something as rare as that."

Pier Luigi spoke shaking his head in disbelief. "Of course we know what a Missal is," he said. "And the Missal of Ludovico da Romagnano is not rare – it's unique!" Continuing his lecture as if he were speaking to a freshman taking an introductory course, "The Guttenberg Bible is rare. One hundred and eighty original copies were produced in the 1450s and some forty-nine partial or complete copies are known to survive today. But the Missal of Ludovico da Romagnano or even one page is unique! Only one was ever produced. It's especially significant because of where it was produced and the archives it's been kept in."

"You're right. So it's unique," the buyer allowed, giving the professor space to exert his knowledge. "Even better. It should be worth more for all of us. But why does it matter where it's been stored?"

Pier Luigi jumped at the chance to explain, "The archives where we are working…." He paused, took a breath and launched into a history lesson with an equal aim to both educate and re-establish his lost sense of self-esteem lost in the earlier negotiation. "The Capitular Archives are on the site of an ancient Roman Theatre. The grounds had been the site of Catholic churches going back to the year 591. At that time, the Byzantine Empire had just won a long war of attrition with the Ostrogothic Kingdom and survived a plague pandemic, both of which left the entire Italian peninsula poor and depopulated. When the Lombard King dedicated the original church, the goal was to maintain the Church's traditions, culture, and values from natural destruction and invasion by the Franks who were then allies of the Ostrogoths. What developed was a very insular, self-sustaining culture."

"I'm not sure I understand," said the buyer.

Pier Luigi looked at Franca and saw her eyes alight with interest. Forgetting the exposed sidewalk where they stood full of passing strangers, he continued, "The Kingdom of the Lombards expanded and contracted over the millennia. It morphed from covering much of present-day Italy to contracting after the Napoleonic era encompassing the north, sweeping eastwards past Venice into Austria. As one of the few constants,

Torino became the intellectual and spiritual anchor of the kingdom and the Capitular Archives the place where those fruits were stored. Since they have been moved and hidden from raiding armies and looters many times, most items haven't been examined in hundreds of years."

"*Certo*, Pier Luigi," Franca added. "We know that the archives and the documents in them are important. That is why we have been asked to make an inventory."

"*Si*," Pier Luigi responded. "But it is more than that. Since its inception, Torino maintained a closed off, inward-looking attitude, protecting its intellectual property from outside influence especially rival cities. Throughout all these years, the church and surrounding buildings, including the archives, expanded, suffered fire and destruction and were re-built again. The result is that the archives accumulated books, codices, and manuscripts, many hundreds of thousands of historical documents and artifacts, have been written and reproduced without the outside influence of Roman tradition."

The buyer's eyebrows shot up at the implication that many of the items found in the Torino archives were derived from a different tradition than those of the rest of the world, most of which were just reproductions – old, for sure – but reproductions of Roman traditions. Pier Luigi recognized that the man who made a living buying stolen church documents saw dollar signs as he thought about selling something with true historical importance.

As Franca looked at her husband, he could sense her admiration and curiosity.

Nonplussed by the condescending explanation, the buyer continued his request, "If you could bring me the entire Missal... it would be worth..." he paused to make sure that he had the professors' interest, "Maybe as much as one hundred thousand dollars."

Pier Luigi couldn't believe his ears. In his imagination, he saw a tiny prison cell, a stained metal toilet in the corner, a thin mattress on an exposed iron frame, a sliver of light cutting in from high above and a steel-barred door slamming. He had only moments ago started breathing regularly when the buyer handed them the money and took the stolen items. That they stood on the sidewalk without uniformed Art Squad policemen arresting them brought an overwhelming sense of relief that would take days to comprehend. Now, blood flushed in his ears making hearing difficult. The buyer wanted him to do it again? Incredible!

Franca spoke up, "The Missal is an important religious item and one of Torino's cultural icons; it would be discovered missing almost immediately." Without waiting for a response, she continued, "The value of the manuscript is beyond measure in the historical and artistic sense. How can you put a price on it?"

But, of course, this man just had. "Besides," Pier Luigi said, "It would take the two of us to carry it out. It is almost the size of a café table and weighs nearly ten kilos." He looked to Franca who appeared uncharacteristically uncommitted at the buyer's request. Pier Luigi knew the couple's finances better than Franca and heard the figure of one hundred thousand dollars – a sum that would go a very long way solving their problems. But at what cost to his nerves?

"It's completely out of the question," Pier Luigi said while leaning forward, his body saying the exact opposite. "But we'll let you know if we find anything else interesting," when he wanted to say that he hoped to forget the day's events as soon as possible.

The man spoke to the two but directed his eyes to Franca, "Even a leaf or two from the Missal could be worth ten to twenty thousand dollars each." He smiled unctuously and finished, "A page – one from a popular saint like San Lorenzo – you could liberate one with far less trouble than these two items you brought me today." He let the offer sit there to make sure the professors understood that their recent success was much riskier than the more lucrative one he was proposing.

"You have my number." The buyer turned and walked away.

The professors watched the man walk up the street and turn out of sight before they dared look at each other. They walked in silence, each to their own thoughts, for nearly fifteen minutes. It soon became obvious that they were walking to their apartment. They entered and went to separate rooms; Franca to the bedroom, Pier Luigi to the narrow kitchen.

When Franca reappeared a few minutes later, Pier Luigi had set out some bread, a few types of cheese and sliced salami. The opened bottle of Barbera d'Asti sat on the table and Pier Luigi was on his second glass.

"We should do it," Franca said. Perhaps expecting a fight, she began to rattle off the financial problems that the money would solve.

"I know." Pier Luigi said without looking up. The visions of the jail cell lost out to thoughts of a happy Franca and being debt free.

"What?" Franca was surprised by the unforced compliance. "So you think it is a good idea?"

"I think it is an idea that will work. And I think we need to do it," he said. "But, it is not a good idea."

He cut another slice of salami and before putting it in his mouth, looked up for the first time and continued, "But after what we did today, what is one more bad idea?" He ate the salami and drained the glass of wine.

"Oh!" Franca exclaimed and leaned over to hug him and gave him a kiss on the cheek. Pier Luigi basked in the emotional outpouring.

"You know? The page of San Lorenzo – the one he suggested – is a very appropriate piece to take," Franca said.

"How do you mean?" Lives of the Saints never interested him as much as it must have Franca.

"San Lorenzo was a deacon in the early church. A Roman Prefect had asked San Lorenzo to bring him all of the wealth of the church. San

Lorenzo asked for three days to create an inventory. He used that time to dispose of all the church's wealth by distributing it to the poor and the orphans. When San Lorenzo returned to the Prefect, he pointed to the group of cripples, lepers, orphans and widows saying that these are the treasures of the Church. The Prefect was so angry that he had Lorenzo roasted alive. That's why you usually see iconography of San Lorenzo holding a pen and near a gridiron, to symbolize the way he was martyred."

"So, San Lorenzo died to save some gold and jewels – *Testun*," Pier Luigi scoffed. "Pretty hardheaded and dumb if you ask me. Isn't the Church rich enough?"

"Come on Pier Luigi, any organization that has been around for two thousand years will accumulate wealth. Property alone accounts for a tremendous percentage of their riches. But what San Lorenzo pointed out seventeen hundred years ago is still true today; that the actual wealth of the Church is in the faithful believers."

"Thanks for the history lesson and comforting sentiment but why does that make it an appropriate piece to take?"

"Because, don't you see? San Lorenzo sold all of the Church's finest possessions and gave away the money to the poor so as not to give it to the powerful Romans. That was in the fourth century. Today, we are the poor and we will take the manuscript to keep it from the Romans of today, the Church." Franca smiled at her rationalization.

Pier Luigi grunted assent and laughed, "So there is profit in San Lorenzo?"

Not to be outwitted, "Or San Lorenzo's treasures are taking the treasure of San Lorenzo."

"I wouldn't go that far. We are nobody's treasures to be doing this." They ate the rest of the meal in relative silence.

***

As they were cleaning up, Pier Luigi began to bounce around the tight quarters of the kitchen with renewed enthusiasm. The events of the day had taken the normal exuberance and energy out of him but all of a sudden he looked to be his old self again. He started opening up and closing all of the kitchen draws, opening and slamming cabinet doors, until he found what he was looking for.

"Ahha!" he exclaimed.

"What is that? Old string?" she questioned the item he held in his hands. "Why do you need that?"

"It's butcher string. Let me show you something." He turned on the tap and let the water run over the string. After about a minute of letting it get wet, he turned off the tap and lightly squeezed his hand to drain the excess water.

"Come with me." He beckoned Franca to walk with him into the living room.

The apartment came furnished and on the bookshelves were several books that had either been those of the absent owner or, more likely, thrift shop purchases to make the apartment seem attractive to prospective renters. Pier Luigi grabbed a thick hardcover book at random and placed it on the coffee table. Opening the book up to a random page, he placed the wet string in a line vertically from the top to the bottom near the spine of the book. When the string was in place and straight, he closed the book and pressed on the cover. He looked at his watch and said nothing for a minute.

When the time was up, and Franca had asked, for the third time, "What are you doing? I don't understand," he opened the book to that page where the wet string had been acting as a book marker. He removed the string tossing it aside absently and firmly grabbed the page that now had a thin line of water where the butchers' string had been. Pier Luigi paused for just a moment. Franca could see now what he was doing. The paper weakened at the water line. With confidence and ease, Pier Luigi pulled the page out and away from its binding producing a clean cut and separated page. Only by really looking at the page numbers or the spine of the book could one even see that the page was missing.

"Very clever," Franca commended. "So you think that all we need to do is place a wet string in the Missal and wait a few moments and pull the page out?"

Pier Luigi nodded and smiled.

"The string solution works well on paper," Franca said. A smile spread across her face. "Did you forget? The manuscript will be on vellum – calfskin – not paper."

Shit, she's right, he thought. Idiot. He smacked his head with his palm. Clearly, he had gotten ahead of himself while trying to be clever.

"We'll need something like a knife or a razor blade to cut it out of the binding."

"Of course it would be vellum. Stupid me!" Pier Luigi said as he got up and rushed to the bathroom. He came back a moment later with a disposable Bic razor and sat back at the kitchen table. Wrapping his napkin around the end of the razor, he snapped the handle off so that he only had the protected safety razor in his hand. He then grabbed the knife that he had been slicing salami with and pried it between the razor and the plastic casing. He wiggled it for a few seconds before the plastic housing broke free and shot across the table leaving Pier Luigi with the two thin razors in his napkin. "*Ecco*, here it is!" Pier Luigi exclaimed.

"Are you sure those thin blades will work? They don't seem very sturdy." Franca said skeptically.

"We only need to use it for two or three pages. They will do the job fine. A box cutter or a real razor blade would be better. But a box cutter is more likely to be noticed by the guard and I don't have a straight razor. We don't have time to buy one before returning. Giorgi will be waiting for us soon."

"I think the vellum will be too thick for those tiny blades," Franca objected again.

With regained confidence, "I will make it work."

"But it must be done soon. This afternoon. The buyer is only in town a few more days," Franca said.

"Agreed. But once we have Giorgi bring the Missal of Ludovico da Romagnano down, we'll still need to get him to leave and give us time to cut the page out."

"Or two," Franca said hopefully.

"Or two. Yes. If we are going to do it let's get more than one leaf. At ten thousand dollars a page, this could make the entire predicament worthwhile."

Franca said, "We can't wait longer than tomorrow because...."

"I got it, I got it." He let his frustration show. "I said I'd ask Giorgi for the San Lorenzo this afternoon. How many more times do you want me to say it?"

Franca ignored his tantrum and said, "I prefer that we get the money right away."

"I prefer that we don't hang on to stolen antiquities for too long. I don't want a knock on our door from the Art Squad," Pier Luigi said knowing that prosecuting all art crime was nearly an impossible task. Similar to finding one particular seashell on a beach of many seashells; it could be done by blind luck or with the concerted focus and resources applied to the task.

"Or if they do come knocking, I don't want to have any incriminating evidence." The statement warbled as the anxiety of the earlier heist crept back into his voice. The key, Pier Luigi knew, was making sure nobody focused on your particular seashell...and that luck kept you in the shadows.

They cleaned up with a sense of purpose and gathered their belong-ings for a return to the Archives. On heading out the door, Pier Luigi had another idea and went to the desk. He returned with a handful of rubber bands of various sizes.

"What do you need that for?" Franca asked.

Pier Luigi smiled, stealing a few pages from the Missal may actually be easier to get away with. "When we have the leaves separated from the binding, I'll wrap them around my leg." Smiling and holding his cache of rubber bands out for examination, "I'll use these to hold the pages up against my leg." He bent down and stepped through a rubber band that he had opened wide demonstrating how it fit snugly around his calf.

"*Bravo*! Pier Luigi," she exclaimed as she leaned over to kiss him on the cheek. "Once we get the pages out of the Missal we will have no trouble leaving the building undetected. *Bravo*," she repeated.

The mission was agreed to.

The plan was laid out.

Their fates, and the fates of many others, sealed.

# Chapter 12

**Basel, Switzerland**
**Wednesday, November 12, 1997**

The woman with the coffee service came into the waiting room where Max, startled, jerked upright. Bending at her hips, she quietly announced, "There is a gentleman here to see you. Shall I bring him in?"

"Yes. Thank you," Max said, rubbing both hands on his trousers in a smoothing motion.

Momentarily, she returned with a small man in a brown suit and brown tie carrying a metallic briefcase. At once Max's ears ran hot for having brought his L.L. Bean canvas messenger bag instead of the cordovan leather hard case briefcase his Aunt Marlene had bought him for graduation.

Max dismissed the thought and regarded the French buyer. At one time, the suit probably fit him perfectly but age or infirmity had shrunk him a bit giving him ample room in his clothing. The man wore a pencil-thin mustache and was losing the battle of the comb-over. His sharp eyes darted around the room jumping from scene to scene with minimal movement of his head as he took in the surroundings. He offered a limp handshake as his eyes continued to survey the battleground and said, "I am Fredric Paquet. How do you do?"

"Hello. I am well and you?"

"*Voulez-vous un café, Monsieur?*" The coffee service lady asked the Frenchman.

"*No, Merci,*" he replied with a dismissive wave of his hands.

Switching to English as soon as she had left the room, "Where are you staying, Mr. Agresta? Here in Basel?"

Max almost scoffed as the man's accent reminded him of The Pink Panther's Inspector Jacques Clouseau. "No, I'm staying in Zurich at the Dolder Grand. I'm speaking at an industry forum." Max responded hoping that he impressed the Frenchman. "Here is my business card," Max said as he handed it over. Before leaving home, Max had thought about printing a new card with just his name and phone number to look more professional and to distance himself from his actual, more pedestrian occupation. He ran out of time, or more likely wanted to save the fifty dollar expense, and instead blanked out the company's main phone number with a Sharpie, leaving only his U.S. cell phone number.

Paquet regarded it carefully and did not make mention of the trucking firm's logo or the ink marks. The Frenchman had his gold pen out and scribbled something on the back. "And this is your mobile number where you can be reached?" he asked.

Max leaned in and squinted, concentrating on deciphering the man's accent. "Yes, when I'm in the States. I don't use the phone here because it is on a different system and it is so expensive," Max explained. The Frenchman maintained a blank expression. Max flushed with embarrassment at his own frankness. He knew it was tacky to complain about phone expenses when he was making a hundred thousand dollar transaction. Max started to sink into minor melancholy at his gaffe which morphed into full force embarrassment and dread as he realized that he just handed his name, business address, and contact info to a counterpart in a transaction that was supposed to be secret. Stupid! Max scrunched his toes into balls and leaned forward contemplating snatching the card back from the Frenchman.

"Mr. Agresta, were you able to bring the manuscript?"

Max jerked back into the present, reached into his bag, and pulled out a mailing tube and handed it over. The Frenchman sniffed, possibly at the mode of transport for so important a document.

Max had been carrying the manuscript in this tube ever since Edgar had handed it to him back in St. Augustine. He hadn't opened it from the protective wrappers and made sure that it never left his sight. Even on the plane, he kept the tube in his bag which he kept at his feet rather than placing it in the overhead compartment.

Paquet seized the tube with both hands and pulled the manuscript out. He took his time unwrapping the cloth which covered it. He laid the page flat out on the table before him and placed small weights on each corner. This was the first time Max had seen the page and was impressed by the vibrant colors and the artistry forming the letters and depiction of a saint. He knew very little about the painted leaf from Edgar. The Frenchman placed a special pair of magnifying glasses on his head which had miniature flashlights attached at the corners and started examining the manuscript.

For something so old and worth so much money, he handled it with a lack of reverence. He felt the paper edges and read through the text, stopping every now and again to examine a section with closer scrutiny. He made barely audible grunting noises as he inspected and turned it over. He repeated the process on the back side. Lastly, he pulled a small handheld light out of his briefcase and pointed it toward the item being inspected. All this time, Max sat hunched forward with his elbows on his knees watching the animated Frenchman inspect the manuscript.

"This is remarkable," observed Paquet.

"What is?"

"Of course, I saw a black and white, very poor quality facsimile that your colleague had sent. But without the details, it was hard to tell. I am fairly certain that this is the San Lorenzo from the Missal of Ludovico da Romagnano."

Max had no idea what that meant but it certainly sounded important...and valuable. "What's San Lorenzo? Is that good?"

"A lot of people will be interested in seeing this," he said more to himself than Max.

"Oh yeah? What is it?"

"A missal is a prayer manual that allows the celebrant to properly say Mass. This hand painted page is part of an instruction book that has been used for generations to glorify and worship the Lord. In this case, we're looking at instructions for the feast day of San Lorenzo…Saint Lawrence, in English. Do you know his story?"

Max shook his head to indicate that he did not know.

"Young man, San Lorenzo, a deacon in the early Christian church, was ordered to turn over the Church's wealth. When he defied the Emperor's order, he was put to death. The story is that he was roasted on a gridiron until he died."

Max leaned in to absorb the instruction.

The Frenchman continued, "There is a wonderful sculpture in marble by Bernini in the Uffizi called the 'Martyrdom of Saint Lawrence'. St. Lawrence is also the patron saint of cooks, chefs, and comedians because of his last words…." Paquet stopped mid-sentence as if he had caught himself being too friendly. He returned to his taciturn and cold manner as he scrutinized the manuscript with greater detail.

When he was finished, the Frenchman looked up at Max and asked sharply, "Where did you find this?"

In the planning stages of this venture, Edgar and Max had worked out the story with enough truth in it to make it sound convincing. Max retold it with, what he hoped would be, convincing authority. "I received it from my grandfather when he passed away. He must have gotten it in the thirties and held on to it."

The Frenchman's eyebrows rose as he asked somewhat pointedly, "Was he a collector of fifteenth-century manuscripts?"

A warm comfort overcame Max and a tear nearly squeezed out as he remembered his grandfather, Nonno Man. Just as quickly a pang of regret stung at the lost opportunity for never having learned Italian from him. It wasn't the first time Max was struck that he hadn't always followed through with the hard work it takes to achieve his ambitions.

Max knew the general basics of his grandfather's life but had called his dad to fill in the details and make the story of the manuscript's history more believable. Nonno Man came to America from northern Italy in the early 1920's leaving behind a mother, brother, and sister. He left Italy, not because of impoverished circumstances but, because he wanted freedom from the structure of the old country. Max could understand the drive; he wanted freedom, too.

Right off the boat, his grandfather worked in a grocery store in Jeannette, Pennsylvania for a month to fulfill his immigration commitment. He made his way to Dago Hills in St. Louis, attending three days of English class, before finding Chicago. Walking around The Loop looking for work, he heard voices from a second-floor pool hall speaking Piedmontese, the Italian dialect of his home. Inside, he met fellow countrymen who steered him to a busboy job at the German-run, Blackstone Hotel where he 'learned the trade' of serving its wealthy clientele. Nonno Man's picture actually appeared in a 1923 newspaper article about a new innovation, the coffee percolator, which made its introduction at the fancy hotel.

One of Max's favorite stories was that his grandfather also served the head table at Al Capone's going away party before the Chicago gangster left for Alcatraz. Max recognized the irony that, as he set up a secret Swiss bank account, Capone went to prison for tax evasion.

Eventually, Max's grandfather visited New York with a friend for the famous Six Day Bicycle race. When they arrived in Manhattan, they went to the friend's aunt's rooming house whose basement served as a speakeasy on West 46th street. The woman who answered the door became Max's grandmother.

Nonno Man returned to Italy for a visit shortly after the Second World War with his wife, Max's grandmother, and son, Max's young father. The family reunion went well. They all committed to maintaining contact but it was difficult to continue the family relationships over the expanse of oceans and cultures. Max knew that his grandfather's siblings had children and were still living in northern Italy. In fact, Max's father, now recently retired and living in New Smyrna Beach, had been dabbling in creating a family tree. He had been in contact with one of his cousins recently; the one who happened to marry a rare book dealer in Torino. The old country connection to rare book dealing made Max's story more convincing and was probably what had set Edgar's idea in motion.

"No. He wasn't a collector," Max finally said to the Frenchman. "He was a waiter."

"What was a waiter doing with a piece like this?" the Frenchman sneered.

Max resisted the urge to return the insult to this arrogant Frenchie with his condescending questions. But he had been expecting the suspicion and said, "After arriving in the States, my grandfather worked at the best hotels and nightclubs in New York. I don't know how he came upon this item but I know that he was a trusted employee of John Paul Getty and one time helped him stop a theft at the Pierre Hotel in New York which Getty owned."

The Frenchman sat back and regarded Max for a moment.

Max continued, "Getty, as you know, was big into the arts and could have given this manuscript to my grandfather as a gift for loyal service."

"Getty also allowed his six-year-old son to go blind because of a brain tumor rather than spend money on medical treatment," the Frenchman replied.

Several moments had passed when the Frenchman finally spoke, "I'm sorry Monsieur. This is not what I was expecting."

Max's ear rang at the rejection and heard, 'Dees eez not whaht eye wuz aspettin'.

"I cannot make this purchase." The little man replaced his tools back in the briefcase, took the four small weighs and put them in his suit pocket, leaving the manuscript page curling dramatically on the corners, and prepared to leave.

"Wait a minute!" Max exclaimed. He lunged forward in his chair with thoughts to stop the French buyer. "I don't understand."

The Frenchman just stared at him, debating whether to speak or not. He chose not.

Max pleaded, "Please explain."

Paquet held his briefcase on his lap in position for a quick departure and, changing his mind said, "That manuscript is a very important document with historical implications."

Max couldn't believe the turn of events. He sat with his mouth open, the words stuck somewhere in the cross signals of his brain. It didn't make any sense. "Then why won't you buy it?" Max saw the dream – the promise of money for Sam's treatment, the hope of an exciting life – falling apart.

The Frenchman weighed his next words carefully. Paquet stood calmly saying, "I buy and sell antique books and manuscripts. I buy from collectors in need of money or at estate sales when the collector dies. I sell to academic institutions and collectors desiring to accumulate treasures. Discretion is of the utmost importance. Many of the items in my trade are church documents, the provenances of which can be a little…shall we say unclear? Some very powerful people…important people have been looking for this," he said indicating the San Lorenzo. "The Church, too, has shown increasing interest in its recovery."

"Good," Max blurted. "It should be valuable then."

The Frenchman sniffed and, although a shorter man, looked down at Max. "Young man, one does not have a successful trade in this business by making enemies, especially powerful ones… and whoever presents the San Lorenzo will surely make one.

Max saw what looked like anxiety in the Frenchman's face.

The Frenchman, his anxious observations jumping from spot to spot, peered at the exit and said, "Besides, I do not purchase stolen items."

"I didn't steal anything!" Max said.

"Perhaps not. But that manuscript is stolen and possession of it is a very serious crime in Europe, punishable by a long prison sentence."

Max stood to protest, slack-jawed and red-faced. His good feelings moments ago had vanished as his world crumbled. Max's brain reeled and tried to process the information and synch it with the ramifications. Prison. His teeth itched and he became lightheaded as thoughts of incarceration played out in his head.

Paquet regarded the young American man for a few moments and said, "Even if you could substantiate your ownership… a manuscript like that, with its cultural significance, competing for powerful forces wanting it…it would be confiscated by the authorities and assumed by the government under the auspices of cultural preservation."

Max understood what that meant; even if the authorities believed his story, he'd lose the manuscript.

"I will not deal in stolen items and have not the energy to fight the bureaucracy for items which they feel belong to all the people."

"I understand," Max said although he didn't.

"Good luck to you, sir," the Frenchman said as he stood and walked hastily to the door. He left the room and said something in French to the receptionist as he left. For a moment, it occurred to Max that he was calling the cops. The thought passed as he heard the Frenchman leave the front door.

Max's head slumped and he stared at his wet shoes, accused of theft and returning home with none of his goals accomplished – a total failure.

# Chapter 13

"I have a manuscript which is very old and rare and could make us some money," Edgar had said that time they ate at the sidewalk café in St. Augustine's historic district. Max thought back to the conversation that led him here.

The oldest continuously occupied European-established settlement in North America, St. Augustine, was an ideal place for Max to let his imagination run wild. Everywhere he looked he saw history. Locals were proud of the city's heritage and fond of calling this part of Florida the 'First Coast' because it is the first place in North America that European settlers landed and stayed. In fact, the locals would tell anyone who would listen that the Spanish settlers shared the first meal of thanksgiving with the Native Americans fifty-five years before the Pilgrims did so in Massachusetts and forty-two years before the English settled in Jamestown, Virginia. And today, Max, a descendent of Italian immigrants, raised across the Matanzas river on what the locals called 'The Island', sat with a local resident of mysterious, Spanish-Lebanese heritage and Sierra Leon/Italian upbringing discussing international business ventures.

Max remembered being relieved to be talking about something other than the recent untimely death of Lady Diana in a Paris car accident.

"So, you've been here long?" Edgar questioned.

"Yeah, I was born in New Jersey but moved here as a kid. I went to elementary school just around the corner on St. George Street," Max said.

"Do you surf?"

"I always wanted to but could never very good...I'm too tall; high center of gravity. Besides, there are too many things in the ocean that want to eat you. I played baseball in high school...a lot less dangerous. But I went to the oldest Catholic high school in Florida; founded by the Sisters of St. Joseph in 1866." Max proudly embraced his city and its roots in Europe and envied the first settlers of his town that braved the oceans and found adventure in the new world.

"But you are Italian?" Edgar questioned.

"Yeah, my grandfather came over from northern Italy in his twenties. I still have cousins over there but I don't know much about them."

"Is that so? I went to high school in Italy and lived with an aunt and uncle because the schools were not very good in Sierra Leone. Civil war broke out so I never returned," Edgar said.

"What were you doing in Sierra Leone?" Max asked, always interested to hear foreigners' stories of immigration.

"I was born there...my father, too. My grandfather moved to Sierra Leone from Lebanon after the First World War."

"How cool is that? I would never have thought." Max said. It never occurred to him that a white guy could be born and raised in western Africa.

"Yes, there actually is...or was...a sizeable Lebanese population in Sierra Leone before the civil war. Most of them are traders and merchants." With little remorse added, "Now I'm here."

"What part of Italy did you go to high school in?" Max asked.

"Near Torino, Italy."

"That's where my family's from! I think one of them is a rare book dealer there."

"What a coincidence," said Edgar. "The rare and antique book world is not that large. Everybody seems to know everybody. Maybe I know your cousin." Edgar's mind raced with the possibilities. "You know, Torino is actually one of the most important cities for the trade. Paris and New York are certainly bigger but, for its size, Torino has a number of important antiquarian booksellers. Especially," he added, "when it comes to fifteenth and sixteenth-century manuscripts. In that regard, Torino is unmatched."

Max and Edgar sat facing the art galleries on the other side of the street so that Edgar could see his used book shop which dabbled in some rare items. Prior to Wilson's promotion and assumption of the role of hall monitor, Max used his extended lunch hours to visit the galleries and bookstores, including Edgar's, with an idea to becoming a collector. But with the tight finances at home, he could never afford anything more than a few postcards for Sam and the twins. Still, he enjoyed his time eating at different spots in the historic district every day and spending time exploring the nation's oldest city.

After his promise to Theodore to stop antagonizing Wilson, Max thought it best to cut the lunches short and settled into a daily routine of eating lunch at Carmelo's Pizzeria, located across the street from the police station on King's Street and a block from his office. The small pizzeria, attached to a gas station, sat outside the tourist circuit and a favorite hangout for the locals where construction workers, politicians, businessmen, and law enforcement could enjoy New York style pizza. It was actually at Carmelo's that Max had first noticed Edgar. The staccato laugh cut through the dining area and, even though they were drinking beer while Max was stuck with iced tea, it struck him that he and the other man were having a business conversation. Max flashed resentment and jealousy picturing Wilson tapping his watch at Max's tardiness while other businessmen had autonomy conducting their affairs.

Max received Edgar's call this morning and, since Wilson was out of the office this week, decided he could afford a leisurely meal which is how the two men found themselves under the umbrella on the sidewalk café across from Edgar's store discussing a new business venture.

"I'm always interested in a little side project to earn money," Max replied to Edgar's inquiry.

"You said that you are going to Zurich for a conference in November. I have an interested buyer for an item and if you meet with them and deliver it…effect the sale, I can figure you in for a ten percent commission."

Edgar looked up and down Avilla Street to make sure no one was listening.

"It must be done in person and I cannot leave my shop. Besides, if we make the transaction in Europe, I can avoid taxes."

"How much is the book worth?"

"It is not a book but rather a leaf or page that, at one time, was part of a book. It's an original 15th century manuscript from a prayer Missal."

"Oh? What's the difference between a book and a manuscript?" Max asked, not being shy when he didn't know the answer.

"A manuscript is an original, handwritten work – not printed," said Edgar. "I don't know for sure what it is worth as we haven't finalized the details but…" lowering his voice to stress the importance, "approximately one hundred thousand dollars."

"One hundred grand! That's amazing." Max didn't need a calculator to know that his cut would be ten thousand dollars or nearly double his most recent bonus.

"Incredible isn't it? The last few years have been very good for the prices of rare books and manuscripts. Plus, I purchased these several years ago for a very good price…so I can afford to be generous in paying commissions."

Max did not argue the generosity – he knew where he could use the money. Laura had talked about going back to work but they both felt that staying home was better for the children and Sam's health. Besides, with the poor pay of Florida teachers, Laura wasn't really giving up much money. The couple had cut back on any luxury item; giving up the beach club membership, canceling cable, and never going out to eat. In financial arguments, Laura never failed to mention that Max ate out almost every day for lunch. He countered saying that bringing food from home was just as expensive. He could see losing that argument soon.

Right then and there, in a sleepy tourist town in northeast Florida, the men struck an agreement. Edgar would make the plans with the prospective buyer for Max to meet him in Switzerland. The one wrinkle was that in order to sell the manuscript, Max and Edgar needed to establish a Swiss bank account. The buyer wouldn't hand over cash, they would wire the money to the account instead. The Swiss secrecy banking laws would mean that the US tax collector was none the wiser. Max would take his commission in cash from the deposited funds and give the bank account information to Edgar. It required a lot of trust on Edgar's part but Max knew he was worthy of it.

"It wasn't easy to set up a Swiss bank account," Edgar said a week later. "It's not like opening an account at First Union Bank. I had to make a lot of calls and pay some people off," he explained when they met just prior to Max's trip.

Max grimaced as he thought about the difficulty in meeting the buyer. Edgar had set it for Basel, which was over an hour away by train, on the same day as the conference's welcome reception. Max had no choice – he'd have to finagle a few hours of unnoticed absence and return on time if he wanted the ten grand and keep his job.

# Chapter 14

Max sat in the banker's office in shock of the Frenchman's statement. The realization of no commission sapped every bit of his energy. He would return home empty handed without being able to afford Sam's surgery. Worse, he'd have to explain to Laura that he spent money… their money…money they didn't have…on another business venture. Just as bad, he had stolen goods on his hands that he'd be smuggling past the United States Customs Agents at the airport when he landed back home. His shoulders slumped and his head hung down.

Mueller entered the room. "I see that your guest has left. That was a short meeting. I trust it went well?"

"Yes, fine," Max lied. He looked at his watch, saw the time and thought of making a quick exit. He rolled the manuscript up without much care and placed it back in the tube. To satisfy Mueller, Max said, "Mr. Paquet will be wiring the money into the account when he returns to Paris."

"This is not what we expected. I understood that we would receive the funds today, after the transaction."

Thinking fast, Max said, "There has been a change of plans. It seems that the item I brought is worth more than originally agreed upon. Mr.

Paquet must make arrangements for the purchase after returning home."

Mueller's eyebrows shot up for a brief moment; they quickly regained form. "Of course. We will await your instructions."

After a pause, he continued, "I believe that originally, you would be withdrawing some of the funds. Do you still intend to do that?"

Max hadn't thought about it but he still had access to an account with ten thousand dollars. This would certainly help with the missing wallet problem and he had the out-of-pocket expenses. He believed that he should get a little something for his troubles and a couple of grand would help ease the tension at home. He was sure that Edgar would understand the situation.

"Yes, I would like to take out two thousand now."

"Would you like it in Swiss Francs or Dollars?"

A big smile spread across Max's face. Cool. "Dollars, please."

"Very well, I will make arrangements and be right back."

Max made his way to the door and saw Mueller lean over to Strauss in the anteroom speaking in quiet tones. Strauss did not hold his emotions as well as Mueller. Max could tell that he had caused an uncomfortable circumstance when the younger banker displayed a look of condescension.

Max stood in the hallway near the receptionist busying himself when Mueller, this time with Strauss trailing him, handed him an envelope with twenty, one hundred dollar bills. After signing the receipt, Max put the envelope in his suit jacket breast pocket.

Mueller shook Max's hand saying, "Thank you for visiting today. Please let us know when we can expect the next transaction." The look from Strauss said that he thought Max an insignificant client and terrible inconvenience – which was the least of Max's concerns at this point, but it still bothered him. Max had struck out on the international stage and felt like crawling back into his cubicle office in Florida and forgetting the entire plan.

\*\*\*

Max stepped out of the building and noticed the sun trying to peak out. Max walked toward the street in the crisp air.

The walk back to the train station would help him clear his head and allow him to take stock of the situation. Mentally, Max made an account of the day's events. He dismissed the missing wallet as bad luck, easily remedied. If he ignored the legal concern of trafficking in stolen items, it wasn't all bad. He got to visit a new city in Europe, he had some money in his pocket and he should make it back to the conference in time. That is if he moved directly to the station and made the 1624 train to Zurich.

He turned left on Angensteinerstrasse and started toward the station when he noticed the French buyer standing with his trench coat askew and rubbing his shoulder. The man's perceptive, anxious twitching was replaced by a pained fear.

"Mr. Paquet, are you all right?"

"Huh? Ah. No. Yes," he stuttered. "I was… those bastards!" The Frenchman struggled to make some sense while tripping to find the right words. Gone was his haughty attitude exhibited just moments ago. "I was robbed. They pushed me down and took my briefcase and ran off."

"Who?"

"The heroin junkies," the Frenchman said. "They destroy everything. It is bad enough that they don't put them in jail but here," indicating Switzerland, "they actually give them the drugs."

Just then, a pale beige Mercedes taxi that had been called for Mr. Paquet pulled up. The mustachioed Serbian driver with four days beard growth leaned across the passenger side and said something in German. Max recognized only one word, '*Bahnhof*. The Frenchman twitched, his hands clenched and face twisted in a low boil rage. Max, recognizing that the Frenchman needed help and that the taxi was headed to the train station, opened the rear door and guided Mr. Paquet in. Max jumped around the back of the car and entered into the back seat from the driver side.

"*Bahnhof?*" the driver repeated. The Frenchman, now with a handkerchief in his hand and holding it to the side of his head, nodded in assent.

"*Ja. Danke shon.*" Max replied, realizing that he had actually picked up some German from watching those war movies.

As he closed the door, Max had a scary thought. There were two international train stations in Basel. Maybe they were going to the wrong one. The panic was short-lived when Max remembered that the Swiss and French lines ran through the same station and, as the Frenchman was headed to Paris, they would be departing from the same place.

The taxi sped off and pulled up to the station minutes later. As it came to a stop at the departures line, the driver leaned back and announced the fare. Max didn't have any Swiss Francs and was glad that the Frenchman reached in his wallet to pay.

"*Servos,*" the driver replied in response saying goodbye.

They had stepped out of the taxi and onto the sidewalk when the Frenchman continued, "It is bad enough that the government gives them free drugs. It is terrible that these bums do nothing but make trouble. Now they have fancy cars and dress like canaries."

Max gave the man a sidelong glance concerned that he had taken a severe blow to the head. Concussion came to mind.

"The drugs are free but they rob me to buy the American clothing. Incredible!"

Max dismissed the Frenchman's rambling and, looking at his watch, realized that his train to Zurich departed in four minutes. "Yes. Terrible," Max said, still deciding whether he had time to make a run for the train.

"Okay. I'm sorry for your troubles. Good-bye."

The Frenchman nodded, grunted a goodbye while Max turned and jaywalked across the street to head to the station's entrance – in too much of a hurry to worry about the Swiss custom of waiting for a signal.

# Chapter 15

"Whadya mean it's not there, Sully?" barked the driver of the rented Peugeot to the man in the back seat.

"Geez, Tommy. You don't have to yell at me," Sully said and slumped back in his seat like a scolded child.

"I'll yell at whoever I want!" Tommy screamed back.

Although of Polish/Irish descent, Tommy affected a Mafioso look with slicked back black hair and all black attire – black leather jacket, black silk tee shirt, black pants, and black driving shoes – always without socks. His square jaw jutted out as he clenched his capped white teeth. His left nostril twitched and he reached in to pull out a stray nose hair. He winced when successful and flicked his find onto the dashboard.

He looked down at the passenger seat where an iconic red handled knife lay open, its box and receipt from a Basal gas station gift shop strewn on the floor. He cursed the airport security guard for finding his Benchmade Pagan. The sleek automatic, out-the-front spring mechanism delivered a razor-sharp four-inch blade perfect for quick in-and-out of pocket use. Known to the uninitiated as a switch blade, the confiscated $400 model was a billed as a gentleman's protection knife – a must have for anyone who put themselves in questionable situations. Now, instead of the chisel-ground steel dagger, he had the Swiss army version of one handed non-serrated knife designed more for slicing cheese and salami than protection. At least it had a locking blade. It was certainly sturdier than the shiv he made from a tooth-brush and razor while at the Southern State Correctional Facility. No matter, Tommy knew from experience that a shank penetrating a hu-man torso would disable a man – kill most – if that's what you wanted.

He grabbed the steering wheel in a death grip and glared into the rearview mirror. His sunken dark eyes bored into a frightened Sully.

Answering his partner's stare, Sully half stated, half whined from the back seat, "It's not here, Tommy." For the past several seconds he had been frantically looking through the stolen briefcase as the car sped away from the scene.

"It's gotta fuckin' be there," He said looking in the rearview mir-ror.

"Tommy, this isn't that big a briefcase. I looked. It's not here." Tommy looked back and wanted to yell at the dimwit some more but it was pretty obvious that the briefcase did not contain the item.

Sully ventured to continue in a tentatively defiant tone. "Watch the road, please."

Tommy jammed on the brakes forcing Sully to slam into the back of the front seat.

"Shit, my nose!" Sully squealed.

Immediately, Tommy slammed his foot on the accelerator push-ing Sully back into his seat. He came to a quick stop at the end of the street where Tommy used the pause to scratch his crotch for at least the tenth time this trip. Relieved, he slammed both hands on the wheel, "I don't believe it!"

"Here, Tommy, look at it yourself," Sully said as he made an attempt to hand the case to the driver.

"I'm fuckin' driving here. I can't look through it!" Tommy spun the wheel to the right and sped up for a block only to come to an aggressive stop at the next intersection. Offering a possible explanation for the missing item, he said, "The old man was probably hiding it in his coat. It's worth a lotta money so it makes sense that he would guard it."

Acting on his idea, he made another hard right, floored the gas pedal and sped down the street in an effort to return to the scene of the robbery. "We've gotta check the guy out again. I ain't leaving without it."

"Tommy, the cops could be there by now. He'll be expecting us. Maybe we should just give up the chase."

"I didn't come this far not to get that book," slamming his hands on the steering wheel.

"I thought it was a page from a manuscript," Sully asked innocently.

"Whatevah!" he screamed. "Shit!" Tommy said as he punched the roof of the car while waiting for the light to change.

He started pulling off the wings of flies at five and graduated to squashing toads with his bicycle by six. When the neighbor's cat was found hanging in the woods, his indifferent parents finally took notice of Tommy Gallagher's strange behavior. When the family dog was 'accidently' lit on fire, specialists were called in. They didn't help. The problems got worse and the trips to juvenile detention became more frequent. By the time he won the Golden Gloves, he was very familiar with the New Jersey juvenile penal system.

On appearance, the discipline of the sport somewhat straightened out his life. Back in his best days, the welterweight who stood five foot, ten inches with a seventy-four inch reach, same as Sugar Ray

Leonard. But he could neither punch nor move like the champ. As he aged, his reflexes got slower and after a young boxer hit him with a left hook that he never saw coming, Tommy retired from the sport. Tommy now had a paunch that made him more of a heavyweight than a welterweight and drank more vodka than Gatorade.

While running numbers for a bookie, Tommy got pinched when a nineteen-year-old, who was in too deep and lost his new pick-up truck, went to the State Police for help. Tommy kept his mouth shut and didn't roll on his bosses. As Tommy awaited trial, the teenaged informant was killed in a hit and run accident in which the driver was never found. Even without the key witness, the State still had enough evidence to convict Tommy on lesser charges and put him away for four and a half years. While serving his time, Tommy's cellmate, who owed him gambling debts incurred in prison, mysteriously hung himself in his cell. No foul play could ever be proved. But Tommy served his full sentence without time off for good behavior; the last ten months in solitary confinement.

"We hardly had any time to set up. I mean, what was he doing outside so soon?" Tommy thought aloud.

"Must have been a short meeting," Sully offered.

After landing in Zurich that morning, the two had rented a car and driven to Basal. They had planned to stake out the bank and be in position long before the French buyer left. However, they had just turned onto the street when they saw the Frenchman standing on the curb, apparently waiting for his taxi.

At first, they thought that their timing couldn't have been better. Tommy slowed the car while Sully, the larger man now in the backseat searching the briefcase, jumped out, said something to the Frenchman and grabbed his briefcase. For as small and old as he was, the French-man put up a fight and, in the tussle, he fell to the ground.

"I told you to take the knife," Tommy said offering the newly purchased blade resting on the passenger seat.

"I don't need it, Tommy. I got the briefcase didn't I?"

"Pussy."

Tommy turned the corner onto Angensteinerstrasse for the second time. This time they could see up ahead a young man enter the rear driver side door of a taxi. Through the rear window, they could both make out the Frenchman's figure holding his hand to his head.

"Who's that with him?"

"How would I know?" Tommy yelled back.

"Can you get a good look at him?" Sully asked.

"Nah. His head's turned." The taxi started to pull away. "But I got an idea who it might be."

Sully leaned toward the front and said, "Follow them, Tommy!"

"What'd you think I'm doing, numbnuts!" Tommy sneered over his shoulder before speeding away.

# Chapter 16

Max ran down the tunnel and turned at the escalator where the sign indicated 'Track 4a'. As he stepped onto the escalator, he looked back toward the station. Even through all the travelers making their way to and from the trains, he could see the small Frenchman looking up at the departure sign. Max bounded up the escalator two steps at a time and, upon gaining his footing at the platform, went directly to the nearest open door of the closest railcar. The conductor stepped onto the car immediately behind him closing the door and, before he could make his first steps, the train began its motion to Zurich.

Max made his way to the bar car and ordered a Duvel. The barman opened the beer and handed it to him and asked for the money in German. Max suddenly remembered that the only money he had was the stack of crisp one hundred dollar bills. "Here," he said handing a Benjamin to the barman.

"No dollars. Francs," the barman said.

"This is all I have," Max said presenting a stack of twenty bills and flipping his thumb over the edge like with a deck of cards. The barman must have decided that Max was more trouble than an unpaid beer and flicked his hand dismissively. Free beer, thought Max as he smiled and bounced back to his seat.

He found a rear facing seat in the second class car, located directly behind the bar car. Looking back at the ground the train had covered, Max reviewed the events of the day.

Max exhaled and lolled his head from side to side to let the stresses of the day escape. He sipped his beer and let out an audible 'ah'. While he hadn't struck the riches he hoped for and career suicide and prison were still potentials, he did feel a guilty pleasure of having accomplished some of the adventures that he desperately wanted. On the plus side, he now had two thousand dollars cash in his breast pocket and eight more readily available through his new Swiss bank account. He was also in possession of a very important, and apparently, very expensive 15th century manuscript. On the negative side, the money was not his to keep and the manuscript was, at least per the haughty Frenchman, stolen.

Max reflected on the problems he faced. Money was the easy one. He already had his argument forming in his head for keeping it. Edgar should realize that a business venture was not without risk. Max had spent his time and energy to meet with the French buyer and set up the account with the bankers. Certainly, Edgar could understand that Max had expenses and should be compensated for them. A few grand that Edgar would lose in the deal should be insignificant and fair compensation for the risk Max had assumed. Max also had a real need for the money –Sam's surgery depended on it. The fact that the deal didn't go as planned was not Max's fault. If the sale didn't make money, well at least it shouldn't cost him. Max practiced these arguments in his mind and promised himself that he would make the strong case as soon as he spoke to Edgar.

The stolen manuscript offered the more pressing problem. As the Frenchman had warned, the mere possession of it could present sig-

nificant legal trouble. Max's feeling of satisfaction waned as he ru-
minated on the possible outcomes of a confrontation with authorities
– all were bad. He could be held for questioning in a foreign country
or, more likely, stopped at the border by U.S. Customs when he landed
in the States. Blaming Edgar at that point would be futile, as Edgar
would surely deny any involvement. He thought of hiring lawyers to
defend him until he considered the expense and the strain that would
put on his family's finances. A couple of days talking with authorities,
or worse, jail, would also mean that he couldn't go to work which
could very likely result in Max losing his job. Of course, telling his
wife what he did and how it affected his family would put even more
pressure on him. Thinking about his predicament wiped away all the
good feelings he'd experienced when he caught the early train and
tasted his first sip of the free Duvel.

However, if he no longer had the manuscript, he wouldn't be subject to prosecution. He debated throwing it away in the bar car's trash
can or at the next train station; anywhere highly traveled. The authorities could link him to the Swiss bankers and the French buyer. From
those contacts, a very motivated policeman could possibly link Edgar
to the meetings he had set up and Edgar to Max. But without the stolen
item in his possession, it would be very difficult for anyone to prove
Max's involvement in stolen antiquities.

A less severe solution was for him to mail it somewhere anony-
mously – but, after a moment's thought, he dismissed the idea. Who
would he send it to? Plus, mailing the manuscript may leave tracks
that could lead back to him.

And disposing of the manuscript wouldn't solve all his problems;
he would still need to deal with Edgar. While Max knew Edgar so-
cially, he didn't know the depth of his connections. Max's imagination
went wild at thoughts of the unsavory characters dealing in stolen art.

Trashing a significant and important historical artifact may be morally reprehensible but it would also represent a financial blow to Edgar and any of the people he worked for. The implications of which were incalculable.

More importantly, the business opportunity would be lost. A new disappointment. Another dead end. An addition to the list of failures. One more explanation to Laura of why he spent time and money chasing another ill-considered business scheme. Max wasn't sure how much longer this could go on. Unless he could fix this, it probably meant the end of his dream of international business intrigue he so desired.

Maybe he could contact his cousin, sell it himself, and exact a bigger commission. Maybe she'd be impressed and make him a representative in America. Or a partner, even. Wasn't this what he had dreamed of? But the reality of making it happen scared him. Probably the safest choice was to keep the two grand as payment for troubles, return the San Lorenzo to Edgar, and regroup to try a different venture with non-stolen goods at a later date.

He realized he had been holding his breath. The stress reclaimed his body and his shoulders tensed. He missed not having someone to talk to. Laura busted his chops unceasingly but maybe it was for the good. Maybe it made him better – focused his thinking. But no way could he tell Laura, or anyone, about this. This was not another vaccine tray deal, this was way more serious. Laura would flip out. This could push her over the edge. At the same time, Max knew that not sharing his struggles with her only added to his anxiety. But fear of her reaction kept him from sharing. He couldn't face disappointing her anymore. He wanted to announce a success…a victory. He knew it was wrong but in this unresolved state, he couldn't talk to her about his situation. However, he promised himself that, when he had returned home safely and unmolested, he would not begin a new venture without discussing it first with Laura. But only after he figured his way out of this mess.

Just then, a mobile phone rang nearby. It took a moment for Max to realize that it was his. He'd almost forgotten that his company had lent him a Nokia cell phone with a European cell phone plan. In a company where only the most important people had mobile phones, he remembered how proud and important he thought himself that he was being trusted with the phone. He picked up the phone and hit the green 'Talk' button.

"Hello, Max Agresta speaking."

"Max, what's happening?" Edgar said.

Max, on his end, imagined the Mediterranean Charlie Brown sitting on Avila Street café sipping a coffee as he checked his affairs around the world.

"Hey Edgar, I was going to call you when I got back to the hotel." Max only just remembered that he had given this number to him before leaving. "This phone call costs a lot of money."

"Well, we're talking about a lot of money. I think this is important enough to use your phone," he said. Max could sense a shift in the man's demeanor. "How did the meeting go?"

"We set up the account. No problem. Do you want the number?"

"Yes...hold on. Let me get a pen. Go ahead," Edgar said. No more Mr. Nice Guy, thought Max.

Max clearly and slowly recited the numbers of the bank account over the phone, unconcerned about being overheard because the number would only allow deposit access. To withdraw the money, one needed to correctly produce a nineteen digit randomly generated number – a number which Max had on a separate piece a paper folded up in a pocket of his bag.

After Edgar had read it back, he said, "Okay, what is the password?"

"Not such a good idea to say that now," Max chuckled. "I'm in a crowded rail car. You do want the money to remain there don't you?"

Edgar hesitated. "Okay. But there is a lot of money in the account now and I want to get access to it immediately.

"Actually, there isn't any money. There was a problem...."

Edgar cut him off. "What," he hissed, "do you mean?" The jolly round-faced man had been replaced by a severely pissed off cold, and calculating man.

"Aside from the deposit you put it, there is no additional money. The buyer was not interested in the document. So I still have it," Max said.

"What?!" he bellowed. A passenger sitting across the aisle from Max must have heard the outburst and looked over. "What the fuck do you mean?" Max could hear Edgar struggling to hold back emotion like horses trying to break free of a burning stable. Edgar's voice mixed the sound of surprise, regret, and fear. In this case, Max also heard Edgar's desire to break things.

"I can't explain right now," Max said, conscious that he was in an open compartment with at least one eavesdropper. "There seems to be a problem with the item and the buyer backed out."

"What the hell, Max? I send you to do one simple thing and you screw it up?" Max could feel the heat rising in his face. He didn't like being made to feel stupid. Max took all the risk. His ass was on the line. The failure wasn't his fault!

Max tried to convey the situation but, given the location of his call, hesitated to go into detail. "I didn't screw up. The problem lies in the product that I have. It was not what was expected," using the words the Frenchman had said only an hour ago.

"I've been in this business for fifteen years. I know what I'm doing. You get involved for two days and undo a lifetime of my work." Edgar said. "You better figure something out. I've worked very hard to get to where I am and I am not going to let you ruin me. Do you understand? Someone will pay for this....and I think you know who!"

Max shook his head to the disembodied voice. He thrust his hand out to the vacant space trying to grasp an answer. "What...What do you want me to do about it?"

"I had to pull a lot of strings to get that account set up and get a buyer to meet you," Edgar said. "Find someone else to buy the manuscript. Remember, you're making money on this, too. A ten percent commission of zero is zero."

"Edgar, I'm going to bring it back and you can figure a way to sell it. I'm not dealing with it anymore."

A long silence followed and Max thought that he had dropped the call when Edgar finally changed tact and said in a more calm voice, "Why don't you go see your cousin – the one who is the rare book dealer in Torino? She can probably help us out." Edgar's use of the word 'us' briefly buoyed Max's spirits. He was still on the team.

"I don't even know her. I've never been there before," Max responded trying to put the issue back on Edgar.

"Go there and meet her, Max. This works out perfectly. You get to see your cousin and we get to sell the manuscript," Edgar said. He spoke now in that easy relaxed manner that Max knew so well. "Have some nice Italian wine and who knows, maybe she will buy the manuscript or put you in touch with a buyer."

Max could feel himself nodding on the phone. If it weren't for the conference, the idea may be worth a shot and certainly better than the previous direction of the call.

Changing the subject, Edgar said, "What about the ten thousand dollars I sent?"

"We still have the account. I had to take some money out, but most of it is still there."

"What do you mean 'most of it' is still there?" Edgar asked.

Max clenched his fist and his body tensed, "I deserve some of it. I'm spending my own money to travel to Basel."

"Bullshit!" Edgar exclaimed. "You have no idea all the trouble I've been through to set this up. If you come back with that manuscript, I've done all that work for nothing. I'm out a ton of money and time and you think that you should get paid?" Max sat stunned on the other end of the line. Edgar waited a few beats, "Unbe-fucking-lievable!" he said before finishing.

Max grasped the situation, "Okay, I'll pay you back the money I took out when I return home." He calculated the drop in his bank account and how to explain it to Laura. "But I can't try to sell the item. I have work to do here and need to concentrate on that," Max said. Trying to put off the discussion for later, "We'll talk about it when I get back."

"No. We'll talk about it NOW! You get to Torino and talk to your cousin." The suggestion had become an order. "Find a buyer and get me my money!" Edgar paused and then added, "Make it right," before the line went dead.

# Chapter 17

Afternoon sun blasted into the west facing windows at number 88 Via XX Septembre, the Torino district headquarters of the Carabinieri Art Squad. On the third floor, Commander Bramante Buratti, Section Chief of the Antique Dealing section, one of the four Art Squad Sections (the other being Archaeology, Fakes/Counterfeiting, and Contemporary Art), was finishing up some paperwork for the afternoon.

The unseasonably warm autumn day combined with the forced radiator heat made Commander Buratti's office unbearably hot. So hot that he even contemplated taking off his jacket and working in shirtsleeves, something few in the Art Squad had ever seen him do. The gray flannel chalk-striped suit was one of his favorites but not in heat like this, its weight better suited for colder weather. He motioned to his secretary who sat with the phone in the crook of her neck taking notes that he intended to go across the hall, if not to see the troops then to get some relief from the heat. There, his inspectors and detectives shared a large, open, cooler, east-facing office cluttered with desks abutting each other and file cabinets running along the walls.

Buratti stood for a moment at the doorway to his section. His team monitored the activities of art and antique dealers, bookshops and booksellers, junk shops, and restorers in Northwest Italy. This afternoon, most of his people were out in the field or elsewhere in the building.

Buratti itched to talk about something other than work when he spied Tommaso Spicuzza sitting at his desk. Buratti approached the diminutive man with the easy confidence of a cowboy approaching a calf trapped in a fence. At twenty-seven, Inspector Spicuzza was ten years younger and about a foot shorter than Buratti's six-foot-four frame.

Their true chronological age gap notwithstanding, Spicuzza looked older due to his thinning premature gray hair and his dark-rimmed spectacles. Buratti, on the other hand, exuded youthfulness with his white teeth and mass of curly dark brown hair which he cropped just close enough on the sides and back to pass Carabinieri regulation but let it flow up top. Maintaining his playboy image, Buratti always kept his face in a stylish, two-day stubble; ready for the cameras when his office cracked the next case. The Commander could be full of himself, especially when promoting himself as Torino's number one most eligible bachelor. But he was fair to his direct reports and handled pressure from the top echelon allowing his investigators the freedom to work without interference. In a force full of bureaucratic pencil pushers, Buratti was an investigator first, one who demanded results but had his people's best interest at heart. Everyone, including Spicuzza, knew that good police work in Buratti's section was required, but good press – with photos – was expected.

Commander Buratti, the current darling of the force, had friends in high places but Spicuzza knew that the Commander was also a learned historian, a first-class detective, and demanding leader. His team followed suit and those who couldn't meet his high standards quickly left for less demanding careers. Spicuzza had personally witnessed Buratti intimidate and pressure subordinates into transferring.

Spicuzza thrived on the accountability and hectic pace. He responded to the boss's pressure and positioned himself to step up his responsibilities. His investigative techniques were solid and work ethic, admirable. His deep sonorous baritone voice gave him additional gravitas when interrogating suspects and gaining confessions. He had been hired by Buratti years ago and felt that there might be a special link between them which could help him advance in the ranks.

It certainly didn't hurt that like his boss, Spicuzza was a fan of Torino's soccer team, Torino F.C. *Toro* fans stuck together and had an underdog group mentality developed from years of losing to their better financed crosstown rival, Juventus. The Bull mascot and love of all things Maroon and White separated the real *Torinese* from the outsiders and hopefully, Spicuzza thought, linked him to Buratti's rising star.

Buratti approached his man as one Toro to another, "Bonomi was *belissimo* last week."

"*Certo*. Two goals against Cagliari last game was nice...But it's still *Serie B*. Minor league," Spicuzza answered.

"We were great once, we'll be great again. If we finish in the top of this 'minor' league, we'll be back in *Serie A* next year." Buratti encouraged the younger subordinate. "You need to believe!"

"Are you going to the next game against Cremola?" Spicuzza asked.

"Of course! I'll be there with all the *Fellissimi Granata*."

"You? A Maroon Loyalist? I thought you'd be wearing that gray pinstriped suit?" Spicuzza said.

"Of course not. I'll be wearing the Maroon and White of the Toro!" Buratti exclaimed. "Besides, this is not pinstriped. It is chalk-striped," Buratti corrected. "Pinstripes are narrower and more defined. Chalk is more subtle and the stripes are wider," he said as if explaining that red means stop and green means go. "Would you get confused and call this a window pane pattern?" the Commander asked. Spicuzza stared blankly not knowing the right response. "Of course not!" Buratti answered for the man.

Continuing with the lesson Buratti asked, "Would you call a Glen plaid, a Glen check?"

Spicuzza probably would. He had no idea of the difference.

Buratti smugly continued his subordinate's instruction on the art of fashion, pacing around the desks. "No. A plaid, sometimes called tartan, is a crisscrossing of multiple bands to create a square or multicolored pattern. A check is a single band crisscrossing to create squares on the fabric. It's ridiculous to confuse the two." Buratti gave a light snort as if he had just explained the most obvious thing.

"I don't know," Spicuzza said. "It all looks like gray to me. The same color you wear every day – just a gray suit."

"Just a gray suit?!" Indignant and kicking up the level of drama to get his point across, "There is a difference between a houndstooth and a herringbone and a sharkskin pattern. You should know better."

"If you say so," said the subordinate.

Buratti strode in a small circle and continued lecturing. "You should know more about art. You work in the premier police force responsible for protecting Italian antiquities. We are responsible for monitoring and controlling the most important archaeological sites in the world! We have forensic analysis capabilities unmatched by anyone."

The younger man sat and listened, thinking that this pomposity was probably the reason the Commander's peers hated him.

"We are tasked with promoting art conservation through the development of educational materials," the Commander continued. "We advise foreign ministries, police forces, and customs bodies. You need to be proud of what we do!"

"*Certo*. I am," the younger man replied, a little nervous that he may have upset his boss.

Unconvinced by the man's reply, the Commander went on, "Don't you know that you work in the former Royal Palace built by the Savoys in the 16th century? Every day you walk through these magnificent halls, steps away from the Palazzo Chiablese and the Chapel of the Holy Shroud, housing the famous Shroud of Turin."

"Of course I know that. These are lovely offices. What's that got to do with suits?"

"For God's sake, the place you work was just named a UNESCO World Heritage Site! You work with some of the finest arts and antiquities scholars. You should appreciate the art of the clothes you wear." Buratti completed his dissertation and leaned on the desk. A smile of satisfaction spread across his face.

Thinking that showing bravery to Buratti's fashion bullying would gain him respect, Spicuzza said, "*Guisto,* Commander, we're a police force not '*fashionistas*'. And if clothes are so important to you, why do you always wear the same thing, gray?" Spicuzza said.

"It's my look." Bramante Buratti flashed his best paparazzi smile. "Besides, nothing looks better for my height than the color gray. And gray gives me excellent options for shirt and tie color combinations. And as I explained, there are many different patterns that make gray the most versatile color. You should ..."

"Commander Buratti," his secretary called out she as rushed across the room. "You have a call from Cardinal Burtone."

Snapping out of his playful dressing down of Spicuzza, he became all business. "I'll take it in my office."

She leaned forward to avoid Spicuzza's sparked curiosity and, so as not to embarrass her boss, whispered, "He seems very agitated and said he needs to speak immediately. I placed the call here."

Stuck between keeping his benefactor waiting and taking a potentially sensitive call in front of his subordinate, he acquiesced, "Okay. Thank you," he said quickly. "Which line is it?"

His secretary indicated the blinking light on Spicuzza's phone and scurried to the safety of her workstation knowing that Buratti would surely castigate her later for the breach of protocol. Buratti looked up at Spicuzza, his eyes indicated his surprise at this urgent call.

"Your Eminence," Buratti greeted the Secretary of the C.D.F. in as cheerful and professional manner as he could muster given the abrupt call that he was forced to take in front of his subordinates.

"Bramante. What's the status of the Torino archive case?" the Cardinal started without preface.

"Your Eminence, you are, I'm sure, referencing the theft of the Capitular Archives some time ago?" Buratti knew the Cardinal was asking about the archive inventory he had championed years ago. "As you know we recovered most of the items almost immediately in London after the theft was discovered. Recently, we recovered a leaf from Florida but I'm not certain of the current status as I'm not directly involved in that. One of my inspectors is. I'll contact him immediately and get you a report as soon as possible," Buratti nervously answered; the words rushing out as he tried to recall the details of a seven-year-old case which he had long ago assigned to one of his inspectors.

"I want you involved in this directly!" the Cardinal said. "Would it surprise you if I told you that I know that page 212 from the Missal of Ludovico da Romagnano, the San Lorenzo, is here in Europe?" The declaration ended in a hiss.

"It certainly would. Please, what can I do to help?" Buratti said, living his worst nightmare. He worked tirelessly to stay on top of his cases and be out front of investigations; always vying for the top spot against the other six Station Chief's located throughout Italy. Even with his region's recent good press, things could quickly change if someone as powerful as Cardinal Burtone had information about his case which his office itself should have developed. The Cardinal had made his career but he could just as easily destroy it.

"You better get on this and find out what's going on. My man at the Capitular Archives discovered the theft because he had the foresight to keep his own inventory," the Cardinal explained. Buratti did not remind the Cardinal that it was the professors he hired who had actually stolen the items that they were now trying to recover.

"Do I need to remind you why that missing page, the San Lorenzo, is particularly important?"

Buratti ran his hand through his thick hair trying to jog the memory. There was something, but what was it?

"The book by Rev. Healy," the Cardinal cried. "The Valarian Prosecution."

It fell into place. "Yes, of course. I understand." Buratti bowed as if the Cardinal could see his supplication.

"Those damned modernists," the Cardinal sneered as if spitting out a bite of a rotten apple. "Trying to 'correct' the record even if it means undermining our traditions!"

"I understand completely. You have my full resources. Of course, we'll find it. What have you learned?"

"Yesterday, my man received a call from a Parisian book dealer saying that he had just met with an American seller. The Parisian thinks he may have been inspecting the San Lorenzo."

Buratti's mind raced. He wasn't surprised that an American was involved. The latest recovery from the Capitular Archive theft was in Florida and was linked to a couple who had purchased the stolen item unwittingly. They produced a receipt and were cleared of wrongdoing but the seller was never located and no arrests were made. Logic followed that the unidentified seller had more stolen property from the Archive theft and could easily be an American.

The Cardinal continued to speak, "Frederic Paquet. Do you know him?"

"I've heard the name. He is out of Paris, no?" Buratti answered. "I've come across his name but I don't believe that our office has had any dealings with him."

"Isn't it your job to get to know these antiquarian booksellers as it is the most likely place that stolen books will be fenced?"

Buratti decided not to point that the Cardinal expected the impossible. Of course, the world of antique book sellers was small, but not so small that the Commander would know everyone on a first-name basis. He let his mentor continue. "Well, someone set up a meeting with Paquet to sell an item that fit the description of the San Lorenzo and Paquet called my man at the archives to authenticate the item. My question is, Bramante, why isn't he calling you?"

Buratti heard the passion and anger in Cardinal Burtone's voice. He regretted taking the call here, next to Spicuzza's prying ears. At the volume the Cardinal was scolding him, the entire office could hear both sides of the conversation.

"I don't know. I'll get on it right away," Buratti said trying to placate his benefactor.

"I want updates from you directly," Cardinal Burtone demanded.

"Yes, sir." Buratti flashed back to his first year of cadet training and then corrected himself. "Yes, Your Eminence. I will be personally involved in the recovery of the San Lorenzo and the arrest of those responsible for its illegal trade."

"I want people in jail! Those damned modernists think we're hiding it! I want this cleaned up and this chapter closed!" the Cardinal said. So the Cardinal did feel some lingering embarrassment for circumstances of the theft, Buratti thought.

"Yes. Your Eminence," Buratti said again.

Spicuzza could see his boss squirm and felt bad for him. He started to walk away from his desk looking for other things to occupy himself away from Buratti.

"I want results by this Sunday." Breaking his rant, the Cardinal toned it down and asked, "You have the information of my flight from Rome on Sunday?"

"Yes. I will pick you up and take you directly to the Stadia d'Alpi," Buratti responded efficiently.

"Bonati was spectacular last game wasn't he? I hope we have a good game against Cremola. We need to get back into *Serie A*. I need to shut my colleagues up about that other team. It's tough being a Torino F.C. fan when all everyone talks about is those zebras."

"I share the feeling." Buratti breathed a sigh of relief talking about the more important and heart-wrenching subject of Torino F.C.'s rivalry with the nationally renowned, black and white stripped, Juventus.

"You are in Torino where it is easier to find loyal *Torinese*. Try to do that in Rome. I swear I don't think Juventus has even one fan who is actually from Torino. They should print a map of the city on the back of the Juventus tickets – this way the fans won't get lost on their way to the stadium," the Cardinal said while laughing at his own joke.

"Yes, Your Eminence. I agree."

"Okay. I'll see you on Sunday and we'll celebrate the recovery of the San Lorenzo, the arrest of the criminal traffickers, and the Bull's victory." The Cardinal hung up without waiting for a response.

"Spicuzza!" Buratti called to the inspector who was now shuffling papers a few desks away. "Get me Frederic Paquet's phone number...both his office and his mobile. Also, I need you to find out about where he's been, his credit card use...you know the drill. You might have to call the local police. Tell them whatever you need to in order to get their cooperation. I want to know what I'm dealing with."

"I'm already on it. I couldn't help overhearing the Cardinal's request and started the search. I'll have something to you shortly," Spicuzza said.

"Very good. This is top priority." Buratti lifted his head and looked out on to the piazza that fronted the offices.

"Commander, of course, it's important to find any stolen item but why the importance of San Lorenzo. It seems particularly sensitive," Spicuzza asked, his curiosity overcoming his fear at poking the man.

Buratti decided not to chide the man for obviously overhearing and picking up on the Cardinal's concern. He explained, "It appears that San Lorenzo's martyrdom – being roasted alive – has been called into question by a group of reformists…modernist, the Cardinal calls them. They want to 'correct the record' to make the death of this Saint more historically accurate. Of course, they don't care that, in the process, they destroy the mystique and beauty of our tradition."

"What does this stolen page have to do with that?" Spicuzza asked innocently.

Buratti took a deep breath and looked around wondering if the effort to explain to his subordinate was really necessary. His desire to expound upon his knowledge won out on his displeasure at being questioned. "A certain Reverend Healy wrote a book about ninety years ago about the Roman Emperor's Prosecution of the early Church. In it, he postulated a theory that had been made years before by Pio Franchi de' Cavalieri that executions at that time were rapid affairs. Of course, we know the story that San Lorenzo was roasted alive; a slow torturous death not in keeping with the express command contained in the edict regarding bishops, priests, and deacons for '*animadvertantur*' which ordinarily meant decapitation. Pio Franchi de' Cavalieri theorized that the myth of San Lorenzo was propagated because of a mistranslation. He claimed, and Rev. Healy furthered, that the Latin phrase '*passus est*', he has suffered, the normal attribution of the executed was improperly transcribed omitting the 'p', making the phrase '*assus est*', he is roasted. Hence, the story of San Lorenzo being roasted alive that we all know. Apparently, this modernist group is claiming that the San Lorenzo, written in the Lombard tradition – not the Roman – has the original and correct translation."

Spicuzza didn't need it explained to him that the modernist group theorized that the missing page was proof of a Church cover-up.

Buratti paced and asked himself, "What's Paquet up to? I'm not real happy that he didn't contact us if he suspected that the work was stolen from Italy. I wonder what he is hiding."

Spicuzza listened, as usual, to Buratti's vocal ruminations.

Buratti turned to Spicuzza as a peer, "The Cardinal made it clear that he expects the recovery of the San Lorenzo and arrests of those trying to sell it.... by Sunday. We've got no choice but to make it happen."

Buratti leaned on Spicuzza's desk and reached over to take the offered paper containing the French bookseller's contact information. "Good work getting started on this – shows initiative." Patting him on the shoulder he said, "I'll be in my office calling some local booksellers to see what they know. Perhaps we'll get lucky. If this seller is casting a wide net for buyers, we're apt to pick up his trail. Until this case is resolved, make it a top priority."

As Buratti returned to his own office, Spicuzza delighted in helping his Commander. He had no doubt that he would be able to track down Paquet's movements and that his help would be critical in recovering the San Lorenzo. A high profile case that involved the Cardinal could make careers. Spicuzza would not let the opportunity pass.

His only concern was if he had time to complete this research and buy a gray suit to wear by tomorrow.

# Chapter 18

Max arrived at the Zurich Hbf a little after five thirty. Even with his rudimentary knowledge of German, he knew that the American Express office address of Bahnhofstrasse was near the train station. He jogged to the address and after four minutes burst into the office, his pulse racing. He put his hands on his knees. "Hi, can you help me?" Max panted.

"Of course," replied the bearded man about Max's age sitting at his desk behind a counter. The man stood and walked over. "How may I be of assistance?"

"I had my wallet stolen on the train today. I need a replacement card," Max blurted out.

"No problem. Do you have identification?" The thin man wore a dress shirt and skinny tie. His brown wool pants rode very low on his waist. Max couldn't help thinking that while he had been considered skinny all his life, compared to these Europeans, he should take up sumo wrestling.

"Yes. I have my passport," Max said as he presented it.

"No problem. It will only take a minute," the man said.

Like a levy bursting, Max's emotions released in a rapid-fire succession of words, "Thanks a bunch. You wouldn't believe what happened today. I had to go all the way to Basel and the meeting didn't go well but on the way there I had my wallet pickpocketed and then on the way back I heard an announcement on the train to be on the look-out for pickpockets and I was like, 'thanks for the warning...a little too late. Couldn't have warned me before? You know? On the way to Basel?' Anyway, I'm running late to meet my boss who is waiting for me in the Dolder. I'm here on business. I'm giving a speech tomorrow. I didn't have any Swiss Francs so I couldn't take a taxi and I knew that you closed in a few minutes so I ran here but I've got to get back soon. I'll need the card to take customers to dinner and now, at least, I can pay for the taxi with my credit card. I was thinking that I'd have to walk but..."

"Here you go," the man said. "And your other card has been canceled."

"Thank you," Max inspected his card front and back and a big smile came to his face. On the back of the new card Max picked up something he considered pretty cool; he now had an American Express Card written in German.

At the corner, Max grabbed a taxi for the ten-minute drive to the hotel. He was going to make it to the hotel at six; in time for a quick change and hustle down to the cocktail reception to meet the big boss somewhat on time.

When he had arrived at the Zurich Airport the day before, a taxi had taken him to a different hotel, the Hotel St. Gotthard in the heart of Zurich very near the train station. Because of limited availability at the site of the conference, the Dolder Grand Hotel, Max booked his AVP into that fancy hotel while he planned to stay at the more modest one with good access to the city's train station.

However, yesterday when he arrived at the Hotel St. Gotthard after the red-eye flight from the States, the ponytailed young desk clerk at St. Gotthard informed him that the conference organizers had experienced some cancellations and had re-booked him as the conference's guest at the Dolder Grand Hotel. The young clerk apologized profusely and assured Max that it was a wonderful hotel with excellent amenities. She had the bellman take Max's luggage to the taxi stand, pay for the taxi and give instructions to deliver him to the hotel.

When the taxi pulled up to the Dolder Grand Hotel that first time, it stopped next to a Rolls Royce. A doorman promptly opened the taxi door, grabbed Max's luggage and messenger bag and handed it to the bellman before Max could protest. For the entire voyage from Florida to Zurich, Max had kept the manuscript by his side during the two flights, a connection in Atlanta, through the Zurich airport and customs and immigration. He had been attentive and neurotic about checking its safety for the past fourteen hours of travel. And now the manuscript that he had guarded so expertly was in the hands of a bellhop.

Had he not been so worried about misplacing the manuscript, he would have had time to feel out of place. The Dolder Grand ranked among the best hotels in the city. The clientele was very chic and dripped of old money... or new money. Max wasn't sure. Either way, he felt like a fish out of water in places that were half this posh. Yet here he was, guest of the conference organizers, being treated like royalty yet unable to recognize it and enjoy it because he was too anxious keeping track of the manuscript.

The bellman carrying his luggage and the manuscript had not strayed far when guiding him to the reception area. The lack of sleep from the overnight flight made Max's head float and he briefly forgot his anxiety as he stepped into the grand lobby for the first time.

It had a crisp, clean, symmetrical look with the registration desk to the left and bar and lounge area taking up the entire right side. Max walked the great expanse of polished marble floors leading to mirror-image curved staircases at one end. The ceiling was supported by Greek marble columns from which hung a large crystal chandelier over a bronze statue of a maiden standing atop a marble pedestal. Max took a moment to enjoy that, in a small way, he was living the life of luxury and intrigue that he desired. He thought of Laura and decided he might not tell her about his room's spectacular views of the city, Lake Zurich, and the Alps.

Now, a day later and just back from Basel, Max bounded up the steps and nodded at the doorman as he went through the revolving doors. Max took the elevator to his fourth floor and hustled down the hallway toward his room. With his damp clothes and wet socks, Max was so focused on a warm shower that he nearly ran into a large man in stocking feet carrying an ice bucket in one hand and using his free hand to open a door. Because he was not wearing his thousand-dollar suit and his trademark Gucci loafers and frameless glasses, it took Max a moment to recognize him.

"Well, hello there, Max," said Theodore, straightening up and putting on his most ingratiating smile.

"Mr. Buford." Max instinctually put out his hand to shake. Theodore, a room key in one hand and an ice bucket in the other, fumbled with the items to shake his salesman's hand.

"Looks like you're busy. You been out hitting the tackling dummies?" Theodore approved of Max's wet, rumpled appearance.

"Yes. I just came back from a good meeting," Max offered. "I'm going to change real quick before going to the reception."

"Sounds good, I'll..." The moment was interrupted when the door flew open. In it, stood a platinum blonde with vivid red lips and brightly painted toenails wearing a hotel bathrobe which she had failed to secure properly. Theodore flushed red in the face.

"This is Corey," Theodore stammered after a pause. He hesitated only the briefest moments before stepping into the room to cover up what the bathrobe drawstring had failed to.

"Oh my!" said the woman more amused than disturbed as she ducked behind the door.

Max could feel his face redden. "Uhh, I'm going to drop these things off and head back down." The words rushed out in a burst. "When you make it down, we'll meet up with the broker I told you about for dinner?" Max said seeking approval rather than issuing a command.

"All right. You get the team warmed up," Theodore said as his shoulders relaxed in relief. "I'll see you down there in a few minutes."

Max walked a few more doors down and entered his room. Max took off his jacket and, for at least the fiftieth time, checked the security of the cash and the presence of the tube. Only after he located the room safe and locked the manuscript and the cash in it did he take off his shoes and the rest of his wet clothes. With his calling card missing, he threw fiscal responsibility into the wind and used the hotel phone in his room to call home. His wife picked up on the fifth ring.

"Hey, honey. How are you?" he said.

"Boy, you put me through a lot of work this morning. Don't you know how to hold on to your stuff?"

"I know. I'm sorry."

"Where'd you lose it?" Laura asked

"I don't think I lost it. I was pick-pocketed on the train."

"Yeah, right. You probably just left it somewhere and didn't remember."

"Definitely not," Max said. "There was even an announcement on the train."

"Well, you should be more careful."

"I'm trying. You have no idea what I'm going through. I'm doing lots of stuff here; lots of distractions."

"Yeah, yeah...well, I canceled everything and we're getting new cards mailed to us." A little concern crept into her voice, "How are you going to be able to pay for stuff?"

"I got it taken care of. I already got a replacement card." Trying to change the subject, Max asked, "How's everything else?" Despite the serious risk of reviving the CHOP conversation which led to money talk and recriminations, Max asked, "How's Sam feeling? How are the boys?"

"Good... and driving me crazy." Mornings were the twins' quietest time – change their pee-soaked night diapers and they could give you as much as six minutes of peace. Their reign of terror ramped up as the day progressed. Except on weekends, Max was absent from the most trying of their behavior. Laura let out a long breath, the weariness of his absence unmistakable. Keeping house, maintaining Samantha's prescription regiment, and running after the twins beat her down. "Did you have good meetings today?"

"Yeah. I'm just back in my room for a few minutes," Max said as he stretched out on the king-sized bed and eyed the mini-bar.

"I need to get ready for the opening cocktail reception and then Theodore and I will be taking one of my clients out to dinner."

"Okay. Well, I'll be having cereal tonight," she said, a common refrain that didn't make it any less true.

"Is your hotel nice?"

"It's fine." There was no way he was telling her how outstanding the accommodations were. He had learned that lesson from previous business trips, the less said about the good parts of travel, the better. Max respected her sacrifice for their children and knew it had to be harder with his interesting travel and fine dining.

"Okay. Well, do a good job tonight." Max didn't miss the insinuation that he hadn't done such a good job impressing the executives in the past. "Maybe Theodore will see what a mistake he made not promoting you when he sees how good you are."

"Yeah. Maybe. We'll see," Max responded, not rising to the un-spoken displeasure that Laura harbored from Max's failure to move up in the company. "Listen, I'll talk to you later." The strain of sleep deprivation rose in her voice, the wedge between them pushed deeper.

"Okay. Bye. I love you," Max responded.

"You better," Laura mumbled as they both hung up the phone.

# Chapter 19

Tommy and Sully followed the cab to the airport and, while Tommy illegally parked in the taxi queue, Sully was able to confirm that the Frenchman got on the train to Paris.

After a brief fight over the pair's inability to quickly meet back up – "What's the matter, you don't see me parking here?" "Tommy, why would I expect you to be in the taxi line?" "I got fucking caught – It's not my fault." "You're driving, Tommy. Whose fault could it be?" "I'm honking and calling you and you're standing with your head up your ass dressed like a neon fucking banana in that jacket!" "Okay, Tommy. Whatever. It's my fault." – Tommy insisted they follow the Frenchman to Paris to finish what Sully didn't accomplish outside the bank.

"We gonna drive to Paris?" Sully asked.

Tommy exploded, "No! I'm not gonna pay for this car for all that way! I gotta pay miles and gas ain't cheap here! Whadya stupid? The train's good enough for Frenchie, it's good enough for us."

Tommy spent a long time searching for the poorly marked rental return. Operating on very little sleep after arriving on the red-eye, he had also forgotten about filling up the gas tank. The exorbitant penalty fee the rental agency imposed for failing to refuel woke him up. Once he made the conversion from Swiss Francs to Dollars, Tommy vented his frustration to Sully, "You couldinah checked the guy's coat when you took his briefcase?"

"Tommy, you were there," holding up his hands in supplication. "I didn't have any time. I didn't know that he didn't put it in his briefcase."

"When we get to Paris you better not screw up again," Tommy said.

"You'll be there, too. I'll let you handle the Frenchie and you can show me how it's done," Sully said while comically striking a boxer's pose.

Sully had a lot of experiences with Tommy's blow-ups – what he secretly referred to as the 'Tommy Vortex'. Supplication, concession, and a little humor usually derailed an outburst – until the next time.

"Whadevah, numbnuts," Tommy said before plucking a stray nose hair.

Patrick Casey Sullivan had been called 'Sully' by everybody for so long that even he sometimes forgot his given name. He and Tommy had been friends since their days on the Jersey Shore and they were partners in this latest venture; although not equal. An odd couple, while Tommy went for the Guido look, Sully dressed in a flannel shirt, jeans and Birkenstock sandals with socks. With the exception of his bright yellow 'Members Only' jacket, he looked more like a tree hugger who had escaped a commune. Sully had a full head of hair with gray on the wings and dyed jet black everywhere else. Hair styling was the one shared practice of the men; they both gave the local drug store reason to keep Vitalis hair tonic in stock.

Sully had worked as an elevator repairman before too much pot smoking and hard drinking ruined his career and marriage. He now lived in his sister's investment property rent-free complaining he couldn't find a job that paid well enough. For some reason, failure had perversely inflated Sully's sense of market value. As the years rolled by, the gap between what employers offered and what Sully thought he should get paid, widened. The entitlement mentality made him susceptible to Tommy's never-ending get rich quick schemes. The schemes rarely enriched – and when they did, only enriched Tommy. Yet, Sully hung with Tommy like a barnacle clings to a boat.

Sully was kind, inquisitive, and enjoyed debating esoteric subjects, although he usually found himself quickly out of his intellectual depth. But his strongest personality trait was his unshakable loyalty and infinite capacity for taking abuse. He provided the perfect dance partner for Tommy's form of tango. Sully would give a stranger the shirt off his back, but he would blindly follow Tommy first. Even if it meant mugging an old man on a street corner in Basel. And that's why it was so easy for him to get caught in the Tommy Vortex, to be inescapably drawn into the center of Tommy's destructive nature.

Now they were headed off to Paris to chase an old man with a rare document. Rather than a quick easy job in Switzerland with some sightseeing thrown in for fun, this trip was turning into another Tommy-created mess. If several stints in the county jail for failure to pay child support and alimony didn't encourage Sully to find meaningful employment, chasing a Frenchman through Europe wasn't going to help either.

"You sure we gotta go to Paris?" Sully asked.

"Numbnuts! We checked the briefcase. There's no manuscript in it. That means, the Frenchie had it in his coat when you robbed him. Makes sense. It's valuable. He wants it near him where it's harder to steal," Tommy said impressed by his logic.

"Tommy," Sully whined. "What if he never bought it? Then he wouldn't have the manuscript at all."

"Don't be an idiot. Of course, he bought it! If he didn't buy it how comes there's no money or a check in his briefcase? Huh? Case closed. We're going to Paris to get my manuscript."

Sully didn't mention the possibility of a wire transfer or the fact that the meeting's location, a bank, might have meant there was never any need for a check or cash. But now was not the time to argue Tommy's decision.

Tommy spotted the train ticket counter and said "Go over there and get two tickets to Paris on the next train," and handed him a wad of cash. "I gotta go over there," pointing to the duty-free shop.

When he returned about fifteen minutes later, he found Sully standing by a coffee shop kiosk trying to get the barista's attention.

"Hey. I got you this," and tossed over a box marked Tissot.

"Thanks," Sully said as he opened the watch box containing a brand new TISSOT T-RACE city race oversized stainless steel chronograph with a white face, red second hand, and a black disc brake motif bezel.

"That's real nice, Tommy." Putting his hand through the rubber belt style band, he said, "This is beautiful. Thanks."

"Yeah, I figured we couldn't come to Switzerland without buying a watch. I got one too," and lifted his left arm sporting his new Rolex Oyster Perpetual, stainless steel with black dial.

"Wow. Is it a good deal here?"

"It's duty-free. But I had to fill out some paperwork to get the tax back."

"I really appreciate it, Tommy. Thank you," Sully said for the third time, truly grateful for the gift and the thought.

"Don't worry. I'll take it out of your cut," Tommy said laughing,

Sully's face dropped. That was typical Tommy, using other people's money to make a splashy show of generosity.

"Just kidding, buddy," Tommy said giving him a light punch on the shoulder. "Now where's my change from the train tickets?"

Sully had been around Tommy long enough to know that he wasn't kidding and that the watch represented a significant cut of his take on this job, money he needed very badly to get back on his feet. That he had been getting back on his feet for nearly fifteen years didn't seem to bother him. Also, typical is that Tommy 'gave' Sully a thousand dollar watch and bought himself a five thousand one. Tommy always made big shows of wealth with big tips and expensive bottles of wine at restaurants, anything where he could play the high roller. Sully noticed over the years that Tommy went out of his way to try to impress strangers yet treated those close to him as his subordinates. He thought, not for the first time, that he needed to separate himself from Tommy.

"Gimme the train tickets," Tommy demanded. There was a local shuttle train to the main train station where they would transfer to the Paris train. Tommy explained that if the train was good enough for the Frenchman, it was good enough for him. Of course, Sully knew Tommy probably chose the train after seeing the flight prices. But by train, they'd arrive about two hours after the Frenchman and have plenty of time to plan the surprise attack.

# Chapter 20

Max, showered and dressed in dry clothes. He took the elevator to the ground floor and crossed the grand lobby, proudly wearing a badge identifying him as a speaker. He made his way to the bar and ordered a Dewar's on the rocks. He didn't drink hard liquor very often but after the day's events, he needed something stronger than beer.

The run-in with his boss and his...wife...mistress...jarred him. Max turned away from the bar.

"Hey, Max, how are you?" said the short man to his right. Spenser Littlefield, an assistant market manager for a southern port that did a lot of frozen chicken exports to Eastern Europe and a fixture at industry events, sidled next to him.

"Hi, Spenser. How are you?" Max replied.

"Good. Good." That could have been the end of the conversation and would have been if Max could have found someone else to talk to.

"They been treating you all right over there at RK Trucking?" Spenser asked in a South Mississippi drawl. Max nodded, not sure how to respond to such a stupid question; As much as he thought working in 'cubical city' at RK was constraining, he wasn't in prison...at least not yet. It wasn't his employer's responsibility to 'treat him right'; they just needed to pay him for the value he created.

"Not working you too hard are they?" Spenser followed up with an equally dumb question.

"No. It's been good." Max responded looking around the room for some excuse to leave the conversation.

"Good location isn't it?" Max said, deciding to continue the small talk. "You've been getting much done here?"

"Yeah. Well, you know. Getting the word out and raising the flag and all," Spenser responded. In his mid-fifties and looking even older, Spenser was the stereotypical empty suit who attended the industry functions and abused his liver. He handled the grunt work of organizing the meetings with customers and attending the events no one else in his organization wanted to. Only to be trusted with the most mundane tasks and never allowed to make any important decisions, he had remained at the same level for over thirty years. Every now and then they would throw him a bone and send him someplace nice which kept him satisfied and towing the company line.

"Yeah…." Spenser continued, "They let us little guys come out to these things every now and again."

Max cringed at the fact that Spenser had just put Max in the same category as him. It was bad enough that his worst nightmare was to become a Spenser but to have it recognized and voiced by the man himself, was just too much.

"Well, you take what you can get. Right?" He finished with a wink and a prod with his elbow.

Max received the light jab to his ribs with a nervous chuckle.

"Who you here with?" Spenser asked.

"Theodore Buford – my AVP."

"Ohhh," Spenser cooed. "One of the big guys. You like him?"

Max thought briefly about dishing some dirt about the scene in the hallway but said instead, "He's fine. Just watch out if you meet him and he says, 'I'm just a country boy, so talk to me slow' or 'I'm just asking to learn'. Those are two of his favorite phrases and he uses them to lull the unwitting into letting down their guard and divulging the information he wants."

"Oh. One of those," nodded Spenser. "A guy who can slide the knife in before you even realize you're in danger."

Just then, Max saw Theodore at the room's entrance fastening his name badge to his suit, positioning it perfectly to make sure his pocket square stayed in place.

Theodore recognized Max and started toward the men. Max hesitated to have Theodore meet Spenser but it was too late to remove himself from his sphere. "Theodore, I'd like you to meet Spenser Littlefield with the port," Max said by way of introduction. "Spencer, Theodore is our area vice president of RK. He has all commercial and operational responsibility of the Southeast United States."

"Well, it's a pleasure to meet you. You have a fine young man here in Max. He really knows his stuff," Spenser said. Maybe not a bad empty suit, after all, Max thought.

"I know he does. We're happy to have him," Theodore responded.

Idle chit chat, true. But he couldn't help but feel happy. The troubles with the stolen manuscript and the bank account receded as Max worked the room with Theodore.

As the cocktail reception wound down, Max found his customer and introduced him to Theodore where they agreed to walk the few blocks to the restaurant. As they entered the hotel lobby to leave, Max saw the blond from Theodore's room sitting at the bar, now completely dressed with freshly applied red lipstick. He could see out of the corner of his eye Theodore's subtle wave to her as they made their way to the door. The blond reacted with a broad smile but did not return the wave.

# Chapter 21

Paquet had a lot of time on the five-hour train ride from Basel to think about the odd meeting with the young American man and the attack that followed. His wife had called him on his mobile phone about an hour out of Basel. Paquet deep in thought didn't want to concern his wife over the phone but he knew that not answering her call would alarm her even more.

He answered but there was no fooling Annabelle Paquet. She immediately picked up the distressed tone of her husband's voice, "What is wrong? Did you not have a good meeting in Basel?" She had been Mrs. Paquet for forty-one years and, while she had never actually worked in the book dealing business, knew that finding and purchasing interesting items was the key to a successful enterprise.

"I'll speak about it when I get home," her exhausted husband responded.

"You met with an American, no? What happened? Was he a problem?" Paquet knew his wife was suspicious of Americans and his reaction only confirmed her strongly held opinion.

"Yes...No. The American was nice enough but he clearly did not know what he was doing. He was more of a courier than the actual dealer."

"But what about the item?" Mrs. Paquet pressed.

"The manuscript was beautiful and in good shape; a very important find. But..." he let the idea hang, "I had a feeling that the items belonged to the archives in Torino. Before you called, I spoke to one of the archivists there. We discussed the piece, all the characteristics that make it distinctive – the size, the margins, the layout and the type of ink used. They all clearly indicate that the broadside I inspected today belonged to the Missal of Ludovico da Romagnano."

"So, you didn't purchase it," she said with a hint of a question.

"Of course not. It is most certainly stolen. I must call the authorities when I return."

"What did the seller say when you told him that it was stolen?

"The American was clearly disappointed that the transaction could not be completed. But he was professional and very helpful after I was attacked."

"ATTACKED! What are you talking about?" she said.

"It's nothing, really. Someone tried to rob me while I waited for a taxi outside of the meeting."

"And you were attacked?"

"They took my briefcase and when I tried to hold on to it, I fell down."

"Are you hurt?"

"I fell and bumped my head. I am fine. Don't worry. It's nothing."

"Your head? Oh, my God. Are you sure that you are not hurt? That could be serious."

"Yes, yes...I'm fine. Don't worry, *Cherie*."

"You say, 'they' took your case? Who attacked you? Did they just walk up to you?  In broad daylight?"

"A large man wearing yellow jumped out of the backseat of a car and grabbed my briefcase. I fell down. When I got back up, the man in yellow had gotten into the car and drove off."

"So he wasn't driving the car? There must have been one other attacker," she said.

"Yes. It seems that way." Paquet began to think about the attack in a different way.

"So at least two men, one driving a car and one wearing yellow…. like a jacket or a sweater?

"A jacket, I think."

"What type of jacket? A rain slicker, a sports coat, a suit jacket?"

"Maybe like a regular jacket. Not a suit jacket and not a raincoat. Something like an American would wear. Like a casual jacket. But yellow. Bright yellow.

"So two men, one wearing a yellow jacket robbed you right after you met with an American courier about purchasing a stolen manuscript?"

"When you say it like that, it seems very suspicious."

"*Cheri*, you know in Paris we have vandals that may break a window, spray paint a building, or scratch a car. But, in broad daylight, a large man with a bright yellow jacket bounds out of the backseat of a car to take your briefcase. It appears too premeditated to be a random event."

"I don't know why I think this…but I immediately assumed that the attackers were Americans. I even mentioned it to Max…the American I met with."

"Could this 'Max' have been a part of the attacker's plan?"

"It is possible…but I don't think so. But even if he were not directing the efforts, there might be some link between the attackers and Max."

"You are too gullible. Of course, they have something to do with each other. But don't worry about it now, *Cheri*. First, let's make sure you are all right. Come straight home and be careful. I love you."

"I love you, too. I'll see you soon," the weary Paquet said as he closed the phone, sat back and rested the remainder of the trip. Paquet knew that as soon as he arrived home, he'd need to inform his contact.

By the time the train pulled into Paris's Gare de Lyon, the train station built for the World Exposition of 1900 with a clock tower resembling Big Ben that always made Paquet sneer at the insult to his nationalist pride, it was early afternoon where he would be calling. He still might have time, after he took the subway to the Richelieu-Drouot Metro station and walked the half block to his apartment on Rue Drouot in the building adjoining his rare book store, to call Special Agent Hemmer.

***

Tommy and Sully had originally planned to head straight to Torino after the manuscript theft. There, they would sell the antique and fly home from Milan the day after next. Instead, the men found their seats on the 1714 train to Paris, placed their small carry-on luggage on the shelf above and closed their eyes to catch a few winks. The train would arrive in Paris at 2240. In theory, they had plenty of time to rectify their Basel failure, retrieve the manuscript, and catch the overnight train to Torino. However, the detour to Paris meant eleven extra hours train travel and another night without a bed.

"You wanna walk or take the Metro?" Sully asked once they arrived at the Gare de Lyon. "I hear it's one of the best mass transit systems in the world."

"You watch too much PBS. We're takin' a cab. We don't have time for your Rick Steves adventure," Tommy said.

Sully chuckled. "How do you know about Rick Steves if you don't watch PBS?"

Tommy ignored the comment and led them to the baggage storage area. After depositing their luggage, they headed straight for the taxis. They seated themselves in the back of the cab and Tommy commanded, "Take us to Rue Drouot," which he pronounced like a period of dryness.

The driver looked at them and put his hands up in the international sign of 'I don't understand'.

"RUE – DROUOT!" Tommy said again only much louder.

The driver responded in French with something that probably meant, "I don't speak English. Do you speak French?"

"I can't believe this guy doesn't speak English. How does he expect to get business from Americans if he can't even understand a simple address?"

The driver pulled out a map and held it up to his passengers expecting them to point to the location where they wished to go.

"I don't know where it is!" Tommy said. "You're the professional driver." He laughed and elbowed Sully, looking for support.

Sully reached into the Frenchman's briefcase and pulled out a slip of paper and handed it to the driver who turned on the overhead light read it and responded, "*Oui, Rue Druout.*" which, off of the driver's tongue, sounded nothing like the address that Tommy had been screaming.

The driver sped up the Rue de Lyon.

"Why'd you do something stupid like that?" Tommy said as the taxi went past the big Bronze statue on an even larger marble pedestal in Square Andre Tollet. "You want everyone to know what we're doin'? What if we gotta rough the guy up?"

"Oh yeah, I didn't think of that," Sully said.

"You are so feebleminded," Tommy grumbled. "Just let me handle everything from now and just do what you do best – sitting there and looking stupid."

Sully chuckled trying to cover his hurt pride, "Geez, Tommy. I appreciate your confidence."

Yelling Tommy said, "Well, you just gave the driver the fuckin' address of where we're goin'! Why don't we just call the police and let them know what we're doin'?"

At that, the driver looked into the rearview mirror and regarded his passengers for more than a passing moment. Tommy realized that the driver may know more English than he let on. The mention of the word 'police' may have gotten his attention. Tommy ceased talking. His eyes shifted nervously as he waited for Sully to point out his slip.

Sully didn't. However, when Tommy had calmed down a bit, he asked, "How are we going to get into the shop?"

"Don't worry. I've got it figured out." Tommy responded not wanting to further alert the driver and because he still didn't have a plan.

They pulled up to the address a few minutes later and the driver pointed to the fare. Tommy handed over the fare in Swiss Francs and the driver responded, "No, No, No. Francs!"

"What's the conversion?" Tommy asked the driver.

"No," the driver responded. "Francs."

"How about American Dollars? Everyone should accept American Dollars."

"Francs!" the driver insisted again for the third time.

"You got any French Francs?" Tommy asked Sully.

"Yeah. I always keep a couple hundred French Francs in my pocket in case I need them in Florida."

For a moment Tommy must have thought him serious and stuck out his hand to receive the bills.

"Of course not," Sully said chuckling. "All I have is a little cash… but it's in dollars."

The driver started driving and the meter kept running.

"Where the fuck are you goin'?" he angrily asked the driver to no response. About one hundred meters later, the driver stopped again and pointed out the window and said, "ATM."

Tommy slapped his head in comprehension. It crossed his mind that they could ditch the driver and avoid paying the fare altogether but the thought quickly passed as he didn't want to draw even more attention to himself. Plus, he realized, he would need Francs anyway for the return trip.

Confusing a random foreign language as the proper language for any foreigner, Tommy called out "*Momento*" to the confused driver and left the taxi to withdraw cash. He returned shortly with a stack of crisp bills to pay the fare. The driver motioned that they should get in the taxi so that he could drive them to their address but Tommy responded using his two fingers in a walking motion to pantomime that they would walk back to the address on their own.

Tommy paid the fare and the taxi pulled away. The men retraced the route to get to the address of the French book dealer. As they were walking, Sully asked, "So tell me your great idea on how we're gonna get in and steal the manuscript back?"

For the past few hours, Tommy had been wondering about the plan. Now, as they approached the address, time was running out to make it happen and still make their train out to Torino.

Sully continued and offered an answer to his own question. "I've been thinking about it. There's got to be an alarm system or something. Maybe we could set it off."

"Yeah, there probably is; we set it off and when the Frenchman comes over to check it out, we make our way inside and get the manuscript," Tommy said picking up on the idea and making it his own.

The two men stopped near the address and stepped back into the shadows across the street from the bookshop. Tommy started searching the ground around him and said, "Look for a rock or something to break the window so that we can set off the alarm."

"Hehehe," Sully giggled, assuming that Tommy was joking – he wasn't. Daring to prod his partner, Sully sarcastically said, "Yeah, that won't attract attention."

Tommy flushed red and his nostril flared.

As he racked his brain for an insulting come back to re-tilt the scales, Sully continued, "No, all you gotta do is go up to the door and disrupt the circuit on the door sensor. If they've got an alarm, they'll have a door sensor for sure." Excited by the idea and proud of his leadership and creativity Sully asked, "Give me your credit card."

Tommy reached for his wallet but hesitated. "What are you gonna buy? I'm sick of spending money! This trip has cost me a lot already."

"Relax, Tommy. Geez. Trust me, will ya? I'm not going to buy anything; I just need a card with a magnetic strip."

"Okay. Why don't you use yours?" Tommy asked forgetting that, six months ago, Sully had his last credit card taken from him for non-payment. Tommy, in one of those surprising moves that keep everything off balance, realized his partner's hurt pride and, clasping his shoulder, said, "Don't worry buddy. After this gig, you'll have plenty of money and credit cards. In fact, not having a credit card has probably helped you save money."

"Whatever. Why don't you get rid of yours then?" Sully responded.

The hand that fed had been bitten and Tommy pounced, "Look around, Sully! You notice anything? How 'bout the way people dress here? Huh?" Compassionate talk over, Sully reeled back. "Look at you.... you dress like a gay lumberjack. We're following this Frenchie on the QT. With that jacket, you can probably be seen from outer space. What are you...trying to be noticed?"

"It helped you find me when you were stuck in the taxi line," Sully snickered.

Tommy's nostrils flared and lipped curled.

Sully put his hands up in surrender, "Okay, okay." he resigned, "I'll turn it inside out."

"That's got to be it," pointing at the sign which read '*Librairie Pa-*

*quet*. It looks like the Frenchman's address is different than the store's address. But the numbers are close," Tommy said pointing to the address on the paperwork from the briefcase. "The Frenchman must live nearby in an apartment and he'll probably be the one to turn the alarm off."

"What if the guy leaves the manuscript in his apartment and didn't bring it to the store?" Sully asked.

"The guy's going to bring keys to his apartment, isn't he? If we don't find the manuscript in the bookshop, we'll just take the keys and toss his apartment."

"What if someone's there? He may not live alone," Sully offered.

"Why you gotta be negative all the time?" Tommy admonished – but it was another good point. If they didn't get what they needed at the shop, they'd have to search the Frenchman's apartment. If it was occupied, he'd have to hurt people; which was no big deal but it added complications – and complications usually cost money. But for this kind of score, the complications were probably worth it.

"Look, nobody knows who we are or that we're here. We paid cash for the tickets so, as far as anyone is concerned, we never left Basel."

***

Sully walked across the street toward the front door of the bookshop thinking about Tommy's last comment. No trace of them being in Paris meant no restrictions on what Tommy would do to recover the manuscript. Loyalty had its price and he'd probably be asked to pay it again tonight. He bit his lip thinking of what he'd see tonight – be asked to do tonight –if they weren't able to pop in and sneak off with the manuscript before anyone realized. Why'd I let myself get drawn into this? It's not my fault. How'd I know it'd get to this point? But I should've known. I've been down this road before.

Sully shook his head like a shiver to clear his mind. He looked up and down the street and when he felt that no one was watching, approached the front door with the credit card. He scanned the frame of the door and saw a security door sensor on the top right-hand corner. Passing the credit card between the door crack and the sensor, he broke the circuit and activated the alarm. Hopefully, the warning system ran to the Frenchman's apartment and he'd come downstairs to investigate. Seeing nothing disturbed, he'd believe it to be a false alarm. When he entered the bookshop to re-set the code, he and Tommy would barge in and have a little talk with the tricky Frenchman.

# Chapter 22

The alarm could have woken the entire neighborhood and called interested neighbors and do-gooders to the rescue. The police could have responded or a private security firm could have come blazing in. An assistant or some other worker from the bookstore could have taken the responsibility of responding and resetting the alarms. Standing alone in the shadow of a doorway only a few feet from the book shop's entrance, these thoughts crowded Sully's mind. While he was with Tommy and following Tommy's orders, Sully had no reason to think of the consequences; so strong was the cult of personality. But while Tommy stood waiting across the street out of view, Sully had a few minutes of thought; and they weren't happy ones.

Sully's life linked to Tommy in a way he couldn't explain. For reasons beyond his control; traditional jobs never seemed to hold Sully's attention or his employment for long. The failure, of course, was always due to someone else or some uncontrollable outside force. He envied Tommy's seemingly charmed life. Upon his release from prison, Tommy's bookie boss rewarded his silence by setting him up with a South Florida car washing business. But when Hurricane Andrew destroyed his client base, Tommy went to work for his dad in the lumber business where he did very well, investing his earnings in flashy clothes, jewelry, and cars. His dad set him up giving him lucrative accounts and helped him in other ways like when he wrote a generous check to dissuade a car detailer from pressing charges after Tommy disapproved of the waxy build up on his Porsche 911 and beat the man into the hospital.

It wasn't fair. Tommy got all the breaks. Sully wanted a guardian angel. He deserved it and in his lowest moments, Tommy sort of filled the bill, coming through with a job offer promising prestige and easy riches. The venture, never well thought out, eventually fizzled long before Sully realized. When the money totally dried up, Sully would reluctantly leave the role of Tommy's sidekick only to come right back with the next promise of a new scheme.

This current plan to steal a valuable manuscript in Switzerland was concocted a few weeks ago after Tommy, with Sully in tow, confronted Edgar Shadi, a local book dealer, at his shop on Avilla Street.

"We gotta talk, buddy," Tommy had opened, the forced smile not offsetting the menacing stride into Edgar's shop.

"About?" Edgar responded in a steady manner. The empty book-shop allowed the men to speak freely. Tommy and Sully surrounded Edgar on both sides. Sully feared Edgar could have a weapon at the ready. He looked over at Tommy who seemed oblivious to the risk either because his fists or the blade in his pocket could take care of the paunchy, bald guy.

Tommy sidled up to the counter like greeting a friend at a bar. "Listen, buddy. We're partners." He looked around the shop making sure no one else was there. He words became more pressing. "You told me when we met at the Chamber of Commerce that you had business connections in Western Africa that could get me low prices on exotic lumber."

"I did," Edgar said without matching his confronter's rising emotions. "And I have delivered."

"I paid you five grand so you'd introduce me to the right people." Tommy said a little louder, throwing in the air quotes around 'right people' for good measure. "...A guy who could connect me to government officials. But I can't even get the product out of customs! We still don't have the required USDA approvals. Your guys didn't fill out the right forms for the export licenses and now we got customs clearances issues."

Edgar nodded, listening to the complaints.

Sully had seen this scene play out before. Business partners, intrigued by Tommy's apparent success, provided contacts, skills or money so that they could chase their dream or make some money. Tommy and this eclectic mix of partners became best buddies until Tommy's empty promises and deceit became too great to ignore. Then came the messy breakup.

When he didn't respond, Tommy barked, "I got a lot a money tied up in this!"

"My job was to put you in contact with the people in Sierra Leone," Edgar explained. "How you arranged your deal is up to you. I'm not involved or responsible for it. You really should be having this conversation with them."

"Bullshit! I'm dealing with you! *You* promised that *you* could clear the way for the stuff getting here. *You* said it was exotic lumber and nearly extinct hardwoods that nobody else could get."

"I was only passing on information. The lumber business is not my business – it's yours. It is your responsibility to complete the due diligence on the product," Edgar made clear. Sully thought Edgar looked like a man who didn't need the hassle and wasn't surprised when he suggested, "Look, if you are upset about the value I provided, I'll refund the five thousand dollar consulting fee."

"You think that's all I'm out? I got material in a bonded customs warehouse costing me hundreds of dollars a day in fees and I can't sell it because it's mostly shit lumber and not what you promised!"

"I can't help you with that. Again, the quality of the product should be your concern."

Tommy paced the room and scratched his crotch while his nostrils flared, "You also told me that you could help open the West African market for U.S. exports of other building materials. I was planning on the cheaper transportation charges of the two-way container traffic."

Edgar stood behind the counter allowing Tommy to vent. Sully watched to make sure there were no sudden moves behind the counter.

"I've won 'Exporter of the Year' award from the Chamber before!" Tommy yelled proudly. "I know what I'm doing!"

Sully knew that the U.S. markets were not as fertile as Tommy thought. But what did he expect? Tommy never conducted market research because it could only either assert what he already knew or undermine his preconceived notions of glory and success.

"The inventory has been sitting on the docks for months. I probably owe more money than what I paid for the product!"

Tommy's rant continued for another ten minutes. He continued pacing around the room and started picking up objects, looking as if he would throw something. Unlike in his other business dealings, here, he didn't have his father to bail him out. "Maybe I should take some of these books as payment?"

Edgar flinched, straightening his shoulders and squinting his eyes. Up until now, Edgar had let Tommy vent as a harmless exercise, like watching a tropical fish blow itself up to appear bigger and more dangerous. But now Sully could see the change in the bookseller's demeanor as his goods and livelihood were threatened.

Tommy and Edgar glared at each other, the counter the only separation. Sully kept his attention on Edgar's hands worried about a reach behind for a weapon.

After a few tense moments, Edgar relaxed his pose and said, "Look, my friend. I don't want to make enemies. I live in this town and have a business here. I don't need an important businessman like you complaining around town about me." Edgar smiled ingratiatingly opening up his arms in supplication. "Maybe we can work something out."

"That's what I like to hear," Tommy said as he flashed his shark-toothed grin at Sully.

Edgar laid out the plan. "I have an unwitting agent helping me sell something of value..."

"A patsy, you mean," Tommy grinned. "I like it."

"Yes, a patsy. Well, this patsy is traveling to Basel, Switzerland soon to sell a very expensive 15th century manuscript to a French buyer. Once the transaction is complete, I suggest that you steal it from the new owner and re-sell it."

"Why would I want to do that? I gotta travel to Switzerland to rob a guy?"

"How much did you say you owe for the lumber?" Edgar asked.

Tommy thought quickly, did the math and then doubled the calculation. "I'm out about fifty-five grand."

Edgar, dubious of the number, played along. "Look, I don't have that kind of money and I don't believe that I owe it to you." Before Tommy could protest, he continued, "However, if you are willing to take the manuscript from an old man in Basel after the first sale, I am willing to give you eighty percent of the proceeds.... after your expenses which we will pay off the top."

Sully could see Tommy making the calculations of a pretty lucrative deal. "So what's this thing worth?"

"About one hundred thousand dollars." Edgar proclaimed.

That got Sully's attention.

Tommy grinned.

"Where are we going to sell it once we steal it?" Sully spoke for the first time.

"That's easy, there are many places in Europe that will buy such a rare and important item. I'll give you some names. However, you'll want to concern yourself more with how you are going to bring the money home."

"Huh?" Sully asked.

"One hundred thousand dollars is a lot of money. It will take up a lot of room in your suitcase. But more importantly, if you get caught by U.S. Customs you could be fined or jailed for bringing in that much cash."

"Yeah. Good point. How are you getting the money for the first sale to the French guy?"

"My patsy...as you say, is setting up a Swiss bank account. The money will be wired into it. This way I can bring the money back here through ...other channels and without paying tax."

Tommy's eyes lit up like a kid in a candy store. Sully had heard him on many occasions talk about being paid in other currencies in the mistaken belief that he could avoid taxes. The promise of access to a Swiss bank account hit the mark.

"That's a good idea. I'll set one up too."

"You don't just walk into a bank and open an account," Edgar responded. "You need to know someone and make arrangements." Edgar paused and appeared to be coming to a monumental decision. "I'll tell you what." Edgar turned on the charm and broadened his smile like he was sharing a secret. "I shouldn't do this, but...if you want, when you sell the manuscript, you can have the money deposited in the Swiss account that I set up. I'll pay you here in the US in dollars, tax-free."

"How do I know that you are going to pay me?" Tommy asked.

"Do you think I want another situation like this?" he said gesturing to the stand-off they had only just diffused. "I'm offering you a great deal and compensation for something that isn't even my fault," Edgar explained. "Like I said, I want to maintain my good reputation here in town and I'm going to be here for a long time. You are too important a guy to make angry." Edgar hoped the gratuitous compliment hadn't gone too far. It hadn't – Tommy bought it hook, line, and sinker.

"All right," Tommy said. "You got a deal. Give me the information for when this sale is going down and where we can sell this thing after we get it. I also want your guy's name and info. And no funny business, or the next time we come here we'll be doing more than yelling."

As they were driving away from their encounter with Edgar, Tommy laughed at how he negotiated a great deal in having the expenses come out before the split. "We're going to screw Edgar 'cause everything we spend is going to get paid by him." Sully didn't argue that their expenses would only reduce their eighty percent cut.

"Besides, we also control the sale. Maybe we can get some of the sale price in cash and only send part of it to Edgar's account. And Edgar ain't going anywhere. He's gotta be good for it. Look at the roots he has in town."

Sully, waiting in the shadows of Tommy's Vortex started to think that maybe Edgar's roots were not so firm. Maybe Edgar would skip town and pay none of the promised commissions. Conceivably, Edgar could recoup two hundred thousand dollars from having two sets of patsies sell the same item twice. Plus, by not being directly associated with any of the people transporting, stealing or selling the manuscript, Edgar stayed arm's length from any illegalities. He could sit back and watch his pawns do his dirty work without risk of discovery while he collected the reward. Sure, if discovered, Max or Tommy could point the finger at Edgar but maybe it would only point to an abandoned shop in Florida and a false name. Maybe Edgar had spent a lifetime leaving very few footprints along his journey and would be out of his schlocky St. Augustine bookstore before any of the patsies returned ready to collect. Maybe Edgar was already past due on his rent. Maybe most of Edgar's inventory was on consignment and the bulk of his net worth in a few, legitimately purchased, highly valuable antique books that could be carried in a small carry-on handbag.

Sully knew, of course, that in Tommy's mind, none of these 'Maybes' caused doubt; he was immune from critical thinking that could adversely affect his desires. Sully swallowed his doubt and chose to stick with Tommy's plan.

He watched the street for activity.

And then something strange happened.

For the first time today, Tommy and Sully's plans worked.

# Chapter 23

After a few minutes of the Parisian bookstore alarm softly chiming, the small Frenchman appeared to come out of the adjoining building carrying a set of keys. Paquet's head remained fixated on his keys looking for the one to open the door. False alarms apparently common by the way the Frenchman walked the fifty meters to the front of the bookshop with only a cursory glance around the street. He unlocked the door and walked a few steps into the shop to the alarm panel, not bothering to turn on the lights.

In an act of perfect timing that comes from knowing someone so well, Sully and Tommy moved with precision. They bounded to the door and grabbed the shocked Frenchman as he turned off the alarm. Sully locked the door behind them and Tommy, putting his hand on the Frenchman's shoulder and waist, bull-rushed him toward the back of the shop, away from the storefront windows. In the back office, they were far enough from the street for casual observation. Tommy pushed Paquet roughly onto the office chair.

"So where is it?" cried Tommy.

The Frenchman stared blankly at him; anger starting to replace the initial fear and shock of the abrupt attack.

"You speak English?" he yelled. "Where is it?"

Paquet looked at both men and pointed to Sully, "You, you are the man who pushed me down in the street."

Sully blanched at being identified. Although he knew to stay silent, the giddiness from lack of sleep made him say, "Yeah, we're bringing you back your briefcase." He lifted the case and placed it on the desk.

Not wanting to be left out of the joke Tommy chimed in, "I'll tell you what, Inspector Clouseau. I'll trade you the briefcase for the manuscript."

The Frenchman's eyes widened. "Ahh, it's the manuscript you want? That's it." His lips parted in a tiny smile of understanding.

"Of course we want it! You think we came to Paris for our health?" looking over at Sully to get the chuckle he desired.

"I'm afraid I don't know you well enough to make an opinion of your traveling habits," Paquet sniffed.

Sully laughed at the man's nerve. Tommy saw it for what it was – a lack of respect – and gave him an open-handed smack. "That should wipe the shit-eating grin off your face!"

Paquet's head jerked violently to the right causing his body to follow. From his slumped position he looked up over his shoulder and directly into Tommy's face.

"I guess being a wiseass in France must be easier," Tommy said, grabbing him by the collar and straightening the Frenchman back on the chair. "Where I come from, you earn the right to be a wiseass by taking the beating that normally comes with it." Releasing him and flattening out his shirt in the manner of an ironic valet.

"Where's the manuscript that you bought from the American?" Sully asked in a pressing yet deliberate manner.

"How do you know about that?" Paquet asked and then... "Of course. It was a trap," the Frenchman said finally understanding that the attack in Basel was not random.

"Listen, just give us the manuscript and we'll leave you alone," said Sully as his gaze bounced from Paquet to the front door and the view of the street. "You can claim a loss on your insurance and everybody wins," he added, somehow believing that committing insurance fraud was a reasonable suggestion after attacking the man in Basel, chasing him across two countries, breaking into his shop, and holding him against his will.

The Frenchman shook his head in distaste and turned to Tommy, who, despite being in the process of rooting out individual nose hairs to pluck, had demonstrated obvious leadership and presented the greater physical danger.

"I did not purchase the manuscript. It was not..." He hesitated and looked away from the thugs. "It was not what I expected. I buy for my clients and they would not be interested in that piece," the Frenchman explained without providing context.

"How do we know you're not lying?" Sully asked, ready to believe him and go home.

"You have broken into my shop and are restraining me against my will. Go ahead and search but you will not find it. The American took the manuscript with him."

Tommy gave the order. "Sully, check the place out."

"Thanks for announcing my name," he responded. Another roadblock, another step deeper into the 'Tommy Vortex'.

"Oh, you're not going to tell anyone." Tommy turned to the Frenchman and smiled peppering the threat with his idea of charm.

The Frenchman ignored the warning, "Do you even know what you are looking for?"

"Yeah, what you said...a manuscript ...uh, uh a book," Tommy said.

"It is a page from an illuminated manuscript," said the book dealer.

"A page? As in a piece of paper?" Sully said.

"All this trouble for a piece of paper?!" Tommy exclaimed.

"What the American showed me was a page of hand painted Latin calligraphy, some of it in real gold, containing the prayers for the Feast of Saint Lawrence. The page was roughly cut out from a larger Missal," he said with a slight smile. Seeing his chance to convince the thugs that he didn't possess the item they sought added, "that is why I didn't want it. I was expecting the entire volume. Not a page in a tube."

"Hey Tommy!" not bothering to keep his name secret. "I think I saw the guy in Basel with a mailer tube sticking out of his bag when he got in the cab." He said it with enthusiasm and conviction he didn't feel. He might have seen the tube being carried by the American or maybe he just convinced himself that he had. At this point, Sully knew he would have said anything to get Tommy and himself out of the shop and away from Paris.

Tommy stared at the Frenchman, pulled at his crotch, and looked around the shop before saying, "So you mean that it's worthless?"

"On the contrary," said the Frenchman, regaining composure in spite of the swelling of his left eye. "It is a very important document and very valuable. It was too expensive for my clients and I couldn't afford it."

Tommy's mood swung one hundred and eighty degrees. "Numbnuts!" calling Sully with a mixture of joy and urgency.

"Why am I numbnuts now?" Sully asked.

"You didn't want to be called by your name so you're numbnuts now."

"Geez, thanks," Sully snickered and shook his head in disbelief; just one more minor abuse to be endured.

"We gotta get find Edgar's guy! Grab some small books to take with us; might as well get a little extra value from this trip."

The Frenchman stood and commanded, "You will not steal from my shop! You have been..." Tommy started for the knife in his pocket but changed direction and threw his weight into the right cross that struck across the Frenchie's jaw. The crushing blow rattled the brain of the older man. Struck with enough power to knock out trained boxers a fourth his age, the wiry book dealer's head snapped to the right, knocking him off his chair – defying gravity until he landed several feet away – his head plopping onto the wood floor with the thud of a watermelon.

"Why'd you do that?" asked Sully.

"He was buggin' me," Tommy said, shaking his fist to relieve the sting.

"You think you killed him?" Sully said with equal parts compassion and self-concern as he went over for a closer look at the Frenchman's body splayed out on the floor.

"Nah…" and then, "look and see if he's breathing while I grab some things."

Sully leaned over the limp form and saw the man was taking shallow breaths. "Yeah. I think he's still alive," he called out to Tommy who was standing over a glass display case with a book propped up on a stand.

Tommy smashed the glass with a stone ashtray and reached into the case to take the small book. He blew off the broken shards of glass and quickly thumbed through it. He flipped through the book - each page a drawing with foreign captions - not recognizing that this rare set of Renaissance engravings depicted f fifteenth century Italian life. What mattered to Tommy was that anything in a glass case had to be valuable. Satisfied of its worth, Tommy placed it in his coat pocket.

"Okay. Let's go," Tommy said as he ripped the phone cord from the wall.

"Should we take the briefcase?" Sully asked.

"Nah," said Tommy as he pushed Sully aside and, using his black designer tee shirt to wipe the case clean of prints.

"You sure he's not going to follow us?" Sully said.

"He'll be lucky to wake up," Tommy laughed and gave the prone man a kick in his side. They left the shop unlocked and walked the half block to the metro station where they hailed a taxi back to Gare de Lyon. There, they reclaimed their luggage, into which they placed the newly stolen book, and went to the ticket counter.

"We going to Torino?" asked Sully.

"Don't you listen? We gotta go to Zurich and get that manuscript back from Edgar's guy."

"How will we find him?" Sully asked.

"Whatdya think I'm stupid? I had Edgar give me his itinerary before we left Florida. He's in Zurich at some conference for another two days. We'll just take it from him and then go to Torino to sell it… plus the book we just got."

"We gonna tell Edgar about what happened?"

"Fuck 'im. He was tryin' to screw us. Remember, Edgar told me that the manuscript was worth a hundred grand. You heard what the French guy said? He said it was a real important document painted with real gold. It's gotta be worth a lot more than a hundred G's. Guys like that don't think a hundred grand is a lot of money. I bet it could be worth a million bucks!" Looking at Sully's disbelieving face modified his enthusiasm a bit and re-stated, "…several hundred thousand dollars, at least."

"Maybe we could have asked him before you knocked him out, then we would've known for sure," Sully needled his partner.

"What?! I barely touched him!" Tommy said shrugging and holding his arms out. "Besides, I'm not so sure that the Frenchman was ever going to buy the manuscript at all. Maybe Edgar raised the price so Frenchie had to pass on it and Edgar's got another buyer." Tommy paused to let the theory sink in. Sully knew that in Tommy's world, you were either screwing someone or someone was screwing you. Since Tommy didn't have the upper hand, someone must be taking advantage of him.

"When you think about it, finding another buyer and not telling us is a clever way to get us out of the picture. We attack the Frenchie and follow him to Paris, leaving Edgar and his guy plenty of time to sell the manuscript for more money to another buyer and cut us out completely."

"But why would they let us in on the deal in the first place? Once we go back to Florida, Edgar knows he'd need to deal with us," Sully asked, not following Tommy's paranoid, off-road logic.

"Maybe they just found a new buyer or maybe they planned it all along... to get us out of the way. You see, by sending us on this wild goose chase, if they get lucky, we get caught roughing up the buyer and the police put us permanently out of the way." Tommy smiled, satisfied with his logic, and continued, "We gotta get hold of that manuscript." He chuckled and playfully punched Sully in his chest, "this could be our big break."

"I don't know, Tommy, we don't have any connections like Edgar."

"How hard can it be? Whatdya think Edgar's some genius?"

"What about Edgar's guy. You think he'll be a problem? He's not some small old man like the Frenchie," Sully said.

"That skinny guy? He's a courier. He'll be happy to get the manuscript off his hands. Unless..." he thought out loud. "Unless he's the one who's playing the game on Edgar...and us." A moment passed between them. "Either way, we'll handle it...and we'll probably take care of him in a way that he can't play games no more."

Sully knew what that meant. And it bothered him. Unsure whether he bristled at the thought of hurting more people or of being locked up, he knew one thing – the price of his loyalty to Tommy kept getting higher.

At the train station, the men purchased two one-way tickets back to Zurich scheduled to arrive at six-thirty in the morning. The train left in less than a half hour, so they bought a couple of sandwiches and beer to bring on the train and made their way to the departure track.

***

At the same time, back in Zurich, Max said good night to Theodore, having spent a great evening of talking, eating and laughing with him and the other conference attendees. The big boss seemed to note Max's knowledge of the industry, his professionalism, and ease with the customers.

Max let happiness wash over him. As Theodore excused himself from the group in the lobby bar, probably to return to the platinum blond with the red lipstick in his room, Max went back to the gang to have his final, final drink with a large, fast-talking Chicago-based warehouseman.

Max sallied up to the bar, the troubles of the day receding from his thoughts. Confident that the day's challenges could be managed easily, Max sat at the fancy bar and talked amiably with colleagues.

Max would not have joked so confidently had he known about two American ex-cons in Paris boarding the Zurich-bound train: both intent on making the San Lorenzo theirs, one itching to use the locking blade stuffed in his pocket.

# Chapter 24

**Thursday, November 13, 1997**
**Zurich**

Tommy could feel the train starting to slow and saw several of the passengers collecting their belonging and heading toward the exits. With a midnight departure, the Paris to Zurich train traveled slower to arrive in Switzerland's most populous city at a reasonable hour. During the fitful night sitting in the passenger coach, it started to dawn on Tommy that maybe he'd been rash punching the Frenchie so hard and then bolting out of the shop. Maybe he shouldn't have hit him at all. What was the guy going to do? He and Sully standing over him? Nothing. Should have talked to the Frenchie more, used some charm, make sure he didn't have the manuscript, get more information on what it was worth, maybe even get him to throw in a book for their troubles…and then shank him, let him bleed out, and hide the body.

Damn! If the beating didn't kill him, he'd left a witness.

Tommy's thoughts turned to the big rumpled dimwit sleeping in the seat next to him. Although he would never admit it to him, Sully was probably his best friend. I mean, he had lots of friends. He was popular at the bars and clubs, with both the locals and the tourist women looking for a good time. He always had plenty of friends wanting to hang out with him. Sure, he always bought, but he could afford it – he was generous. Bartenders and wait staff loved him. They were actually some of his best friends. It wasn't just 'cause he tipped big. They truly liked him. You had to see how happy they were when he showed up. It wasn't true what his ex-wife said that his only friends were people depending on his money. He didn't pay the girls he dated from the clubs! I mean, at first you have to – when they're dancing – but they're not hookers. You don't pay them for the date. Sure, you gotta pay for dinner and stuff – like if they needed groceries or something, like a video game for their kids. These young girls need someone to look up to – a role model. Someone to take care of them, treat them right. It's not his fault that it never worked out for long. It's not his fault they don't recognize his goodness. That's why they'll never get out of their rut. They're not mature or smart enough to realize how good he is for them. Even the guys around town couldn't be counted on all the time. Everyone usually bailed out eventually –everyone except Sully. Only Sully, sitting next to him and slobbering on the rail car window, remained loyal to him.

Tommy and Sully alighted from their railcar, the second night without a bed, stiff, tired, unshaved and grumpy. They needed a shower, a warm cooked meal and a long rest.

"Where are we going?" Sully asked Tommy as they exited the main doors of the station into the brisk morning air.

"Edgar's guy is staying at a hotel right near the station."

"How do you know that?" Sully replied.

With pride, Tommy reached into his bag and pulled out a piece of paper folded over several times that read, '*MAX AGRESTA - HOTEL ST GOTTHARD.*' The handwritten note contained a phone number and several doodlings. The information had been traced over several times which left a deep impression on the paper. Tommy held the note up for inspection, his hands quaking 6.5 on the Richter scale.

"Let me have the note…or hold it still," Sully said. "What are you? Nervous? I can't read it when you're shaking it so much."

"I don't need you to read it! And it's cause I had coffee."

"When did you have coffee?" The men had not left each other's sight for over fifteen hours. "You could have gotten me a cup."

Tommy ignored him, "Let's just walk around here and find the hotel! It can't be far."

"Why don't we ask someone?" asked Sully.

"Do you speak German, numbnuts?"

Sully took the insult as water off the back of a terrapin and tried to get a few of the industrious commuters' attention saying, "Excuse me". Without exception, the busy people passed by and refused to make eye contact. The commuters had to work hard pretending not to notice the big man with the yellow coat.

"Come on!" Tommy grabbed Sully by the shoulder. "There's a bunch of hotels up this way. Edgar said that he was staying near the train station. I bet it can't be far. Maybe it's one of these?"

They crossed the road directly in front of them and walked up the Bahnhofstrasse, the main thoroughfare reserved for pedestrians and tram traffic. Sully gawked like a tourist and cheered like a kid seeing Space Mountain for the first time when he spied the sign for the Hotel St. Gotthard. Tommy approached the front desk clerk while Sully investigated the lobby's design and architecture, appreciating the craftsmanship of the detailed features.

The desk clerk stood behind the counter filing some paperwork when Tommy interrupted him without greeting or preamble and said "My partner," indicating Sully who at this moment stood in the middle of the lobby with his neck craning up staring at the ceiling, "and I just got in on a train from Paris. We've been traveling all night. Actually, we came in the day before from Florida and flew into Zurich. Then we went to Paris. Well," Tommy smiled flashing his capped teeth, "we've been traveling a lot."

The clerk stared at the babbling man. He clucked at the American's propensity to over-share. "Just arrived from a train?" he asked in a tired voice. "What a coincidence, this hotel is located only one block from the train station. What are the odds?"

Missing the sarcasm, Tommy took the retort as a sign that he had won the man over and continued. "Say, we have a friend of ours staying here a…" Tommy said discreetly looking at his note, "Max Agresta. Can you call him for us?"

"Sir," the clerk responded stiffly, "We cannot disturb our guests at this hour." The clerk had noticed the man's shaking hands as he read the note containing his 'friend's' name. "I'm afraid that I can't help you."

Tommy shuffled from side to side, looking around. Frustration built as he reached for his knife before a less violent idea dawned. "Do you have any rooms available?"

The clerk's suspicion did not extend to rejecting paying customers. "How many nights?" he responded.

"Just one," Tommy answered quickly.

"Let me check." The clerk completed a perfunctory search of his log book and grabbed a key from the wall behind him. "Yes, we have one double available now. Will you be paying cash? Or credit card?"

"Cash," he said and reached into his pocket pulling out a wad of French Francs mixed in with U.S. dollars but very few Swiss Francs. "Ah damn! I gotta change the money," he said more to himself than to the clerk.

"Don't worry sir, I can change it for you, no problem," the clerk said pointing to the sign behind him listing all the currencies and the hotel-favored exchange rates. "I just need your passport, please." Tommy handed over his passport without hesitation and the clerk went to the end of the counter where he made a copy of it. "Hey. Why do you need a copy of that?" Tommy asked a little too late.

"I must have your information to register you. I can give it back before you leave."

"Okay. Don't forget to give it back to me. I don't want my information all around town."

The clerk returned the passport to Tommy and, after using a small calculator to show the conversion results, counted out the bills in front of Tommy.

The transaction completed, Tommy paid for the one night of the room and received the room key on a heavy brass fob. Tommy and Sully took the phone-booth sized elevator to the 5th floor. They opened their door and walked into the tiniest hotel room they had ever seen. The two, twin beds were so close together that you couldn't drop a magazine between them.

"Ah shit, look at this crappy room," said Tommy.

"Don't worry about it, Tommy," Sully said popping his head into the bathroom. "The bathroom looks nice and at least we got a bed."

"Yeah, but I don't wanna sleep with you. Look at that!" pointing out the beds rammed up against each other. "Why would he give us this room?" Tommy continued talking to himself as Sully started using the facilities. "Doesn't he know we're two guys? Why would we sleep this close to each other?"

Sully laughing and calling out from his seat on the throne said, "Maybe he thought you were one of 'those' guys."

Tommy's eyes grew wide with embarrassment and heat flashed up his face, "He didn't think that!"

After a moment he sniffed the air and grimaced. "A courtesy flush would be nice! And light a match or something. Holy crap, what did you eat?"

Tommy hurried over to the phone to call the front desk. "We wanna different room," he said as soon as the front desk picked up. "Whatdya mean this is the only one?" he yelled into the phone and wrapped his knuckles on the table as the clerk answered. "Ah, this is bullshit!" Tommy finished and hung up the phone.

Tommy shouted over the sound of the sink faucet running, "We're stuck in this room. They don't got anything else."

Sully stepped out of the bathroom, his shirt already off, showing his pale, freckled, and flabby body. "Okay, well we're not staying here long anyway. Are we?"

"Nah. Let's get cleaned up and rest a bit. Then we'll find this 'Max' and take the manuscript."

"We're not going to hurt him are we?" Sully asked.

"I'll do whatevah I need to do to get that manuscript!" he yelled. "Who cares what happens to him? He wants to play, he's gotta be willin' to pay the piper." Sully got the message that he was serious. He should've remembered how the car detailer looked months after he was released from the hospital.

"Edgar said that Max is here speaking at some conference. He might want to carry that manuscript around him when he can, but I bet that when he's giving that speech, he won't have it on him. We'll be able to snag it from his briefcase or, if he leaves it in his room, we could get a hotel maid to get in his room and take it from there."

"Okay. Good idea," Sully agreed, glad to have a non-violent option.

"But..." Tommy continued. "If he stays close to the manuscript the whole time and he wants to protect it, then I'm gonna take him out."

Sully realized what that meant – someone would die and someone would take the fall. Hopefully, neither would be him. "I'll take a shower first if you're okay with it and then we'll rest till about ten o'clock and then find Max's room," Sully offered.

"Yeah. Max is here for a conference for work. He ain't going any-where."

# Chapter 25

Max arrived a little earlier than the conference's opening remarks, surprised to be one of the first people there. The woman in charge of coordinating the administration of the conference greeted him warmly, "Mr. Agresta. Good Morning. How was your room?"

"Oh, wonderful! And thank you again for getting me in this hotel. That was very nice of you."

"Of course. Thank you for speaking today and taking the time to make the long trip. You will be going on the panel directly following the luncheon speaker."

Max absently tugged and twisted his lip. Morning had brought back his concerns but it was too early to call Laura. Anxiety wore down his thin veneer of calm.

"Oh, really? Great! Thank you," Max said even though he already had memorized the schedule; opening remarks from the association's chairman, a panel discussion on global economic trends followed by a lunch where Rudolph Frank, Member of the Executive Board of the European Community Bank and Chief Economist of the ECB, would give the luncheon address on the monetary union of Europe and the objectives of forthcoming move to a single currency. Max's panel would be held in a smaller room down the hall after lunch. He had already checked it out while the hotel workers set it up.

At nine o'clock on the nose, chimes rang to announce the start of the conference. Max found seats near the front of the audience, on the side furthest away from the doors. He saved the one next to him and looked over, waiting for his boss to arrive. He hadn't seen Theodore at breakfast and he took a break from reviewing, for the hundredth time, his presentation notes to scan the growing crowd. He fended off conference goers trying to take his prized extra seat and succeeded until a wily Belgian slid in at the same moment that Theodore appeared. Max turned to say something to the man but it was too late. Regretting the lost opportunity to impress his boss, Max sneered at the Belgian.

The conference began and the speaker, with a heavy French accent droned on, way past the allotted time, about the aims and goals of the industry association. Max's mind started to drift away from the conference and even away from the thoughts of his speech and landed on his predicament. Namely, what to do with the manuscript. As he had done for many years when making an important decision, he made a list of pros and cons of a particular action. The mental exercise worked equally well for him on both major and minor decisions. Ironically, for the biggest decision of his life, that of asking Laura to marry him, he didn't use it. The decision was really quite simple; he loved Laura and his child was going to be born to two loving and married parents.

While a trade official made a word salad explaining newly proposed levy increases, Max started on his list. The thought of just getting rid of the manuscript and forgetting the whole deal jumped out front. No. Even if he got rid of it, most of his problems – returning home a failure without money for Sam's surgery and making an enemy of Edgar – would remain. But something else bothered him. Like a small pebble in his shoe that became more uncomfortable the further he traveled, an idea, a realization – something the bookseller had mentioned – grew in significance.

Max started thinking about the item rolled up in the mailing tube as more than a commission check. What was it the Frenchman said? The San Lorenzo was some kind of prayer manual that had been used for generations to glorify and worship God. Max pictured a lone monk in the fourteen hundreds creating the beautifully decorated page – alone in a stark cell surrounded by unadorned gray stone walls, wearing a brown roughhewn cassock, bent over his desk in the cold, pen in hand, concentrating on each stroke, his eyes straining in the fading light to accurately apply the precious paint to the page. This thing was an important work of art. The Frenchman had said as much. Plus, it had spiritual and historical importance. Strangely, Max even felt drawn to St. Lawrence's story. No. Regardless of the fact that not having the manuscript would make it nearly impossible to produce a conviction, he could not destroy it.

Besides, a 'conviction' was not Max's biggest concern. Just being questioned by the authorities would cause irreparable harm. A clear trail of evidence linking him to the stolen manuscript could be built; the Frenchman and the Swiss bankers, to name a few. Police questioning would delay his return or tie him up in Customs. The delay would need to be explained to both his wife and his company. Laura would be furious and feel betrayed that he'd risk his job to go off on this wild goose chase. His employer would wonder, quite justifiably, if his manuscript dealings were on company time and with company money. Theodore's support would dissipate and the incident would indelibly ink him on the headcount reduction list. Not to mention that defending himself from any possible charges would take money; money he didn't have.

Max flipped the page on his yellow legal pad and continued on his list of whether he should return the San Lorenzo to Edgar in Florida or go to visit his cousin in Torino and seek a sale or assistance. On the 'pro' side of Florida – simplicity, requiring no change in plans, and over in three days' time.

But the 'cons' outweighed the 'pro' by a landslide. First, returning to Florida with the San Lorenzo meant no money for Sam's surgery. It meant the failure of another business idea. It meant defeat. Second, if San Lorenzo was actually a stolen item, he'd be continuing his complicity in trafficking stolen goods by returning it. He'd also increase his chance of being caught by U.S. Customs when he landed in the State which could mean jail time or, at minimum, substantial fines. Playing dumb and denying involvement would not work. At best, he could turn state's witness against Edgar but a long, public trial with plenty of publicity and plenty of lawyers to pay would drain Max, emotionally and financially. In all cases, life as he knew it would be over.

Even successfully returning the San Lorenzo to Edgar would not relieve Max from future complications. For the rest of his life, he would be waiting for a knock on his door by authorities wanting to hear an account of his role in the trafficking of the stolen 15th century manuscript.

There was a chance, and Max hoped fervently that it was true, that the San Lorenzo was not a stolen original or that the manuscript in his safe was only a competent reproduction. If it was a reproduction, Max could demand compensation from Edgar for the wasted time and effort traveling all over Switzerland. Or maybe the Frenchman's assessment was wrong and it wasn't stolen. If so, going to Torino might represent a chance to sell it to someone else. Thinking on his feet and finding an alternative buyer could convince Edgar to actually increase his commission. The only way to find out was to go to Torino and have it evaluated by another expert.

The only 'cons' for going to Torino was that he had never been there before, didn't know his cousins, and didn't speak that language.

Moreover, in order to see his cousin and return to work by Monday, he'd somehow need to sneak out of the conference early. And he'd have to call his father to arrange the impromptu weekend side trip to see the extended family.

The most pressing difficulty was getting out of the conference, and away from his boss's attention, with enough time to make his return to the U.S. The conference extended until mid-day tomorrow. Max mentally played with different excuses for why he would leave first thing tomorrow morning and how he could change his return flight from Zurich on Saturday to Milan on Sunday. As the EU tariff expert finished his speech, Max decided to go to Torino as soon as possible and seek the advice of his cousin about the San Lorenzo manuscript.

# Chapter 26

Even the most experienced special agent in the Jacksonville office had to make the coffee if they were the first to arrive. And at a little after six in the morning, Grace Hemmer was the first one in the office.

Back in her office, she saw the red message light blinking on her phone. She picked up the receiver, dialed her voicemail code and retrieved her messages. Having left early for a dentist appointment yesterday, she expected to be swamped with several messages. She was pleased, yet surprised, to only have three.

The first one was from her supervisor, "*Hey, it's Merriman. Listen, I'm going to need your help doing the background on the Salvatierra drug case. Mullaney is out next week on deposition and I'm not going to get through all the interviews in time for the grand jury. If you're around tomorrow, we'll talk. Thanks.*" Grace deleted the message — she didn't care if he was the group supervisor and, technically, her boss. She was sure that if Merriman hadn't hooked someone else into doing the crap work that he saved for the last minute, he would be at her door at 8:31 begging again.

She pressed the button for the next message, "*Hello, this is Fredric*

*Paquet. Please call me. I met with the American buyer today in Basel, as we discussed."* A long pause followed. Grace found herself holding her breath while listening to the next part. *"As you asked me to find out... Yes. I believe with near total certainty that it is the San Lorenzo. I will be at my library tomorrow and we can discuss then. You will want to act quickly."* Grace saved the message and hit the button to play the next message.

Grace hit the button for the next message and listened distractedly, still thinking about what the Frenchman had said. The message played, but nothing was recorded. Or rather, there were sounds but no voices. At first, Grace thought that the answering voicemail system was malfunctioning. She let the recording play and noted that the call went on for almost fifteen minutes and terminated when the system was at full capacity. Upon listening to it a second time, she realized that there were sounds, scraping, and shallow breathing sounds... possibly even some paper shuffling sounds, but no voices and definitely no one speaking into the phone.

Perplexed, Grace saved the message and looked in her Rolodex for Fredric Paquet's phone number. She dialed +33, the international code for France and then the number to Paquet's rare book shop and listened to the strange ring tone from the other end of the line. She let the phone ring for what seemed like an eternity and thought it strange that no one answered. At a quarter after twelve in Paris, the phone of one of the most prominent rare book shops in all of Paris should be attended.

On the fifteenth ring, she saw the RAC, Cecil Pond, walking into his office. She hung up the phone and hurried over, practiced in cornering Pond in these early morning tete-a-tetes to press him for the best assignments and additional resources before her colleagues arrived.

∗∗∗

"Morning, bossman." Grace stood at his door with a painting on smile, perkily bobbing her head.

"Grace," Pond replied wearily, knowing that the more chipper Grace was, the more she wanted. He dreaded the demands for resources which rankled the many egos in the office but, for all the headaches Grace presented, she got results.

"Okay. Let me hear it. You seem to have a knack for getting the attention of the boys in Washington..." Maybe with her help, he hoped, he'd be on the fast track to Tampa as the Special Agent in Charge.

"I received a call yesterday from my French source. He said he knows where the San Lorenzo is."

"Were you able to put together the case on the locals who were fencing the manuscript?" Pond asked.

"I still need to talk to him – he only left a message. I've reviewed my notes from the previous case of the stolen manuscript and following up on loose ends that always seemed to bother me. There's a rare book dealer in St. Augustine whose name keeps popping up. And the more I dig into him the more aliases I get. Seems pretty shady and I think that he's involved in this transaction as well. I've got a pretty good file on him and was thinking about heading down for a little talk with him this afternoon," Grace said.

Pond knew that she loved getting out in the field uncovering truths. No fact went unquestioned. No lead forgotten. And once the suspect was within her reach? She was an artist at gaining confessions. He had watched her in admiration as she interrogated a suspect – a Michelangelo painting a scene for the suspect to walk through, leading him through a maze where the only exit was pleading guilty.

"If my contact can link the San Lorenzo with a U.S. citizen from here in our district – that means Federal illicit trade and trafficking charges can be filed from our office," she finished.

"Sounds good, Grace. Keep me informed. But I suggest that once you get the file built, you hand it off to Bramante Buratti at the Art

Squad. And take a vacation. You work too hard!" Pond called out with a chuckle.

***

Grace redialed her informant's cell phone when she got back in her office. A voice answered on the third ring. "*Bonjour.*"

"Hello, Mr. Paquet?"

"Who is this, please?" said the voice in heavily accented English.

"I would like to speak to Mr. Paquet. This is his cell phone, I believe?"

"Yes, this is his mobile phone. Who are you?" said the voice.

"I'll ask you the questions. Who are you and may I speak to Mr. Paquet? It is his phone after all," Grace said, agitation crept into her voice.

"I'm sorry but Mr. Paquet cannot come to the phone right now." He paused. The weight of this statement sank in. "Now, I ask you again, who are you?"

"I'm U.S. Customs Special Agent Grace Hemmer of the Jacksonville, Florida office in the United States. Now tell me who you are or put Mr. Paquet on the phone!" Grace said, the words spilling out of her in a rush.

"I am afraid that I can't. I'm Inspector Jacques Leverd of the 9th Arrondissement and I am investigating a suspected homicide of Mr. Paquet." Grace's mouth dropped open and she leaned on her desk.

Before she could ask any questions, the inspector said, "Very curious. The number from which you are calling... it was the last phone number dialed from this mobile phone. We've been trying to reach it for several hours."

"I didn't receive any messages. Of course, I wouldn't," she said more to herself than to the Inspector in Paris. "The voicemail system was full and no longer accepting messages after Paquet's call last night."

"Can you tell me, Special Agent Hemmer, what your association is, was, with Mr. Paquet?"

"We were professional colleagues," she said, wary of giving the dis-embodied voice too much information. "Many months ago, I located and recovered a 15th century Italian manuscript that Frederic Paquet had a professional interest in. We checked in with each other from time to time." Grace told the truth but without the context. She did not want the French police to link the Paquet homicide with the San Lorenzo…at least until after she recovered it. It would be hard enough to keep the Carabinieri Art Squad out of her case and away from her deserved glory. Getting the French Police involved and linking the art theft to a homicide would take it to another level which she could not control. She needed to use this opportunity to learn from them, not the other way around. "What have you learned so far? What is the situation?"

"Mr. Paquet was found by his assistant before noon, lying on the floor in the back of his bookshop near his office. We will not have a time of death until the forensics department arrives but he does not look like he's been dead for long. He suffered a severe trauma. Mr. Paquet had bruises on both sides of his face caused by hard objects or perhaps large fists. Papers lay strewn across the floor and a thin metallic briefcase sat open near the body. An item is missing from a smashed glass display case. I have put a notice out to all European authorities. The rest of the shop is in good order. We found no signs of forced entry but the front door was unlocked when the assistant came in today…a little later than usual… around eleven. We're questioning him now and we still need to question the deceased's wife."

Good, Grace thought. This inspector offered the evidence more freely than she would have expected. It could be an inside job with no relation to the San Lorenzo but her instincts told her not. The case just got more complicated.

"Why do you think he would call you as he was dying?" Inspector

Leverd asked.

"He called me earlier in the day to check in," she said. And trying to minimize the connection suggested, "I think it is merely coincidental. He probably reached for the phone and hit the redial button by mistake; making me the last call of a dying man," Grace answered.

"You are in Florida, Yes?" asked the inspector.

"Yes. Jacksonville, Florida."

"Is that near St. Augustine?" The inspector asked seeming to already know the answer. "Are you familiar with a company called R.K. Trucking? Employer of a Mr. Agresta?"

Grace bent over her desk writing everything down.

"What about the Dolder Grand Hotel? It is handwritten, presumably in the hand of the dead man, on the back of the card. Maybe that is where they met? Maybe the meeting had something to do with his death? At this time, I don't know. What I do know..." he teased out, "is that it is coincidental that a dead man has this Max Agresta's business card in his wallet and the man is from some small provincial town in Florida, United States and on the same day of his death, the dead man makes two phone calls to the police in that same provincial town."

"Jacksonville is not St. Augustine and we are not provincial towns! At least Jacksonville is not. We have a professional football team here," Grace said defensively.

"Well, I am going to speak to this Mr. Agresta. Anything that you have on the man would be most useful. Perhaps we can speak later?" the Inspector finished.

"Okay. I'll see what I can find out. What is your phone number; how can I reach you?" Grace asked.

"It's not necessary. I have your number. I will call you when I need something," he finished before disconnecting the line.

Grace almost jogged over to Pond's office. "Cecil," she called out.

"What is it, Grace?" in a manner that told her that her allotment of time had already been used up.

"I just called my contact in Paris. He's dead... Murdered, they think."

"Murdered?" Pond dropped his pen and looked up.

She had his full attention. Unlike in the movies, informants rarely got murdered for working with the authorities. Grace retold everything she had been working on since their last discussion. Pond leaned forward as she continued, "And there is a wrinkle...there seems to be another local player involved that I didn't know of. I need to get basic research done on him but I've got his name, his employer in town and the hotel where he's staying now. But the good news is that it looks like we have two potential traffickers in our midst."

Grace knew that Pond and the U.S. District Attorney, Weidenfeld would like that. Two suspects were better than one. Not only did it look like a greater, more threatening conspiracy, but two suspects made it easier to get convictions because one criminal was bound to rat on the other in exchange for a lighter prosecution for themselves.

"What about the murder?" Pond asked reasonably.

"We're not sure it's even related. At this point I think we should focus our attention on the stolen manuscript and the two Floridians trying to sell it," Grace said.

"Sounds logical. How much time do you need to make the case? When are you going to call the Carabinieri Art Squad?" Pond asked.

"Well, I can't ask my informant anymore. I'll just have to go on what he told me; that he saw the San Lorenzo at his meeting in Basel." She paused for a moment to think about the directions her pursuit could take her. "The Inspector seemed to believe that this Max Agresta from the trucking company met with Paquet recently. I'm sure that he'll follow that path. However, what he doesn't know is how Paquet's meeting with Max Agresta links to the stolen San Lorenzo," she said putting it together.

"We need to keep it that way...at least until I recover the manuscript."

"I don't know, Grace. I don't like even the hint of us withholding information on a homicide."

"We're not withholding anything. He didn't ask anything about a manuscript and when he mentioned the name Agresta, I had never heard it before. Whatever I find out about this guy, I'll tell the French police. That is if they ever call me."

"What do you mean? Why can't you call them?"

"Oh. Didn't I tell you? The little prick didn't even give me his number. Just said, he'd be in contact with me."

"Weird."

"I'm thinking I need to go to Switzerland tonight and meet up with this Agresta guy and squeeze him. I'll have the travel documents typed up in an hour. I'd like your approval so that I can track him down in Switzerland and get a confession and the San Lorenzo."

"What?!" Aren't you moving a little fast here? Listen, this really belongs in Buratti's hands. Why don't you call him and hand him the information? He would be much better at tracking this guy down and recovering the stolen manuscript," Pond tried to reason. "Or if you really want Agresta for yourself, why don't you wait until he returns to the US and meet him at the airport with silver bracelets?"

"Because by then, the French police may already have him in custody for murder and we'll miss our opportunity to recover the San Lorenzo. You know as well as I do that the Art Squad can't be too far behind. It'll take half a day to zip over there. I'll be there in the morning. I bet half the continent already knows that the San Lorenzo is on the market. Besides, if we don't get to Agresta soon, he might dispose of the manuscript and then we'll have nothing," Grace countered.

"Grace. Listen. It's not that easy for you to 'zip over' to Switzerland and interview a suspect on foreign soil. Do you realize the paperwork that needs to be done? You'll need to coordinate with the attaché office in Rome, which covers Switzerland, and then you'll have to coordinate with Swiss authorities. More importantly, once you're there, you don't have any legal authority of your own."

Grace already knew all that but she chose to respond to only a portion of Pond's viable objections. "I'll let Buratti know. But only after I get the San Lorenzo and get this Max Agresta in cuffs."

Having failed to dissuade Grace's travel plans to pursue Agresta, Pond dropped the ultimate roadblock, "Besides, we don't have the budget for that kind of unplanned travel expense."

"If you don't want to pay for it, I'll pay for it myself." Grace proclaimed. "Besides, you told me to take a vacation. This will be it. I'll vacation in Switzerland...that's normal, right?"

"If you want to go on your own, I can't stop you. But I'm not paying for it and I'm not approving it as government business." Grace knew that she could never win the argument with the bureaucratic Pond. "But I think you'd be better off handing this over..."

"I know, I know," Grace interrupted, "....to the Art Squad and Bramante Buratti." Grace stormed out of the office but not before grumbling, "If you like him so much, why don't you go out with him."

# Chapter 27

**Zurich**

The luncheon speaker, the Chief Economist of the ECB, had just taken the podium and prepared to read his introductory remarks. The wait staff swarmed the room clearing plates and serving coffee. Max's table of ten was fully occupied except for the seats on either side of him. His boss appeared to be listening to the presentation politely, if not attentively. Spenser Littlefield, who had glommed on to Max at the first coffee break and hadn't made a move without him, sat next to Theodore. Three young Germans who sold industry-specific tracking software and two Polish trucking men who sat with their heads together throughout the entire lunch without even bothering to look up comprised the rest of the table.

The large refrigerated warehouseman from last night approached the table as the speaker took the podium. Putting his meaty hands on Max's shoulders, he bellowed, "You got room for me, Maxy? Whad-I-miss?"

Part cowboy, part Chicago playboy, the man leaning on him had a big personality and an even bigger head. Not ego, but, literally, the largest head Max had ever seen on a human. His blondish/grayish locks flowed in a hockey hair mullet. Puffy cheeks framed his Fu Manchu mustache and soul patch, what some people called the Zappa. His head sat on his burly shoulders without the benefit of a neck. He dressed in black cowboy boots, big silver belt buckle, and nicely pressed jeans. Under his black silk blazer, he wore a white cotton dress shirt unbuttoned to display a bouquet of gray chest hair and enough gold jewelry to make any hip-hop rapper jealous.

Max blanched at the man's presence but couldn't find a reason to say no. "Ah...sure, Sylvester," he whispered.

He didn't take the hint, "Snowman," he responded loudly. "I used to be Sylvester the Cat." Proving his point he called out, "Suffering Succotash", with a lisp in the manner of the eponymous cartoon cat.

Max cringed. The social lubricant who caused screams of laughter at the lobby last night didn't seem so amusing now.

"But now my friends call me 'Snowman' 'cause I'm big like a snowman and my last name is Snow.

"Sylvester Snow," he said as he shook his hands with Theodore. He similarly introduced himself to the others at the table before sitting down, oblivious of the need for quiet during the speech.

As he dropped to one of the seats, he slapped Max's knee saying, sotto voce, "You are Oh-Kay, Maxy! I don't care what anybody else says about you." Sylvester seemed a knowledgeable guy who could probably be a good contact. But at lunch today, before his speech and in front of his boss, Max cringed at associating with a musclehead calling him 'Maxy'.

Preoccupied with Snowman's arrival, Max felt a tap on his shoulder and turned to see the conference organizer woman bending down to speak to him. She sat partially on the empty seat next to him. Max turned and offered her the seat to which she refused.

"You have an important phone call....at the front desk." She remained calm but the voice projected urgency.

And while her statement did not invite questioning, Max blurted out, "What?" A phone call at the front desk could only mean bad things at home. Even with Samantha's ongoing health issues, strangely, Max's first fear was that he hadn't screwed in the bookshelves as securely as possible and one of the twins had hurt himself...badly.

For the one and a half minutes it took Max to walk to the phone at the front desk, he thought of every negative possibility that could happen to his wife and kids. His heart raced a mile a minute as the clerk handed him the phone. "Hello, this is Max. Is everything all right?"

"Is this Max Agresta?" said the voice on the other end of the line in a heavy French accent. The hotel clerk stood nearby making a show of doing paperwork.

Immediately, the fear of his family's safety waned as the fear of the manuscript situation waxed. "Yes. This is Max Agresta."

"This is Inspector Leverd with the Paris police."

Max's heart nearly stopped and his mind raced trying to comprehend the Paris connection.

"Do you know a Monsieur Paquet?"

"Who?" Max had a hard time understanding the man's accent.

"Paquet. Frederic Paquet. He is the book dealer you met with."

"No. Not really," Max answered.

"Are you denying that you met with Monsieur Paquet in Basel?"

"No. I met with him in Basel at a bank." Max sounded defensive. "But that's it. I don't really know him. I never saw him before and didn't see him after the meeting," Max explained.

"What was your business with Monsieur Paquet?" Leverd pushed.

"What is this about?" Max asked. "How do you have this number?"

"Routine questions. What is your dealing with Monsieur Paquet?"

Not wanting to give this inspector any link to the stolen document nor to fulfill the desk clerk's growing curiosity said, "We just had a business meeting. That's all,"

"And he left the meeting and you didn't see him again?"

"Correct," Max stated.

"Interesting, so you are saying that you didn't share a taxi with him?" He paused and added, "Strange. I will need to check with the receptionist again because she says that it looks like you and Monsieur Paquet were fighting before getting into a taxi; in front of the bank."

"We weren't fighting. I was helping him. He had been attacked," Max corrected.

"But a moment ago you said that you last saw him in the meeting, now you are changing your story and telling me that you shared a taxi with him."

Max flushed. His heart pounded and breath became shallow. He looked down at his hand where his thumb absently fidgeted, wiping the sweat from his fingers. "I did share a taxi with him to the train station. That's what I meant to say." Max tried to keep his thoughts straight but knew he only sounded guilty. The hotel clerk lifted his head with interest.

"Maybe it is my English." The inspector took a different tact. "You say someone attacked him? Who?"

"I don't know. Why don't you ask him yourself?"

"Don't tell me how to do my job," he warned. "Please answer."

Chastened, Max responded, "When I arrived on the street, he had already been attacked. I gave him a hand up and then helped him to the taxi."

"And so the last time you saw Monsieur Paquet was not in the meeting but in the taxi? Or did you spend time with him at the train station?"

"No. As soon as I got out of the taxi, I ran to catch my train back to Zurich."

"Certainly; you are in Zurich...now." The inspector let the suspicion hang. "Do you have any idea who attacked Mr. Paquet?"

"No. I didn't see anyone. Why aren't you asking him these questions?"

"I'm afraid I can't." Leverd paused for a few moments before saying, "Monsieur Paquet is dead."

"Dead?"

"Yes. It appears that Monsieur Paquet may have been murdered last night."

"Murdered!" Max exclaimed. The clerk stopped all pretense of paperwork and hung on to Max's half of the conversation.

"I am with the Paris Homicide Department. In fact, I believe that you, Max Agresta, are the last one to see him alive. Perhaps you could shed some light on his death," Leverd said.

Max looked up to see his face, devoid of all color, in the mirror behind the desk. A stolen manuscript in his room and now being linked to the murder of the man who informed of its theft – incomprehensible.

"I have nothing to do with his death," Max said. He forgot all discretion before catching himself and looking up to see the hotel clerk eavesdropping like it was his job.

"But the attack....who could have done it?"

"I didn't see it. The attackers were gone by the time I came out. Paquet told me it was drug addicts."

"Interesting. Why would he say that?"

"He complained that the men were probably American drug addicts because they wore American clothes and drove an expensive car."

"Really? He said that?" Leverd sounded surprised at the response.

"Yes. He also said that one of the men dressed like...like a canary."

"*Incroyable.* So some American birdmen attacked Monsieur Paquet? A very creative story."

"That's what he said. And that the men stole his briefcase," Max tried to explain.

"Can you describe it?"

Max felt on firmer ground here and started to describe in detail the Frenchman's slim line silver metallic case that had made such an impression on him.

"Would you find it interesting, Mr. Agresta, if I told you that a briefcase matching that description was found in Monsieur Paquet's office this morning? I can only assume that it is the very same briefcase that you claim was stolen in Basel."

"I'm not 'claiming'. I'm saying that's what he said."

"Mr. Agresta, *that* is precisely the definition of the word."

Max's mind spun to catch up to events.

"Mr. Agresta?"

"I didn't have anything to do with his death," Max said.

Leverd pressed, "How do you think a briefcase, stolen in Basel, finds its way to Paris within a few hours? How does that happen?"

"I don't know... Maybe, after I left him at the train station, Paquet returned to the bank and found it?"

"Hmm. That is a good answer. Produced rather quickly, don't you think?" Leverd complimented unctuously. "Perhaps you and he traveled together and the attack you describe happened in Paris?"

"I didn't go to Paris with him!" he said. "I'm here in Zurich."

"But to believe your story, after you met with Monsieur Paquet, two American men dressed as birds attack the bookseller and steal his briefcase. You then share a taxi to the train station and go your separate ways. The next morning he's found dead with the stolen briefcase by his side. Coincidental, no?" The inspector said nothing for a few seconds before adding, "Perhaps you didn't kill Monsieur Paquet but your involvement seems pivotal."

"I am in Zurich and couldn't have committed the crime," said Max, becoming both agitated and defensive.

"You are speaking as if you planned your elaborate alibi." He paused to turn the discussion back in his favor. "True. You are in Zurich now but it is only four hours by train... even shorter from your meeting in Basal. It would be easy enough to follow Paquet here and return back in time for your conference. You are at a conference, aren't you? The front desk clerk said that you were registered under the conference rates. You will be staying until tomorrow?"

Max ignored the detective work the inspector had done to find him. He responded to the main accusation that he would kill the Frenchman. "That's crazy to think I would kill him. Why would I have any reason to do that?"

"That's what we will find out. There is enough evidence to have a further talk with you." Max's worse nightmare flowered and took on new life. "Perhaps when the pathology results and the fingerprints analysis are complete, your involvement will become clearer. But there are many questions and all the answers seem to point to you."

"But I had nothing to do with any of this. I just told you." Max pleaded. He looked around for help but only saw the face of the interested clerk.

"It's better to talk in person. If you are telling the truth, then you have nothing to worry about. Oh – one more thing." Leverd had left the best for last. "I find it curious that the last two phone calls Paquet made were to a Special Agent for the U.S. Customs Service in Florida, United States."

"Huh?" Max's senses hit their highest level of alertness. He could clearly prove that he didn't kill the Frenchman but the U.S. Customs connection could only mean that Paquet's murder related to the stolen manuscript.

"Surprising coincidence? No? Two people from the same town in

Florida being associated with a man's murder in Paris."

Max had nothing to say.

Leverd continued, "I have arranged for two Zurich plainclothes detectives to pay you a visit later this afternoon. Please make yourself available. And of course, if your story checks out and you had nothing to do with the unfortunate demise of Mr. Paquet, then you will be free to go on your way."

With that statement, the Inspector discontented the line.

# Chapter 28

Max replaced the receiver in its cradle and pushed the phone back to the nosy hotel clerk. Max struggled to make sense of the competing thoughts running through his head. He hadn't killed anyone but the Inspector's litany of circumstantial evidence tied Max to Paquet. If no forensic evidence turned up at the man's shop to put the blame elsewhere, the attention would focus on Max.

Max realized that anything he said would only link himself closer to the dead man and make him a more likely suspect. He'd already contradicted himself in speaking with the policeman and seemed eager to present an alibi. His guilt at having the stolen San Lorenzo must have spilled over to his discussion with the homicide detective; making him appear guilty of murder as well.

Max made his way across the lobby to rejoin the conference, worried that his absence had irritated his boss. Conference attendees exited the ballroom and Max saw Theodore, Spenser in tow, coming toward him. "Everything okay?" Theodore inquired.

"Oh yeah. No problem. Strange – they didn't need to call me out of the meeting for that," Max responded. "How was the speech?"

"It was fine. You know... lots of Eurozone talk. Not much to do about us," said Spenser.

"Well, The Maastricht Treaty that creates the single European currency is going to be a big deal for ease of trade," Max said, momentarily forgetting his talk with the Inspector. Theodore tilted his head back and looked at Max. "But could also put a lot of pressure on our dollar by making a stronger single European currency," Max explained. "The currency exchange rates have a lot to do with what we export and the price of any equipment we might buy here."

"You're right about that," said Theodore. "Right now, we're dealing with eleven currencies. If they get a strong one and flip on us, we could find it very hard to purchase here but it would sure help our exporting and that could be very good for our business," Theodore said. Max didn't miss that he included Max in the 'our'.

"Well, I'm glad I'm hanging out with you guys. You sure know a lot about this stuff," Spenser said.

Theodore put his hand on Max's shoulder and said, "There might be some questions about that in your panel discussion, Max. I'm sure you'll know how to handle it."

"I'll try to say something that sounds logical," Max said, forcing a smile and wondering if the Inspector thought he sounded logical.

"That's all you need to do – you'll do fine. All that lunch speaker did was throw out big words and fancy concepts. But he doesn't know any more than the man on the moon about where the currency is heading," offered Theodore.

"Well. We going to head over there?" asked Spenser.

"Sure," said Max. And the three moved down the hallway to the panel discussion.

Theodore found a seat in the audience while Max headed to the dais and sat behind one of the three microphones. Even though Theodore had seemed preoccupied during the morning sessions, he now sat with his legs spread, his elbows resting on his knees and his chin propped up on his clasped hands. He leaned forward and watched the speakers being introduced. In any normal circumstances, this attention from his boss and the strangers in the audience would have made Max nervous. However, with the Zurich police about to question him in a murder investigation and a stolen 15th century document in his room, all thoughts of stage fright vanished.

As the other two speakers gave their opening remarks, Max revisited his list of pros and cons. A lot had changed and, yet, nothing had; only the stakes had gotten higher. Sure, two cops were coming to question Max about a murdered French bookseller, but he was innocent. Max's first thought was to remain and tell the truth – just wait and tell the policemen what he knew. Yes, he stood accused of murder but he could prove he didn't do it. Or could he? A bunch of people saw him last night. They could vouch for his whereabouts. But that meant getting other conference goers or his boss involved. At the thought, his heart rate sped up and perspiration squirt from every pore.

No way.

Maybe the bartender from last night remembered him? When did he come on duty? Would the investigating policemen wait until he showed up for work to verify his alibi? Maybe in the meantime they'd want to search his room? No. They'd definitely want to search it. Could the policemen enter his room without a search warrant? Did they even have search warrants in Switzerland? Maybe they'd just ask the hotel manager. Why not? They open the safe and find an ancient manuscript – what then? The cops would certainly be suspicious. What was a logistics industry conference attendee, suspected of being involved in the murder of a French antique bookseller with whom he had just met, doing with an ancient manuscript? With that type of connection, proof of being in Zurich last night may not be enough to keep Max from the swirling gravitational pull of a murder accusation.

Even if the policemen believed he wasn't involved in the Frenchman's death, and even if they didn't search his room, and even if they only needed routine background info and politely let him go after questioning, he was screwed. Theodore would know about the police involvement, unanswerable questions would be raised, headcount discussions would be brought up, and Max would be ruined. But if he could solve the manuscript issue, maybe he would be cleared of involvement in the murder during the interim. Maybe his cousin could help him answer the San Lorenzo question.

In his head, he knew that leaving Zurich before the police showed up and skipping the conference with the police on his heels provided only a short-term solution with significant downside. But he couldn't stand the pressure. Eventually, they'd probably catch up to him. He'd use a credit card or show up on a hotel registry or train manifest. If the Paris police wanted to implicate him in a murder, they'd probably get him. Being caught was not a matter of if, but of when. Unless they found the real culprit in the meantime. Worst case, in two days' time, he'd be stopped at passport control on his scheduled flight home. By leaving Zurich and missing his appointment with the police, he only controlled the when. Max also realized that the sooner he left, the better chance he had in making it across the border to Italy, through both Swiss and Italian passport control without detection, and maybe, a resolution.

And so, as the second speaker from a freight management company based in Antwerp finished his opening remarks, Max decided he'd leave the conference without checking out of his hotel room and go to Torino on the next available train.

Theodore presented a significant challenge and Max started thinking about excuses he could offer that would minimize the damage to his reputation. The call from the front desk already implied trouble at home.

Max had to take the chance. His wife chided him that he covered himself well. Max counted on it working now.

"Max? Max!" The moderator said.

Max roused from his strategizing to the sound of the moderator's voice. "Max, we'd love to hear your thoughts."

"Well, thank you," Max said and covered his mental absence by remarking, "My fellow panelists raised several interesting concepts and I just wanted to modify my remarks to reflect their learned opinions." Max vamped as he collected his thoughts. Even though he hadn't heard a word of the previous speaker's remarks, he launched into his prepared remarks without abandon.

Max resisted the urge to give a glorified commercial of his company and spoke at length and in detail about the trends and outlook of the U.S. trucking industry. He pulled statistics from the Bureau of Labor to support his statements about the impending shortage of drivers. He researched government budget data for infrastructure spending on roads, highways, bridges and tunnels. For twenty minutes, Max explained the challenges of his industry and the customers who relied on it. He held the audiences' interest and, during Q&A, the first question was to him.

The Belgian man who had earlier taken Max's saved seat asked, "Based on the driver shortage and the failure of your government to increase their support of port and roadway infrastructures, how is your small company able to improve the situation and adjust for the future?"

"Thank you for your question...." Max said to the Belgian. Max went on to explain his company's strategy for driver retention and how they used their knowledge of the market to drive efficiencies, bridge economic development gaps, and open new markets. When he was done, Max looked up to see Theodore smiling from ear to ear.

More questions followed and Max tried to repress his anxiety. Would the cops be waiting for him outside the door? When no more questioners raised their hands and the panel looked weary from the barrage of inane comments, the moderator stepped in to thank the panelists and announce the afternoon coffee break.

After a round of applause, Max stepped off the podium and approached Theodore and Spenser beside him. "You did a fine job, Max," said Theodore.

"Yeah, you did real good," Spenser concurred. "Boy! They were asking you some tough questions. I don't know how you keep all that information in your head." Max suddenly knew the definition of a useful idiot.

Max worked so hard to get himself invited to give the speech. He researched the information, spent hours preparing the slides and tirelessly rehearsed the presentation. When it came time to perform, he did so without fail. Yet, he couldn't enjoy the adulation he so craved with one eye out for the expected policemen. Also, he dreaded telling Theodore that he needed to leave the conference early. Various excuses vied for prominence in his mind. He said a small prayer that whatever came out of his mouth would make sense.

Max pulled his boss to the side and said, "Theodore, I need to speak with you about something."

Before he could continue, Theodore interrupted him and looked at his watch, "Max, you did a fine job here today. Listen, I promised the little lady that I would take her to see Lake Lucerne. You seem to have this conference in control. We've got a car taking us there and they're probably already waiting in the lobby. She wanted to leave earlier but I wanted to see you speak. You hold down the fort here at the conference and I'll see you back at the office on Monday."

A wave of relief washed over Max and he almost hugged Theodore, "Uh, okay. No problem. See you on Monday."

"Bye, Spenser, it was a pleasure meeting you," Theodore said and after a quick handshake vanished in the crowd.

"Well, you know those big executive types, can't stay for the whole conference. I guess it's just you and me, buddy, for the rest of the event," said Spenser to Max who did a mental jig for his good fortune.

Max again considered staying until the cops showed up and proving his case but the thought of being detained – for even a few days, not making it home as scheduled, calling home for help, handing over the San Lorenzo and losing his chance to turn this situation around – convinced him to stay with his plan, "Yeah, Spenser. Hey, I need to hit my room real quick before the next panel. I'll see you down here in a bit," said Max as he headed across the lobby.

# Chapter 29

Max went straight to the phone as soon as he got to his room. Putting the charge on the room, he dialed '9' for the external line and then his parent's phone number in New Smyrna Beach. After three rings, his father picked up, "Hello?"

"Hey, Dad. It's Max."

"Hello, Max," he cheered in a sing-song voice. "Listen, I can't talk right now. I'm just walking out the door to a community architectural review committee meeting I need to attend. I'll put your mother on the phone. Louise! Louise!" It always baffled Max why his parents would answer the phone when they didn't have time to talk; why not let it go to the answering machine? This time he was very glad they picked up.

"What is it, Tony?" Max heard his mother yell from across the house.

"Dad. Dad!" Max shouted to get his father's attention. "Listen, I need to talk to you. It can't wait."

"Are you in trouble?" The board meeting was forgotten and concern leaped into his voice.

"HELLO? HELLO? MAX? Is that YOU?" his mom chimed in after having apparently picked up the second phone.

"Yeah, it's me, Ma. Listen, Dad, I need you to..." his mother cut him off saying, "Where ARE you?"

"Louise, Please!"

"You sound like you're calling from a tin can," she shrieked.

"I hear him fine, Louise. It's because you're using that crappy phone. I told you to throw that one away."

"Oh. This one? I thought you told me to throw the other one away. Are you sure?"

"Sure, I'm sure," his father bellowed, not the first time using the opportunity to speak to each other on the phone instead of him.

"Mom! Dad! Listen! I need you to be quiet."

"Is there something wrong?" His father remembered to be concerned. "Louise. Hang up the phone! I can't hear Max with you breathing so heavy."

"All right," she sulked. "I'll hang up the phone. Call later Maxy... when your father is not around."

Max hated being called Maxy.

"What's wrong? You are in Switzerland, right? Is everything okay? Is Samantha okay? The boys?"

"Nothing is wrong." His father concern bordered on frantic. Max's father didn't operate well under pressure so it was important to turn this around quickly.

"Everyone is fine. Don't worry. Listen, do you remember asking me if I'd have time to visit your relatives in Italy on this trip? Well, my schedule has cleared up and I'd like to do it."

"Terrific!" Max's father said. "That sounds great. Max, I really appreciate you doing that. You know. I want to keep the family ties going but it's been tough. I haven't really done a good job getting out there myself..."

"Dad!" Max had to stop the man from droning on and on.

Time was of the essence.

Zurich Police.

"Dad. I'm getting on a train in a few minutes to Torino. That's where our relatives are...aren't they? I need you to call your cousin...what's her name? Marisa? The one whose daughter runs the bookstore? Tell them that I'll be in town tomorrow and I'd like to see them."

"Okay. My Italian is not so good. Only a few of those people speak English over there."

"But the book people do...don't they?' Max asked.

"Oh, sure they do," Tony said. "My cousin's husband does. And of course, the daughter does. They go to London and New York each year for the book fair. But I'm not so sure about my cousin, Marisa. I don't think she speaks much English."

"Well, you'll figure it out."

"All right, I'll make the call but what if they're not in? Or out of town? Then what will you do?"

Max hadn't thought of that. He'd assumed all along that the bookstore cousins would be around to give him advice and, hopefully, solve his problem. "I'll see the old country anyway. So it won't be a lost trip. But listen. Dad, you need to do this now. I'm heading to the train station."

"I don't know if I can get to it right away. I've got my board meeting and then I've got to take your mother to the doctor. You know she's having a problem with her wrist. She..."

"Hey, Dad. I'm leaving right now. You bugged the crap out of me to visit your family," Max reminded his father. "And now I made the time to see them. If you want to 'keep the family going' or whatever you say, call your cousin and tell her I'm on my way."

"Okay. I'll call her right now," Max's father relented.

"Now listen...one more thing, here is my cell number," and Max told him the phone number. He repeated it several times due to either his father's hearing of the poor quality of the international call. Wilson and the accounting department be damned. "You can call me on it anytime. And you can give it to your cousin. I'll have it with me on the train."

"That's amazing! You mean I can call you anytime from my phone and I can reach you in Italy on your cell phone? You know when I was your age, you couldn't even call overseas without going through an operator..."

"Yeah, Dad. It's called technology. Anyway, when you get in touch with your cousin and make the arrangements, call me right away. Thanks. Love you."

"Love you, too. Okay. I'll call Marisa now and I'll call you after I arrange something with her."

"Thanks again." Max hung up the phone and threw his clothes and effects into his roller style carry on suitcase and retrieved his toiletries from the bathroom. Lastly, he opened the room safe, took the remaining cash from his Swiss bank account withdrawal, and put the mailing tube containing the manuscript into his messenger bag. He really didn't need to check out; the hotel had his credit card on file and could fax him the bill later. In fact, Max thought that he really should avoid the front desk and any of the conference goers altogether. He'd rather the Zurich Police believe that he was still here because the time wasted searching for him would give Max distance. After five minutes, Max had everything packed up and in order. He stepped out of his Dolder Grand Hotel room for the last time.

***

A car horn, a loud bus, a street vendor, or maybe some construction noise, something...something pierced Tommy's deep, enjoyable sleep. And when it did, Tommy knew all too soon, that they had overslept.

"What de fuck time is it?" a startled Tommy said to a still sleeping Sully. "Wake up Sully, you dimwit! You were supposed to wake me up!"

"Wha...? What? What's going on?" Sully said as Tommy punched his shoulder.

"Come on. We gotta go!" Tommy said. "It's almost four o'clock. We were supposed to get up at ten."

Tommy buttoned up his shirt and stuffed the shirt tails in as he left the room. A groggy Sully, his shirt completely unbuttoned and trying to work the sleep sand out of his eyes, trailed behind. The room door slammed in his face as tried to catch up to Tommy. At the elevator, Tommy continued, "We gotta get downstairs and find Edgar's guy at the conference. I wanna get that manuscript before the meeting breaks up and I don't know where he'll be. We gotta get him now."

Tommy bounded out of the elevator into the lobby and ran up to the young female clerk, "I'm trying to reach a friend...a Max Agresta."

"What room is he in?" the petite young woman with a sharp chin, aquiline nose, and straight brown shoulder length hair, asked. Her slender eyebrows arched gently as she smiled. She was nobody's pushover. She may not have been as suspicious as the clerk this morning – after all the men inquiring were now hotel guests – but she responded with the proper discretion saying, "I'm sorry, I cannot give out the room number... but I can connect you to his room by phone."

"Okay. Yeah. Call his room for me." Tommy flashed a big shark toothed grin at Sully that said, 'we got him now'.

"I'm sorry. What did you say the gentleman's name is?"

"Agresta, A-G-R-E-S-T-A," spelling it out, slowly and over pronouncing, like he would to a deaf person. "Max Agresta."

"There is no one here by that name," the clerk responded.

"Whatdya mean? No one here by that name? He told me he would be here!" Tommy charged, faulting the clerk.

"I'm sorry sir. I can only tell you he is not here now," she explained. She typed feverishly on the computer and after some loud keystrokes looked up. "Ahh, I see. He was originally booked here, but now he is at another hotel."

"Which hotel?" Tommy leaned far across the counter invading the clerk's space and sharing his three-day-old breath.

"The one that is hosting the conference," the clerk said as she leaned back away from the encroaching guest. "Most of our guests are going there every morning."

"You mean the conference isn't here?" Sully asked.

The clerk replied, "No, sir. We do not have conference facilities," she said, pointing out the tiny lobby with only one entrance and the front desk and elevators occupying less space than most Americans had in their family rooms.

"Holy Shit! You mean I been in the wrong place the whole time!" Tommy said.

"I do not understand what you mean," the clerk said, becoming a little unnerved. While she didn't feel threatened exactly, she did not understand this strange man's outburst.

Tommy started pacing around the lobby like a caged tiger.

Sully stepped forward and said, "I'm sorry for my friend; he gets a little nuts at high altitude." He giggled. Aside from the warm smile and the twinkle in his eyes, Sully looked scary. He held his coat in the crook of his right arm. He hadn't bothered to button up his shirt and his pale, freckled skin, covered in gray chest hair, was not a sight anyone wanted to see, least of which a young Swiss hotel clerk. But his smile was genuine and his apology sincere. "We overslept and we're very tired. It's not your fault," he said putting his hand out attempting to stroke the clerk's arm. With the most charm he could muster after having been roused from slumber, Sully asked, "Can you tell me where the conference is?"

The clerk pulled her arm back behind the counter in a reflexive manner. After a slight hesitation, she decided that divulging the information broke no privacy rules and would result in them leaving her alone. "The Dolder Grand Hotel," she responded.

"Thank you. See that, Tommy?" Sully poked Tommy with his easily gained information. "Ask nicely and you get the information you want." Turning back to the clerk he said, "Now, I'm not familiar with the city. Is that hotel close by?"

"It is not too far. But it is best to take a taxi. Ten minutes by taxi."

"You see that Tommy? Ten minutes by taxi," Sully said, speaking to him as if he were talking a jumper down from the ledge. "We'll be at the conference in ten minutes."

"Okay. Let's go!" Tommy said as he stormed out.

Sully followed but not before bending down and reading the clerk's name tag and saying, "Thank you...Lucie."

# Chapter 30

What should have been a three-minute walk to the taxi stand turned into fifteen. Tommy insisted that the taxi stand lay in the other direction. Sully tried to argue but ended up following him instead. Sully turned out to be correct yet still got yelled at by Tommy and blamed for the delay.

"Do you even know what he looks like?" Sully asked Tommy once they finally got into the cab.

"You're the one that said you saw him getting into the cab in Basel with the old man. Didn't you tell me that you saw the mailer tube in his bag?" Tommy asked.

"Yeah. I mean..." Sully backpedaled, "I saw him from the back but I kind of have a general idea of what he looks like."

"I'll be able to find him! They'll be wearing name tags, you dimwit," Tommy sneered. "Plus, I think I may have seen him before – at Carmelo's. Edgar says I'll recognize him; he's a tall skinny kid."

***

Max stepped out of the elevator into the lobby, his eyes scanning to avoid conference goers and plainclothes Zurich policemen. Hoping the coast clear, he took quick steps toward the entrance. Before reaching the revolving doors a bell boy stepped up to him to help him with his luggage.

"Allow me, sir," the young man said as he reached for Max's luggage. Believing that refusing would probably slow down his exit, he allowed the bell boy to take the roller bag but held on tight to the messenger bag containing the mailing tube.

"Did you have a pleasant stay?" the bellboy continued.

"Yes, thank you."

"Taxi to the airport sir?"

"No, the train station."

"Do you have your tickets already?"

"No. Can I buy them at the train station?"

The bellboy passed the roller luggage to the valet and gave some instructions in German. "Come with me, sir. You can purchase your tickets here and it will be much easier and faster. The lines at the train station can be very long."

Max looked toward his bag being rolled outside to the valet stand outside. He grabbed hold again of the tube in his messenger bag seeking reassurance.

Sensing Max's concern the bellboy said, "Don't worry, sir. Your bag is safe and will be waiting for you when you're done." The bell boy guided Max to the concierge and introduced Max, "François, this is Mr...?"

Max responded, "Agresta, Max Agresta." Unhappy about the time and attention his departure caused, he still almost laughed at the way his name came out like 'Bond, James Bond.'

"Where will you be going today, sir?" the concierge asked.

"Torino, Italy."

"Maxy!" The big man bellowed as he slammed his meaty hand on Max's back. "You gave a damn good speech up there; the only guy who knew what he was talking about. What you up to?"

The concierge tapped his pen on his desk as the big man asked his guest about his plans.

"Hey, Snowman. I'm trying to sneak out of here to see my cousins in Torino." Turning to the concierge who'd begun typing on his computer, "I'd like a one-way ticket on the next train to Torino."

***

Tommy reached into his pocket to pull out his remaining Swiss Francs to pay the taxi fare as they pulled up to the front of the hotel. A doorman ran over to open the rear passenger door, "Checking in, sir?"

"No, we're here for the conference," Tommy said as he brushed by him. The two men, one of them still tucking in his shirt, walked into the lobby without tipping.

"Wow, this is a fancy place," said Sully while buttoning the last button on his shirt and then running his fingers through his Vitalis hair. Sully wandered a few steps, took a deep breath and did a 360 to soak in one of Europe's great hotel lobbies.

"Shit – there he is," said Tommy under his breath.

"Wha? What?" Sully came to attention beside Tommy.

"Over there, standing next to the guy with the silver cowboy belt buckle and the rapper jewelry."

"Maybe that's his partner in this thing."

Sully's suggestion hit the mark – Tommy wished he'd been as quick to make the connection.

Sully pointed out, "Look. His bag's got a tube sticking out of it."

"Let's go sit over there at the bar and keep an eye on him," said Tommy.

***

"What class, sir?" the concierge asked. Normally, Max would have saved the money and gone second class but in this fancy hotel in front of the concierge and his new best friend from Chicago, Max said, "First Class, please."

"The next train you say?" asked the concierge to clarify. "Let me check. I believe it leaves in less than an hour."

Snowman noticing that he'd interrupted placed his paw on Max's shoulder saying, "That sounds nice. If you got time, let me buy you a shot before you leave. I'll be right over at the bar." He pointed to the bar across the lobby and stepped away from the concierge's desk.

The concierge continued, "Hmmm. Sir, the next train departs in fifty minutes. Shall I put it on your room bill?"

"That will be fine," said Max.

"What room number are you, sir?"

Max wanted to slip out of the hotel and the conference unannounced. But with the train ticket purchase and meeting Snowman in the lobby, Max was leaving a pretty healthy trail for the police to follow. Still, he'd cross the Italian border in two and half hours. Max told the concierge his room number.

"Do I have enough time to make the train?"

"Yes, of course. No problem. It is only ten minutes to the train station; so no worry. The train goes to Bellinzona, Chiasso, Milano Porta Garibaldi and then to Torino Porta Nuova. You must change trains three times."

\*\*\*

"The big guy is coming over," Sully announced to Tommy when he saw the man who had been talking to Max walk straight to them in the lobby bar.

Snowman sat on a stool and got the barman's attention. Behind the bar, a short, bald man with only the faintest wisps of hair on the sides arranged bottles in preparation for the evening. "You got any Fernet Branca left?"

"I'm sure we do, sir," said the bartender.

Tommy saw his opening and asked the big man, "What's that drink you just asked for? Is it a Swiss thing?"

"Nah. It's Italian," said Snowman, "I just tried it last night for the first time. My friend Maxy, introduced me to it. It's an *amarro*, which means bitter; supposed to be good for your digestion. But Man, it pops a kick!"

"Did you say Max? Max Agresta?" Tommy asked feigning innocence.

"Yeah, that's him. You know him?" Snowman answered. "We were just talking over there at the concierge and I told him I'd buy him a shot before he leaves."

He partially stood and halfway extended his hand, "I'm Sylvester Snow but everybody calls me Snowman."

"Oh, yeah. Hi," Tommy responded without meeting the man's proffered hand. "Where's Max going?"

"Torino. He's over there now buying train tickets for the next train; leaving like in less than an hour – thought he might have time for a quick drink."

"That's interesting. Hey," Tommy said turning to Sully, "I just remembered that we were gonna meet those guys right around now."

Sully stared at him dumbly and only slowly nodded to Tommy's ploy. "It was nice meeting you, Snowman," Sully said as they left the bar.

"Don't you want to wait for Max and have a shot with us?"

"Maybe later, we gotta go." Sully and Tommy headed toward the front door to catch a cab back to the train station; making sure to stay as far away from Max and the concierge desk as possible. Tommy thought there was little chance that he would recognize them but it was better to be safe than seen.

As they stepped out the front doors and into the portico of the Hotel, the same doorman, having been stiffed on the way in, glanced at the men's return and indifferently asked, "Taxi, sir?"

"Yeah, to the train station," Tommy barked without reaching into his pocket. When they were on their way Sully asked Tommy, "Why didn't we just take the manuscript from Max there in the hotel lobby?"

"Whadya crazy? You see how many people were there?" Tommy scrunched up his face and shook his head in disbelief. "We'd never get away with it. Plus, he's leaving anyway. We know where he's going and how he's getting there. We just get on the same train as him and we'll have plenty of opportunity. When he's on the train, he's gotta go to the bathroom sometime. When he's alone, we'll just pop him and take the manuscript."

Sully nodded at the explanation.

Tommy continued, "But, we still gotta get our stuff at the hotel. We left in such a hurry that we didn't check out or pack our crap. When we get to the train station, I'll run back to the hotel and take care of packing our things and I'll meet you back at the train station. You buy us two tickets on the next train to Torino. That's very important. We wanna be on the next train! That way we'll have several hours to steal the manuscript and take care of Max without witnesses."

***

"You get straightened out with your tickets?" Snowman asked Max when he approached the bar.

Max nodded, "I'm heading out now in a few minutes. Last night was a lot of fun."

"Snowman is a social lubricant," he said of himself. "Barkeep!" he called. "Two Fernet Brancas, neat." The barman turned to fulfill the request.

"So you headed to see your family, huh? That's nice."

"Yeah, I'm a little nervous. I don't speak any Italian."

"Ahh, don't worry about that. You'll do fine."

The barman placed the two glasses down, "Two Fernet Brancas. Am

I missing anything?"

"Hair!" Snowman responded and let rip a belly laugh. The barman's face fell and turned up his nose. Max cringed in embarrassment.

"I'm just kidding. Look at me, I'm no better" Snowman said as he continued to laugh and point to his own receding hairline. Swallowing the first sip and grabbing his chest, Snowman said, "I don't know how you drink it. It tastes like cough medicine."

"I had this for the first time when I was nine years old," Max explained. "I had just come home from a carnival and after eating tons of cotton candy and chili cheese dogs and going on the rides. My stomach was upside down and I wanted to puke. When I got home, my father had me drink this…as a digestive."

"And it settled your stomach down?" Snowman asked.

"No – I threw up all over the floor." Max gave the punch line with great comic timing. "But I did feel better after that."

Snowman gave another hearty laugh, raised his glass and said, "*Cent anni.*"

"*Salute,*" Max responded with a huge smile. Tension in his neck and shoulders released. Since making his decision to go to Torino, everything had worked out right. They drained the shots and Max went to the front entrance relieved to be reunited with his luggage and glad to be catching a taxi to the Zurich Hbf.

# Chapter 31

Tommy's chest heaved trying to catch his breath from lugging the two bags the three and a half blocks from the hotel. For once, Sully's stupid, yellow 'Member's Only' jacket didn't annoy him. Frustrated and wondering how he would meet up with Sully at the train station – Boom! There it was – the bright yellow jacket, like a beacon in a storm of drab Zurich train travelers.

"Did you get the tickets?" Tommy asked throwing Sully's bag at him in the process.

Sully held his arm out, pushing the tickets further away to allow him to read the fine print.

"You need longer arms," Tommy joked.

"I left my readers back at the hotel."

"Shit!"

"Wha…?"

"I left my fuckin' knife back there!"

"Don't look at it like it's my fault," Sully whined.

"If you woulda woken up!" Tommy glared. "Where we going?"

"Ground level, Track 8," Sully responded calmly. "We gotta move fast. Train's leaving in six minutes."

"The train to Torino?'

"One of them," Sully replied.

The men started to move without delay toward the track. Between breaths, Tommy squeezed out, "Have you seen him?"

"Yeah, I saw him coming out of a sandwich shop with a bag. He'll be on the train."

After reducing their jog to a brisk walk, "Let's get on the first car and then walk toward the back. This way we hit every car looking for him. Once we see him, we can keep an eye on him from behind and decide when to make our move."

Sully countered, "Maybe we should go to the last car and walk forwards, this way we can see him before he sees us...in case he recognizes us."

"He's not going to recognize us!" Tommy yelled.

"Whatever you say, Tommy." Moments later the train rolled up to the island platform. From where they were standing, the middle of the train would be in front of them when it completely stopped. Tommy turned to the right and started to run alongside the train as it slowed to a stop. In his haste, he jostled several other passengers who had already positioned themselves along the platform. The conductor stepped out of the first car behind the locomotive, and Tommy called to him, "Is this the train to Torino?" The conductor had his other duties to perform at the stop but quickly glanced at Tommy's proffered ticket and said, "*Ja, Ja,* this train."

Now that they were on the train, Sully screwed up his face and winced as he told Tommy the news he had been withholding. "Tommy, this train isn't going to Torino, it's going to Bellinzona and then we change to another train going to Chiasso." He said this butchering the names of the cities with his American accent.

"And then we go to Torino?" Tommy asked.

"No. That one goes to Milano – Porta Garibaldi and then we get on the one for Torino Porta Nuova."

"Holy shit! How many changes is that?" Tommy asked.

"Three." Before Tommy could start yelling the train lurched forward and they were on their way to Torino – with three changes in between. "Tommy, you told me to get the next train to Torino and that's what they sold me. When you showed up and threw the bag at me, I was looking through the tickets and almost had a heart attack. I was going to ask you if we wanted to change maybe to a simpler route."

"No. If this is what Max is taking then we gotta take it too." Tommy paused for a second and thought, "Actually, it could be a lot better for us. Three changes in three different stations means we'd have a lot more opportunity to swipe the manuscript from Max...and maybe throw him off the train," he laughed.

"You're not serious about that," Sully asked with concern, mindful of their actions in Paris and scared of exposure with a second attack on the American.

"Why not? You don't think if he had a chance that he'd do the same to us? He's our only link to the French guy; we get rid of him and we're home free. Isn't it obvious that he's playing a game and double-crossing me, you and Edgar."

"That would be a triple cross," Sully offered.

"Whatevah. Let's check out the passengers. And remember...if you see him, don't react, just walk past him. We got the element of surprise 'cause we know where he's goin'."

***

Max grabbed a sandwich and a beer for the trip and headed toward the underground walkway to his train. When he got to his designated track, he checked his ticket for the car number against the bulletin board posting the train 'consist' which listed the order of every railcar number for every train using that particular track for the day. Max made his way to his seat, the third to last window seat in the last car, and placed his luggage on the rack before sitting. With his messenger bag and manuscript at his feet, he set out his sandwich and beer on the fold out tray.

The train started moving while passengers moved to find their seats. From half a car away, he saw a pudgy man approaching wearing a sports jacket, silk tie, and slacks. The short, bearded man had longish gray-shocked hair which stuck wildly out of place either by design, neglect or having been disturbed in his hurry to catch the train. The man sat down next to Max in the aisle seat after placing his Louis Vuitton carryon bag on the luggage rack above the seat.

"Hello," said Max, still in his suit, tieless and feeling underdressed next to the man.

"Hello. That is a good idea," the man said indicating Max's lunch. "The food on this train is not good."

Max chuckled. "You come on this train often?"

"Yes...well I used to, quite often – in my previous business. You must, too, because you are so well prepared."

"Actually, no – this is only my second time in Europe. It is really my first time because I visited Rome as a kid but I don't really remember it."

"*Bravo*. You must have remembered something because you are a real European traveler now." The man had a slight accent. "You are here for work?"

"Yes, I spoke at a conference in Zurich. I'm Max Agresta." And put his hand out to shake.

The man shook his hand with a faint grip but did not introduce himself. Rather he said, "That's very nice to give a speech, especially for someone so young. Will you be traveling here in Europe often?

"I hope," Max said, basking in exactly the kind of conversation with exactly the kind of European businessman that Max he had always wanted to have. They continued the small talk.

***

Tommy and Sully made it through three of the seven railcars before being stopped by the conductor who checked their tickets and pointed them back to their seats at the front of the train. Tommy insisted that they walk toward the rear but the conductor found it difficult to understand his accent and tortured grammar.

Sully finally said in a loud slow voice while pantomiming, "We want to drink." The conductor nodded, took his ticket puncher to their documents, and moved on. To continue the rouse, the men decided to grab a beer at the bar car.

"Have you seen him?" asked Sully.

"Not yet. We got three more cars to go. Let's take these beers with us." Tommy smiled. "The bottle will make a nice weapon."

As they continued their walk toward the rear of the train, Sully noticed his partner's frustration starting to grow. It concerned him that they hadn't found Max yet and the longer it took to find him, the angrier Tommy would get. If Max wasn't on the train, Sully thought, Tommy would break the beer bottle over his head instead of Max's. Even if they found Max in the last car, Tommy appeared so amped up that he might just attack the man on the train. Either way, the result would not be good.

They continued searching through the remaining three railcars and when they got to the end of the train, Tommy spun on Sully and said, "He's not fuckin' here!"

"Maybe we missed him in the first cars while the passengers were still finding their seats?" Sully said hopefully. "Or maybe he was in the bathroom when we checked his car. Let's just calm down and think this through. He's gotta be on this train."

Tommy, for once, actually listened. It was possible that they missed him; Sully had seen Max at the train station, and they knew that Max was headed to Torino. He had to be on this train. If they missed him now, at least they had three train changes to catch him.

***

"And I just got passed over for promotion," Max continued on, "and now my boss is a guy I used to work with. He's being a real jerk and he put me on a list of people to be fired from the company. Part of my mission here was to prove my value and hopefully keep my job."

"I hope you succeeded," his seat neighbor said. "But even if you leave the company, maybe it is for the best. It may be the push you need to follow your dreams and pursue what you really treasure."

They had been talking nonstop for about an hour.

"Yeah, and the director's job was not really the one I wanted anyways. It's all paperwork crap, anyway," Max said.

His companion let out a huge roar of laughter. The man, realizing that Max was not in on the joke, said, "Do you know the meaning of the name 'Agresta'? That is your name, No?"

Max shook his head indicating that he did not know the etymology of his surname.

"In Italian, it means rustic...But it also has a second meaning of... how do you say? Sour grapes," he laughed again.

Max swallowed his smile in embarrassment.

The man said, "Don't worry, we all feel that way sometimes. It's a defense mechanism. We all have ways of protecting ourselves from being hurt. You know, when I was your age, I was consumed by making money to pay for my lifestyle instead of building my career."

Max tilted his head looking at the man quizzically.

"You don't understand the difference? If you focus on doing good, honest work, the money and promotion will follow. Build the career first and the money will follow. Build the money first, and the career...?"

He paused and looked off out at the passing scenery. "I took shortcuts...I cheated, more precisely. It paid off at first. But ultimately, it cost me my family, my wife, my reputation, my career and, eventually, my freedom."

Max turned in his seat, enthralled by the story.

"I had a lot but kept none of it. What I treasured, I lost." Turning to Max and looking him in the eye, "Always remember, it's not what you make...It's what you keep."

"I'm afraid that I'll spend the next thirty years in the same position doing the same thing and never get promoted."

Laughing, the man said, "Max, I've known you for less than an hour and I highly doubt that. You are a force to be reckoned with. Someone will recognize your talent."

"There is a real big concern that is even worse than getting fired," Max confessed. His fellow passenger listened with concern and, for some reason, Max trusted him enough to voice his deepest fears. The concerns, damned up for the past few days, released, "I've got this business situation where my partner has led me into a very difficult position. I'm risking a lot of money and even my job. To be honest, it could be worse than that. My wife doesn't know anything about it. I was trying to surprise her with the money I would earn. But she's going to be pissed when she finds out what I've done. She's already warned me about my business ventures before. I'm afraid that this one will push her over the edge."

The passenger didn't directly address Max's admissions. But after several moments he spoke. "I've learned that the choice of your spouse is probably the most important decision you will ever make. It is nice to pick a pretty and nice girl, but the one that is a true partner of yours and makes you a better person, one that lifts you up. That is the one to marry!"

"My wife is pretty and smart," Max said.

"Ahh. But she must be good for you too?" he questioned.

"Very much so."

"Then you must share with her your situation. She will help you. You are meant to work together."

"But I feel like I'm shirking my responsibility if I put this burden on her."

"Nonsense! In a marriage, you are to build upon each other and pull each other up!"

Max's travel partner became more serious. "Your decisions affect her and she needs to be part of it. Besides, if she is smart like you say, she will help find a solution to your problem."

"Maybe she'll just be disappointed."

"Maybe. But imagine how disappointed she'll be if things fall apart and you never told her?"

"You're probably right."

"Of course, I am right."

Max's seatmate gave him a lot to think of. To change the subject and relieve his musings, he probed rather aggressively, "What happened to you? Are you still married?"

"No. Not anymore. We were one of those couples who were not good for each other." Max was taken aback by the frank response. The seatmate continued, "She was certainly beautiful…and smart! She was at the top of her field, but she was not good for me," he said sadly. "And maybe I was not good for her." Looking off in the distance he was lost in reminiscence. Shaking himself from the reverie and admitting to himself, perhaps for the first time, "But I don't blame her; it is not her fault."

The man leaned over and looked at Max, placed his fingers together like he was holding his thoughts at the tips of his fingers in a gesture to focus the listener's attention on a fine and critical theoretical point, willing it to become tangible, and explained, "But with her, I became a worse version of myself. I should not have let that happen. I should have been the spouse to make her a better version of herself. Instead, we both let each other down. And believe me, in that case, you're better off single."

"Was she a good partner?" Max asked. He sensed the man's heartbreak.

"Yes... I guess you could say we were good partners in crime," he said.

\*\*\*

The train slowed to the station by the time Tommy and Sully finished walking to the front of the train. They even checked all of the bathrooms along the way. Still no sign of Max. Sully looked out of the window and said, "This is it – Bellinzona. We gotta get out here and change to the next train."

"Okay good, get out fast and head to the exit. Make sure nobody passes us without us seeing them," Tommy said.

As soon as the train came to a stop, Tommy bounded out and headed toward the only exit. He and Sully positioned themselves on either side of the steps leading to the underground passage. The only other means of getting to the passageway was an elevator where two elderly people were waiting. Several passengers departed the train and walked past the men. After about two minutes, a whistle sounded and the conductors got back on the train which pulled out of the station. Within thirty seconds the platform was clear of all people. Tommy and Sully were staring at each other, alone on an empty platform at the Bellinzona rail station.

"What de fuck?!" He's not here, Sully! He wasn't on the train!"

Sully kept his guard up, happy that they had thrown the empty beer bottles in the trash instead of keeping them for weapons.

\*\*\*

The conductor announced the train's arrival into Milano Centrale. "Don't we need to go through passport control?" Max asked, surprised at how quickly the time had flown.

"No, with the European Community they've done away with much of that. They treat it as a domestic route...no problem now."

Max breathed a sigh of relief, "You know, I almost didn't take this train. When I purchased my tickets I asked for the next train to Torino and they wanted to give me a ticket that had three connections."

"Yes, the train that goes to Bellinzona," the man said.

"Fortunately, I also asked the concierge if the next train was the fastest way to get to Torino. He told me no, that for a quicker trip, I could leave a little later on a train that would arrive earlier. And I'd only need to change once, here in Milan."

The man laughed, "Ha ha, you need to be careful how you ask the Swiss questions. They are very exact. Ask for the next train and that is what you will get. Ask for the quickest train and it might be a different answer."

"Good thing I thought of it; by leaving fifteen minutes later, I'll get to Torino thirty minutes earlier. Plus, I got to meet you," Max said.

"It was my pleasure," the man said and smiled.

While the train came to a crawl pulling into the station, the man leaped from his seat, as if he had forgotten something, and squeezed past Max. "Excuse me. It was nice meeting you," he nodded as he made his way to the exit. "*Arriverderci.*"

As the man became swallowed up in the mass of passengers exiting, it suddenly dawned on Max that he had been so self-absorbed that he never bothered to ask the man's name. He cringed, ground his teeth and dropped his head. Stupid. Self-centered. Rude. He looked down at the floor of the vacated seat and spotted the man's business card which must have fallen out. Max picked it up and read it, thinking he'd send a thank you note or email his neighbor when he got home. The card read, *Professore Pier Luigi Scarsi, Licei Classici di Milano.*

# Chapter 32

Max grabbed his luggage and stepped off of the train in the Milan Central Station, the largest train station in Italy and one of the busiest in all of Europe. Built during Benito Mussolini's rule, the station's architectural style borrowed from both the schools of Liberty and Art Deco. Sculptures portraying the power of the fascist regime adorned the façade and interior. A great canopy of structural steel arched across the twenty-four platforms of the terminus style station creating an impressive indoor terminal. Each day, more than three hundred thousand passengers traveled through the busy hub.

On this day, one American man, Max Agresta, hounded by police and carrying a stolen antiquity, made his way from the inbound ICE train from Zurich to the tracks servicing the slower, domestic service that would take him to Torino's Porta Nuova.

Max made his way to the correct platform and the waiting train to Torino. At his hour, the passenger traffic was light. Several people boarded the train without stopping while a few milled around, enjoying the conversations with the people that came to see them off or grabbing a quick smoke in the huge open space.

In all the time he spent talking to his seat neighbor, he forgot that he was waiting for a call from his dad confirming the arrangements with his cousins. He set down his bag and pulled his cell phone out. He saw that he must have inadvertently turned it off and corrected the issue –wondering if he had missed his father's call.

The pay phones were a short walk back but Max thought that if he kept his call short, it shouldn't be a big deal with his accounting department. The decision was made for him when the phone started ringing. He picked up on the first ring.

"Hello, Max?" his dad's voice sounded clear and strong.

"Hey, Dad. Did you talk to your cousin?"

"Yes. Everything is set. Marisa will pick you up at the train station. When you get to the station in Torino, you need to go outside to the street. She can't come in to meet you because parking is impossible there. She drives a red Fiat 500 *Cinquecento* and she'll be wearing a red coat. She says to come straight out and she'll see you."

"Dad, she doesn't need to do that."

"She insisted. You'll stay at her house tonight. Her daughter, Carlota, is in Bologna today, but she'll get back tomorrow. You're going from Milan, right?"

"Yeah."

"Then she'll know the train," his dad said. "Where are you now?"

"I'm at the Milan train station."

"Terrific. I hear it's beautiful."

Suddenly realizing how long they had been on the phone Max said, "Dad, thanks a ton. I've got to go. I'll talk to you when I get there. Love you."

Max hit the end button and relaxed. Before he could put the phone back in his bag, it rang again. "Hey, Dad. What do you want?"

"Max Agresta?" a woman's voice inquired.

"Yes," Max replied. "Who is this?"

"This is Special Agent Grace Hemmer from the U.S. Customs Service in Jacksonville, FL."

"How did you get this number?" Max blurted out. His mind raced as his fears coming true.

"Rhonda in your accounting department was very helpful. I've learned a lot about you in the past few hours since I received a call from the Paris Police."

"I had nothing to do with that man's death," Max said.

"That is a subject for the Paris police to discuss with you. I'm more interested in a certain manuscript and how you came to possess it." Grace thread a fine needle so as not to spook her prey. "I only am interested in recovering the San Lorenzo. Besides, you're not a killer. Are you?"

"No! Of course not."

"Good. But what do you know of the San Lorenzo? You met with Mr. Paquet about it recently. Right?"

"I don't know what you are talking about!" Max said. His eyes stung around the edges as his tear ducts reacted to the news – a special agent from the U.S. had tracked him down and knew everything. The bile in his mouth tasted of fear.

"The manuscript was stolen from the Capitular Archives of the Archdiocese of Turin several years ago."

"I didn't steal it!" Max cried.

"But you had it with you when you met with Mr. Paquet in Basel yesterday. Your business card was found in a dead man's wallet and your name was written in his planner scheduled for a meeting in Basel." Grace let the information wash over Max.

She continued, "It seems that you were there to discuss the sale of the San Lorenzo and today, the man is dead."

"I really don't know anything about his death. As I told the police inspector, I saw him for the last time in Basel." Max's worst case scenario was coming true. Shortness of breath and cold clammy skin returned as it had several times in the past two days. The stress changed his physical appearance and became nearly debilitating.

"There is every indication that the death of Mr. Paquet involves the stolen San Lorenzo." Max looked up to see a few straggling passengers darting for the train and noticed that aside from the conductor, most of the people previously milling around were gone. He had to get on his train.

The special agent continued, "Are you denying that you tried to sell the San Lorenzo to Mr. Paquet?"

"I don't know what to say," Max replied. No truer words could have been spoken.

As Grace neared her objective, she applied more pressure. "These are very serious crimes and every bit of evidence points to you, Mr. Agresta. Maybe you didn't kill him, but you are somehow involved."

Max heard the echo of the Parisian homicide detective.

"I can help you," she said earnestly. "But only if you let me. Returning that manuscript would be a good start," she said.

What was it he'd just heard from his neighbor on the train? It's not what you make, it's what you keep. Max knew now he was keeping nothing. Certainly not the San Lorenzo. The jig was up. Now, the only thing he could keep was possibly his freedom by staying out of jail. "I'll bring it back to you when I get back to the States." Time had run out. He'd have to throw himself on the mercy of this special agent lady.

"No. I'm coming to get it," Hemmer had found her mark and was going to be the one to bring him in – even if it meant traveling to Switzerland as a private citizen on her own dime. "I'll be in Zurich tomorrow morning. Stay where you are and don't talk to anybody."

Max thought of withholding his destination and letting her fly to Zurich. But this woman meant business. Once she learned of the deceit she'd probably pursue smuggling and money laundering charges with greater vigor. The murder charges were bogus but they would cloud the case; especially if they implicated him as a conspirator to the murder.

At this point, she sounded like his best…only option. In the end, he was frank. "If you want to meet me and get the manuscript back, come to Torino. I'm headed there by train right now to see my cousin. She's a rare and antique book dealer. "

"Who is your cousin and where can I find him?"

"Her. Her name is Carlota Principe, her mom is my dad's first cousin. I've never even met her before but I thought that she could help." Max said. The wind had been knocked out of his sails but a wave of relief passed and he saw a potential exit.

"I'll find it," Special Agent Hemmer said. She paused before finishing her conversation, "Mr. Agresta, the first rule about getting out of a hole is to stop digging. You go to your cousin's bookshop tomorrow and sit tight. I'll meet you there in the afternoon and when you return the San Lorenzo to me, we can discuss your…situation. Until then, don't talk to anyone."

"Agent Hemmer, you've got to believe me. I didn't know this manuscript was stolen. I was just selling it for a friend and I had nothing to do with Mr. Paquet's death. I'm just trying to make a little money. I didn't want this mess."

"I'll see you tomorrow around noon," Hemmer said.

Max hit the 'end' button and put his phone away as he jogged to the train. Before he found his seat, the train started moving backwards out of the station. Special Agent Grace Hemmer was coming to meet him in Torino and take possession of the San Lorenzo – nothing he could do to stop that. But it left him about sixteen hours to develop his alibi and collect evidence against Edgar and hopefully minimize the damage to him and his family.

# Chapter 33

**Torino, Italy**
**Friday, November 14, 1997**

Max woke to the sunlight streaming into his aunt's apartment. Last night, he had fallen asleep before his head hit the pillow and awoke now, unsure of his surroundings. As he brushed off the night's sleep, he thought about the woman who had taken him here last night, his aunt, technically his first cousin once removed as she was the niece of his grandfather, and her rare book dealing family in Torino. He lay in bed recalling some of his grandfather's stories; trying to build the link to the relatives in whom he had placed his last hope.

Max thought back to his time with his grandfather at the dinner table. Long after the meal was served, Nonno Man, who had cooked the meal, sat back and peeled fruit for dessert and talked about the old country, serving famous people at the hotels, and his first weeks and months in America. One story Max never got tired of was about when Nonno Man served a brief stint as a grocery store clerk in Pennsylvania. Max had pleaded to be told over and over how one day when his grandfather worked in the basement rearranging the produce, another worker yelled, "Look Out!" The phrase sounded very similar to the Piedmontese phrase,

'*Lau Caud*' meaning "I'm hot." To which Nonno Man responded, "*Lau Caud Anch'Io.*" (I'm hot, too!). Max never failed to laugh as Nonno Man explained how the box that the co-worker had thrown down, struck him on the head.

Max also delighted in his grandfather's stories about waiting on famous people like Al Copone and Frank Sinatra. But there were other stories, stories about the old country that had a tinge of sadness and regret. Reading between the lines, Max could tell that his grandfather had left to get out of the shadow of his older brother, his aunt's father, a wounded WWI war hero and medical doctor. Nonno Man's attempt to join the army was stymied by his protective brother and he saw no alternative for obtaining self-determination other than to leave the small Italian village for America.

Along with three friends, Max's grandfather purchased a second class ticket for the ocean voyage from Genoa. Irritated that his younger brother would squander his limited financial resources on a second class sea-passage, the older brother went to the shipping line office and traded it down to steerage class to save his brother a few dollars for the New World. Maybe, Max hoped, the protective nature of his distant family extended another few generations and would help him now.

So far it had.

Last night, just as his dad had arranged, his father's cousin, a tastefully dressed woman with slender, erect posture and perfectly coiffed black hair, waited in front of the Porta Nuova train station, wearing a red coat in front of her tiny red Fiat. She must have noticed Max searching the street because she started waving and calling him by his Italian name, "*Massimo!*" Her smile lit up the night as she waved and held out her arms. Max approached the car cautiously and said, "*Zia Marissa?*" His aunt rushed up and grabbed him in a hug, kissing him on both cheeks and speaking to him a mile a minute in Italian.

Not stopping to take a breath, she motioned Max into the car, got into the driver seat and took off. She sped down the narrow streets paying only minimal attention to the road ahead. All of the time, save for a few moments when she honked the horn, she used her hands for talking as much as steering. Every few minutes, his Aunt looked at him sadly and said, "*No si capisce niente?* (You don't understand?)", and then continued to speak rapidly in her language.

One bit of information he did pick up along the fifteen-minute drive was the confirmation that Marissa's daughter, Carlota, who now ran the family rare bookshop, would be returning mid-day tomorrow. He hoped to meet with her earlier and find out the truth about the manuscript and hopefully devise a strategy to minimize his trouble. At this point, there was not much to do but worry and wait.

After rousing from the guest bed, Max made it to the kitchen where his Aunt prepared coffee and arranged a few biscuits on a plate. She rambled in Italian while Max smiled and nodded politely; the strain of feigning comprehension emotionally draining him. The few hours of sleep had provided a little relief but the pressure began mounting as espresso hit his bloodstream and awakened him to the reality of his possession of a stolen manuscript, the accusation of murder, and the imminent arrival of a U.S. Special Agent eager to arrest him.

He needed to clear his head.

Max produced a tourist map that he had picked up at the train station and pointed to it for the benefit of his host. Using pantomime, he asked his aunt's help in marking locations on the map. His aunt put on her glasses and pointed to the location of the apartment, "*Casa,*" she said. In English repeated, "House. My House."

"Thank you. *Grazie,*" Max said and then asked, "Where is the shop, the bookstore? The shop?"

"*Ahh. Libreria?*" his aunt said and pointed to a location of the shop which appeared to be about 15 minutes walking distance from the apartment, noting that the route took him past the Cathedral of Saint John the Baptist which held the Shroud of Turin.

"Thank you. I will walk," Max said trying to keep the English to a minimum and simple.

"No. No. I drive. It's okay," his aunt replied.

"Thank you. But I want to sightsee," Max said holding his hand over his head in an effort to pantomime looking for something.

"Oh, *Va bene*. I see you. *Un po 'più tardi?*" his host replied.

"Yes. Later when Carlota arrives." Max didn't add, 'Hopefully before the Special Agent arrives.'

He said his goodbyes and left the apartment with his bag containing the manuscript. He jogged down steps instead of taking the ancient elevator and burned off his nervous energy walking briskly for a few blocks. He thought about checking out the Shroud of Turin – maybe a miracle would happen. He didn't know what lay ahead but one thing was certain; his life was about to take a dramatic turn…and not for the better.

***

Tommy and Sully left the small used bookstore in a huff and hurried around the outer edges of the Piazza Castello. Not even Sully bothered to notice the grandeur and beauty of Torino's medieval castle and the elegant, baroque 18th century Palazzo Madama. Along the perimeter of the square, they walked blindly past the small cafés, restaurants and bars and small shops like the rare book store they had just left.

"I can't believe that asshole wouldn't even make an offer for this!" Tommy said holding up the book they had stolen from Paris bookstore. "What'd he call it? He had a name for it."

"He flipped through a few pages. Maybe it's just not his thing," Sully reasoned.

Tommy ignored him and left the square and stepped under the covered sidewalk porticos so common in Torino. He strode with purpose looking for the next rare book shop on the hotel clerk marked tourist map hoping this one would buy his Paris loot.

"Yeah, but did you see his face when I showed it to him?" Tommy stopped and said to Sully mid-stride. "He knew what it was. He called it ah, ah… *Tarochi.* That's what he said, *Tarochi.* But he wouldn't make an offer," he grumbled.

"Could he recognize it and know it was stolen from Paris?" Sully asked.

"There's a million fuckin' books in the world! How could they know all of them? Don't be stupid, you moron."

Sully allowed the verbal shot to roll off his back but wondered if his guess had been right.

Tommy took the silence as a need to explain, "It's probably Edgar trying to screw us. He said that Torino would be hopping with antique book dealers interested in this crap. Think about it." Tommy stopped to explain his theory of how Edgar had conspired all along to get him into this unfavorable position. "He sets us up to steal the manuscript. Then he sends us here to sell it and we strike out. So what do we do? We sell the item back to Edgar for a song. Edgar has us do his dirty work and he gets the profit."

Sully could see Tommy working himself up into another tantrum. Convincing himself he was getting screwed.

"Tommy. That was just the first place," Sully said, another outburst would only worsen the situation. "We've got plenty of time to check out the other dealers and sell this stuff."

Tommy's nostrils flared and he shook his head looking down like a dog after being tapped on the nose with a rolled up newspaper. They continued walking down the arcaded sidewalk. Trying to extract his partner from his stewpot, Sully asked, "You know where this is, Tommy?

This is where they filmed the Michael Caine movie '*The Italian Job*'. I thought I recognized it earlier but this is definitely it!" he said as if he had finally solved a great mystery and expected Tommy to present him with an award.

"Why would I care about that? We got other problems to think about."

Sully continued as if Tommy hadn't responded, "I recognized it from these covered sidewalks, this is where the Mini's drove down."

"Holy Shit!" Tommy exclaimed.

"Yeah – this has to be where the chase scene was filmed," Sully explained, glad to get Tommy excited about the subject.

Tommy grabbed Sully's shoulder, pulling him back.

"What?" Sully asked.

"Is that him?" pointing to a figure across the street.

"Who, Micheal Caine?" Sully asked with more interest.

"Is that Edgar's guy? Look across the street, by the pastry store! The tall skinny guy."

"No shit," Sully said in surprise. "You're right."

"Of course I am, numbnuts! Just stand here like you don't know anything," Tommy said. "That shouldn't be too hard for you." Then, adding unnecessarily, "we don't want to be noticed."

The men watched Max continue walking down the arcaded sidewalk; this time a little faster. "I think he saw us. We should cross the street and grab the tube," Sully suggested.

"Nah. He doesn't know we're here. Let's see where he goes first. He'll be easy to follow; he looks like a two by twelve. We need to get him alone – without all these witnesses."

"What are you goin' to do?"

"Whatever we need to in order to get that manuscript," Tommy said.

His cold dead eyes sent a shudder through Sully. Knowing it was too late to escape the vortex, he followed through with Tommy's plan. Sully walked down the sidewalk, keeping pace with the prey. Tommy followed with caution and clenched his fists.

The American stopped again, this time in front of a luggage store. Tommy and Sully stopped and tried to gauge what Max would do. Suddenly, their subject started walking with defined purpose to the corner, turned right and headed down a narrow street with a tram track running down the middle. The sudden move surprised the men but their quarry wasn't acting as if he was being chased. It was more like he suddenly realized that he was late for an appointment and starting walking with determination. The American kept to the narrow sidewalk on the right side of the street.

Tommy and Sully split to opposite sidewalks and maintained their distance. Neither was confident that they could win a footrace with the younger man so stealth was necessary. After two blocks of following, their prey had not looked back even once. He appeared to be headed to the cathedral where the street opened up onto the piazza. Tommy signaled Sully to continue following directly behind the pursued while Tommy took a more roundabout path to approach his target from the opposite side.

Tommy took quick steps across the piazza; never taking his eyes off his quarry and not even looking back to see if Sully was following. He wasn't even sure that Sully had understood his instructions. Their target, rather than walking to the front of the Renaissance-Baroque style cathedral with its wide flight of steps leading to the raised, main entrance, was walking around the southeast side toward the smaller side doors.

Tommy closed the gap and reduced his speed to a walk; keeping light on his feet like he did on his best days boxing. When his mark stopped to further investigate the ornamentation on the side of the church, Tommy turned his back and faced the piazza. His prey's head lifted like a buck twitching in the woods listening for the sounds of the hunter in the tree stand. Tommy didn't want to spook him and took his time making a wide loop around him. Sully, unable to keep up with Tommy, was forty yards behind and walking directly toward the man.

As Sully approached, his prey looked up with a glint of recognition. Realizing his jacket was bright yellow, he hoped it hadn't been recognized before, at the Basel train station or maybe the hotel in Zurich. But his prey's attention was held on Sully just long enough that he didn't see Tommy come up behind him. In a split second, Tommy's fist impacted the man's jaw forcing the target to fall head first into the stone pavement.

Tommy flashed his capped teeth in triumph and shook off the sting in his fist before grabbing the mailer tube from the victim's bag. He walked toward Sully who spun around to reverse course. Before tourist witnesses looked up from the man lying on the pavement, Tommy and Sully had exited the bricked arch leading away to an adjoining piazza.

***

Max saw spots at first and then some light. As the sun grew brighter, he thought he was at his aunt's guest bedroom again. Shapes started to become clearer and he saw the words, "Juventus," with a red lettering. He felt a hand on his shoulder trying to revive him. His face pressed on the pavement staring at the sports page dropped by the man shaking him.

He accepted the help getting up but didn't understand a word the scrawny uniformed security guard was saying. Only the word 'la polizia' made sense. The guard pointed to his post set just inside the small glass side door motioning for him to sit and wait for the authorities.

Max thanked the man and pulled himself from the growing crowd of Good Samaritans. He put his bag on his shoulder and straightened himself out as best he could and walked toward the cathedral.

There was no need to check his bag for the manuscript. It was all clear to him now. The man with the yellow jacket had taken it. That man and, presumably, the man who hit him, had been in Basel to steal the San Lorenzo from the Frenchman. They stole his briefcase thinking it contained the manuscript. When it didn't, they followed him to Paris believing he still had it. And when the Frenchman couldn't produce it, they killed him.

Max squeezed his eyes tightly to hold back the forming tears. But how'd they follow him? He guessed it didn't matter. They finally caught up to him in Torino. His carelessness had reached epic proportions and the resulting trouble became monumental. His emotional pain outstripped his physical pain but his body still ached. His eyes felt like they'd been jammed with ice picks and a searing migraine started forming at the front of his head. He needed to sit, recover and gain strength for what lie ahead; the dark church beckoned.

# Chapter 34

Grace perched on the edge of a sturdy metal chair. Her carry-on bag and purse sat atop a metal table in the center of the small, windowless room. At the international arrivals area of the Malpensa Airport, the red customs light had flashed. It was supposed to be a random check but Grace doubted it. Something, or someone, must have flagged her. When a cursory inspection of her luggage revealed her U.S. Customs badge, the indifferent Italian official, a chubby, defeated looking, and poorly shaven man became agitated and escorted her to this room. The man, who had the eyes of a basset hound, had kept her passport and boarding passes after he left her alone.

That was twenty minutes ago.

The door opened and the basset hound entered followed by an officer she had not seen before. The second official was slim, and despite his thinning hair and gaunt, angular face and beak nose, had a youthful spring to his step – like a juvenile Golden Retriever.

"Grace Hemmer of the United States Customs Service – Special Agent in Charge," the man said in a heavy Italian accent. "I'm Lieutenant Luca Bozzonetti. Sorry for the delay." He said his name as if he were singing an aria. There was no way Grace could remember it let alone pronounce it so she settled on thinking of him as Trigger...the name of the golden retriever she had as a child.

Trigger tilted his head and furled his brows while looking at her. Grace could almost see his pupils focusing, scanning her for clues. She knew what he was doing. She'd done it herself a thousand times. He kept silent while shifting his gaze – looking her over, then back down at his paperwork, and then over to the basset hound – until he finally turned toward her, stared, and broke the silence, "It has been a busy morning. I have a few questions...and then you can go."

Grace nodded. So he's the good cop, she thought.

"What brings you to Italy?"

"Tourism," her voice cracking and strained from the long overnight flight and dehydration.

"Why did you bring your credentials? If you are not here on business, you will not need them."

"I'm so used to carrying my badge; I forgot to leave it at home. And I didn't want to leave it in my car because it might get stolen," she smiled trying to speed the process. She had a suspect to meet and stolen art to recover.

"You were in a rush?"

"Yes. You could say that."

"You purchased your ticket a few hours before the flight here? That is strange for a tourist."

"It was spur of the moment," she smiled, tilted her head and blinked forcing an overly friendly disposition.

"And you flew from...?" he said looking down at his notes.

"Jacksonville to JFK. JFK to Milan," she answered.

"Yesterday afternoon you just decided to drive to the airport and purchase a ticket to Italy?"

Grace didn't answer.

"Quite the jet setter," Trigger remarked. At the jibe, the basset hound nodded his head knowingly. Grace had been on the other side before and she knew that the less she said, the better the outcome. Trigger waited for a response and continued, "To be honest, that sounds like an emergency business trip."

"It's not. My boss told me I needed a vacation and so I booked the trip." She needed to convince them that she was harmless. She had a small window of time to affect her plan.

"Your boss knows that you are here?"

"No."

The lieutenant wrinkled his brow and narrowed his eyes…just like Trigger used to. "So you left without permission?" The officer smelled blood.

"No, I was granted leave. But he doesn't know where I am. We are not required to tell superiors our every move while off duty."

Changing tacks, Trigger said, "Did you touch any of your bags while waiting here?"

"No. The official," indicating Basset Hound, "warned me not to touch my bags."

Trigger motioned for his colleague to check the luggage. Grace kept one eye on the inspection as she tried to engage the officer and answer his questions.

"May I ask? Where are you planning to go?"

"I'm not certain. I'm renting a car and will probably just drive around – see the sights. Italy is known for that, no?"

Trigger sniffed at her and motioned with his eyes to his colleague.

Earlier while waiting, she had practiced her carefree delivery. Hopefully, her easy demeanor, professional courtesy, and luck would get her through this hurdle. Taking the hard approach and asking for Trigger's supervisor would only delay her several hours.

"Am I doing anything illegal?" she questioned. "I am an officer of my government and in the same profession as you. Our countries are allies," she said. "I'm surprised that I'm being treated this way. I expected more..." She let the last sentence trail off under her breath as she turned to see the other official and his discovery.

The basset hound smiled grandly as he produced a set of handcuffs that Grace had hidden in her bag. The grinning official handed the contraband to Trigger who observed the cuffs as if they were an alien device never seen before. Saying nothing, he stared at Grace and let her squirm.

Next, the basset hound pulled out a very thick manila folder. Despite her best efforts, Grace gasped audibly. The folder contained all the information she'd gathered about the San Lorenzo, Max Agresta, and the other suspects. She could make a plausible excuse for the cuffs but the evidence about lost artwork and suspects...probably not.

"These are interesting items. What possible use could handcuffs have if you are not here for work? Do you know that it is a serious offense to do policing in our jurisdiction without the proper approval? Do you have a mutual legal assistance treaty request from the Italian government?"

"I'm not conducting business here," Grace said. She was getting nowhere and time was wasting. She could be delayed for long enough to be inconvenient and let the San Lorenzo escape out of her grasp. She decided to tell the truth or at least a part of it.

"I'm here because I need to see somebody at the Carabinieri Art Squad and deliver that folder." The Lieutenant started to open the folder as Grace raised her voice and continued, "Which is highly confidential and cannot be read by anyone else." Her warning resonated and the officer closed the folder. "I am not here on official capacity but I have some information about a stolen artifact. It's a piece of Italian heritage and I'd like to help you get it back." Playing to their pride might work.

It didn't.

"So send it by mail. Why the last minute flight? Why the hand-cuffs?" the basset hound grumbled.

Grace pulled out her last card. "The officer I'm bringing this information to is...sort of a friend of mine." At that, the men glanced at each other. Office romances were nothing new and they were immediately jealous that this good looking American agent was making a personal visit to some other Italian policeman. Grace saw that they had taken the bait but needed to add a bit more. "We met each other in another case. When I discovered this new evidence about an art theft here, I thought that I'd bring it to him in...person." She was not practiced in the art of flirtation but made her best attempt at batting her eyes.

"This Carabinieri, what is his name?" said the Lieutenant. Every time he said the word 'Carabinieri', the Basset Hound laughed.

Grace hadn't wanted to get into details but said, "Bramante Buratti. He is Commander of Art Squad in Torino."

The men snickered. "Does he know that you are coming?"

"No. It is a surprise."

"So if we call him, he will know your name and can vouch for you?" Trigger asked.

"He would certainly know me." She paused, "But I'd like it to be a surprise."

"Bramante Buratti," the interrogator said as he was writing on his notepad. "What did you say his rank was?"

"He is a Commander, I believe."

"In the Torino Command Center?"

"Yes."

"I'm sorry Miss Hemmer but I will need to ruin your surprise. We will give him a call to check out your story. Of course, at this time of the morning, he will probably be too busy drinking champagne in his fancy office to take a real policeman's call."

The basset hound snickered again this time bordering on a guffaw.

"Because of professional courtesy," – and the fact that you have nothing on me, Grace thought, "I'm going to let you go now. But I keep the handcuffs."

He motioned for his colleague to zip up the luggage and hand it back to Grace. "I'm sure that you are not lying to me about Commander Buratti and your reasons for being here," he said. "It would be most unfortunate for you and your career if you were to cross me."

"I won't," Grace said.

"And I suggest that you leave your credentials in your bag. They mean nothing here." With his last statement, Trigger and the basset hound left the room.

With no time to waste, Grace grabbed her bag and made off to the rental car counter for the hour and a half drive. She needed to move quicker to get the confession and recover the San Lorenzo now that Buratti was going to be contacted. Hopefully, Trigger was right and Buratti would be too busy gallivanting to receive the warning.

# Chapter 35

Max walked up the steps and into the doors of the St. John the Baptist Cathedral. Cool and dark, he immediately felt better moving away from the crowd gathered at the Chapel of the Holy Shroud. He looked for a quiet place to sit and about halfway down the nave, found an alcove lit with several candles and numerous displays of fresh flowers. Above the shrine was a large oval portrait photo of a young man sitting in a relaxed manner with one hand in his pocket and the other on the armrest. Starkly different than any church painting Max had ever seen, the subject wore a modern sports jacket with a white open collar shirt and looked to be in his twenties. Underneath the photo, the words "BEATO PIER GIORGIO FRASSATI" were engraved on a plaque affixed to the marble altar.

Max noticed the prayer kneeler in front of the shrine and, for the first time in a long time, got down on his knees. Unlike every Sunday at Mass when he normally just went through the motions, today Max talked to God.

"Hey, ah, it's been a while. But if you're listening," Max said aloud. "I am in a jam." He hesitated a few seconds "Please God, help me get through these next few hours. I'm sorry for all that I've caused to happen and I promise that I'll learn and be better next time. Amen."

Max made the sign of the cross.

"That was a very heartfelt confession," said a man tucked back in the dark only a few feet away.

Startled, Max jerked his head up looking in both directions before seeing the man dressed in a priest's black cassock sitting to the side of the shrine in a chair.

"What? Who are you? You heard me?"

"Yes. Were you not here for confession?" said the older man. A mop of gray hair framed his block face, lantern jaw, and bushy black eyebrows.

"Oh. No. I'm sorry." Max said embarrassed at having spoken aloud.

"Don't be. You showed the proper element of a confession."

"Who are you?"

"I'm Fr. Giorgi. What you said is enough, but would you like to tell me more. I am happy to complete the Sacrament of Penance."

Max nodded.

"Please, unburden yourself," the priest said. "What is bothering you? What kind of …jam…are you in?"

The frustration and angst that had been building up for the past days rushed out of Max like water rushing through a breached levy. "I had this thing that I was trying to sell. Well actually, I was selling it for someone else but he was going to give me some of the profits from selling it. See, it turned out that the thing I was selling was stolen. And now the Paris police think that I killed a guy and in a few hours I'm going to be arrested by a cop from the U.S. and I can't even return the stolen item because some guys just stole it from me. So, I'm probably going to jail which might be safer than seeing the guy who got me into this whole thing who probably wants to kill me."

The priest's caterpillar eyebrows shot upward but he remained attentive and silent.

Max paused and explained what bothered him the most. "And I lied to my wife…well, really just kept things from her, which is kind of like lying. So yeah, I lied to her. And my job…well…It's all just a mess." Tears formed in Max's eyes as he unburdened himself and heard his complicity. "I kind of knew there was something suspicious about the item. I mean, why would someone pay me ten thousand dollars to go to a meeting in Switzerland when you can fly yourself there for a thousand dollars?"

Max contemplated his naiveté. "I wanted to believe that I was important. I told myself that my silence saved my wife from worry. But I probably kept it from her because I didn't want her to point out that my plan was full of crap." Max wondered if his curse would negate his profession of sorrow.

After several moments of silence, the priest asked, "Is that everything?"

"Yes. I think so."

"First, I must ask you about this murder in Paris you spoke of…"

Max cut him off, "I didn't murder anyone. I've never even been to Paris…. but I have a good idea who did. It's the same guys that stole the item from me."

"Okay good. I'll expect you to work with the authorities to help."

"Of course," Max said.

Fr. Giorgi leaned closer, said some words in Latin and made the sign of the cross. "There, you are forgiven."

"That was easy," Max said, feeling strangely relieved of his burden.

"The absolution is easy, it's the examining of one's soul that is the difficulty. Would you like to talk someplace more private? Your soul is now healed but it sounds like you have more earthly issues to deal with."

"I don't think that you can help me, Father."

"Sometimes just talking helps. The beauty and grace of the confessional are a lot cheaper than a therapist." He laughed until he coughed.

"Well, you heard my situation…I guess I need to tell my wife about what I did and prepare her for what's about to happen. But I'm afraid that she will be angry."

"She may be. And probably has the right to be."

"But I was just trying to help my family. We don't have enough money to pay the bills and we're really struggling to make ends meet…"

"This does not excuse theft. I understand that financial pressures could make one fail to examine the moral implications of business dealings. But money, fame, and glory are false gods. They get in the way of the true treasure."

"You're right," Max admitted. "Someone else I was just talking to said basically the same thing."

"It is a concept that is sometimes difficult to live – camel through the eye of the needle and all – but the more times you hear it, the easier it is to follow."

Max thought about his pressing situation, "What do I do about my situation, now?"

"Explain to her that your desire to succeed blinded your ability to make good decisions. That is essentially what you just said."

Max nodded his agreement.

"You were joined together through the Sacrament of Holy Matrimony. I would suggest that, in the future, you discuss these ideas with her before you set off into these ventures. ….." The priest stopped for a moment and reconsidered his approach saying, "to put in your American way, you need to get your wife's 'buy in' first."

Max smiled saying, "she'll keep me from doing stupid things and if she agrees to my crazy ideas at least I've covered my butt.'"

"Something like that," Fr. Giorgi laughed. "You don't have an organization last for two thousand years without providing some sensible guidance for people's daily lives."

Max's shoulders relaxed for the first time in days. A calm overtook him yet he soon became uncomfortable with the silence. To fill the void, he said, "You know, Father, if I go to prison here, at least I'll learn Italian. That's something I've always wanted to do."

The priest laughed, "San Lorenzo is smiling down on you."

Max's head rocked back as his face flushed. He hadn't mentioned the stolen manuscript – had he?

"You know about San Lorenzo and the story of his martyrdom on the gridiron?" Fr. Giorgi said, mistaking Max's reaction for ignorance about the saint's story. "He's the patron saint of comedians. His final words while being roasted alive were, 'Turn me over, I'm done on this side'."

"Is that really true?" Max asked.

The priest shrugged his shoulders and laughed, his caterpillar eyebrows dancing. "Some people say Lorenzo's story is derived from poor handwriting." Fr. Giorgi chuckled again. "A missing 'P' made the announcement read '*assus est*' which in Latin means '*he was roasted*' instead of the more common '*passus est*' or 'he suffered'… that is, was martyred."

Max nervously looked around to make his escape from this priest and the uncomfortable subject.

"The archives here in this building used to have a beautifully illustrated missal but the page for the feast day of San Lorenzo was ripped out and stolen with several other items." The priest looked at the mosaic floor lost in thought for a moment. "Some people, people trying to take away the mystique of the Church, are now saying that we have hidden the San Lorenzo because it proves the saint was not burned alive."

Max's head rocked back and face turned red recognizing another victim of his reckless behavior.

"Ridiculous!" the priest continued. "They miss the point. The actual form of San Lorenzo's execution is not what makes him admirable, someone to emulate. It is the fact that he understood, and died for declaring, that the treasure of the Church is its people and not the earthly possessions. Besides, regardless of the 'actual' truth, being roasted alive is a good metaphor for how many of us live our lives under constant and growing pressure. The practical answer…San Lorenzo gave us… is to respond with humor."

Equal doses of guilt and amazement gushed into Max's mind as he pondered his role in this story. "Uhhh, thank you for your help, Father," Max said quickly as he tried to get away from the priest before his guilt overcame him and he told the details of the manuscript, "that saint stuff is kind of irrelevant anyway. I mean it was so long ago. It doesn't really pertain to today's problems."

Fr. Giorgi became serious and ducked his head close to Max's, "You don't believe that the saints play a role in our lives today?" His eyes penetrated Max's ambivalent exterior. "Somehow you were drawn to the Frassati shrine. The Beatified young man showed courage against the fascist and was so charitable that he even contracted polio from ministering to the poor. This was recent…at least in this century. Not such olden times. I cannot help but believe that your journey was guided by him."

"Maybe, Father." Max stuck out his hand to shake. "I should be going, though. Thank you."

The priest took Max's hand in both of his and looking at him with warmth said, "God bless you, Max and good luck."

Max left the darkness of the cathedral and stepped into the piazza. Irrationally fearful of a second attack, he struck out toward his cousin's bookshop. With only a few hours before the authorities would surely arrest him, his most pressing thought was calling home and explaining.

# Chapter 36

Spicuzza, wearing a new gray suit, carried a stack of folders to Buratti's office. The pants had been quickly hemmed but a proper fitting would have to come later. The subordinate stood by his boss's opened door before being waved in.

"Where do we stand on the San Lorenzo?" Buratti barked.

"For the past day and a half, we've been issuing special addendums to the *"Bollettini delle opere d'arte trafugate."*

"Who is going to notice an addition to the *'Arte In Ostaggio'* – Stolen Artworks Bulletin?" the boss asked. "That thing is at least two hundred pages and takes years to publish. The information is years old by the time it gets out to the public."

"We cast a wide net with the Bollettini. Anyone who might tangentially come into contact with the San Lorenzo received a notification." Spicuzza defended himself with his description of the proper protocol. "That includes used and rare bookshops, antique dealers, universities, libraries, cultural foundations and research centers including ICCROM, as well as the local *soprintendenze* and ecclesiastical bodies. We've also notified UNESCO, UNIDROIT, ICOMOS, ICOM, the FBI, and INTERPOL."

"Lost in a sea of information," Buratti said.

"I agree that it's good to also make a focused effort," Spicuzza said. "I've been thinking. We know that the seller is in Europe and has already attempted to sell to a Parisian dealer. It follows that the seller may likely continue trying to fence the piece until they are successful."

"Okay..." the Commander said leading his investigator on.

"There are only a few antiquarian booksellers who would have the knowledge to recognize the authenticity and value of a 15th century manuscript. There are even fewer who would have the money readily available to purchase one. Normally, these types of transactions would happen at one of the big shows like the one in London or New York. The sellers obviously would rather keep this sale quiet so they are setting up appointments individually." Spicuzza was laying out a nice case for his investigation but Buratti picked up the thread and couldn't contain himself.

"And since they couldn't sell a stolen Parisian book in Paris, Torino, Milan or Rome would be the next logical choices," Buratti said finishing the man's thought process.

"*Exacto*. And Torino is closest to Paris. I've sent a more focused notification via fax to private collectors and antiquarian booksellers located in those three cities who specialize in rare manuscripts," Spicuzza announced.

"Do you think that a private collector will pay much attention to our Notice of Theft? They are just as likely to purchase the San Lorenzo and keep it for their own use. But with our warning, they'll buy it at a lower price knowing that it is stolen." Buratti had been battling art theft for many years and was cynic when it came to the good intentions of art collectors.

"Perhaps. But they'll also be on notice and might give us information to do the right thing. We don't really have many options. The San Lorenzo was stolen seven years ago and we have it on good authority that it is being shopped in our backyard. This might be our best chance to recover the San Lorenzo."

"And arrest the traffickers," Buratti added. "Good police work," the Commander complimented. "I'm picking up the Cardinal on Sunday. Try everything you can. I want some good news to report."

"We'll send another alert later this afternoon," Spicuzza continued. "I think if we keep their fax machining ringing, we are more likely to get noticed and get a hit."

Spicuzza changed course and mentioned another interesting development. "The faxes did bring some interesting responses this morning." Buratti looked up and leaned his head forward and nodded for his subordinate to report. "Do you know the bookshop a few blocks away from the cathedral St. John the Baptist?"

Buratti nodded.

"Of course, you do," Spicuzza mumbled apologetically. "Well, they were on my initial fax list yesterday. This morning, only a few minutes ago, they called and left a message. They asked that someone from our office contact them."

Buratti was paying attention but perturbed at how his subordinate in the ill-fitted gray suit was dragging the story out. "What's the headline? Fill in the details only if I'm interested," he huffed.

"Sure," Spicuzza said, moving to the point of the story. "Two American men approached the dealer this morning trying to sell a complete set of 15th century engravings, very rare. They had no proof of ownership and seemed to have no idea what they possessed or what it was worth. I checked the list of stolen items from the original Capitulars Archive theft and it's not on that list." He was losing Buratti's interest and quickly asked, "Have you heard of the so-called, *Man-*

*tegna Tarocchi?"*

"The *Mantegna Tarocchi*? Yes. I think I saw something on that just yesterday...or this morning. Let me check," he said as he checked his email. "Yes. Here it is. It was reported stolen from a Paris book shop in connection with a homicide of the shop owner. A Paris Homicide Detective, Inspector Leverd, posted the 'Notice of Stolen Art' late last night."

"Apparently these thieves are in Torino this morning trying to sell the *Mantegna Taroccchi*. I'm heading over there now to get a better description of the men." Spicuzza said.

"Excellent," Buratti said. "I will call Inspector Leverd to see what more he has gathered." Bringing in killers and a stolen work of art should make for good press and be good news to report on Sunday...even if he made no progress on the San Lorenzo.

He added, "Be careful, Spicuzza. These men have already killed and may kill again."

# Chapter 37

Max found the bookshop on Via Academia Albertina, a small side street running perpendicular to Via Po, the main shopping street that ran down the center of town toward the Vittorio Emanuele Bridge. The shop set back from the street along a small side road. Above the door in large block letters hung the sign, '*Libreria Principe*'. Max could see from the street that the rare bookstore fronted the street for about seventy meters but there was no telling how far back the shop went. The store appeared to be split in two; on the left side was a two story open shop with book-shelves going from floor to ceiling, on the right side the shop had been split by a wooden loft serving as an office.

A petite, wiry woman with stylish, short black hair greeted Max as he opened the door. Her clear blue eyes sparkled when she smiled and her dramatic dimples took a decade off her looks. She welcomed him with two arms and pulled him close to give him a kiss on both cheeks.

"You must be Massimo...er...Max," she said in heavily accented English. "What happened to your face?" she said with concern.

Max put his hand up to touch his cheek having forgotten the mark the punch must have made. "Carlota?" Max questioned, bending down to accommodate a face to face discussion.

"Max, I'm up here!" called a voice from the loft up above. Max looked up to see a smiling blond woman leaning over the railing. "Welcome, cousin. Come up here please." She addressed the woman standing next to Max, "Silvana! You can wait for my mother and let her know that I'm busy."

"*Certo*," said the woman coldly.

Max walked up the spiral wooden staircase and stepped up into an office containing two large desks on either end of the room, both piled high with papers and antique books. A Persian rug sitting over the marble floor bridged the desks. Large bookshelves packed with antique documents, books, manuscripts, codices, illuminations and such lined two of the three walls. The wall facing the street contained a few smaller, half bookshelves with gilded framed 18th century painted landscapes hanging between the windows. In addition to the natural sunlight, the room was lit by two large crystal chandeliers. The light filtered through a faint haze of cigarette smoke which hung in the air.

When Max was a kid his father had built him a 'fort' to play in. The fort was more than an 8' x 10' piece plywood elevated a few feet off the ground; no walls, no roof, just height. For a kid who wanted to see far and go far, elevation always made him feel more in control. Now, standing in the loft office, perched above the library, surrounded by wealth and beauty of antique books which contained western civilization's greatest ideas composed by its greatest minds, a peaceful ease overcame Max. He breathed easy and was present in the moment.

"Please sit down. I want to talk to you. Get to know you," his cousin said.

Max smiled and looked around. "I would like to do that... and I do have something to discuss with you. But before I do, would it be all right if I called my wife? She hasn't heard from me in a few days."

His cousin hesitated. "Ah...Of course. Here, you can use this phone," indicating the phone on her desk.

"If you don't mind I prefer to speak in private. If, that is okay?" Max was nervous about being impolite but the conversation he was about to have was not for public consumption. It was bad enough that he talked aloud at church. That seemed to work out all right, but he'd rather have this conversation in private.

"Yes, you can use the back office in there," and pointed to a room about fifteen feet away.

Give me the number and I will dial it for you and you can pick it up there.

Max wrote down the number on a notepad and handed to his cousin and went into the back office. "It's ringing!" she exclaimed after she had dialed.

Max hit a button on the phone, which had several lights blinking, just in time to hear Laura's voice say "Hello?"

"Hey, honey it's me."

"Hey, babe. Where are you? What time is it?"

"I'm at my cousin's bookstore in Torino. It's about one in the afternoon."

Laura launched into her events of the past day, "Well, I've had such a past few days. You know your oldest son, yesterday, climbed up the book shelves. Of course, the little one thought that was hilarious so he had to do the same thing. Thank God you bolted the bookshelves to the wall."

"Honey. They're twins. Why do you keep saying the older and the younger?"

"You can't treat them the same. All the books say that you need to allow them to develop their own personality. You know you should read..."

"Honey. Honey! Laura!" Max interrupted. "Listen. I'm using someone else's phone so I can't talk for long but I've got to tell you something."

Max could hear the tension in Laura's silence.

Max stated, "Remember that guy I mentioned, earlier? Edgar?" He paused and took a deep breath. "Well, when I told him that I was coming to Zurich on business, he asked if I wanted to earn some money by helping him sell a rare manuscript he had."

"Okay?" Laura drawled out. "And...?"

"Well, it turns out that the manuscript might be stolen. So the guy who was supposed to buy it didn't. And then he was robbed outside of our meeting and later was found dead in Paris."

"Oh my...that's awful. But what does this have to do with you?"

"Well, I got a call from the Paris police asking me questions and they think I killed the guy in Paris."

"WHAT! What are you even talking about? You have a meeting with a guy and then he dies and the police call you? What are you not telling me?"

"I'm trying to tell you... I was doing it for the surgery for Sam." Max rushed out defensively.

"Did you go to Paris?" she interrupted Max and started interrogating him.

"No."

"Have you ever been to Paris?"

"No."

"Where were you when this guy died?" Laura continued.

"Zurich, at the conference."

"Do you have proof that you were there?"

"I mean, yeah. Several witnesses, the customers I went to dinner with and of course, my boss, Theodore."

"Well, you won't want to use him as an alibi," Laura answered. "I can see where getting screwed up in this could damage your credibility and career. Did you use a credit card?"

"Yeah. Twice; once for dinner and then at the bar afterward."

"Then you weren't in Paris and couldn't have committed the crime. What are you making such a big deal about?" she said. "Unless there is something else you're not telling me..." she questioned.

"Well, I got a call from a Special Agent from the U.S. Customs Service. They know about the stolen manuscript and they want to meet with me."

"I'll find us a lawyer, I think my friend Libby's husband could help. He's a lawyer. When you get back here..."

"She's coming here."

"Who? Libby's coming to Europe?"

"No, the Special Agent...it's a woman, Grace Hemmer, and she's coming to meet me here at my cousin's bookshop to get the manuscript back."

"Well, give it to her. Then you're done."

"But, she thinks I'm involved in trafficking stolen items. It's a serious crime," Max said trying to lay out the facts as Laura's questions kept pounding him.

"Did you steal it?" Laura asked.

"NO!" Max said. Defending himself was exacerbating.

"Then what are you worried about? Just return it. You'll probably get a reward."

"I can't. Remember I mentioned that the Frenchman got robbed outside the meeting? Well, I think I know who did it...because they must have followed me here and stole it from me."

"What do you mean they stole it from you? Stole what from you? The manuscript? What'd you do, leave it somewhere?" Laura in her questioning had a way of being both accusatory and condescending.

"No!" Max said. "They punched me in the head and knocked me

out. When I awoke, it was gone."

"Shit, Max! What have you got yourself into?" she said. And then with concern, "Are you okay?"

"I'm fine, just a little sore." The embarrassment of the attack was greater than the physical pain.

"How do you know it was them?" Gone was the tone of condescension and accusation. Max heard Laura enter full problem-solving mode.

"I recognized one of them by his jacket. I've been seeing him around for the past two days but never really put the coincidence together."

"Dammit, Max! You can't keep walking around with your head up your butt. Start paying attention! Now you've got this Special Agent on your back."

"Okay. Maybe they will come after me for originally having the manuscript and selling it and not believe my story about what really happened."

"Who cares what they believe?" Laura now shifted from problem-solving manner to full 'Mamma Bear' protection mode. "They've got to prove it. Right now, the only person who placed you with the 'stolen' manuscript, and we're not even sure that it even was stolen, is a dead guy. You have an airtight alibi and this special agent lady probably can't even substantiate that there even is a stolen manuscript, to begin with."

"Well, there are two bankers too," Max added.

"Who?" Laura questioned. "How many surprises do you have for me? What bankers?" The accusation side started to rise.

"The meeting was at a bank in Basel. There were two bankers there when I set up the Swiss bank account and had the meeting with the French buyer."

"What bank account? You can't keep giving me information in dribs and drabs."

"The bank account was established with ten thousand dollars that

Edgar sent so that the buyer could deposit the money in the account for the purchase of the manuscript."

"You didn't tell me that but... did the bankers see this supposedly stolen manuscript?"

"I don't think so. No. They saw the mailing tube it was in but not when it was sitting out."

"So, they don't know anything. Besides, I don't think Swiss bankers are known to be Chatty Cathies. They won't say crap."

"You're right. If we are discussing all the issues, my company might be mad that I used my time to go to Basel for this meeting."

"Did you put the expense on the company?" she asked – firing questions at her husband.

"No."

"And are you there for the speaking engagement at the conference and did you give the speech?"

"I was in Zurich for the conference, Basel's where I went to try to sell the manuscript. I'm in Torino now. But, yeah, I went to Zurich for business," Max answered starting to see her point.

"Okay, but you paid for the trip to Basel and back with our money? Right?" Laura didn't wait for the answer, "So what's the problem?" she demanded.

"Well, they might be upset that I took some time for myself to do something other than company business."

"Really?" she said sarcastically. "You think they're going to make a big deal about this when Theodore is running around with some woman on a business trip?"

"Okay. So the company really shouldn't have a problem but I'd prefer that they didn't know," Max said. "If this special agent flew all the way here, she's going to want to come back with something; if not the manuscript, then maybe a suspect or an arrest."

"You might be right, Max. But have you thought that she may be in on this scam? Maybe she's crooked. Seems awfully strange that she just mysteriously pops up claiming you stole something that you didn't and then flies all the way to Italy to retrieve it. Don't be so naïve; she could be part of this rip off plan."

"I never thought of that."

"Of course you didn't. You are too gullible. That's what got you into this mess in the first place." It was an accusation, but one made with love and one which Max had to, if he was honest with himself, agree with.

"I think she's legit but I'll make sure I check her identification and I'll have my cousin check her out or call the local police just to make sure," Max assured Laura.

"Okay. In either case, your best bet is to see if you can help retrieve the manuscript or get the guys that beat you up...or somehow get Edgar."

"Edgar?" Max questioned.

"Yes. Edgar. Clearly, he set you up. He knew the manuscript was stolen. That's why he sent you instead. If you could sell it great, if not, he knew how to get it back from you. It was a no-lose proposition for him. He played you."

"You're right." The thugs didn't just 'happen' upon the Frenchman. They'd been sent by Edgar. The thugs had been after him all along. "Why didn't I see that? I should have talked to you about this sooner."

"Damn right you should have," she demanded. "Listen, the customs lady has got a lot bigger fish to fry than you with your little stunt. You are no catch for them, just a minnow."

"Geez, thanks," Max said feeling a bit dejected.

"But you are my catch and a big fish here. So hurry back home," she said. "And don't worry about meeting that special agent lady. See what you can do to help and it will all work out in the end. Love you."

"Love you, too."

"Oh crap...how the heck did he get ahold of a sharpie?! I gotta go!" Laura said as she hung up the phone.

Max was not sure if the conversation was over and heard a click and then another click before hearing the dial tone. He put down the phone and walked out to the office with a little more confidence and stillness of heart knowing that his wife supported him and loved him.

Max needed that confidence as he walked back the twenty feet to the main library office and saw the Charlie Brown looking man seated comfortably talking with his cousin.

# Chapter 38

"Hello, Max," Edgar said. "I'm glad you took my advice." Edgar was sitting in an ornate leather chair in front of his cousin's desk, looking very relaxed and in control. His cousin was sitting behind her desk regarding the interaction between Max and Edgar with extreme interest. The surprise of finding Edgar made him forget to greet his cousin.

"Edgar, what are you doing here?" Max questioned. His heart hit staccato beats and his throat constricted.

"I was just in Milan conducting some business. I think that I have a buyer for the San Lorenzo."

"I mean...What are you doing here? In this store?" Max asked again.

"Didn't I tell you to come here? Your cousin's bookshop is very well-known in the rare book community. Right after you and I got off the phone, I called to see if she'd be here today. I've met her father at book fairs but until today, I've never had the pleasure of meeting her." He smiled at Carlota.

She regarded him suspiciously.

"What do you want, Edgar?" Max said.

"What do you think I want? I want the San Lorenzo. It's mine, after all," said Edgar. It was all very matter of fact and said with the ease of asking someone to pass the salt and pepper.

Max knew that he had been set-up and he scrambled to turn the tables. What did Edgar know? Information was power and Max needed to gain it, not give it. He could only imagine what a first impression he was making in front of his cousin. Boy, would his father be angry about getting his cousin involved in this deceit. His grandfather was probably rolling over in his grave.

"What are you talking about?" Max asked.

"You know exactly what I'm talking about," Edgar said as he lurched forward in his seat. Carlota backed up in her seat and regarded the events. "Where is it? Did you sell it?"

Max put on his most innocent blank and confused face and slightly shrugged his shoulders.

"You had it when I called you on the train. You better either produce it or give me the fucking money for it!" Edgar's face reddened by the moment. Gone was the jolly-faced man that he had met in St. Augustine. Now, Max met the man hardened by African civil war.

"I don't know what you're talking about." He kept his voice easy and relaxed, trying not to implicate himself or lie.

"The San Lorenzo! It is mine! I purchased it! I want the money for it! What did you do with it?" Edgar enunciated each word in a loud, threatening manner. Sounds carried in the loft office and Max heard the door chime and clients talking to the woman downstairs.

Max wasn't sure what to say next. His normal inclination was to spill the truth and tell both Edgar and his cousin the tale of how he had traveled with the manuscript from Zurich but had it stolen this morning. But he wasn't sure how that would help.

As he processed Edgar's reaction, a thought crossed his mind; could it have been Edgar who knocked him out in front of the Cathedral and stole the manuscript? Clarity overcame Max as he processed Laura's idea that Edgar had been working with the man in the yellow jacket all along, perhaps even in Basel.

Edgar stood and started to pace. Max stepped back defensively, unsure that his cousin's presence would prevent a physical confrontation. His cousin spoke up for the first time, "What seems to be the problem? Maybe I can help?" she said as if the danger were not so obvious. It appeared that, at least for the moment, Edgar wouldn't physically attack Max.

"He had something of mine and now he's lost it!" barked Edgar.

"What was it?" she looked toward Max who kept quiet.

Edgar responded for him, "It is a page from a Missal, known as the San Lorenzo, showing the hand-painted depiction of the saint with the gridiron and dalmatic." He sneered spitting the words out of his mouth like a sour grape, "I asked him to bring it to you so that you could inspect it and possibly buy it."

"So it's yours and you planned to sell it to me?" Carlota said.

"Yes, and now this...this incompetent shit doesn't have it," Edgar pointed at Max.

"Oh, I understand..." Carlota said and stopped as the woman from downstairs walked up the steps.

"Silvana, I thought I told you that we were not to be disturbed," Carlota said in a stern voice.

Silvana paid no heed and walked around the desk and bent down to speak in her ear. After a few moments Carlota, still seated, responded, "No. Bring them up now."

Silvana looked disappointed in the response but returned downstairs. She looked back to give Max a look of sympathy before descending the stairs to the main floor.

"We need to figure this out now!" Edgar said.

"I need to speak to these clients of mine, please. Maybe after I speak with them, we can figure out a way to resolve the situation," Carlota said.

Max stood by the back door to the office and winced as a bit of bile came up in his mouth. His stomach heaved and his head dodged back. Stupid! He could only image that it was the police or the special agent coming from the United States to arrest him for murder and trafficking. His plan of coming to his cousin to seek her help had not worked out. In fact, in the several seconds it took for the people to walk up the stairs, Max realized how absolutely stupid the entire idea was. To show up unannounced to long lost relatives and expect to be bailed out of a murder charge and a stolen art trafficking charge, was ridiculous. Max kicked himself as he waited for the other shoe to drop.

All eyes went to the staircase where several feet were trotting up the wooden steps. Even though the man in the black leather coat walked in front, Max's attention fell to the man behind him wearing a yellow Members Only jacket. Edgar turned to see the men stepping onto the loft floor.

"Huh, figures you'd be here," said Tommy to Edgar. Turning to Max he charged, "You double-crossed us with that stunt with the Frenchman – trying to keep the manuscript for yourself?"

"What are you talking about?" said Edgar addressing Tommy and then faced Max. "Max, you're working with these guys?"

Carlota's head went back and forth like a spectator at a tennis match.

Max recognized the man in the black leather jacket now; he had seen him at Carmelo's Pizza with Edgar. It was the time he felt jealous of the two entrepreneurs enjoying a beer during a lazy long lunch.

"We're not working with him," Tommy said. "You guys are the ones trying to screw us!" Tommy confronted Edgar, "We checked the French guy after the meeting in Basel and then at his store in Paris. He didn't have any manuscript. That's a lot of traveling for nothing!"

Pressing the issue with Edgar, Tommy continued, "You sent us out here so that you cut us out and make more money. But the joke's on you 'cause I got it now."

Edgar's eyes became slits. "You have the San Lorenzo?" he seethed.

Max's head moved from Tommy to Edgar trying to follow the action and make sense of the past three days.

"Yeah. Got it right here," he said as he produced the mailing tube. "Sully and I happened to run across him," indicating Max, "in front of some church. Sucker never saw it coming." Tommy laughed, recalling the attack. "Right, Sully?"

Sully didn't say anything. His hands twitched and he rocked on his heels.

Carlota cut through the accusations and counter accusations and spoke up. "Let me get this straight. You have the San Lorenzo?"

Tommy nodded.

"May I see it? I'm very interested in it." Tommy hesitated and eyed Edgar.

"I'm a professional," Carlota said reassuringly. "If you say it is yours, I will give it back to you."

Tommy held the mailing tube aloft and sneered at Edgar. He found a potential buyer and had the upper hand, literally.

Carlota, rebuffed by Tommy, turned her attention to Edgar. "But you say it's yours?"

"It is," Edgar said.

"Is not," Tommy retorted.

"It's mine!" They both said at the same time. Max couldn't help thinking that these two grown men, men who he thought were successful, accomplished entrepreneurs, sounded exactly like five-year-olds fighting over a toy truck in a sandbox.

"Ya evah hear of the 'Golden Rule'?" Tommy asked with the thickest possible Jersey accent. Apparently trying for a menacing effect, it came off pathetic. "Whoevah has the gold, makes the rule. And this here is my gold," holding up the manuscript. "So I make the rules." Tommy snarled at Edgar.

Max watched Edgar, his eyes scanning the room analyzing the angles of approach and searching for potential weapons, no doubt weighing the odds of a successful attack on Tommy and escaping with the manuscript.

"Okay. Enough!" Carlota commanded. She was standing now trying to take charge of the fighting going on in her office. With the situation as bizarre as three grown men from Florida fighting over a valuable manuscript in Torino, it was strange that the first thought in Max's head was how good Carlota's English was. He remembered his comment to the priest about learning Italian while incarcerated.

Door chimes indicated that customers entering the shop downstairs. Max heard people talking and the woman below speaking rapidly in Italian. He looked around the library office embarrassed to make eye contact with his cousin. His presence had to be hurting her business. He flushed as he remembered that his aunt was coming to meet them at the shop. There was nothing he could do about it now, but the fact made him feel even more guilty; another innocent victim of his scheme.

When the men had quieted down, Carlota continued, "I know why you are here," indicating Edgar. "You knew that my cousin, Max, would come to me for help." Turning to Tommy and Sully, she said, "But why are you here?"

"Because we want to sell the manuscript and another book I have."

"Another book?" Carlota asked in genuine surprise.

"Yeah, I found this old book in... a garage sale in America so I brought it here to see what people here would pay for it."

"May I see it, please?" Carlota asked.

"Yeah. But I don't wanna let them see it," nodding his head to Edgar and Max.

"Don't worry," Carlota said. "Edgar, do you have anything to do with any other book which Mr.? I'm sorry. What is your name?"

"Tommy Gallagher," replied Tommy as if everyone should know him. He reached into his bag and pulled out the small book bound in a gray binding, took two steps to handed it to Carlota. "What's it worth?"

"I really couldn't say. I'm not sure what it is," Carlota responded, truly perplexed at the turn of events.

"Let me take a guess," said the tall, solidly built man wearing a well-tailored, glen plaid gray suit, white shirt, and yellow silk tie. He had just stepped in the back entrance – the same one that Max had entered minutes ago after calling home – and was leaning nonchalantly on the door jamb.

Standing only a few feet from Max, the new man peered at the group and answered his question, "It's the *Mantegna Tarocchi;* most recently the property of Frederic Paquet of Paris prior to his death and the robbery of his bookshop."

# Chapter 39

"Bramante!" Max's cousin exclaimed.

The broad-shouldered man looked like he had just come from a photo shoot for Italian GQ magazine; his wavy hair was perfectly out of place and his strong chin sported the two-day growth look. He smiled in an easy manner and winked in greeting to the woman behind the desk, "Grace."

'Grace'? Max thought...is that Italian for something? Why is he calling Carlota, Grace?

Sully didn't like the turn of events. Standing to the right of Tommy, he had a good view out the window of the three police cars parked outside. Looking over the banister, he saw several policemen near the shop's entrance training their sights on the happenings of the loft office – that escape route impossible. Escape through the back door exit was more likely, but it meant getting past Tommy, Edgar, Max and the gray-suited sculpture of David, incarnate. In an instant, even that choice disappeared when two additional armed policemen entered the rear door.

The GQ model made quick work rattling off instructions in Italian. He pointed to Tommy and Sully and nodded his head to Edgar and Max. "I'm Bramante Buratti, Section Chief and Commander of the Carabinieri Art Squad. You gentlemen are under arrest."

Two uniformed Italian police officers, Carabinieri, both of them heavily armed with flak jackets, moved toward Tommy and Sully and roughly cuffed them. Two chairs were pulled over and the American men shoved into the seated position.

Similarly, but with less animosity, Edgar was sternly told to stand. A policeman cuffed him and made him sit back down.

Max's heart leaped to his throat while only he remained standing. All of the panic and stress of the past few days was nothing compared to the reality barreling at him like a freight train. His worst nightmare came true as a short, gray-haired detective in a baggy gray suit handcuffed him behind his back.

Bramante barked something in Italian to which the diminutive gray-haired man, whose name Max understood to be Spicuzza, responded by adjusting the handcuffs so that Max's hand were in front of him. In English, Spicuzza asked, "Should I find another chair or leave him standing?"

"Standing." Buratti looked to Max in the sternest possible manner and pointed his finger at him. The message was unambiguous; 'stay exactly where you are, don't move and don't say a word.' It was a message that Max was all too happy to comply with.

While Max stood, Tommy, Sully, and Edgar were seated, hands shackled behind their backs and facing the Carabinieri Commander who leaned back on the edge of his desk with his arms folded.

"Why the hell don't you make him sit?" Tommy interrupted as he struggled in the chair trying to regain some dignity.

"I think he has enough sense not to move," he said responding to both Spicuzza and Tommy.

"You, on the other hand," Bramante said, turning his attention to Tommy, "have no such sense."

He opened a manila folder and pulled out fax papers. "You are Mr.

Thomas Gallagher; of the New Jersey Penitentiary System?" Tommy glared at him and, except for his left nostril which flared wildly, stopped fidgeting.

Shifting and looking at Sully, he said, "And you are Patrick Casey Sullivan; of Duval County Florida County Jail fame?"

The two, defiant at first, sat with their heads down in realization that this Italian policeman knew more about them than they cared to admit. Tommy had been telling the lie about who he was for so long and so often, that even he forgot the truth. Now, this cop was shining a Maglite on his past. The worst part of it was that he was being embarrassed in front of strangers.

Tommy rallied from this setback and defiantly yelled, "I know my rights. I ain't sayin' nothin'! I got the right to remain silent. I wanna call the embassy. I gotta get my phone call."

Buratti laughed, this time a full hearty laugh. "It's funny what you Americans think with your movies and TV shows. You have no such rights here. 'Miranda Warning' as you call it, is an American thing. Look around. This is not America."

Buratti continued, "Let's talk about what happened in Paris. You have left quite a trail of evidence on your little escapade. Rental car bill for a return in Basel airport, electronic parking ticket with photograph evidence for parking in the taxi lane at the Basel airport....you know you're not allowed to park in a taxi queue?" he scolded. "Train tickets from Paris to Zurich immediately following the time of the attack on the Parisian bookseller. Interesting. Hmm, no train tickets from Basel to Paris – You must have paid cash."

Buratti had a flair for the dramatic and was clearly having fun with this. Max was not sure how to feel. It was nice to see the evidence piling up on these two guys. On the other hand, this Bramante Buratti seemed like a no nonsense guy who would make every one of them pay.

"You can't be talking to me about this! You're Italian police and that was Paris. You don't got jurisdiction," Tommy countered.

"Just because you have experience in the U.S. penal system does not mean you know anything about ours."

Spicuzza, apparently dying to get into the act, added, "The Carabinieri Art Squad works across many jurisdictions and many countries to stop the illegal trade of stolen antiquities."

The Commander gave a sideways glance at the interruption. Spicuzza shrunk a bit and stepped back. His boss continued, "Why do you think I'm working here with Grace?"

"Grace? I thought you were Carlota?" Max blurted out.

Buratti shot Max a cold look admonishing him for breaking the unspoken command and interrupting his dissertation of compiled evidence.

"I'm Special Agent Grace Hemmer from the U.S. Customs Service," said the woman Max had, until moments ago, thought of as his cousin. "Your cousin is the woman you met downstairs when you came in." She indicated Silvana, the short black haired woman who silently stood at the office back door, having appeared without fanfare during the excitement of the arrests.

Turning to the three handcuffed men seated in front of her and lifting a recording device that she had on the desk, she said, "That's right, boys. You've been very helpful in implicating yourselves."

Edgar took note of the device and twisted right and left looking to get away. An armed policeman stepped forward menacingly causing Edgar to sit back and wait.

"Yes, we'll get to that," Buratti said, trying to regain the theatricality of the arrest and the recitation of the long list of evidence that pegged these two men to the Frenchman and the theft at his bookshop.

Rifling through more papers, "Oh, look, Grace." He flashed the paper to Grace. "It seems that Mr. Gallagher purchased two watches in the Basel airport. Are you wearing them now?"

He leaned over toward Tommy. "I hope the handcuffs don't scratch the fine finish on them," he mocked. "I see that you filled out the paperwork to get your VAT tax back. Make sure to give them your address in prison so that they know where to send the tax refund." He chuckled while Tommy seethed.

"I'm sure that you also registered at a hotel or changed money somewhere. The trail will become clearer. But for now, the good stuff." At that, Buratti clapped his hands together. "It seems that you withdrew one thousand Francs from an ATM machine just two blocks away from Mr. Paquet's bookshop around ten o'clock at night. It's a good picture of Mr. Gallagher, don't you think?" as he flashed the fax at Grace and then went back to reading the file.

"Great," she said sarcastically.

"That don't mean nothing! So I took some train rides and visited Paris and I gotta fuckin' parkin' ticket. Big deal! You ain't got shit," Tommy said.

Buratti raised his eyes from the manila folder without lifting his head but did not respond to Tommy's outburst. The Commander continued to look through some more of the fax pages and found the one he wanted and continued, "Here it is. This is the one I wanted, the fingerprint analysis of the bookshop. Perhaps this one means something to the man preoccupied with scatological references." He raised his eyes and stared at Tommy. "It seems that you left your fingerprints just about everywhere in Mr. Paquet's bookshop and especially on the briefcase."

"I wiped the briefcase off!" Tommy yelled.

Everyone in the room stared at Tommy. He knew that he had made a mistake. Bramante Buratti chuckled and said, "I wish this was one of those cases where we had no evidence and you just provided us with the link we needed...but no, you really did leave your prints everywhere; the front door, the desk, the inside of the briefcase, and on a stone ashtray. They found yours too, Mr. Sullivan....although not as many. Apparently, you were more careful." Sully couldn't suppress the little smile which he stifled as soon as he noticed Tommy glaring at him.

"Wait a minute...apparently, Mr. Gallagher, you are correct. You must have wiped the outside of the briefcase well. No prints were found there...*Bravo*," he finished.

"You also admitted visiting the Frenchman...on tape," Grace said as she held the tape recorder for all to see.

The facts were out there and the men were clearly linked to the Paris robbery. Buratti switched gears. "You two have had a busy morning. I hear you have been trying to pawn off this stolen book to several book-sellers in town."

Holding up the book that Tommy had handed to Grace, he asked, "This is it? The one he tried to sell you?"

Grace's reaction was non-committal.

Buratti continued, "Very well. Do you know that this book, the *Mantegna Tarocchi*, is a compilation of 50 plates created in 1465? It actually explains the Big Bang Theory? Amazing, all the way back then they had the same theory." He almost gushed as he displayed his knowledge of the rare and extremely valuable item. "We have lots of time to talk about it back at the station," Buratti said and then rapidly rattled instructions in Italian.

Following orders, two armed Carabinieri officers escorted Tommy and Sully down the stairs and into the awaiting police cars with Spicuzza in tow, monitoring the activity.

Buratti turned his attention to Edgar and Max and regarded them carefully. "And what do we have here?" he asked of the two remaining men, one scared stiff, cuffed and standing against the wall and one like-wise cuffed yet seated calmly. "I was not expecting you – Messrs. Gallagher and Sullivan, yes. But I'm not sure what to make of you two." He looked at Max whose deep red welt stood in stark contrast to his ashen face. Max shifted his gaze from the floor to Buratti failing to keep eye contact for more than a moment.

Buratti looked at Edgar who sat expressionless, staring directly at him. Unlike the others whose emotions tended to play on the surface, Edgar's ran deep like a lava-rich volcano whose heat and turmoil churned thousands of meters below the cool facade.

"This is Edgar Shadi," Special Agent Grace Hemmer stated. "Or Eduardo Sadurni or Eddie Shade. Actually, the list is pretty long of your known aliases and I assume even longer of your unknown aliases." Grace had mimicked Buratti's pose and was now leaning on the desk alongside him in a tag team interrogation.

Buratti asked, "And why are we interested in Mr. Edgar Shadi?"

"Because he's linked to the San Lorenzo," Grace responded.

Max's lower body clenched as he heard the answer and prepared to be pulled into the fire. Carlota, who had been standing at the door, took a slight step forward and gave Max's hand a slight squeeze of encouragement. This was a woman that he had never met but their grandfathers were brothers; not much of same genetic material ran through their blood but in a world of six billion people, it was much more relation than total randomness. At this moment, it was the only lifeline Max had.

"Yes, this man, Edgar, is the one who called me claiming that he had the San Lorenzo for sale," Carlota, Max's real cousin, said in heavily accented English.

Both Grace and Buratti looked over at the bookstore's proprietress as she continued, "Max called me to say that this man," indicating Edgar, "had a stolen item and he was coming to return it. I was calling your office, Commander Buratti, after I had a chance to look at it. But when *this* woman came..."

"What *are* you doing here, Grace?" Buratti asked as if now, for the first time, he realized the strangeness of an American Customs agent being in this Italian bookstore interrogating suspects.

"I was working with Paquet. He called me to let me know that he had found the San Lorenzo. I linked the owner back to Mr. Shadi here and his accomplice," she said indicating Max. "Both of these men are from St. Augustine which is in my area of responsibility."

"And you didn't call my office? Of course, we would be very interested in that." He made the last statement politely but the message was clear; Grace had overstepped her bounds and was on thin ice. The only thing saving her was that the return of the San Lorenzo was a timely victory for Buratti.

"I only found out yesterday and I decided to come right here. I was going to call you but the opportunity to get confessions out of them was too good an opportunity to pass up. I knew that you'd understand." Acceptable logic, great results, and a flash of her green eyes encouraged Buratti to overlook the breach of protocol.

He let her off the hook, saying, "A Lieutenant Bozzonetti at Malpensa mentioned that you would be seeing me." With a clearly flirtatious intent, he asked, "He didn't give you too hard a time, did he?"

Unhappy with the chumminess of the two and feeling deceived by the female agent, Carlota charged, "She forced me to switch places with her."

"I'm glad you did. Our mutual friend will be very pleased with the results," Buratti said with a smile to Carlota's confusion.

"I didn't force you," Grace countered. "I convinced you to switch places with me so that I could acquire an honest and full accounting of how the San Lorenzo came to be in Torino."

Turning her attention to Buratti she explained, "I knew from my research that Max was probably just a minor player in the scheme to sell the manuscript. He hadn't planned the theft or the sale."

For once Max appreciated not being thought of as important. He hoped the tide had turned.

"However," Grace continued, "I believed him to be the key to finding the true culprits. Edgar Shadi's name had surfaced as a possible suspect in the previous recovery of a 15th century manuscript in Florida several months earlier. When his name showed up on a flight manifest for arrival in Milan just the day before, I thought the possibility too remote to be a coincidence. I figured that the two could be working together. By impersonating Carlota, I was able to get Edgar's full confession of ownership."

"I can't believe this!" Edgar said. "When I came here I didn't have the San Lorenzo, he did!" pointing to Max.

Max was about to respond but Grace spoke up before him, "I have the entire conversation on tape," she said as she pointed to it. "When I was posing as the owner of this shop you, Edgar, clearly claimed that the San Lorenzo was yours."

"But those other two guys had it when they came in here!" Edgar insisted.

"I'm not sure I understand," Buratti interrupted. "A moment ago you said that this man had it," indicating Max, "and now you just said that those other two men, Tommy Gallagher and Mr. Sullivan, had it. Please try to keep your story straight."

Carlota interjected, "That man!" she said pointing to Edgar, "came here to sell the San Lorenzo and claimed that it belonged to him." She looked Edgar fully in the face before adding, "You contacted this shop to arrange the sale. That is why I came back from Bologna this morning." Carlota added somewhat gratuitously, "Max informed me of this stolen antiquity and he did the right thing to try to get it returned."

Grace screwed up her face. Max knew that, while this wasn't exactly

the sequence of events, the sequence did fit together nicely and that trying to tie his involvement into the story of the San Lorenzo may actually
muddy the waters and take the focus off of the confessed culprits. Grace
had gone out on a big limb pursuing the San Lorenzo. Max realized with
relief that the current recovery story offered her a way back to secure
footing.

Speaking to Commander Buratti, Grace said, "That sounds right. I
also have a lot of evidence to link Edgar to my contact in Paris, Frederic
Paquet. Mr. Shadi is the one who arranged the sale."

"So Max, it looks as if you're mixed up in this...but without more
evidence..." Buratti nodded to one of his men who went over to Max to
take the cuffs off. Max forced himself to remain silent; so far not talking
had worked out all right.

Buratti motioned to the remaining Carabinieri and Edgar was escorted away. No words were spoken but Edgar's stare burned a hole in
Max.

"I will need to take full statements from you so that I can write up
my report. May I have the tape from your earlier interview?" Buratti inquired. Grace popped the tape out of the recorder and handed it over to
him. The excitement over, the drudgery of compiling the reports, completing the forms and filing the proper paperwork had to be completed
to button up the case.

"Those two Americans caused quite a stir while trying to sell the
stolen *Mantegna Tarocchi* this morning. The inspector working the case
in Paris, Inspector Leverd, posted the bulletin last night and when we
heard about it being shopped this morning, Leverd faxed me the rest of
the information he had gathered."

"Plus, they need to answer for the murder of Paquet," Grace said.

"Murder? No. Paquet's death has been ruled natural causes, a heart
attack. The time of death was long after those two goons arrived back

in Zurich. Paquet's wife said that he came to bed around midnight. She heard him make coffee in their kitchen around six. He was found dead on the floor in his office."

"Then why did the French police think it was murder?" asked Grace.

"When Paquet's assistant arrived at noon, she saw the broken display case and signs of a robbery and then found her boss dead on the floor. Until the forensic information was gathered and Mrs. Paquet interviewed, they suspected foul play. Paquet did have bruising on his face and it is possible that the stress from the attack contributed to his untimely death. But I don't believe that the French police will pursue murder charges."

"Once the bulletin was posted, it became primarily an art crime," Buratti explained. "I think Inspector Leverd was glad to close the case and hand it off to us."

Holding the mailing tube containing the San Lorenzo, Buratti said, "Grace, it looks like you recovered another important part of Italian Culture. Is there any chance we could get you to join the Carabinieri Art Squad?"

Grace flushed at the compliment.

"We need to thank the U.S. Customs Service for coming all this way and spending their resources to help us. How long will you be here?"

"Actually, I came here on my own time and money. I am technically on vacation," Grace said, only now fully realizing the danger she had put her career in by traveling to a foreign country and taking unauthorized law enforcement actions. She avoided an international incident if only because of her success in recovering the San Lorenzo and Commander Buratti's willingness to accept her involvement.

"Even better! Then you must allow me to take you to dinner and show you around Torino. It is truly an Italian gem that most foreigners do not know."

"What about the suspects?" Grace asked.

"We have the artworks and the suspects are locked up. They will not be going anywhere soon," Buratti said.

Turning to Carlota he said, "I'll need to call Cardinal Burtone on this and tell him the good news before your mother does and takes the credit." He laughed.

"Cardinal Burtone? I was wondered why I saw a note from my assistant that he had called the bookshop yesterday. Of course..." a light bulb went off in Carlota's mind. "...He was calling us to warn about the missing San Lorenzo."

"Of course he did," Buratti chuckled. "That is why I said 'our mutual friend' will be happy."

Grace interrupted asking, "Who is Cardinal Burtone and why would he call your mother?"

"They are childhood friends," Carlota explained. "In fact, my grandfather, Max's great uncle, saved the Cardinal's young life. He called yesterday. Apparently, he had some information..."

"I should have known that he wouldn't have rested by just letting me handle the hunt," Buratti said. It didn't surprise him that his mentor was playing different angles to accomplish the same goal.

Looking at Max, Carlota added, "I think he'll be very happy that his childhood friend's cousin from America was responsible for helping it be returned."

Dubious of Max's innocence, Buratti stared at him for a long while trying to understand Max's involvement. For Buratti, it had been a very successful day but it seemed a little too neat, to the law enforcement officer, that the hunt for the San Lorenzo started with a U.S. Special Agent's pursuit of Max but ended with the arrest of three career criminals who possessed the item and confessed, on tape, to their ownership of it.

Criminal cases were not neatly gift-wrapped but said to no one in particular, "*A caval donato non si guarda in bocca*." Buratti offered Max a conditional pass by not looking in the horse's mouth.

"I hope that you enjoy your time here in Torino with your family," Bramante said. Having no desire to let Max completely off the hook continued, "Things seemed to work out this time. However, if we cross paths again in similar circumstances, I can assure you that it will not work out so happily for you."

Buratti smiled and turned to the U.S. Customs Special Agent, "Grace, I will see you this evening around seven?"

"Where will we meet? You don't know where I'm staying... I don't even know where I'm staying," Grace said.

"Don't worry. I know a nice boutique hotel nearby. I'll have one of my men take you there," Buratti said with a wink. He escorted Grace downstairs with a spring in his step.

# Chapter 40

Alone in the office with Carlota, Max held his head in his hands, not only to hide the moisture in his eyes but also the sense of shame and embarrassment.

"*Massimo,*" Carlota said, her eyes a pool of sympathetic melancholy interrupted with flashes of joy at meeting her cousin for the first time.

"I'm sorry..." Max started but was cut off.

"Don't worry. You don't have to explain. I know everything." The warmth and compassion in her eyes grew. "I'm sorry, but I listened to your phone call to your wife."

Max was a little taken aback. He had forgotten the clicking sound but now remembered that, at the time, he wondered if someone had been listening in. "You were listening to me?"

"I'm sorry. That policewoman, Grace, she said that you were involved in something illegal. She said that if I helped, she would be more lenient on you. I was picking up the phone to make a call and you were talking...explaining the situation. I didn't realize you were talking to your wife. But then I heard what you were saying and I thought that I could help. I hope you understand. I didn't mean to invade your privacy," Carlota said.

"It's okay...I would have told you the exact same thing that I told my wife."

"What you were doing could happen to anybody. You trusted the people you were dealing with and they put you in a bad position."

Max nodded but sat silently in his thoughts. It was more than trusting the wrong person. He knew that now but what was the point in dragging his cousin into it. Finally, he said, "The San Lorenzo...the buyer, Paquet, seemed very excited when he saw it. And here today, there seemed to be a lot of intrigue about it. What's the big deal? Is it worth a lot of money?"

"Yes, of course, but its value goes well beyond its monetary value," Carlota explained. "The San Lorenzo has tremendous artistic and spiritual value as well." Leaning forward and speaking in an insistent tone, "You know, here in Italy, we have more items on the UNESCO World Heritage List than any other country. The theft is a crime against Italian culture itself."

"I can see. You have a whole police force to combat art theft."

Carlota nodded her head in agreement. "Do you know what is so ..." struggling for the right word, "...coincidental? Is that the San Lorenzo was stolen from here in Torino from the Capitular Archives, the library, of the Archdiocese of Torino, next to the Cathedral of St. John the Baptist."

"Right near where those guys knocked me out and stole it from me this morning," Max said.

"Yes! Interesting – stolen twice from almost the same location," Carlota thought aloud.

"Did they ever find out who stole it from the library?" Max asked.

"Yes, they found out almost right away. It was two professors from Padua, a married couple, who had been hired to make an inventory."

"Wow, how did they find them?"

"One of the helpers, a priest, who was working with them, suspected something and started to keep his own inventory of the items he handled. After the professors had completed their work, the two lists were compared and the discrepancies discovered. Of course, the professors admitted to the theft right away but the objects were gone, sold to private collections and unscrupulous dealers."

"Did they go to jail?" Max was curious what his future could have looked like.

"Yes, but they received light sentences because they cooperated as best they could. But they never could identify the buyer of the San Lorenzo. It could have been that man here today, Edgar. The couple went to prison for a few years but I think they are out."

"Really?" Max was surprised at the short sentences and interested in what they were doing now. "Are they still professors?"

"No," she said shaking her head. "They are disgraced. I heard that the woman went back to her hometown in Sardinia and became a recluse. The husband, he is a teacher in Milan at a small high school with many immigrants from Morocco. I heard that he is trying to make restitution and sometimes the Art Squad calls on him to give an opinion on some technical matter. They don't quite trust him, but he is trying to rebuild his reputation."

Max's head spun thinking that a bookshop owner in St. Augustine had drawn him into a chain of events that started with two professors stealing objects from a church library here in Torino.

Carlota tried to emphasize the lesson, "Max, you must be very careful with whom you place trust," she said. "Any respectable dealer will check an item against the Bulletin of Trafficked Art Works first. That is why Edgar asked you to sell it. He hoped the buyer wouldn't check the directory, but if he did, you would be blamed, not him. If it seems too good to be true, it is." Max didn't have any older siblings but he thought that the warmth he was feeling with Carlota may have given him a taste of what it would be like.

"What about faking who you were and switching with the special agent pretending to be you?" Max wondered only now realizing how sneaky that was.

"I'm sorry about that. She showed me her badge and mentioned Commander Buratti's name. She seemed knowledgeable about the art and rare book community and she claimed that she was trying to help you. She said that she needed to hear your story honestly and frankly as if you were telling a friend or family." Now it was Carlota's turn to be a bit embarrassed at her naiveté.

"But I didn't completely trust her so while you were upstairs talking to Grace, I called the local Carabinieri Art Squad to validate her credentials and ask that somebody come here. They told me that they were busy tracking down the item stolen from Paris. I was especially upset that no one could come to help when Edgar showed up here..."

"How did he know to find you... and me? Max interrupted.

"He called the shop yesterday to make inquiries about buying some items that I have in my catalogs. He also said he wanted to sell some books that he had. I was actually interested in a Juvara and a Guarini that he claimed to have," she explained. "So an appointment was made for today."

"But Edgar didn't have any books to sell when he came here, did he?" Max asked.

"No, perhaps he never had any and used that as a way to get an appointment or maybe he sold them earlier – he told me that he arrived in Milano yesterday. There are many rare book dealers there, too." Carlota continued her explanation of the events, "Once the other two men showed up I realized that the situations were related, so I called the Carabinieri office again and told him that my cousin and I had sct a trap for these thieves and to come right away."

"So do you know this Commander Buratti?" Max questioned.

"In this business, it is good to know some people at the Art Squad. But I'm not sure if he even received any of my messages. Maybe he only showed up here because he was chasing the two Americans."

"They were trying to sell a book too, right?" Max said.

"Those two buffoons? Ridiculous! The *Mantegna Tarocchi* is very well known and worth about a million dollars. Everyone knows that set of engravings; it is one of the rarest and most enigmatic group of prints in the history of western art. Any respectable dealer would be suspicious of two uneducated men like them trying to sell such an important work. I'm sure that the first shop they went to called Commander Buratti as soon as they left. They had no chance of selling it to a legitimate dealer."

She smiled and held both of Max's hands in hers. Shaking them in a way that meant all is forgiven and forgotten. "My mother is coming now. Let's enjoy the rest of your time here. I want to show you my city."

# Chapter 41

**St. Augustine, FL**

**December 1997**

"RK Trucking and Logistics, Max speaking."

"Hey, Hon," Laura said. "I got a sitter for tonight, I talked to Nella and she said Gabbie, can do it."

"Great." Getting babysitters was always difficult. Not only because the twins were a handful but because Laura was so protective of her kids that she rarely felt like leaving them. "You sure Gabbie can handle the three of them?"

"Sure. We'll get the boys in bed before we leave....we don't need to get there right at six do we?"

"We don't need to go to the company Christmas Party if you don't want to. You don't sound like you're that excited."

"I am. I've got a lot of stuff to do to get ready," Laura said sharply. Max recoiled from the rebuke until Laura said, "It'll be nice to leave the house for a while. We never get to downtown to see all the white lights on the buildings and I'm sure the Casa Monica will be beautiful. You're coming home early to get dressed, aren't you?" Laura asked. "Your golf shirt and khakis aren't dressy enough for this event." Without waiting for an answer she said, "Hey, you got a big envelope from Italy."

"What is it? Go ahead and open it," Max said. His mind raced through the possibilities, very few of them good.

"I don't know what it says. It looks almost like a diploma or something. You'll have to ask your dad to translate it. Wait a minute, there is a letter stuck in here."

"What's it say?" Max said, patience not being a strength.

"Hold on a sec, I'm reading it," Laura responded. "It's a letter to you thanking you for your help in protecting Italian cultural heritage."

"The letter's in English?" Max asked.

"No, I just learned how to read Italian in the last ten seconds. Yes, it's in English," she scoffed. A scream of delight or anguish came from the other room. "Got to go. See you soon." The line went dead.

That was pretty cool, Max thought, getting a commendation from the Italian government. In the weeks that followed his return to Florida, Max followed the news releases pretty closely. In the U.S., the return of the San Lorenzo was a one-day local interest story highlighting Grace's involvement. Even though she was not on official government business at the time of the San Lorenzo's repatriation, U.S. Attorney, Don Weidenfeld, was extensively quoted in the press release and appeared in every photo when the consul general for the Italian Consulate in Miami visited the Service's Jacksonville office to present the commendation.

Max stayed in touch with Carlota who kept him informed on the prosecution of Tommy and Sully for the theft of the *Mantegna Tarocchi*. Tommy's father had hired a well-respected and expensive French criminal defense lawyer who bailed him out of jail. He returned to his old job at the building supply distributor within a week and went on about his business as if nothing happened. Fortunately, Max hadn't seen him eating pizza at Carmelo's lately.

Tommy's sidekick, Sully, was not so fortunate. While Sully was marking time in jail, hopeful that Tommy's lawyers would beat the rap for the both of them, Tommy's lawyers were having their client testify that Sully was the mastermind. Tommy had apparently learned from his four years in prison. Besides, Sully could never muster the same threat of retribution as the New Jersey bookies.

Max reviewed all of the press clippings and news articles that Carlota sent. Most were from the Italian newspapers and, because he didn't read Italian, Max spent much of the time looking at the pictures of the repatriation ceremony. He recognized Commander Bramante Buratti, Grace and Carlota in one of the pictures that accompanied the article. Obviously, Grace had made a special trip to be at the ceremony...and perhaps to see Bramante. Carlota mentioned that the two of them were quite an item at the reception. He wasn't sure, but he also thought he recognized one of the church's officials who had attended, a grey-haired man with bushy black eyebrows in the picture looked similar to the priest he met at the Cathedral.

Some international, English language publications did pick up the story of the San Lorenzo's recovery and return to the Archdiocese of Torino especially after its inspection by church leaders and academic scholars. When the recovered manuscript supported the legend of San Lorenzo's death, the group claiming that his martyrdom was a myth advanced by a misspelling quickly pivoted to a different argument.

The prosecution of Edgar was also complicated. Special Agent Grace Hemmer called Max about a week after she returned from Italy and asked him to meet her at a coffee shop across from the Plaza de la Constitución in old town St. Augustine. Before they ordered their coffees, Grace opened, "Have you been in contact with Edgar Shadi?"

"No. Of course not," Max replied. He was shocked at the accusation. "Isn't he in jail?"

"He didn't appear for his first pre-trial hearing. Frankly, I can't see him returning to face trial."

Max was troubled by the development.

Grace continued, "He had an Italian passport which allows him to cross borders to almost anywhere in Europe without a trace. He may decide to contact you. If he does, I want to know immediately."

"Why would he contact me?" Max asked trying not to let his concern show.

"I have a hunch. Your dealings with him are still unclear to me," she said. "You could still be working together for all I know."

"No way. I'm on your side. I'm as upset as anyone about the way he played me," Max said. "Won't the Art Squad be pursuing him in Italy?" Max asked.

"The retrieval of the items usually takes precedence over the conviction of the thief. The San Lorenzo was repatriated, so the thief may get away."

"That's not good," Max said. "But he won't be able to do this again, will he?"

"Who knows? There is such a large underground network for the illegal trade of antiques and ancient artifacts that I wouldn't be surprised if he pops up somewhere else doing the same thing. Although, I doubt he'll do it back here in Florida; probably not even in the U.S."

"So you don't think that he'll come back here?"

"Not to his old life. I checked with his landlord, he's four months past due on his shop and he's got several liens placed on his inventory by vendors. It looks like he was planning to leave for a while. He's probably smart enough to know that, after what happened in the bookshop, I'm on to him and determined to gain a conviction. We have less art theft so we can afford to be more persistent. Plus, he'll face stiffer sentencing if convicted here."

"Good. I'd rather not have to deal with him again."

"But if he does contact you, I want to be informed the very moment it happens. You don't want to be guilty of conspiracy after the fact, do you?"

"Absolutely not. You have my word."

"As long as we have that straight." She added the warning, "You got away with being naïve once. It helped that your cousin vouched for you. The next time, though," she said, "there will be no benefit of the doubt."

Max put his head down in conciliation but remained silent.

"Good luck, Max. Let's not run into each other again in a professional manner," she said.

***

Wilson let the sales team leave the office at four the afternoon of the company party. Max got home and went to the kitchen table where the twins were sitting in front of their mac and cheese. Laura was busy in the kitchen cutting up strawberries for the boys. Samantha was playing with her American Girl doll in the living room. "Hi, Daddy," she called out without looking up.

He kissed the boys on their heads and Laura called out, "As soon as I get these cut, I'm going to take a shower and get dressed. You watch them and make sure they eat their fruit before you let them play. The sitter will be over at five." Laura walked toward the master bedroom and before entering said, "You have a FedEx I threw it on your desk. It's postmarked from Basel, Switzerland. Are there any more issues I need to know about?"

Before Max could answer, the door closed with authority.

# Chapter 42

Laura had a difficult time getting the boys down for bed and they had already missed dinner by the time they pulled up to the Casa Monica Hotel. Max handed the keys to the valet and Laura adjusted herself as they wordlessly communicated their shared frustration at not being able to arrive on time. They silently walked up the few steps into the Moorish Revival styled lobby. The couple was too preoccupied with their tardiness to enjoy, or even notice, the frescos, fountains, and beautiful chandeliers as they walked to the private party.

"Merry Christmas, Max, Laura," Max's immediate supervisor greeted the couple as they stepped into the ballroom.

"Hey, Wilson. Merry Christmas," Max said. "We had trouble getting out on time. The boys wouldn't go down."

"That's all right. Most people have finished eating but the buffet is up for another half hour so get yourself something to eat." For a guy who had put him on the list to be fired, Max thought, he sure was happy...or tipsy.

"Thanks, Wilson. We appreciate it. Is Jennifer here?" Laura asked about Wilson's wife.

"She's out on the dance floor. The company is raffling off cash and prizes all night long....but you need to be on the dance floor to win," Wilson chuckled. "Jennifer swears she's not leaving without getting something."

"That sounds like fun," Laura said. "We could use the money too. I'll eat fast and join Jennifer in a bit."

With just about everyone on the dance floor, Max and Laura each made a plate of food and found a quiet table in the corner. Max went to the bar to pick up two glasses of red wine and returned to the table with Laura. He was about to sit down when a middle-aged blonde wearing bright red lipstick and a cleavage-enhancing holiday dress approached his table.

"There's my favorite person!" she hollered. "Why I didn't think I'd ever see you," the woman said in a southern accent as thick and sweet as honey. Laura furled her brow when she noticed the southern belle speaking to her husband.

"Max, give me a big Christmas kiss." Max recognized the woman as Theodore's companion in Zurich. While he had been very forthcoming with Laura about the details of the European trip, somehow running into Theodore and this woman in the hotel hallway never came up. Max hoped she didn't mention that the last time Max saw her she was only wearing a bathrobe...and not too well.

"You must be Max's wife?" the woman said as Laura stood, either to greet or to attack the intruder. "Hey, I just got to tell you that I love your husband!" the 'love' was drawn out for at least five seconds. "I'm Corey Armistead, Theodore's wife."

That answered one question, Max thought. He was still confused about this woman's exuberance – but he wasn't complaining. For the time being, the conversation seemed like it was going in the right direction.

She continued speaking to Laura and holding her hand like a dear friend, "You know we were in Switzerland together and those conferences can be so boring and I told Theodore I am not going to spend our 25th anniversary at this dreadful meeting." She rattled on, speaking a mile a minute.

Laura stood there, her hand being held, smiling at Corey's confident, enthusiastic and cheerful gyrations. "I wanted to let you know how much I appreciated Max taking over and allowing Theodore some free time to spend with me. After all, you're not married for twenty-five years every day, honey!" Corey hooted.

"Why, thank you," was about all Laura could say.

Corey was on a roll. "You got yourself a good one there, honey. Theodore says Max is one of the best young talents in the company."

Max watched Laura nodding her head absently, seemingly pleased with the compliments yet helplessly speechless by the refreshingly bold, outspoken independence of a woman who was clearly no two-faced butt kisser.

"Theodore. Theodore! Come over here please sweetie and talk to me and Max and his beautiful wife." Max and Laura basked in the wave of adulation.

Theodore, wearing a tuxedo with gold studs and cuff links, ambled over with his confident gait like a lion approaching a kill. Max could tell that the black silk bow tie with small gray polka dots was not a clip-on.

"How are you doing, Max?" Putting out his hand to shake, said, "Laura, a pleasure to meet you. This is my wife, Corey." Max didn't realize that Theodore knew his wife's name – must be another one of his talents.

Corey gushed, "Hush, Honey, I already know Laura and Max. Let me tell you, Laura, your husband is very impressive. Theodore couldn't stop talking about how good his speech was and how well he handled all the different customers and conducted himself over there. You going to go real far with this company and believe me, honey, I've seen a lot of folks. I know what goes on – I can tell you that."

Theodore fidgeted uneasily from foot to foot at the effusive praise Corey heaped on his subordinate. Probably, Max thought, not because it was untrue but because he would like Max's loyalty directed to be to him and not his wife.

"Ladies, if you'll excuse us a moment." Theodore put his arm around Max and turned him slightly to peel off from the women. Once they got to a remote corner of the room, Theodore continued. "Max, I'm not sure the best way to say this but Wilson won his internal battle and your name is on the final headcount reduction list."

That little shit, Max thought. No wonder he was so happy when he greeted me this evening. "I don't understand..." Max started.

"Now before you say anything, let me finish. I told you that antagonizing him was not going to work."

Max disregarded Theodore's request and interrupted, "but I stopped doing that..."

"Well, either the damage was done or you kept doing it less obviously," Theodore said.

Max's head dropped. Fear and sadness mixed together.

The big boss continued, "I've counseled Wilson that a good manager doesn't discard talent just because of a personality conflict. A good manager fixes those problems."

"Yeah, but he's the one with the job," Max said.

"Now, Max, being on that list means that you're off of Wilson's team, not necessarily out of the company."

Max's heart leaped for hope.

"You did a fine job there in Switzerland and I think a case can be made for focusing some of our sales efforts in Europe, especially Eastern Europe and Latin America as they become more economically viable."

"I couldn't agree more," Max said. He had been pushing this concept with Wilson and his predecessor for months. Either it had just reached

Theodore or he was developing the plan on his own after seeing the opportunity in Zurich.

"The business development group had two retirements and one of the guys is moving to fill a sales post in Cincinnati. We only needed to reduce by two, so it leaves an opening. If you want it, it's yours. It's a chance to show us your creativity."

"That would be great." Max had no idea what the business development group did but at this moment, it was exactly the job he always wanted. "This is exactly the group I've always wanted to be part of."

"Well good." Theodore smiled like a man accustomed to effusive praise and enduring loyalty. "In your new role, I'd like you to put together a presentation on how we would structure an international sales focus, model its costs and forecast its impact. If the board likes it and we can justify the expansion, we may even be able to create a new international sales and marketing group right here in our area."

"Great! I can do that."

"Now, don't let me down," Theodore said.

The men made their way back to the table where their wives had been joined by Wilson and his wife, Jennifer. Max's situation may have improved but he still sneered at the weasel move Wilson had made.

Theodore recognized the tension and started holding court, "Do you know where the name of this Casa Monica hotel came from?" His audience awaited the answer as if their lives depended on it. "It is named for Saint Monica who was the mother of the Bishop of Hippo in North Africa. Of course, you know who the bishop was, don't you? St. Augustine." He smiled a big grin and watched as others did the same.

The little group broke up, Max and Laura hit the dance floor but didn't win any of the raffled prizes. During one of their breaks, Laura asked, "What was Theodore saying to you. I was trying to listen but Corey kept asking me about the boys."

"It's all good," Max said. "He wants me to move over to the business development group and help justify a new group focused on international sales."

"So it will be a promotion? Will you make more money? Maybe with the raise we can pay for Sam's surgery?" Laura asked.

"Maybe. I hope. I'm not sure. Remember, my quest to make extra money almost got me in major trouble. I have a job and with all the headcount reduction, that's a good thing. We're better off now than we were a month ago. No matter what, we need to remember that our treasures are home asleep, honey."

"I know. I just worry about Sam," Laura said. "Sounds like a good opportunity, Max. I'm so proud of you." Laura said as she gave Max a big hug.

"I have something else sort of interesting to tell you," Max said as Laura's face turned skeptical and suspicious. Looking around to make sure that nobody was around, he continued, "I opened that FedEx envelope. Inside it was a letter from the Swiss bank that I set up the account in."

Laura finished his sentence to clarify, "The one where Edgar put the ten thousand dollars and you took the two?" She was well versed in the accounts and had used what remained of the two thousand that Max brought home to apply to some of the bills.

"Yes, that one. The bankers closed the account and sent me a check for the balance. Apparently, they didn't appreciate having the French police calling them asking about their clients who were either murder suspects or murder victims. Plus, when I went there, the younger banker wasn't crazy about the small size of the account. The police involvement was probably a convenient excuse to close it."

"So we got a check for eight thousand dollars!" Laura nearly jumped up. "I'll contact the hospital right away and get Sam scheduled!"

"We got a check all right...actually for more. There were a few more deposits made after Switzerland; possibly from items Edgar sold in Milan right before coming to Torino. He had the account number but never got the password. He must have had the purchasers of his books deposit the money in the account assuming he would be able to retrieve it after he got the password from me."

"But he didn't get the password from you?" Laura questioned. "Why didn't he ask you for it?"

"Because when I saw him, we only had a few minutes together before the two thugs showed up and then the Carabinieri Art Squad arrested him."

"So is that money illegal? Did he get the money from selling stolen items?" Laura questioned.

"I don't think so and neither does Special Agent Hemmer, who just got promoted to Resident Agent in Charge for Jacksonville, by the way. She checked Edgar's last movements and the books he sold in Milan were not stolen. Even Carlota followed up later with the rare book dealer who bought them and the transactions themselves were legitimate."

Laura questioned again, "Are you sure the money is legal?"

"Totally; as far as I can tell. We just need to pay taxes on it."

"Let me get this straight..." Laura pulled slightly at her ear as she tried to get her head around this latest development. "Edgar set you up to sell a stolen manuscript, but he had no problem selling his legitimate and perfectly legal items to dealers in Milan a few days later...and proceeds from his sale went into the account which you opened and have the only access to?"

Max nodded that Laura had summarized the situation correctly. Laura continued, "Edgar is missing, didn't show up for his court dates in Italy and no one knows where he is. When... or if he is found, he'll be arrested again."

"That's what I understand. I spoke to Hemmer yesterday. She thinks Edgar went back to Sierra Leon." Max continued, "And she said that he can't come back to the U.S. But for all of her research and investigation, she says that Edgar came by the books he sold in Milan, legally."

"So the only person besides you who could make a legitimate claim on the money is a criminal and fugitive from justice? Sounds like the money is ours," Laura said as a statement of fact.

"What are the chances he'll make trouble for us? I don't want to spend it all and then have him come after us. I mean, I will. Sam needs it, but hopefully he's got a lot more problems to worry about than eight K." Laura said.

"I agree. But just to be clear, it's a bit more than that. The books Edgar sold in Milan were pretty valuable."

"How much was the bank check for?" Laura asked.

Max hesitated. Unfamiliar emotions coursed through his body. The past few weeks had kept his shoulders and neck in constant tension. Now, light-headed yet feeling relaxed and solid in his core, he danced on his toes like a kid on a moon bounce. He realized that most of the past week's stress came from trying to tackle the issues on his own. He thought of the failure to close the deal in Basel and when the police accused him of murder and when he had the manuscript stolen from him in Torino outside of the cathedral. He remembered not knowing where to turn. He thought about calling his wife to tell her the mess he was in. With the police, U.S. Customs Service and the Carabinieri closing in and the very high likelihood of him losing his job, Laura had given him sound, logical advice with a dose of compassion thrown in. He recognized the assistance his father gave him in setting up the meeting with his cousin who was sharp enough to help parry Max's involvement and point the authorities in the direction of Tommy, Sully, and Edgar.

Now, everything had worked out. He kept his job, had an international business experience, and made some money. More importantly, he realized he wasn't alone. With his wife as a full participant, they could make good decisions moving forward and achieve the goals and happiness they desired.

"How much was it?" Laura asked again.

Max paused and said, "It was more like three hundred and twenty thousand dollars."

Laura just stared at Max, speechless. Tears of joy sprung from her eyes. Max felt it too and as Laura bear hugged him and collapsed in his arms, he finally realized the emotion of success.

***

# Author's Notes

A few years ago, I set out to tell the story of a train ride. I have always liked trains—especially train stations. There is something exciting to me about different people—each with their own concerns—occupying the same space as they go to and from places unknown to those around them. Their lives briefly intersect and thousands of people with unique histories share, forever and for always, a common moment.

It's the same with airports, you might say. But since my job requires me to travel nearly every week by plane, airports don't carry the same romantic allure that railway stations do. So I started writing a story about a man on a train, heavily influenced by my first business trip to Switzerland. However, the story of a man traveling from Zurich to Zug in order to visit pig-iron traders does not hold one's interest (even mine) for long. So the man got a new destination and a new purpose, with which came new challenges and foes. And thus, my novel came to life.

This is a work of fiction, which—for those friends of mine buying and reading a book for the first time—means "made up." The story was inspired by the actual theft in 1990 of the page known as "The San Lorenzo" from *The Missal of Ludovico da Romagnano* from the Capitular Archives in Torino, Italy by a married couple of Italian antiquities professors, but the events, circumstances, and characters are purely conjured from my imagination. An exception is the background information of Max's grandfather, for which I used the actual facts of my grandfather's immigration to the United States and some of his early American experiences. Also, my grandfather's brother, as the town doctor, did save the life of a boy who became a cardinal in the Roman Catholic Church.

No author's work is completely his own, and I must thank many people for helping me. First, I thank my parents, Peter and Anita Massoglia, who have always supported me, stressed the importance of education, and exposed me to the broader world with numerous trips to Europe. Thank you for your love and support. I love you.

I've been fortunate in my life to travel the world and meet thousands of interesting people. A storyteller's craft is learned over years, and the retelling of my adventures—great and small—has honed my craft. To all those who listened and laughed, thank you. To those who glanced at your watch while I recounted my latest tale, you've hopefully taught me to carve out unnecessary story elements and quicken my pace. Thank you, too.

To all the people (school teachers, Boy Scout leaders, coaches, priests and CCD teachers, work colleagues, relatives, and friends) who taught me to think, donated their time and talent to pass on knowledge, and encouraged my creativity… thank you.

Some specific people who leant their time and talent to dispense advice and encouragement that helped make this book a reality include Victor DiGenti and the members of Florida Writers Association - Ponte Vedra Writers Group, Nancy Quatrano and the fine folks at the Ancient City Writers Group, author/book-coach Rick Feeney, Matt Hook, author Andy Brumbach, author and friend Don Hutton, Jennifer Cox, Karen Latzko, Fred Betz, author Michael Arnold, and writing instructor UNF Professor John Boles.

I thank my editor, Allison Erin Wright, for her encouragement and her intuitive and considered feedback, which resulted in a quicker-paced, suspenseful plot with deeper characters.

I offer special thanks to those who read nascent versions of my manuscript and offered expert advice about some of the subjects in the novel. DHS, Homeland Security Special Agent (retired) Eric Pond was critical in helping me understand the nature of the US Customs Service in the late 1990s. Umberto Pregliasco, my cousin and an antique book dealer, offered valuable insight into the rare book trade. Captain Guido Barbieri, the commandant of the Carabinieri in Torino, helped me gain understanding of the functioning of the Art Squad at their Torino Via XX Septembre offices.

Others who gave feedback on the actual novel include Alixia Bermak, whose Hollywood savvy set me on the right direction in the first few chapters, Anne Burton Walsh and Joe Walsh, who read through an early version and provided pages of notes, and my mother-in-law, Rita Forrer, who offered me a copy edit.

Both my son, Graham, and my daughter, Gabbie, have been extremely supportive and helpful. Thank you, Gabbie, for reading not one, but two, of my complete drafts and providing constructive feedback. I love you both very much.

I save the greatest thanks for my wife, Kathy, whom I love with all my heart and dedicate this novel to. Her encouragement brings about the best version of me, and this story would never have seen the light of day without her. She was the first person I let read my scribbling—which I did with much trepidation. As a first-time author, I felt exposed and vulnerable offering my writing for critique. Kathy's loving support gave me the confidence to continue, and for that I can't thank her enough.

Made in the USA
Columbia, SC
16 December 2017